Praise for Don Wright

"Inspiring. Don Wright has the knack for writing stories based on real people that present a gritty, accurate, and inspiring portrait of those who endure and triumph—a testimony to the human spirit." —*Romantic Times* on *Gone to Texas*

"Historical fiction of the first order....A ripsnorter, fast-paced and delightful from first page to last."
—*Chattanooga Times* on *The Woodsman*

"A breathtaking adventure of power and scope....A captivating wilderness adventure of love and courage during the French and Indian wars." —*Publishers Weekly* on *The Woodsman*

"Marked by high adventure, strong characterizations, accurate historical background, and authentic knowledge of treacherous wilderness, the book is sure to take its place among the classic stories of the American frontier."
—*Nashville Banner* on *The Woodsman*

"Wright has woven old family rivalries and historical footnotes into a compelling and entertaining narrative....A thoroughly exciting adventure!"
—*Publishers Weekly* on *The Captives*

"Good, clean, grisly fun, with scalps coming unstuck like Velcro, arrows thwacking into bodies, and Morgan Patterson leading the charge." —*Kirkus Reviews* on *The Captives*

"Engrossing, realistic, and very human....Marvelous."
—*RAVE Reviews* on *The Last Plantation*

GONE TO TEXAS

DON WRIGHT

A TOM DOHERTY ASSOCIATES BOOK
NEW YORK

GONE TO TEXAS

A Tor Book
Published by Tom Doherty Associates, LLC
175 Fifth Avenue
New York, NY 10010

www.tor.com

Tor® is a registered trademark of Tom Doherty Associates, LLC.

ISBN: 0-812-58908-4
Library of Congress Catalog Card Number: 98-14622

First edition: July 1998
First mass market edition: October 1999

Printed in the United States of America

0 9 8 7 6 5 4 3 2 1

This story is dedicated to my wife, Pat.
Heroines are alive and well today—thank God!

ACKNOWLEDGMENTS

Most authors know that writing a book is a long, drawn-out process. Many times, before it is finished, it leaves the writer burned out with the story line and the characters as well. Therefore, without the objectivity and special insight of a group of diverse people, whom I call "manuscript readers," many books would never come to fruition. Mine is no exception. I owe my readers a debt of gratitude. They, for the most part, are typical Americans from all walks of life, and as such, contributed greatly to my most recent endeavor, *Gone to Texas*, by giving generously of their time, honesty, and much needed suggestions and criticisms.

Many thanks (in no particular order) go to: my wife, Patricia G. Wright, office manager; Judy Russell, accountant; Peggy Bandy, administrative assistant; Tina Butler, executive; Geneva Williams, retired teacher who has a Master's degree in English; Betty Belote, homemaker; Bettie Lord, business consultant; Marila Fuqua, nurse; Elizabeth Pollard, retired school teacher; Jane Wright, national sales manager; Betty Wright, fine-art gallery executive; Mae Harrodda, M.D.; Gail Atkins, homemaker; Paul Akers, truck driver; Joe Rittenberry, shift supervisor; David Wright, world renowned artist; Bill Fuqua, retired United States

Air Force Colonel; and Don Hickerson, Tennessee Highway Patrolman.

In addition, I must thank the following people. Without the perseverance and patience of my typist, J. R. Williamson-Sorrell, this book may have never been completed. Many people consider professional writers an odd group because of their unusual lifestyle and chaotic hours. Fortunately, J.R. is a professional writer and keeps unusual hours. After this book was written, then revised, expanded, edited, and retyped ten complete times, both of us were certain we had ventured beyond odd and had slipped into insane. Fortunately, we have both recovered, and are working on our next project.

I would be remiss if I failed to mention perhaps the most important people who, because of their interest, insight, and expertise, made this story come together. Ms. Claire Eddy, my editor, who is exceptional to work with and knows what she is doing, and Ms. Elisabeth Tinsley, who made me stop and think about what I had written.

INTRODUCTION

I enjoyed writing this story about a journey to Texas for several reasons.

First and foremost, it afforded me the opportunity to boast about my forefathers and the stories that were told to me during my growing-up years not only by those who heard them first-hand but in many cases by those who lived them.

In rural Kentucky during the 1940s—the Second World War and after—we had never heard of television, few homes had electricity, and fewer still a radio. As a result (and I, as a writer, can only thank God), we children were entertained by stories told by the adults, many of whom were eyewitness to the incidents and people who helped carve America into the greatest nation on earth.

The stories of the exploits of my great-grandfather, Warden Clay Taylor, were spellbinding. As a young man, Great-grandpa Taylor went to Texas when it was still a raw frontier. He worked longhorn cattle and cowboyed with the best of them. He returned to Ohio County, Kentucky, and became sheriff of said county.

My great-uncle, Ike House, carved himself a ranch out of a section of land in the Oklahoma Territory. I have the lever-action rifle he carried. He was a real cowboy who made his living and reared his family ranching. In the early 1950s, Uncle Ike told me that he and most of the cattlemen he knew owned two pairs of boots—a plain-looking, forty-dollar pair that he worked in, and a five-dollar, fancy-stitched pair that he wore to church. He also told me a cattle rancher seldom put his initials on a brand; it was considered a greenhorn vanity. Uncle Ike's brand was in the shape of a house.

UNCLE IKE'S BRAND

My great-grandfather on my dad's side of the family, John Henry Wright, fought in the Civil War, and in later years drove a stagecoach. I have his stagecoach driver's license and a copy of his discharge from the army.

My grandfather on my mother's side, Van Owen House, was a wonderful storyteller, and on many a rainy or snowy day, sitting around the stove, he would keep children and adults mesmerized with his accounts of days gone by.

Van Owen (Papaw) House was a Kentucky mule skinner during his young life, and as were many stockmen before and after the turn of the century, he was expert with a bullwhip. He told me that during his days as a teamster (driving horses or mules), a man was judged by how accurate he was with a whip. He said it was a simple matter of pride, and that every man worth his salt wanted to be the cock-of-the-walk with a whip. He taught his children and grandchildren to make a bullwhip of nearly any desired length with strips of bark from hickory sapling trees. They were fine platted whips, but unless we put them in the creek each night, they would dry out and become brittle and useless. He gave me the remnants of one of his rawhide bullwhips. I treasure it to this day.

When I was visiting my great-uncle Ike House back in the early 1950s, my family and I observed in a Texas museum exhibit the charred remains of a stagecoach burned by the Comanche. It made a lifelong impression on me.

Also in the young and wandering days of my growing-up period, I was fortunate to have the opportunity to know and talk at length with several cowboys whose young lives were spent in what is now referred to as the Old West.

One such gentleman, Hewey, who allowed my brother, David, and me the privilege of hunting on his Montana ranch, told us many stories about his life on the prairies, the Indians, the cattle, the sheep, and the famous western artist, Charlie Russell, whom he cowboyed with in his youth.

Hewey told me once—"let me in on a secret," actually— that when he was a young man, he used to drive the Indian maidens wild: "When I kissed 'em, I would slip my tongue in their mouth. They'd go crazy! Worked every time."

I can't help but wonder what he would think if he watched a sexy scene in a movie today.

GONE TO TEXAS

PROLOGUE

February 14, 1901

The mid-February temperature was a cold forty-three degrees, yet nineteen-year-old Kate Edmons was perspiring by the time she reached the top of the hill. Silhouetted on its crest stood Peyton Lewis, tall, broad-shouldered, hair as dark as coal except for a touch of silver at the temples. He reminded her of a statue, unmoving, rock hard, as he surveyed an oil derrick on a knoll a quarter of a mile away. The roar of the crude oil was as deafening as a tornado as it exploded two hundred feet into the sky before crowning and then raining down its lovely aurora of purple, pink, green, blue, and black droplets. This was the fifth day of the phenomenon, with no end in sight.

Kate topped the rise and halted to catch her breath. She studied the man she had climbed the hill to interview, and was surprised to feel a ripple of awe constrict her already pounding chest, making it even more difficult for her to breathe. Peyton Lewis, at fifty-three years of age, was still lean and muscular, ramrod straight, and in spite of, or possibly because of, the permanent squint etched into his sun-browned face, a face that looked as though it had been crafted by a sculptor's knife, he was very probably the handsomest man she had ever seen—and by far the wealthiest. It was rumored that he had just sold two oil wells for the astounding sum of one million dollars each.

Clutching her pad and pencil more tightly, Kate took a deep breath and walked toward him.

"Mr. Lewis!" her shout could hardly be heard above the roar of the gusher.

He turned toward her and her breath caught; she was staring into the coldest, most magnificent gray eyes she had ever encountered. *It's true,* she decided, *he can see right through a person, intrude into one's most secret places.* She was thrilled yet disturbed by the revelation, for never had she faced a man who, with a look, left her feeling naked and vulnerable.

Transferring her writing pad to her left hand, she offered her right. "I'm Kate Edmons, sir. The *Waco Times Herald* sent me to Beaumont to do a story on you."

He hesitated for the merest instant before shaking her hand, but when he did, she found his grip firm, his palm callused from hard work. "Ma'am." His voice was cool and low-pitched. Then, disengaging his hand, he touched the brim of his Stetson in the age-old manner of man acknowledging woman.

Kate found his discomfort at having shaken her hand both intriguing and amusing, for he was widely respected as a tough, hard-driven man who was absolutely ruthless in the life-and-death struggle that comprised the intricate industry known as "big business."

Kate smiled, her confidence bolstered by her belief that her gender and credentials had intimidated him.

"Mr. Lewis, my newspaper wants to do a series of stories about your life—how you came to Texas, the early days, the cattle drives, the rustlers, the sheep wars, everything."

She considered including "and most especially the details concerning your lifelong relationship with a woman who the rumormongers swear was a prostitute during the War Between the States," but she did not, for his eyes had narrowed suspiciously as he appraised her, and again she heard her editor's warning that seeking an interview with Peyton Lewis would be nothing but a wild-goose chase; Lewis was a private person who would, in all likelihood, refuse to meet with her.

Kate experienced a smug satisfaction. He was meeting with her, all right. She had made that a certainty by watching and waiting for just the right moment to approach him, and it had finally presented itself after three days of monitoring his every move. Now she had him alone on a Beaumont hill called Spindle Top, and she would do what she came to do—get a story.

The wind on the hilltop whipped a loose strand of hair from beneath her hat and plastered it across her cheek. Absently, she brushed it aside.

"You are a Texas hero, Mr. Lewis. Yes, indeed, a living legend . . ."

She hesitated, gauging his expression for the expected reaction to her vocal applause. Seeing none, she quickly added, "You're as true a Texas hero as Moses and Stephen Austin, Sam Houston, Joe Lovin, Charlie Goodnight, and Chisholm." His face remained passive. "And, sir," she faltered, her confidence wavering, "the *Waco Times Herald* wants an exclusive to your life story. We're planning on publishing it in segments—one chapter each week—beginning with your decision to come to Texas in 1866.

"We understand that after the war between the states ended, people from all parts of the South merely walked away from their homes, their jobs, their businesses . . . that they stuck a sign in their window or yard that stated, 'Gone to Texas.' And from what we've heard, sir, 'G.T.T.'—Gone to Texas—was as famous a slogan in those days as 'Go west, young man, go west!' Men, women, and children headed west on horseback, in wagons. Some were even on foot. We want to write about that migration, Mr. Lewis— the trials, tribulations, joys, and excitement of *your* trip."

Peyton Lewis smiled sadly at her, and Kate Edmons was shocked by the unexpected pity that lay deep in his eyes as he studied her. Trials and tribulations? Joys and excitement? He looked away, at the oil derrick silhouetted against the distant, silver-gray skyline, and something in his stance suggested to Kate that he was not seeing the derrick at all, that he was looking beyond it, to a Texas she had only heard and read about, and a story that, if it was ever told, would astound her.

One

February 14, 1866

Snow eddied and swirled about the twelve men cloaked in Federal army greatcoats who rode their horses at a walk up the main street of Liberty, Missouri, toward the brick building that housed the Clay County Savings Association. They paid little attention to either the snow or the penetrating cold.

Upon reaching the hitching rack in front of the bank, three of the riders stepped down from their saddles and handed their bridle reins to the horse-holder, a seventeen-year-old youth named Fletcher Rucker.

The leader of the three, his coattail billowing in a sudden gust of wind, nodded to his companions, and together they opened the bank door and took long, purposeful strides to the cast-iron stove in the center of the dimly lit room. They thrust their hands close to the flue pipe that glowed a dull red and rubbed them briskly.

William Bird, the bank teller, glanced up from the pile of gold coins he was separating by denomination and appraised the trio. They were young men, lean, with the look of hard usage about them. Their faces, what little he could see of them beneath their low-pulled hats, were deeply tanned. Not the surface brown of a warm and gentle sun, but the burned-in kind that comes from spending most of one's time in constant exposure to the unrelenting savagery of nature's harshest elements. The brims of their slouch hats were frayed, and sweat stains darkened the dingy gray felt around the band. Had Bird looked more closely, he would have noticed puncture marks on the hat brims where Confederate cavalry insignias had once been pinned. He did not look. Instead, he noted that their greatcoats were threadbare and their gray woolen trousers, slick at the knee, were stuffed into tall riding boots that were scuffed and run-down at the heel. *Travelers.* The word carried a stigma; hundreds of wanderers had passed through Liberty these past ten months since the war had ended, drifting, moving, going someplace, but in truth going no place. Bird dismissed the men at the stove and returned his attention to the gold coins he was separating. The clock on the wall struck twice, a hollow, metallic sound that accentuated the bleakness of the sparsely furnished room.

Eighteen-year-old Peyton Lewis chafed his frost-nipped hands as heat from the stove sent prickling sensations the length of his fingers. He surveyed the room.

Gracing one of the plastered, whitewashed walls, which did little to brighten the gloomy interior, was an oval-shaped, framed lithograph of George Washington. Facing George from the opposite side of the room was Abraham Lincoln. Beside Lincoln was the Seth Thomas clock that had just chimed. Several cane-backed chairs were pushed against the chair rail of an oaken wainscoting, and a walnut counter, behind which Bird stood, ran the width of the room. It was the walk-in vault beyond the teller, however, that caught—and held—Peyton's attention. Greenup Bird, the teller's father, had just moments before unlocked the vault and stepped inside.

Peyton's eyes met those of his two companions at the stove, and he smiled; their timing was perfect. Unbuttoning his greatcoat, he walked unhurriedly to the teller and shoved a five-dollar bill across the counter.

Unable to hide his astonishment that a young and shabby traveler was in possession of such a large sum of money, William Bird snatched up the bill and studied it front and back in the feeble light that penetrated the small-paned front windows. Satisfied that the currency was not counterfeit, he looked at Peyton.

"We give paper for paper, no gold." He laid the bill on the counter. "You want it changed to five ones?"

Peyton raised a Spiller and Burr, a .36-caliber Confederate revolver, and leaned across the counter to push its icy muzzle against the soft skin of Bird's forehead.

"And all the rest of the money in your bank."

Bird took a cautious step backward.

"What is this, mister?" His eyes swiveled from Peyton to the two men standing at the stove. They were watching him. "Are you boys funning somebody?"

Peyton cocked his pistol.

Incredulity caused William Bird's mouth to drop open.

"Nobody robs banks!" It was both a question and a statement.

Peyton's unwavering gray eyes penetrated into and through William Bird, leaving the man shaken with the reality that it was indeed a holdup and chances were good that he had only one heartbeat left to live.

Nineteen-year-old Jesse Woodson James opened his greatcoat and drew two Colt Dragoon revolvers from the waistband of his trousers. With an eye on the safe where William Bird's father had disappeared, he thumbed back the pistols' hammers and motioned for his brother, Frank, to watch the front door. Jesse laughed aloud when he glanced again at the counter where Peyton stood with his gun barrel pressed against Bird's face. Bird, shaking like a man with the ague, appeared to be trying his best to touch the ten-foot ceiling with his raised hands.

Seeing William Bird on the verge of hysteria sent a thrill of power through Jesse. It was a self-sustaining intoxicant that would carry him into and through a glorified life as an outlaw for the next sixteen years.

Jesse pointed his pistols at Bird, then laughed even harder when the young man squinched his eyes closed, certain that he would be shot. "Get a move-on, Peyton! Somebody's apt to come in here any minute. If that fellow gives you any sass, pull the trigger on him."

Peyton jerked a grain sack from beneath his coat and flung it at William Bird. He tipped his pistol barrel toward the cash drawer and the stacks of money on the countertop. "Put every last nickel in the sack . . . now!"

Out of the corner of his eye, Peyton saw Jesse dart into the vault, and he was relieved. Shooting the teller was not part of the plan. In fact, the unnecessary scaring of the young man into cowardice gave Peyton reason to question the validity of Jesse's actions, for he, Peyton Lewis, achieved no personal thrill from intimidating a man who was at a disadvantage.

William Bird, having also seen Jesse enter the vault, faltered, and in spite of the chill of the room, sweat beaded his forehead. "What's he going to do? My father's in that safe. He's an old man . . . his heart's not very strong."

"That depends on you, sir. You fill that sack real quick and easy, and we'll walk out of here an' nobody gets hurt. I suggest that you do as the man said: move!"

William Bird, taking nervous glances at the vault, shook open the grain sack and began raking the stacks of gold coins into the container. They made a dull, clinking sound as they struck one another in the bottom of the bag. Then he removed the cash drawer and dumped its contents into the sack.

As Bird laid the empty drawer on the counter, Jesse James emerged from the safe, straining under the weight of a similar sack that appeared even heavier than Peyton's. Jesse swung the bag onto the counter, then grinned at Peyton. "You ready?"

Peyton nodded.

Pointing with his chin, Jesse motioned William Bird inside the vault. The young man scrambled quickly across the floor to the safe and rushed inside.

Jesse slammed the vault door, then leaned close to its thick metal facing and tapped it with his gun barrel.

"You boys should feel right at home in there! You know birds are supposed to be caged." With a howl of laughter, he swaggered toward the counter.

Peyton's stomach tightened into a knot. The robbery had gone off like clockwork, smoothly and efficiently—then Jesse had ruined it. Peyton looked at Frank to see if he, too, had heard the foolish mistake, and was relieved to find that Frank was also scowling at Jesse.

Frank turned his back on his brother and hastened toward the door. "Let's get out of here, Jesse. We've been lucky so far. Let's don't press it."

Irritation marred Jesse's face as he shouldered the heavy, gold-laden gunnysack and stepped into the seat of a cane-backed chair, then onto the polished countertop, where he stood wide-legged and menacing.

"Hell, Frank, we probably just pulled off the first broad-open-daylight bank robbery in the history of America, an' it was easy as pie. What do you mean, we were lucky? Luck didn't have a damned thing to do with it."

Frank jerked open the front door and glanced up and down the street. It was clear. He turned to Jesse.

"I mean, let's walk out of this bank, mount our horses, and ride out of this town like we rode in—slow an' easy."

Jesse bounded to the floor and sauntered across the room to the front door. Without a sideways glance at either Frank or Peyton, he pushed through the opening and onto the steps of the bank, where new snow had already covered their entry tracks, made only minutes before.

He grinned at the nine mounted men. "We did it, boys. We got us more money in these sacks than you ever have seen."

Ignoring the film of snow that covered his saddle seat, Jesse snatched his bridle reins from young Fletcher Rucker and swung up on his horse. Wheeling the animal into a hard canter, Jesse spurred his mount savagely down Liberty's main thorough-fare. His henchmen, with Peyton bringing up the rear, galloped after Jesse, the hoofbeats of their horses muffled by the newly fallen snow.

George Wymore, a student at Liberty's William Jewell College, chose that precise moment to cross the street. He was thinking of sledding after class, of asking Norma Clendining to join him. As a result of his preoccupation, the dozen horsemen who thundered out of the swirling blizzard were on him before he knew it.

For a split instant, Wymore froze. He could see the steaming breath of the horses, the whites of their eyes, the cutting edges of their flashing hooves. Then he was running, his books tumbling from his arms, leaving a paper trail that followed him toward the wooden walkway at the far side of the street.

Jesse James, screaming a Rebel yell that shattered the tranquility of the deserted street, spurred his horse directly at the boy and leveled both of his heavy Dragoon revolvers at Wymore's fleeing back. Four quick shots, sounding like muted thunder in the snowstorm, slammed Wymore to the frozen earth and sent him skidding face first for several feet before coming to rest with his cheek pressed against the edge of the walkway.

Peyton Lewis reined his horse to a sliding halt and gaped down at the body. A moment ago, Wymore had been a living, breathing young man with an entire lifetime before him. Now the only thing that showed any signs of life was the boy's hair, ruffled by the wind of the outlaws' horses as they galloped past.

Fletcher Rucker, who had held the horses during the robbery, saw Peyton Lewis rein up abruptly, so he, too, pulled his horse to a skidding stop. Dancing his skittish mount up beside Peyton's, he peered nervously at him.

"Why'd you stop, Peyton? Your horse throw a shoe?"

When Peyton didn't answer, Rucker became even more apprehensive.

"We've got to get out of here, Peyton. This place is goin' to be covered up with folks any minute now." Rucker glanced anxiously down the street in the direction his comrades had fled, then back the way they had come. People were emerging from buildings, calling questions, demanding answers, and Rucker knew, with a sinking feeling that added to his anxiety, that it was only a matter of moments before their escape route would be sealed off.

"For Christ's sake, Peyton!"

"He's crazy, Fletcher." Peyton stared at the young body lying broken in the snow. "Jesse is just plain crazy."

Rucker's horse reared, then shied sideways away from the smell of blood, blowing through its wide, distended nostrils in an attempt to expel the odor.

Rucker jerked his horse back into line. "Jesse might be crazy, Peyton, but he ain't loony enough to hang around here an' get hisself shot by a bunch of townspeople. An' I ain't either."

Sinking his spurs into the animal's flank, Rucker jumped his mount into a canter that sent clods of snow flying in all directions.

When Peyton looked up from George Wymore's body, several people were standing on the walkway staring at him. There was no sound, only an eerie mixture of faces that bespoke horror, anger, disbelief, curiosity—and accusation. It was the latter that struck Peyton like the kick of a mule, leaving him sick to his stomach, disgusted not only with himself but with mankind in general, for they were all guilty of the murder of George Wymore—he, Jesse James, the onlookers, the government, the nation—because each had created the times they were living in, and those times were giving birth to men like Frank and Jesse James, like Fletcher Rucker, like Peyton Lewis.

Turning his horse, Peyton walked the animal slowly down the street, following the tracks of the men with whom he had ridden into town, men with whom he had fought the Union army, men with whom he had eaten and drunk. He knew, with that hollow feeling of one who turned his back on everything and everyone he called friend, that after today, he would never embrace them again because something, perhaps his last semblance of youth, had died along with George Wymore.

Two

Five miles west of Liberty, Missouri, the bank robbers sought refuge from the storm in an isolated, large, one-room clapboard church that was sheltered from the howling gale by a thick grove of oak trees. The men dismounted and led their horses through the double front doors of the building and down the long, narrow aisle to the open area before the pulpit.

Jesse wasted no time upending both grain sacks and dumping their contents on the rough pine floor. He stood back, grinning triumphantly at his companions as they abandoned their horses in a rush to get a better view of the fortune that spilled across the planks.

For the most part, they were country boys from hardscrabble farms that had barely eked out a living before the war. Since the war, there was no living at all. The gold that lay haphazardly scattered in all directions was spellbinding, the first coined money many of them had seen in more than four years and most definitely more wealth than any of them had ever beheld in their entire lives.

A horse blew and another stamped its hooves, but not a man moved as Jesse counted the plunder into twelve equal piles.

When he looked up at them, there was an insolent grin on his youthful face.

"Well, boys, our first holdup got us more than sixty thousand dollars. Sixty thousand dollars!" He raised his eyes to the picture of Jesus that adorned the wall behind the pulpit. "Look at it, Lord! They ain't never been this much money in one of your churches before, never!"

Jesse scraped together the few hundred paper dollars intermingled with the gold and stepped up to the pulpit. Making a production of stacking the currency neatly on the lectern, Jesse leaned on his elbows on the rostrum and gazed at the men below him. A slow smile curved his thin lips.

"How many of you men believe, come Sunday mornin', when the preacher of this church house figures out where this ill-gotten money came from, that righteous man of the cloth will march into that bank an' give it back?" Everyone laughed.

Jesse jumped down from the pulpit and raked his portion of the gold into a pair of saddlebags.

"We'll split up here and head for home, boys." He swung the leather bags over his shoulder. "In six or eight months, when things die down, I'll send word and we'll rob the bank over at Lexington."

Peyton Lewis, who, along with the rest of the men, was busy filling his own saddlebags, looked up at Jesse. "Don't send for me, Jess. I won't be coming along on the next one."

Jesse's smile vanished, and his long eyelashes fluttered spasmodically, as they had a habit of doing when he became excited or angry. Every man watching was aware that in Jesse James, either of those sensations could prove dangerous.

"You have five thousand dollars gold in your poke, Peyton. Do you have a problem with how we got it?" The eyelashes again.

Peyton shouldered his saddlebags. "I have nothing against robbing Yankee banks, Jess. It's probably the only revenge we'll ever get."

"Then what is it?"

Fletcher Rucker, along with the rest of the group, nervously watched the exchange. What had come over Peyton Lewis to cause him to openly brace Jesse James? Peyton was a fine pistol shooter—probably as good as Jesse or Frank—but Rucker would have been lying had he said that it did not bother him that Peyton had defied a man whom they had all seen flare into a killing rage with less provocation than they had just witnessed. Rucker licked his dry lips and inched his hand closer to his pistol.

Frank James closed the flap to his saddlebag and stepped to Jesse's side. He, too, was afraid for Peyton; it showed in his young, hard face. "What's the trouble, Peyton?"

Peyton let his breath slide through his teeth, angered at himself with the realization that he should have just ridden out without voicing his opinion. "We held up the Liberty bank, Frank, to pay back the Yankees and the carpetbaggers for what they've robbed from us these past four years. It was retribution. It was justified."

Jesse made a cutting motion with his hand. "We hit them sons-of-bitches a lick, Peyton, sixty thousand dollars' worth! And that's just the beginning. Before we're through with our retribution, the damned blue-bellies who have taken our homes, our farms, our country, will wish they'd stayed up north where they belong."

Peyton knew he was on shaky ground, but for the sake of everyone in the room, someone had to speak out and tell the truth about the robbery. "It's not the Northerners I'm concerned with, Jess; it's the Southerners." He had their attention. "In time, folks around here will laugh about the holdup, but what they'll never forget—or forgive—is the killing of that kid who was crossing the street. He was a Southerner, one of us. We killed one of our own people."

Jesse eased the saddlebags off his shoulder and dropped them on the floor. The solid thud as they struck the planks sounded loud in the stillness.

"We don't know that for certain, Peyton. The Yankees an' carpetbaggers have taken the South, brought their wives an' children down here. Why, hellfire, that boy was trying to head us off!"

Peyton shook his head. "All he was trying to do was get out of our way, Jess."

Jesse's eyelids fluttered like the wings of a moth, and he began unbuttoning his overcoat.

"I won't have a man riding with me who questions my leadership, Peyton."

Frank James put a restraining hand on Jesse's arm. "Peyton wasn't questioning your leadership, Jesse. Were you, Peyton?" He looked hard at Peyton. A warning.

Peyton shrugged, aware that Frank was giving him a way out. "I wasn't questioning Jesse's leadership." He slipped his hand inside his coat and gripped the handle of a five-shot Colt revolver, aware that a shootout would very likely erupt, but at that point not really caring. "I was questioning Jesse's judgment. We're the first men who ever robbed a bank in broad daylight, and it was simple. Heck, it was a joke. And that's how folks would have looked at it—a joke. But killing that boy was a mistake—an unnecessary mistake."

He was pushing Jesse hard and he knew it, but he could not stop. "It was also a mistake when Jesse called me—and you, Frank, and the Birds—by our given names. Sooner or later those bankers will remember his remarks, and it will dawn on them that the robbers had to be local boys."

Jesse scowled at the men around him, taking note of the uneasiness that suddenly filled their faces; Peyton had scored a point. Jesse laughed hesitantly. "Those bankers were scared out of their wits. Why, they won't even remember there were only three of us inside that bank."

Even with the braggadocio, it was a weak argument, and everyone knew it. Fletcher Rucker stepped closer to Peyton. They waited.

Peyton backed toward his horse, his hand on his pistol, his eyes watching Jesse's every move. "I'm taking my money and riding out of Missouri, Jess."

Jesse nodded. "I think that's the smartest thing you could do, Peyton. In fact, I think you'd better get out of here . . . now." The eyelashes again, faster than before.

The men watched in awkward silence as Peyton flung his heavy leather bags across his horse's rump and strapped them behind the saddle cantle. When he led his horse down the aisle to the front of the church, Frank walked with him, being careful to keep his body between Jesse and Peyton.

At the door, Frank caught Peyton's hand and shook it firmly. "Ride out of here and don't look back, Peyton. Good luck to you."

Peyton nodded at Frank and took one last look at the men who had been his friends for so many years. They were busy gathering up their money, laughing and discussing the robbery. Not one person glanced in his direction except Fletcher Rucker, who was studying him through bewildered eyes. Then someone spoke to Rucker, and he, too, looked away.

Peyton led his horse through the double doors, and a moment later, both man and beast were lost in the swirling blizzard that burst into the church like an angry preacher on a rampage.

When Fletcher Rucker left the church, he was only thirty minutes behind Peyton Lewis. He pushed his horse hard through the howling blizzard, expecting to overtake Peyton at any minute, but it was ten o'clock the next morning at the confluence of the Missouri and Kansas Rivers, thirty miles southwest of Liberty, when he finally came upon him.

Peyton had dismounted and was standing beside his horse, gazing across the wide expanse of slate-gray water.

Rucker rode up beside him and, sitting hump-shouldered because of the cold, he, too, looked out across the river. Even though the snow had stopped momentarily, a squall moving toward them from the west had effectively blotted out the far side of the stream, giving one a sense of murky water that stretched into infinity.

"Ferry on the other side?" Rucker's cold lips barely moved when he spoke. He licked them, and the saliva instantly froze.

If Peyton was surprised by Rucker's sudden appearance, he did not show it.

"I talked to the woman up at the tollhouse. She said it should be on its way back if it hasn't gotten lost in this blizzard."

"Any hot coffee up there at the tollhouse?"

"She didn't offer."

Rucker leaned forward and rested his forearm on his saddle pommel.

"That was a dumb thing you did, Peyton. Bracing Jesse."

"Maybe so."

"Why'd you do it?"

"Jesse killed that boy in Liberty for no reason."

"Why, hell, Peyton, durin' the war, we killed lots of men for no reason."

"The war's over, Fletcher."

Rucker shrugged. "Nobody but the Yankees believes that, Peyton."

The snowstorm that had been moving across the river hit them with heavy, wet flakes. Rucker drew his coat collar up over his ears to the brim of his tattered campaign hat.

"Where you headed, Peyton?"

Peyton did not answer.

Rucker lifted his hat from his head and brushed the snow from its brim. The wind plastered his long, ash-blond hair close around his chiseled cheeks. For that brief instant, one could easily have envisioned him a warrior standing on the windswept bow of a Viking ship.

Rucker shoved his hat firmly down on his head and drew the throat string snug under his chin. "I'd allow that, considerin' you're crossin' the Missouri an' headin' west, you're goin' to Texas. I'd kind of like to see Texas again myself."

Peyton's mouth tightened. Fletcher Rucker was his cousin; they had grown from adolescence together, worked the farm together, gone off to war together, and while Rucker had proven himself to be trustworthy and fearless in battle, he was childish and indifferent to matters concerning the responsibilities of real life and human emotions, which, unless there was fighting involved, made him a liability instead of an asset. Furthermore, even though Peyton would never consider vocalizing the sentiment, he was not at all sure he liked Fletcher Rucker.

"It's a free country, Fletcher."

"Well, now, Peyton." Rucker straightened in the saddle, and his face turned petulant. "That ain't no answer."

The sad truth of the matter was that Fletcher Rucker, although only a year younger than Peyton Lewis, had always depended upon his cousin for leadership and direction; it had been that way since childhood. Now, once again, like a younger sibling, he awaited the elder's approval.

When the ferry materialized out of the squall and made its way sluggishly toward the shore, Peyton Lewis, without a word or gesture to Fletcher Rucker, led his horse down the slippery incline to the river's edge.

Three

Assuming that a Clay County posse would be in pursuit of the bank robbers, Peyton and Rucker crossed the Missouri River, then turned their horses south by west and rode into a bleak stretch of Kansas prairie where the howling, snow-laden wind whipped across the endless flat country as though it were searching for a permanent landmark upon which to vent its pent-up energy. Finding none, it turned its fury upon the two riders and flailed them unmercifully.

They rode throughout the day and into the night hunched against the cold, their bedrolls, which were simply one moth-eaten blanket each, draped over their heads and wrapped close about their bodies.

Near midnight, Rucker suggested they stop and sit out the storm in a sheltered ravine, but Peyton declined, telling him they needed to put as much distance as possible between themselves and Liberty, Missouri.

Two hours later, when Rucker complained that he could no longer feel his hands or his feet, Peyton tied Rucker's bridle reins to his horse's tail to ensure against their becoming separated in the darkness and pushed on.

Dawn broke bitter cold but clear, and although Peyton did

not believe it possible, he must have slept, for he could not remember it having stopped snowing.

Twisting in the saddle to inspect their back trail, he was surprised to find that the path they had opened in the snow was a
fairly straight line all the way to the horizon. Even more incredible, they were still traveling south by west.

Rucker's horse followed a quarter of a mile back, having
sometime during the night broken the inflexible, ice-hardened
leather reins. Rucker, his blanket covered with snow, sat upright
in the saddle, and for a terrible instant Peyton was certain he had
frozen stiff. A moment later, however, a puff of cigarette smoke
spiral up from beneath Rucker's hat brim. Peyton drew rein and
waited for Rucker to catch up.

When Rucker rode abreast of Peyton, instead of being a
solid block of ice as Peyton had feared, he was reeling drunkenly
in the saddle and grinning like a dolt. Peyton threw out a restraining hand to keep the boy from falling.

"What in the name of God do you think you're doing,
Fletcher?" Peyton's words were slurred through lips that were too
numb to form the proper syllables. When Rucker merely
shrugged, Peyton caught up a handful of his overcoat lapel and
shook the boy until his head snapped.

"Where'd you get the liquor, Fletcher?"

"Had it all 'long, Peyton." Rucker fished clumsily in his saddlebag and withdrew a pewter flask. "You oughta try a shot, Peyton. It's a damn sight less painful to a body to be dead drunk
than dead hungry . . . an' we ain't ate since day b'fore yesterday."

Disgusted, Peyton released Rucker and touched his horse's
flank with his spurs. He rode on without looking back.

A bleak sun that reminded Peyton more of a sphere of cold,
gray ashes than a ball of fire stood two feet above the horizon
when he noticed a thin tendril of black, oily smoke rising from
what appeared to be a snowdrift a mile or more to his left. Drawing his horse to a halt, he studied the odd spectacle.

Then it dawned on him that on days like this, freezing cold,
knee-deep-snow days, folks who lived miles apart would often

lace their kindling with axle grease to send up a signal that they were alive and well. It also acted as a beacon to travelers who were unfortunate enough to find themselves stranded on the open prairie in such weather.

Rucker nudged his horse up beside Peyton, and he, too, watched the smoke. "I been real understandin' with you about puttin' distance 'tween us an' Liberty, Peyton. But I ain't goin' to be understandin' a'tall if you're figurin' on ridin' past that house without stoppin'."

They rode toward the smoke.

Caleb King shouldered open the door to his soddie and stepped outside. Having spent the last two days holed up in what was little more than a cellar with a sod roof, he was nearly blinded by the sun, weak as it was. He squinched his eyes shut and immediately began unbuttoning the fly of his trousers. A moment later, in the middle of urinating, he opened his eyes to find two mounted men not thirty feet away, watching him. King grinned sheepishly, which amounted to little more than a parting of his thick, rust-colored beard.

"Well, boys, you durn near caused me to piss all over myself—an' they ain't nothin' more degradin' than for a man to be caught with his pants down. I wasn't expectin' no callers. Not this early, nohow."

King buttoned his trousers and closed his coat. "Must be ten below zero out here." He glanced out over the unbroken space of prairie which stretched like a white carpet to the horizon, searching for wagons, packhorses, fellow travelers, anything that would give him a clue as to the identity of the two men. Shifting his attention back to Peyton and Rucker, then their horses, and finally their heavy saddlebags, he waded through the knee-deep snow toward them.

"Name's Caleb King, gents. You might as well climb down an' come inside an' warm yourselves for a spell. It's cold enough out here to freeze the brass balls off'n a pair of horse collar hames."

Peyton attempted to kick his boots free of the stirrups; they were welded to the leather by solid sheets of ice. "We can't dismount."

He watched King closely, bothered by the speculation that flickered in the man's small, piggish eyes as they again strayed cunningly to Peyton's saddlebags. It was the same expression Peyton had seen in the eyes of his Confederate commanders when they were evaluating the strength of an enemy position prior to their attack.

King grinned sympathetically at Peyton. "Froze to your saddles, eh?"

Peyton was certain there was a sound of satisfaction in the man's tone, and he forced his numb hand inside his greatcoat to fumble awkwardly for the butt of the revolver housed in his waistband, praying that King would not guess he was unable to so much as feel the hammer or the trigger of the weapon.

The significance of Peyton's hand disappearing inside his coat was not lost on King, and he hesitated as he approached the rider. Indecision played across his rugged face as he gazed up at the youth: the boy was cautious—too cautious—to be merely a greenhorn kid on his way west. He was hiding something. Or protecting it.

Watching Peyton from beneath his shaggy brows, Caleb King waded the rest of the way to Peyton's horse and twisted the stirrups from Peyton's boots. With a ripping noise that left particles of ice clinging to the frozen cloth, he peeled the fabric of Peyton's trouser legs free of the saddle fender.

King moved on to the second horse. Because Rucker's hands were in plain sight and posed no threat, he addressed Peyton as he ripped Rucker's legs free of the leather: "Jest who might you boys be? An' what brings you out in god-awful weather like this?"

Peyton leaned forward on his horse's neck and worked his leg over the cantle. He debated answering the man's question, then decided he and Rucker were far enough from Liberty to chance telling the truth.

"I'm Peyton Lewis. He's my cousin, Fletcher Rucker."

Peyton dropped to the ground and would have collapsed in the snow had he not hooked his elbow around the saddle horn for support. For a long moment, he hung there, feeling nothing from his knees down. When he and Rucker staggered in King's footsteps to the soddie, Peyton was surprised that his feet functioned at all, for they were as dead as lead weights, and had he not seen them rise and fall, he would have sworn they had not moved.

By the time they reached the soddie and tied their horses to the rickety hitching post, the wind, as though aware that its quarry was escaping, attacked with renewed vengence. When they ducked their heads to negotiate the low doorway of the soddie, snow blasted into the room as if it were unafraid of and could overcome the feeble heat that would spell its demise. King hurriedly slammed the door behind them and walked to a small potbellied stove at the far end of the room. Shoving his hands into the steam that was rising from a pot of stew that simmered on its cast-iron top, he squinted through the dim light of a single candle lantern at the two young men, again sizing them up. Nobody but a crazy person would venture out in weather like this unless they had a darned good reason. "It's a pure wonder you boys are still alive." When neither of the men commented, King shrugged his shoulders. "It'd be a heap easier to talk to you fellers if you'd talk back at me."

Peyton thrust his hands into the heat above the stove and attempted to flex his fingers. They were too stiff to move. He swung his gaze to King, and eased his hands closer to the stove top, splaying his fingers to catch as much warmth as possible. "Our horses need seeing to, Mr. King. Have you got a barn? Some grain or hay?"

King studied Peyton's frozen hands, and for a split instant the man's face shone with a cunning that caused Peyton to physically force his stiff fingers to slowly curve into fists.

When King spoke, his words were guarded. "We ain't had time to build no barn, not even a lean-to. I'll turn your horses loose like we do our oxen. They won't stray far."

Peyton turned his hands over to warm their backs and again flexed his fingers into fists. It was easier this time. He watched King out of the corner of his eye, concerned by the brief, crafty look that had crossed the man's face. "The horses stay, where they are, Mr. King."

If King heard the apprehension in Peyton's comment, he ignored it, and shrugged his shoulders good-naturedly. "Suit yourself. But them animals of yours is plumb wore out. And, from the looks of you, ain't neither one of you boys in no shape to ride nohow."

When neither Peyton nor Rucker answered, King grinned widely at Peyton, exposing a row of crooked, tobacco-stained teeth. "Aw, hell, Lewis. The truth is, me an' my woman would be plumb tickled if you boys would stay a day or two with us. Why, we ain't had no company in a coon's age. That's why I greased the firewood, to attract company!"

Peyton mulled over King's words. Something the man said . . . Then it hit him: "me an' my woman." Alarmed, he quickly scanned the interior of the soddie, which was no more than twelve feet wide by fifteen feet long. The room was lit by a single candle lantern that hung from an overhead beam in the center, its dull flame doing little to dispel the gloom of the dreary, cellarlike chamber. Nor did its waxen fumes alleviate the stench of damp sod, unwashed bodies, and other odors peculiar to closed-in humans. Firewood was stacked floor to ceiling along one earthen wall, and shelves that housed foodstuffs and personal items, one of which was a large leather-bound Bible, had been hacked out of the dirt of the opposite wall. Beneath the Bible, a new .44-caliber Henry repeating rifle stood upright with its front sight resting against the holy book's thick, black leather cover. Peyton's eyes narrowed in speculation. A Henry repeating rifle was not the type of weapon favored by most farmers. His gaze swiveled to a pallet on the floor that served as a bed. It was barely wide enough for one person. Nowhere in the soddie did he see anything that indicated a woman's touch—no rugs, no frills, not a dress or a bonnet.

Skepticism pushed two quick questions to the forefront of Peyton's mind: If there was a woman, where was she? Or was King suffering from cabin fever?

Amid a blast of frigid air, the door of the soddie was forced open, and a heavily bundled figure tromped in, stamping her feet in an effort to dislodge the ice and snow that clung to her brogan work shoes and the hem of her ragged woolen skirt.

As she stood there, blinking against the blinding change from outside brilliance to interior darkness, Peyton used that instant to appraise Mrs. King. His surprise was total: she was tall for a woman and young, probably a year or so his junior. Her face was narrow, hollow-cheeked, and incredibly dirty with what appeared to be an accumulation of woodsmoke, soot, cooking grease, and just plain everyday living. Her hands were gloveless, red and chapped, the fingernails broken and grimy.

As her eyes adjusted to the dimness, she became aware of Peyton's critical scrutiny and glared at him with open animosity. Peyton touched his hat brim in the customary salute, but she ignored the gesture and addressed Caleb King.

"The brindled ox froze to death last night." Her voice carried the dull, unemotional tone of one who was used to talking to herself. She removed her floppy-brimmed black felt hat and hung it on a wall peg near the door. "The red one won't make it through the day without shelter."

Her hair, more the color of tarnished bronze than gold, hung in limp, greasy strands to frame a gaunt face whose only claim to animation was a pair of intelligent, oversized, almond-shaped brown eyes that cut like a knife through the feeble light cast by the candle lantern.

Her words hung in the air as though they were a planned assault on King's credibility, for he had, just minutes before, insisted that Peyton turn his horses loose as he had done his oxen—and now one of the beasts was dead and the other dying. Caleb King's hands slowly balled into fists, and his mouth drew into a thin line of accusation as he stared at the woman.

Peyton was certain King intended to strike her, and she thought so, too, for she visibly steeled herself for the blow. A second ticked by, then another, and the woman's face grew tenser.

With a look that said he would deal with her later, King draped his arm over her shoulders and pulled her close against him. He grinned at Peyton. "If you boys will stay the evening, my wife, Molly"—he tightened his arm around the woman's shoulders until she flinched in pain—"will traipse back down to the pasture and butcher that ox that froze."

He smiled even more broadly at Peyton, but the mirth never reached his eyes. "How does a big, sizzlin' beefsteak sound to you gents?"

The thought of a hot meal twisted Peyton's stomach into a knot. Still, he hesitated. Something was not right in this house; the man was much too eager to please, and the woman was either too agitated—or frightened—to make even the slightest attempt at hospitality.

Peyton glanced at Rucker to see if he, too, sensed the tension between King and his wife.

Rucker did not; indeed, he mistook Peyton's gaze as an invitation to express his opinion, which he did without thought. "Why, that's right generous of you, Mr. King. Me an' Peyton ain't had a hot meal in over two days!"

Peyton felt the woman's gaze penetrate him like a blast of cold air. When he looked at her, her eyes slid away, but not before he saw what appeared to be alarm glimmering in their depths. Why would she feel threatened? Did he know her? Peyton studied her more closely. No, he had never met Mrs. King.

He swung his gaze back to her husband. "Much obliged for the offer, Mr. King, but we'll just be here long enough to thaw out, then we're riding on." Out of the corner of his eye, he saw Molly King release her pent-up breath.

King removed his arm from his wife's shoulders. "Well, at least take breakfast with us. Surely you ain't in that big of a hurry."

Rucker's mouth dropped open at Peyton's refusal of a hot meal. Had his cousin gone daft?

"You bet we'll stay for breakfast!" He looked hard at Peyton, his silent challenge visible to King and his wife.

Peyton saw Molly King's face stiffen, but other than that momentary tenseness that drew her jaw into knots, she revealed nothing as her cold fingers fumbled clumsily with the buttons of her dingy, woolen gentleman's topcoat. It was a slow process as she negotiated the fasteners through the eyelets, but she finally shrugged the coat off her shoulders and hung it on the same peg

that held her hat. She was thinner than Peyton had first imagined, but that was all he could tell concerning her figure, for the
colorless, homespun dress she wore hung like a sack from shoulder to floor, and like the rest of her, it, too, appeared not to have
seen soap or water since its threads came off the spinning wheel.

As Molly approached the stove, Rucker snatched off his hat
and held it reverently over his heart. "We hate to be a bother,
ma'am, but we surely are hungry."

Molly hesitated for the briefest instant, studying Rucker's
face. The smell of liquor, which she abhorred, was heavy on his
breath, and his eyes appeared unfocused as the undulating glow
of the candle lantern highlighted the planes and peaks of his features. Yet, even under those unflattering conditions, Molly was
aware that it had been a long time since she had seen a man—
no, two men; her eyes strayed to Peyton—as handsome as these.
For the first time in months, she struggled with a sensation she
had thought long defeated: fear—not for herself, never for herself—but for the two unsuspecting young travelers. The emotion
staggered her, for she had been truly convinced that the last
three years with Caleb King had left her callous to any feelings
whatsoever.

Molly stepped past Rucker and retrieved two wooden bowls
from a hand-split board shelf suspended by ropes attached to an
overhead beam.

Caleb King, as though he were afraid for his wife to be more
than a step or two away from him, sidled up to Molly until his
thigh brushed hers. Again she visibly tensed. And a moment
later, when King made a show of patting her backside, she cut
her eyes quickly to Peyton to see if he had observed the intimacy. He had. Stepping away from Caleb, she began vigorously
stirring the stew.

Peyton watched the two from beneath his low-pulled hat
brim, certain that had Molly and Caleb King been alone, she
would have verbally rebuffed her husband's crude show of pro-
prietorship.

The animosity that stirred the very air itself inside the small
enclosure was suddenly so thick Peyton could almost taste it. He
glanced again at his cousin, but Rucker, oblivious to the intrigue

that was manifesting itself so belligerently throughout the soddie, seemed to be engrossed with this tall, thin woman who was
young enough to be Caleb King's daughter instead of his wife.

Rucker grinned with loose-lipped drunkenness at the girl,
and asked her how far it was to the Missouri River.

Peyton groaned under his breath, and his fingers itched to
reach out and attach themselves to Rucker's throat. Why did
Fletcher not pay attention? Something was wrong with these people; any fool could see that!

As though Molly had heard Peyton's apprehension, she
glanced over her shoulder at him. A guarded wistfulness crept
into her eyes. Or was it a warning?

Before Peyton could reflect on her latest expression, Caleb
King answered Rucker's question. "I'd guess it's maybe eighteen,
twenty miles to the Missouri River, as the crow flies."

Twenty miles! Rucker glared accusingly at Peyton; they had
nearly frozen to death to put only twenty miles between them
and the Clay County law. He had a good mind to tell Peyton to
go on to Texas without him, that he would lay over with the
Kings for a week or two until the weather cleared. Hell, what
was their big hurry? Texas wasn't going anywhere.

Molly King dipped stew into the bowls and handed one to
Peyton. A calculated yearning was in her gaze. "Are you going
east? Kansas City, maybe?" She extended a bowl to Rucker, but
her gaze stayed riveted to Peyton.

It was on the tip of Peyton's tongue to lie to her and say yes,
but her eyes demanded the truth. He said nothing.

Caleb King observed the silent interchange between his wife
and Peyton Lewis, and a smoldering anger began in the pit of his
stomach. He and Molly had enacted this very same scenario to
its sordid conclusions many times in the past. She knew exactly
what was expected of her, but she was not playing her part well
at all.

"Accordin' to their tracks"—he eyed Molly with slow delib-
eration—"they came from Kansas City."

For a split instant a cloud of doubt obscured the woman's
face, then it was gone. Rucker took his bowl of stew from her and
ladled a spoonful into his mouth.

"Me an' Peyton are on our way to Texas." He grinned at her. "We're goin' to build us a ranch, be the biggest cattlemen in the whole darned state."

Peyton frowned at Rucker. Every time his cousin opened his mouth, he said too much.

King threw a significant look at the woman, and something passed between the two that upset her, for she blanched a deathly shade of gray before turning quickly to the stove and busying herself by lifting the iron lid and adding more firewood.

Caleb King wore a smug countenance as he addressed Rucker. "World of land down there in Texas. Thought a time or two about goin' down there myself. But I ain't never had enough money. . . . It takes money to buy land an' build up a ranch." He raised his eyebrows as though he expected a reply.

Rucker wiped his mouth with the back of his hand, but before he could answer, Peyton changed the subject. "Did you homestead this place, Mr. King?"

King's mouth tightened with annoyance. He had expected the talkative one to reply, for the truth was, he had already written Peyton Lewis off as a source of information.

"Homestead? Naw. I bought this place outright. I got a deed. Hell, the Homestead Law ain't nothin' but the U. S. government bettin' some fool a hundred and forty acres he can't live on it! And nine times out of ten, Uncle Sam wins!"

King shifted his attention to Molly as she handed him a bowl of stew. "I'm a farmer, gents. Just a hardworkin' tiller of the soil." He spooned a chunk of meat into his mouth, then, chewing vigorously, steered the conversation again to Rucker.

"Now that the war's over, I expect folks will flock to Texas. Yes, sir, there'll be Conestoga wagons rollin' past here in droves with 'Gone to Texas' painted in big red letters on their sides." King's eyes narrowed. "Land's mighty cheap out there, I hear tell a man can buy some prime property anywhere from ten cents to a dollar an acre." It was not a question, nor a statement; it was a probe.

Rucker, the worse for the liquor he had drunk, grinned with foolish importance at the man. "Well, if land's that cheap, Mr. King, I reckon me an' Peyton's goin' to own a passel of acres."

Peyton took a bite of stew to hide his disgust. Would Rucker never learn to keep his mouth shut? Probably not. Peyton's thoughts shifted to King's remark that he owned his land free and clear. Yet he had built no barns or sheds—not even a wind-break to keep his livestock from freezing to death. Even more pe-culiar was the sparseness of the soddie itself. The first thing a man usually did when moving into a home, soddie or not, was to build his woman a bedstead, something that would raise her off the cold, damp dirt floor. Something permanent. Something in-timate. There was nothing in this dugout that suggested either of those. Peyton's eyes traveled to the expensive Henry repeat-ing rifle. Caleb King was lying about being a sodbuster. Why? Peyton pushed the question from his mind; it did not actually matter one way or the other because he and Rucker were leaving here as soon as they finished eating.

King kept up a constant dialogue with Rucker. On the sur-face his questions appeared innocent, but to Peyton they held an underlying intensity that bordered on interrogation. It was a re-lief when the meal was finally over.

Peyton handed his empty bowl to Molly. "My cousin and I are obliged to you for your hospitality, ma'am." He withdrew the five-dollar bill he had used in the bank robbery and offered it to her.

If he had expected the Kings to protest payment for the less than meager fare, he was mistaken. Caleb King snatched the money from his hand and held it up to the light of the lantern, where he inspected both sides of the bill. Molly eyed the money longingly, almost reverently, as though it were a savior of some sort. Peyton would have been amazed had he known that his five-dollar bill was the first legal tender she had seen in three long years—since Caleb King—and she was thinking that with a sum that large, she could leave King and this forsaken prairie behind and purchase a ticket on the next stagecoach going any direction. The dream showed on her face. Again, Peyton was struck by the oddity of the couple's deliberate rudeness—but most especially hers—and he determined that they had been cooped up on this windswept prairie much too long. The quicker he and Rucker got away from them, the better.

Peyton walked to the door of the soddie and waited for

Rucker to join him. Caleb King watched him through slitted eyes while Molly studied him through wide, frightened ones.

Rucker stopped at the door and doffed his hat to Molly. "A finer fare I ain't never eaten, Mrs. King." He grinned boyishly at her. "General Lee said that to one of his soldiers when they was suppin' on acorns, ma'am."

Peyton waited until Rucker stepped outside, then he, too, tipped his hat to the woman. Watching the pair closely, he ducked beneath the doorjamb, then quickly waded through the snow to his horse. Placing the animal between himself and the house—an automatic precaution learned from his cavalry days, when soldiers used their mounts to shield themselves from enemy fire—he threw the stirrup of his saddle up over the horn and quickly tightened the cinch.

Rucker forwent tightening his cinch and immediately swung himself into the saddle. As he shifted his weight to straighten his riding gear, his horse sidestepped to balance itself. At that instant, a shot exploded from the doorway of the soddie, and the bullet slammed into Rucker's back, driving him halfway out of his saddle.

As the blast reverberated across the open prairie, Rucker's horse fishtailed into a mad dash through the knee-deep snow, and for the first time in his life, just to keep his seat, Fletcher Rucker, one of the finest horsemen in the Confederate cavalry, was forced to grasp his saddle horn.

Before that first shot had become an echo, Peyton was in action. He drew his revolver from his waistband, dropped to one knee, and thumbed off two quick shots beneath his horse's belly at the soddie's partially open door. The horse trembled and quivered, but, being a seasoned cavalry mount, it set its legs and stood firm as Peyton emptied the remaining four chambers into the darkened interior.

Caleb King slammed the door, and for a long second there was total silence. Then, his voice muffled by the thick wooden boards, he called a truce. "All right, Peyton! Stop shootin', damn you. You done knocked off my kneecap. I'll be crippled for life!"

Peyton eased his small, five-shot new model Colt pocket pistol from his saddlebag and cocked it. Resting his arm across his horse's back, he fired a round into the door, then another.

Caleb King howled his protest, shouting again that he was already wounded.

Peyton kept his pistol leveled at the soddie. "I'm walking my horse out of rifle range before I mount up, King." He watched the door expectantly. "If you so much as stick your rifle sight outside that house, I'll come back on your blind side and smoke you out of there. And I'll shoot you dead when you come out. And if you've murdered Fletcher Rucker, I'll come back and shoot you anyway."

When the door remained closed and Caleb King did not respond, Peyton, careful to keep the horse between himself and the gunman, walked the animal two hundred yards out onto the prairie before climbing into the saddle.

With a final glance toward the soddie, he spurred his horse toward Fletcher Rucker, who was now but a speck on the seemingly endless expanse of snow-covered plains.

From behind the stove where she had taken refuge when the shooting began, Molly Klinner watched Caleb King crack open the door and bring his rifle to bear on Peyton Lewis.

King laughed aloud and thumbed back the hammer. "That damn fool ain't got a suspicion that this Henry rifle will shoot plumb dead center at three hunnerd an' fifty yards if you hold the front sight two inches high. . . ."

As King lifted the rifle barrel to the desired height and settled his sights two inches above Peyton's head, Molly raised a .34-caliber Bacon and Company single-shot boot pistol and pointed it at him. "If you shoot him, Caleb, I'll kill you."

King's finger froze on the trigger, and for a long instant, time stood still. Wind-driven snow gusted into the room and settled on King like a swarm of small white butterflies. He did not move. When he finally turned his head toward Molly, his face was nearly comical in its incredulousness, and the sight of her pistol brought a sneer to his lips.

Dismissing Molly as though neither she nor the pistol existed, Caleb King turned again to the cracked door and searched for his quarry. Unable to see Peyton in his limited field of vision, he shouldered the door open another six inches and peered in all directions. Finally, he saw the rider emerge from a low place on the prairie five hundred yards away.

With an oath of obscenities directed at Molly, King abandoned the rifle and turned his attention to his shattered leg. His face was a mask of pain as he ripped his trouser leg to expose the wound.

"Damn you, woman. Get over here an' stop this bleedin'. Can't you see that half my goddammed knee is blowed away?"

Molly watched, fascinated, as King clutched his shattered knee with both hands in an attempt to stop the flow of blood that surged down his leg like molten volcanic ash and splattered like lava on the instep of his boot. She wondered how long it would take Caleb King to bleed to death: two minutes? Two hours? Never? The fact that she even considered allowing him to die concerned her; but the realization that she actually wished he were already dead scared her. What had happened these past years to make her so callous, so uncaring? She gazed into King's face. He was perspiring in spite of the cold. He had changed her—he alone. His meanness. His baseness. His hatred for everything and everybody he touched. Had it truly rubbed off on her?

King saw the reluctance in Molly's eyes, and his pale face blanched even more sickly as the truth that she would not lift a finger to help him penetrated his pain-ridden brain. He lunged for the rifle wedged in the doorway, and Molly pointed the pistol toward him.

"Don't touch that rifle, Caleb. Don't make me shoot you."

King's fingers hovered near the stock of the Henry. He peered up at her, taking in her ashen face and a hand that trembled so badly that the pistol she held was aimed spasmodically at nearly every part of his body. His face twisted into a mocking taunt.

"You better come to your senses, girl. You ain't goin' to get but one shot outa that popgun, an' you know as well as me that a pistol at twenty feet is as worthless as tits on a boar hog."

Molly drew back the hammer and steadied her hand. The pistol bore yawned menacingly at a spot between King's eyes.

King, sincerely believing Molly would not have the courage to challenge him, was startled by the metallic sound of the hammer clicking into full cock. He gazed from the pistol barrel to the woman standing across the room. She couldn't shoot him. Not her! Not that sniveling piece of trash whom he had beaten into submission these past three years. Not she who never spoke unless spoken to. Not she who had finally embraced him and his way of life.

He gazed into her unblinking eyes, and for the first time since having abducted her in 1863, fear welled up in him, for even his slow-witted, mean-spirited mind understood the significance of her newfound courage. King grabbed the rifle stock, and Molly squeezed the trigger.

Four

It took Peyton more than an hour of hard riding to catch Rucker's horse. Every step of the way, as he tracked the animal through the knee-deep snow, he had expected to find his cousin's body. Somehow, Rucker had managed to stay in the saddle. Peyton knew, judging from the amount of blood that covered the boy's coat and trousers, that Rucker was hanging on to both his horse and his life by sheer determination and stubbornness. Neither could last much longer. Peyton also knew that if Rucker were to lose consciousness and fall, he, Peyton Lewis, would not have the strength to lift him back into his saddle. Peyton dismounted and tied Rucker's boots to his stirrups.

Rucker clung to his saddle horn and stared down at Peyton, his face drained and haggard.

"Two years, Peyton. Two long years of war an' we never got shot—not once. . . ." Rucker tried to smile, but it was a grimace instead. "Ain't this the shits."

Peyton nodded to himself: Rucker had summed it up nicely.

The blue shadows that highlight snow when evening falls were already creeping into the pockets and low places before Peyton found a suitable location for a campsite. He was forced to dismount and physically drag Rucker's horse down a treach-

erous incline into a broad gully that housed a shallow, frozen
stream. Leaving Rucker in the saddle, Peyton searched the
sparsely wooded banks of the ravine for enough kindling to fuel
a fire, and in less than twenty minutes he had a substantial flame
gnawing greedily at the frozen twigs.

Peyton untied Rucker and eased him out of the saddle, then
seated him beside the flames. Squatting in the snow, he carefully drew the boy's bloodied greatcoat down over his shoulders
until it lay in a heap around his waist. Peyton unbuttoned
Rucker's shirt, then his long johns, and peeled back both gar-
ments until the wound was visible. The .44 slug had passed
through Rucker's back and exited his shoulder just above his
pectoral muscle. It was a messy, ugly puncture.

Rucker peered at the wound, then grinned weakly at Peyton. "Why'd he shoot me instead of you? Nothin' ever happens
to you, Peyton. It just ain't fair." Rucker's feverish eyes closed,
then opened. "I should have stayed with Jesse and Frank. At least,
when we rob banks, it's us doin' the shootin'!"

When Peyton remained silent, Rucker looked fearfully at
him. "Has he killed me, Peyton?"

"He shot you clean through, Fletcher. You'll live."

Rucker closed his eyes and relaxed, and Peyton was glad he
had lied to his cousin about the wound. The truth was, he had
seen men with lesser wounds die agonizing deaths.

Peyton climbed to his feet and hurried to Rucker's horse,
where he retrieved the pewter whiskey flask from the saddlebags.
Disappointment caused his shoulders to sag; the decanter was
nearly empty. Kneeling beside Rucker, he debated whether or
not to pour the remaining whiskey on the open wound or attempt
to numb the pain from the inside. Rucker made the decision.

"I need about two fingers of that liquor in a number-two
washtub, Peyton."

Peyton held the flask to Rucker's lips, and the boy drank
deeply. When the whiskey was gone, Rucker moaned and gritted
his teeth. "Not enough, Peyton. . . ."

Peyton cast the flask aside. Untying the knot of his cotton
neckerchief, he ripped the fabric in half and folded the two pieces
into compresses. After applying them firmly to the entrance and

exit holes, he slipped Rucker's clothing into place and drew the greatcoat up over his shoulders.

The weight of the garment against Rucker's wound was like a hot brand being driven into his flesh, and the boy clenched his teeth to stifle the cry that was forcing its way into his throat.

"I'm sure as hell glad I ain't stone sober, Peyton . . . I ain't for certain I could handle this."

A minute went by, then Rucker's eyes closed and his chin inched down to his chest. Peyton thought he had passed out, but a moment later, the boy's eyes flicked open.

"Come mornin', Peyton, I'm goin' to ride back to that soddie an' shoot Caleb King, an' see how he likes it."

You'll be lucky to be alive in the morning, Fletcher. That realization left Peyton shaken. Suddenly he was homesick for the good years before the war when he and Rucker were boys, hunting and fishing together. Peyton blinked away the memory and reached out and took Rucker's cold hand.

"We'll ride over to Caleb King's in the morning and we'll both shoot him, Fletcher."

Rucker did not hear him; the warmth of the fire, combined with the loss of blood, had finally pushed him into unconsciousness.

Peyton retrieved Rucker's blanket roll from his saddle and draped it over the sleeping man. Then, unsaddling both horses and dropping the gear next to the fire, he led the animals down the gully to a windswept field where stems of natural hay showed above the snow. He slipped the bridle bits out of the bone-tired horses' mouths and turned them loose. They wearily began pawing away the snow and ripping up mouthfuls of summer-cured grass.

Thirty minutes later, when Peyton rounded the creek bend and had an unobstructed view of the campsite, he was startled to see Molly King seated beside the fire warming her hands. Even the thickening twilight which had settled over the entire area like a flimsy blue blanket failed to conceal the cold and weariness that showed in her face. Peyton unbuttoned his overcoat and drew his pistol.

As he approached, Molly made a deprecating gesture to-

ward the gun. "You won't need that, Mr. Peyton." Her voice was
flat, emotionless. Then, with only the slightest hint of curiosity in
her eyes, she pursed her lips at him. "Is Peyton your last name or
your first?"

Ignoring her, Peyton followed her trail up the embankment
to where her horse was tied to a bush at the edge of the ravine.
The animal stood with its head drooping nearly to its knees. It
was so gaunt that every bone in its body showed beneath its dull,
shaggy coat, and Peyton wondered how it had found the strength
to endure the five-mile trek from the soddie to his campsite. He
backtracked the animal for a quarter of a mile before he determined that Molly King was alone.

When he turned toward camp, he was stunned to find her
not twenty feet away with Caleb King's rifle pointed at his chest.

The gun seemed more a challenge than a threat, and after
a long moment of silence, she shrugged. "Do we shoot each
other, Mr. Peyton?"

The unwavering rifle lay with loose assurance in her grip.
Her stance was hipshot, relaxed. She was calm and waiting.

"No." He slipped his revolver into his waistband and rebut-
toned his overcoat. "We don't shoot each other."

Peyton made his way to the fire and hunkered down beside
Rucker, his back to Molly as she approached.

She propped her rifle against Rucker's saddle and knelt beside Peyton.

"Coffee will be ready in a minute." She indicated a tin pot
nestled in the embers near the edge of the fire.

Resentment welled up in Peyton. Without so much as a by-
your-leave, the woman had commandeered his camp and made
herself at home.

He glanced beyond her to the Henry rifle. The only way
she could have gained possession of Caleb King's weapon was
over his dead body—and he was not certain whether he should
be elated or bothered by that truth.

"What are you doing here, Mrs. King?"

"I followed you."

Anger pushed color into Peyton's face. "Don't fool with me,
Mrs. King. You didn't simply follow me."

"I didn't say following you was simple. Your horses broke the trail; mine merely walked in their path."

"That's not what I asked you, Mrs. King."

Molly ducked her head and began rummaging in a gunny-sack that lay in the snow beside her rifle. A moment later she withdrew a tin drinking mug. Using the hem of her skirt as a pot holder, she lifted the coffeepot out of the embers and filled the mug. After taking a sip, she handed the steaming coffee to Peyton.

"I only brought one cup, Mr. Peyton. I didn't take time to pack properly. Just threw some things into the sack. . . ."

Her voice trailed off, and Peyton wondered if she was apologizing.

"Don't explain a damned cup to me, Mrs. King. Explain what happened in that soddie. Explain why your husband tried to murder Fletcher and me."

Molly gazed steadily at him, her dark eyes deep and fine and uncompromising. The wind whipped loose strands of hair across her face, but she made no move to push them back.

"Caleb King assumed that because you were on your way to Texas to buy a ranch, you must be carrying an impressive sum of money." She smiled at him. It was a sad expression, without warmth or friendship. "Your actions indicated as much . . . that you had something of value. You were too nervous; you didn't want anyone to go near your horses. Elusive. Like you were hiding something . . . or protecting it."

She looked away and studied the silent landscape. "And when you offered that five-dollar bill, well, that proved his suspicions. Actually, it didn't make any difference. . . ." Molly King sighed, and her voice dropped to a murmur, as though she were speaking to herself. "Caleb would have killed you for your guns and horses, anyway."

Without waiting for Peyton to reply, she flicked her hand toward Rucker. "He's lucky to be alive. Caleb King didn't usually miss when he set his mind on killing somebody."

Peyton's mouth tightened; he did not like this woman. "He didn't miss, Mrs. King. Fletcher's shot clear through. He'll probably die before sunup."

Molly shrugged. "Fletcher's lucky to be drawing breath, Mr. Peyton. Take my word for it."

Peyton took a sip of coffee. He supposed she was right. Perhaps Rucker was lucky to be alive—but that was beside the point.

"Is there any whiskey in that sack you brought?" He made no effort to hide the contempt in his voice, or to erase the disgust for her that showed plainly on his face. "We could at least ease his pain, and clean the wound."

Molly shook her head and told him Caleb King had been without whiskey for weeks. She walked around the fire to Rucker and dropped wearily to her knees beside him. Without asking permission, she removed the blood-soaked compresses and studied the wound. Then, using the snow-soaked tail of her topcoat, she sponged away the blood that flowed freely from the punctures. Thirty minutes later, her shoulders sagging from exhaustion, she cleansed the last of the dried blood from Rucker's body, then raised her eyes to Peyton.

"I have a tin of sulfur in the gunnysack, Mr. Peyton, but it would be a waste to apply it to a wound that's still hemorrhaging."

Peyton watched new blood fill the ragged holes and trickle down Rucker's body. He knew she was right, but fear for his cousin's life, and a streak of stubbornness, kept him from admitting it. Furthermore, he would be damned if he would sit idly by if there was the merest chance of saving Rucker's life.

"Do it anyway."

Molly shrugged and reached into the gunnysack for the can of sulfur. She unscrewed the lid, then sprinkled the yellow powder on the wounds.

She returned the tin to the sack, replaced the compresses, and drew Rucker's clothing up over his shoulders.

Peyton watched her every move, untrusting, skeptical, cautious. "Your husband let on that one of my bullets broke his leg, Mrs. King. Is that true?" Eyes narrowed, he rocked back on his heels, studying her face for a reaction.

Molly laughed. It was a hollow sound without mirth.

"That's the first time I ever saw Caleb King surprised by anything. He had nothing but contempt for handguns, Mr. Peyton.

Caleb always complained that a pistol was no account unless the shooter was standing within three feet of the person he intended to kill." Three feet! Well, Caleb had certainly been mistaken about that; a handgun was just as accurate at fifteen feet. "Yes, Caleb was definitely surprised, Mr. Peyton. He wasn't even expecting you to shoot back at him, much less hit him."

"How bad was the wound, Mrs. King?"

His concern for Caleb King's well-being irritated her, and she eyed him defensively. "It was fatal, Mr. Peyton."

Peyton's first impulse was to apologize for shooting her husband, but, in truth, he was not at all sorry. Caleb King had tried to murder Rucker and him, and now he was dead. It was the price one paid when plans went awry.

"He should have let us ride away, Mrs. King. I had no fight with Caleb King."

Molly stared into the fire. "You had a fight with Caleb King the moment you rode up to the soddie, Mr. Peyton. That's the way he was. That's why he sent up the smoke signal—to lure unsuspecting travelers."

Suddenly cold, she shivered and buttoned her overcoat at her throat. The turned-up collar caused her face to appear even more hollow-cheeked. "Well, there is one thing for certain, Mr. Peyton. Caleb most assuredly underestimated his victim this time. You are an excellent shot with a revolver."

Peyton let that pass. He considered it just plain good luck that his bullet had hit Caleb King.

An amused smile dimpled the corners of Molly's lips. "You're a modest person, Mr. Peyton. I like that in a man. You could have said something silly like, 'I got lucky,' or some other such foolishness, but I've a notion"—she studied him through long, heavy lashes—"that luck had nothing to do with it. You're one of those rare individuals who make things happen . . . usually for the best, I'd say."

Her flattery disgusted him. He could not remember a time when he had actually *made* something happen. Even the successful bank robbery had been planned and executed by Jesse James.

"Don't patronize me, Mrs. King. The truth is, your opinion

of me doesn't matter one whit." Molly's eyebrows shot up, and
color crept into her face. She opened her mouth to protest, but
he was going on: "From what you've stated, Mrs. King, you and
your husband are the ones who make things happen. By your
own admission, you lure unsuspecting travelers to your house
and then murder them."

She raised her chin defiantly. "I admitted nothing of the
kind . . . and my name is not Mrs. King. It's Molly Klinner. Caleb
King was not my husband."

She watched his face for a reaction. There was none. His indifference left her empty, as though nothing she had said had
meaning for him. "But, yes, Mr. Peyton, Caleb King murdered
and robbed several people, including the man who had home-
steaded the soddie."

She looked straight into Peyton's eyes. "I had nothing to do
with those killings, Mr. Peyton."

Although Molly Klinner's denouncement of the murders
rang with authenticity, Peyton found himself increasingly suspicious of her. Hell, no one need tell him that an hour ago when
she had held her rifle pointed at his chest, she would have shot
him dead if he had so much as blinked.

Peyton climbed to his feet and brushed the snow from his
trousers. "I'll take your horse down the draw and leave it with
ours. There's a stand of bunchgrass down there."

The excuse to leave sounded lame even to him, but he had
to get away, to sort through what she had said and, more importantly, what she had left unsaid.

Molly Klinner watched Peyton disappear down the gully. He
did not believe her. Could she blame him? She closed her eyes
and felt the weariness of the long day seeping into her bones.
Picking up the coffee mug, she touched its cold rim to her lips,
and her gaze crept again down the draw. She wished he had
asked her to explain the circumstances that had shackled her so
steadfastly to Caleb King. If he had known the truth, perhaps he
would have judged her less harshly. Had he asked, what would
she have told him?

Molly emitted a long sigh. Could she tell him the truth
about her past . . . all of it? Any of it? How did a woman confide

her private—no, not private—her most *personal* self to a man she had just met?

Molly mulled that over. Her past was her Achilles heel, her one vulnerable weakness. Yet, by the same token, it was also her stability, the single most compelling factor that had enabled her to survive mental and physical atrocities unimaginable to men or women who had not seen, heard, or endured them. Still, if she were to travel to Texas in his company, he had every right—indeed, it would be in his best interest—to know who, and what, she was.

An uncompromising stubbornness which had been Molly's constant companion and source of strength these past four years sent her to her feet to stare after Peyton. Damn him for his arrogant disinterest. Damn him! Damn him!

Five

Fletcher Rucker smelled the coffee long before he opened his eyes. When he did open them, it took a full minute for his vision to clear. How long had he slept? An hour? A day? A week? With an effort, he turned his head toward the fire. Molly Klinner, seemingly in deep thought, appeared to be basking in the heat that radiated from the undulating flames whose reflections danced like nymphs off the brass receiver of the Henry rifle next to her.

Rucker was halfway out of his blanket with pistol in hand when a wave of white-hot pain seared through his upper body. With a strangled moan, he collapsed back into the snow, his head swimming, his teeth clinched tightly to stifle the sound. Sweat beaded his brow as he again forced his head over so he could watch the woman. He was surprised when, instead of looking toward him, she climbed to her feet and for a drawn-out interval peered down the gully as though something in that vicinity was of the utmost importance to her. He was even more bewildered when, shrugging as though she had reached a conclusion, she turned again to the fire and noticed that he was watching her. With a smile, she walked to him and placed the rim of the coffee mug between his lips.

Rucker drank sparingly, stopping often to rest. Finally, he turned his face away, indicating he had had enough. With one last look at Molly Klinner, he drifted back into unconsciousness. Neither he nor she had spoken.

As Peyton approached the camp, Molly Klinner refilled the mug with the remainder of the coffee, then set the empty pot aside. It sizzled and popped as it melted down into the snow. Taking a sip of the hot coffee, she indicated Rucker with a tilt of her head.

"Even though he's half out of his head with pain, he has more manners than you, Mr. Peyton." Peyton's inquiring frown brought a faint curve to her lips. "At least he didn't demand to know why I'm here."

Ignoring the scowl that twisted Peyton's face, Molly opened the gunnysack and lifted out the tin of sulfur. She walked to Rucker and knelt down beside him. To her surprise, Peyton squatted beside her and raised Rucker to a sitting position. Together, they again stripped the boy to his waist and inspected the wound. The bleeding had slowed to a seep, but the swollen blue-black mass of flesh around the bullet punctures was grotesque.

Peyton steadied Rucker as Molly dusted the wound with the medicine, and he was forced to admit a grudging approval for the woman's quick reflexes because, even with Rucker flinching and twisting, her ministrations were careful and precise, and little of the powder was wasted.

When she returned the tin to the sack, then calmly washed her bloody hands in the snow, Peyton could not help but speculate on the number of times she had treated gun-shot men. Several, if her cool professionalism was any indication. He was not certain whether he should be elated or concerned.

Peyton stood and stretched the kinks out of his muscles, then walked to the far side of the fire across from Molly Klinner, whose hands were thrust toward the heat to dry. "When I asked why you were here, Miss Klinner, you danced all around an answer. So I'll ask it again: why are you here?"

"You didn't ask why I was here, Mr. Peyton. You demanded to know what I was doing here . . . and I told you."

"You knew what I meant. You're still sidestepping an answer, Miss Klinner."

Molly's brow furrowed ever so slightly. "I suppose I'm here simply because I want to go to Texas with you, Mr. Peyton."

Peyton sat back on his haunches and stared at her. The woman was incredible!

"Fletcher and I are traveling light and fast, Miss Klinner. Texas is a long way from eastern Kansas, and we don't need excess baggage."

Molly Klinner appraised Peyton as though she were assessing a simpleton.

"You're not traveling light and fast, Mr. Peyton. In fact, you're not traveling at all. And you won't be unless someone attends to Fletcher Rucker's wounds. Without help, he'll not last ten miles in the saddle. And the nearest town in the direction you're going is more than forty miles from here." She flashed Peyton a bittersweet smile. "And as far as me being excess baggage, well, you and I both know you're not the kind of man who would leave a woman stranded in the middle of nowhere."

She prayed that she was right. Then she realized it did not really matter whether she was right or wrong because she had no place else to go. Nor anyone to go to.

Peyton glared at her, making no attempt to hide his displeasure. What she had said concerning Rucker was true. He needed help. The second part was also true; he would not abandon her on the high plains.

"Miss Klinner, you can travel as far as the next town with us. And my name is Lewis. Peyton Lewis." He frowned darkly at her and ran his hand wearily over the three-day beard stubble that darkened his jaws. "After that, you're on your own."

Molly cocked her head to one side and pursed her lips as though she had not heard a word he had said. "Peyton Lewis? Peyton Lewis. That's a nice name."

She turned her back to him and took an iron skillet and

canvas package of dried meat from the gunnysack. She laid the meat aside, then scooped the skillet full of snow and set it over the flames. When the snow melted, she added the meat. A smile of contentment sprang to her lips; for the first time in three years she was preparing a meal without Caleb King standing over her, watching her every move. She felt free, and it was wonderful.

Molly grinned at Peyton, her white, perfectly formed teeth strikingly out of place in her grimy face.

"Although you've beaten around the bush instead of coming right out and asking, Mr. Peyton Lewis, I will enlighten you as to my involvement with Caleb King. If we are going to be traveling companions, you have a right to know."

Peyton waved her proposal aside. "Save your confession for a priest, Miss Klinner. It doesn't make any difference one way or the other what your involvement with King was. I told you I'd carry you to the next town, an' I'll do it." He surveyed her coolly. "The truth is, Miss Klinner, after what you've already told me, I think I'd be better off not knowing any more about you than is absolutely necessary."

Molly angrily snapped off a branch from a nearby bush, and for an instant Peyton was certain she intended to flail him with it. Instead, she used the big end of the stem to stir the food in the skillet.

"You're an arrogant, ignorant, self-righteous, pious bastard, Mr. Lewis. You pass judgment on me without knowing the facts. You condemn me because I lived with a murderer, while, if the truth were known, you yourself are running from the law."

She had his unwavering attention. "What makes you think I'm running from the law?"

Molly smiled mockingly at him as she raised the stick to her lips and tasted the food that clung to its end. Ignoring his threatening posture, his narrowed, dangerous eyes—indeed, seemingly totally indifferent to them—she continued to stir the skillet with a vengeance.

"I can tell by the way you move, Mr. Lewis. You're always on guard. Defensive. Watchful—like now. Like a criminal."

"What makes you such an authority on criminals?"

The question annoyed her. She had already explained to him that she had lived with Caleb King for nearly three years and that King was a killer. Surely he had sense enough to realize that in three long years even a dolt would have learned something of the intricate workings of an outlaw's mind.

"I ate, lived, breathed, and slept with an outlaw for nearly a fifth of my life, Mr. Lewis. I believe that entitles me to be somewhat an authority on the criminal element."

She eyed him hotly, growing more angry by the second. "The truth is, Mr. Lewis, I probably know more about being an outlaw than you do about soldiering, because I've been a fugitive for more years than you were in the army!"

She took a deep breath, and he thought she was finished, but she slammed the stick down into the skillet and jumped to her feet. Glaring at Peyton across the campfire, she made an angry cutting motion with her hand.

"I ran from the law when Caleb King ran from the law, Mr. Lewis. I slept in the cold when Caleb King slept in the cold, Mr. Lewis. I went thirsty, and hungry, and dirty. I suffered all the things an outlaw suffers, Mr. Lewis, but I never got to enjoy whatever it is that outlaws enjoy. Yes, I *am* an authority on no-account men, Mr. Lewis. I learned it the hard way!"

Peyton regarded her thoughtfully. "Are you finished?"

"Perhaps. Perhaps not!"

Peyton walked around the fire and towered over her, forcing her to look up at him.

"While you're trying to decide if you're finished or not, keep this in mind, because I'm only going to say it once: don't ever yell at me again!"

Molly squatted down and snatched up the stick. She stirred the skillet angrily. She would not tolerate ultimatums, not from him, not from anyone. Biting back an acute desire to shout an obscenity at him, she glared up at him through her lashes.

"Just answer one question, Mr. Lewis, and I want the truth." His gaze was level. Waiting. She took a deep breath. "Are you a murderer? Is that why the law is after you?"

Molly watched his face for a reaction and was relieved to witness genuine anger registered there.

"No, Miss Klinner, I'm no murderer. I helped stick up a bank."

Her eyes grew wide with incredulity.

"You robbed a bank?"

He nodded.

She burst out laughing.

"You find that amusing?"

"Why, mercy, yes, Mr. Lewis. You're no outlaw. Everybody in the South will hail you as a hero. Lord knows, Southerners haven't got two thin dimes to rub together, much less to put into a bank. You did us all a service!"

Molly's eyes swam, and she wiped them on her coat sleeve, hard-pressed to tell if they were tears of mirth or if her eyes were merely brimming because of the intense cold that came with sundown. No matter. It was a relief to know he was not a murderer.

She took two hand-carved wooden spoons from the gunnysack and offered one to Peyton. "I didn't bring any bowls."

Again he wondered if she were apologizing.

Molly lifted the skillet out of the fire. "If you will hold Fletcher upright, Mr. Lewis, I'll try to get some food down him. You and I will eat whatever is left." She was not apologizing.

Feeding Rucker was not nearly so simple as Peyton had imagined. The wound caused the boy to toss and turn, and Rucker had trouble holding down what little food Molly forced him to eat. Finally, they gave it up as a bad job and allowed Rucker to drift into unconsciousness.

Molly eyed the scant portion of food in the skillet. She was ravished, having eaten nothing since the day before. Hunger drew her stomach into knots, and her hand crept there in a protective gesture, and she wondered if the child that had been forming in her womb these past six months was as starved as she.

Feeling Peyton's eyes on her, she quickly moved her hand and glanced at him out of the corner of her eye. He was watching her, veiled, a personal look. Was it pity? The thought both shocked and angered her. She wanted no man's pity and most certainly not Peyton Lewis's.

Indeed! What would he think were he to know that she was simply using him and his desire to get to Texas as a ways and means to provide her with what she needed most: an opportunity to become a real person—her own person—instead of an object of indiscriminate usage by those who viewed her as nothing more than an available, accommodating female body.

The muscles in Molly's jaws tightened into knots. Peyton Lewis had unknowingly given her a chance to prove to all who cared to look that she was more than just a convenience. She would show them, show the world if need be, that she was a real, live person, an individual, a woman with feelings, needs, desires. . . . A soon-to-be mother who longed for something better for her child than the life she had been leading. Something better? Molly's shoulders slumped. Anything would be better.

She pushed the skillet toward him. "Eat it before it gets cold."

Peyton studied her for a moment more, then turned toward the draw where the horses were tethered. "I've got to gather firewood, and the horses need to be hobbled. I'll be back directly."

Peyton struck off toward the gully. When he was certain he was far enough from the light of the campfire to be lost in darkness, he turned and watched Molly Klinner. She appeared small and forlorn as she knelt beside Rucker and wolfed the contents of the skillet. Indeed, she was an unusual person—one who would rather go hungry than have a man know that she was practically starved. A flicker of approval drew his lips into the faintest hint of a smile: she was tough, he'd give her that much.

An hour later, when Peyton returned to the camp with an armload of firewood, he was surprised to find Molly Klinner sitting where he had left her, fast asleep. The coals had burned to embers, yet the snow illuminated the night with an iridescent glow that resembled twilight more than late evening.

As Peyton stealthily laid the firewood beside the coals, he studied Molly Klinner from several different angles. Determining she was indeed fast asleep, he reached for the Henry rifle that lay loosely cradled in the crook of her arm.

When he touched the rifle barrel, Molly's eyes opened, and mockery danced in their dark pupils. "I saved the leftovers for you, Mr. Lewis." She tilted her head toward the skillet. "So there'll be no need for you to take my rifle and hunt for game. I'm sure that's what you had in mind."

Peyton removed his hand from her rifle and walked to his side of the fire. He ate in silence.

Molly moved closer to the light of the fire and rummaged in the gunnysack. Peyton was amazed when she withdrew the large, leather-bound Bible that had adorned the shelf cut into the soddie wall. She opened the book to a passage marked by a length of frayed ribbon.

Peyton frowned. The Bible must have weighed at least eight pounds. Why on earth would she choose to lug it all those miles through the snow? Common sense would dictate that a person carry food, or medicine, or something useful, not a collection of beautiful stories whose sole purpose was to sustain one emotionally and spiritually!

Molly saw the displeasure on his face as he squinted at the Bible and guessed, accurately, that once again he thought her a very foolish woman. She raised her chin defensively.

"My only link to my family is written in the pages of this Bible, Mr. Lewis . . . and furthermore, today is the Sabbath."

Peyton looked off into the night and cursed her impracticality. It would not be Sunday tomorrow, but the book would still weigh eight pounds.

Molly settled herself more comfortably in the snow and silently began reading.

Peyton laid another stick on the fire and watched her through the flickering flames, intrigued by the hypocrisy of a woman who admitted to living out of wedlock with an outlaw, then searched for solace in the Scriptures of the Good Book.

He studied her face as she read the passages, amazed that in the firelight, with the book in her lap, Molly Klinner appeared as pure and innocent as a child. Peyton laughed under his breath at that, because without a doubt Miss Klinner, or Mrs. King, or whoever she turned out to be, was the most contradictory woman he had ever encountered.

"Would you read aloud?" Peyton was as startled as Molly by his request, and he quickly averted his gaze, wishing he had said nothing.

For a long moment Molly simply sat and stared at him. When she spoke, there was a catch in her voice.

"You haven't heard the gospel since you left home to go to war, have you, Mr. Lewis."

Peyton did not answer. Her habit of making statements instead of asking questions irritated him, especially when she was right. His mother had read the Bible aloud every night when he was a child. But she was gone, and he had not heard one word of Scripture since her death. In truth, the only time he had set foot in a church in the past three years was when Jesse James divided the money from the bank robbery.

Molly turned the pages to Proverbs. In low, clear tones, she read about the seven deadly sins concerning adultery and the wiles of a harlot.

Peyton silently questioned her choice of Scriptures— uncomfortable with them—for it was unbecoming for a woman to read about sex, even if it was in the Bible. He listened to her, but he avoided her eyes each time she raised them to him. Still, her voice was nice, soft yet throaty.

Although he would never have admitted it, he was sorry when she closed the Bible and returned it to the gunnysack.

Her eyes held a challenge as she looked at him. "Have you ever required the services of a fallen woman, Mr. Lewis?" She did not expect an answer, so she continued. "Like those women I just read about, Mr. Lewis. That's what I am."

Peyton fidgeted, uncomfortable with her disclosure and his reaction to it. He silently cursed the heat of uncertainty and embarrassment that suffused his neck and worked its way to his forehead, but he was powerless to stop it.

Molly watched with interest as Peyton laid the skillet aside and examined her from head to toe. Men had visually undressed her many times in the past, but instead of the certainty of conquest she normally experienced when she knew she had captured a man's attention, Peyton's prolonged scrutiny filled her with an unexpected surge of disappointment—and that shocked her, for suddenly, deep down inside her heart, she had hoped he would be different from other men. Curiously, for the first time since becoming a soiled dove, Molly Klinner realized she had hoped to find something deeper in a man—him—than mere sexual lust.

Peyton climbed to his full height and gazed down at her with a look that she could not read. "You have just answered a question that's been bothering me, Miss Klinner."

Molly was startled. Instead of the patronization she usually heard in the voice of a man she had propositioned, she heard plain, unconcealed contempt. He was going on:

"And although it's a subject I'd rather not discuss with a . . . woman, you asked me a question and I will answer it. I was a soldier, Miss Klinner, no better or no worse than any other soldier. I have killed men in battle, and I have slept with whores. The truth is, Miss Klinner, that after the fact I found neither of the events very fulfilling."

Molly's face drained, causing her frost-nipped cheeks to resemble a white canvas that a lackluster artist had splotched with red paint. She watched him walk to the saddles, where he knelt and began unlashing his bedroll. It infuriated her that he would dismiss her as though she were so much rubbish. Eyeing his bedroll, she, too, jumped to her feet.

"I didn't ask you for a sermon, Mr. Lewis. I merely asked if you wanted me to share your blanket!"

When Peyton ignored her and continued working with his bedroll, humiliation sent a flame of very real embarrassment to her cheeks, the first she had experienced in years. She did not like the feeling, nor the sensation of baseness and cheapness that accompanied it. She slept with men, yes; but she was *not* a whore. How dare he deliberately make her feel like one!

Molly Klinner sneered insolently at him. "I yelled at you, Mr. Lewis. Did you not hear me? I yelled at you, and you didn't do a thing! You're just a boy, Peyton Lewis, nothing but a know-it-all kid who robbed a bank and now thinks he's all grown up!" She knew that was not true. In spite of his youth, Peyton Lewis was no kid—and she was experienced enough with men to know the difference.

Molly took her bottom lip between her teeth and silently cursed herself for her foolish outburst; she had just alienated the one man she desperately needed as a friend. She considered apologizing for her flare-up, but when he untied her quilt and carried it to the fire and dumped it unceremoniously in the snow, the regret died on her tongue.

Peyton walked to the other side of the fire and squatted down before the flames. He draped his blanket over his shoulders, pulling it tight against his throat. From beneath his hat brim he watched Molly Klinner snatch up her quilt and spread it out next to Rucker. Without so much as a glance in Peyton's direction, she plopped down full length on the coverlet with her feet toward the fire. She snuggled her body close against Rucker and arranged her blanket so that it covered them both.

Peyton was surprised by her knowledge of wilderness survival. Then he recalled that she was an experienced outlaw and had probably spent many such nights wrapped up in her quilt with some man with her feet held to the fire. He laughed silently at his sorry pun.

Peyton studied the dark silhouette of her body mingling with Rucker's under the blanket, and it irritated him to find himself envious of Rucker for sharing her warmth on this miserably cold night.

Six

Peyton awoke when Molly Klinner added new kindling to the coals and blew the embers into a full flame. He sat up, stiff and cold, concerned that she was up and about while he lay abed. He glanced at the eastern horizon: dawn was just a suggestion.

He climbed to his feet and stretched his aching muscles. When he took a deep breath, he went into a spasm of coughing as the frigid air burned its way into his chest.

Molly packed the coffeepot with snow, then dropped a handful of crushed coffee beans into it and placed it in the embers at the edge of the fire. She would repeat the process of melting the snow several times before having a full pot of water. "I wouldn't do that if I were you. This kind of frigid weather can sear a person's lungs."

He knew that.

Molly set the skillet in the flames to preheat it, then removed a slab of frozen salt pork from her canvas bag and dropped it into the pan. As the meat thawed and the grease began to sizzle and pop, Molly laughed, enjoying herself, because the sound of cooking meat was applause for a job well done.

The flickering light cast by the campfire as she bent over the skillet created a curious radiance to her complexion that emphasized the fine planes of her angular face and added golden highlights that transformed her lank hair into a soft luxuriousness that made her almost pretty. She was unaware of that, however, as she squinted up at Peyton through the woodsmoke.

"I'm curious, Mr. Lewis. What did you and Fletcher intend to eat while traveling to Texas? I haven't seen one morsel of food, or one coffee bean, not even a biscuit. And you've nothing to cook with." Small creases appeared between her eyes that suggested true perplexity. "Most men who ride the high trails plan things like that in advance."

Peyton rolled up his blanket and carried it to his saddle. As he tied the bedding behind the cantle, he peered down the draw toward the horses. Even though daylight had broken, the shadows lay too thick and heavy to make them out.

"I guess I'm just not as slick an outlaw as most of the men you've known, ma'am."

If he thought his sarcasm would intimidate Molly Klinner, he was mistaken. She sat back on her heels and laughed delightedly.

"You're no outlaw at all, Mr. Lewis. You're a bank robber who doesn't have the least idea what being a desperado is all about."

"The truth is, Miss Klinner . . ." He hesitated in an attempt to get a grip on his mounting temper. "I didn't make up my mind to head for Texas until after the robbery. I reckon I figured Fletcher and I would pick up supplies at the first town we came to in Kansas. I didn't count on a blizzard, or the fact that towns are mighty scarce once you cross the Missouri and Kansas Rivers. I assumed that the Missouri law would check the closest towns first, so we passed them by. It's as simple as that."

Peyton scowled at her as he walked back to the fire. He did not understand nor particularly enjoy the fact that he had felt compelled to explain his actions to her. Indeed, that was a sensation he had never before experienced with a woman. Casting an irritated glance at the open coffeepot, he vowed it would never happen again.

With a flick of her wrist, Molly expertly flipped the salt pork she was frying, and the grease in the skillet hissed as though it were alive.

She grinned up at Peyton. "A watched pot never boils, Mr. Lewis."

Peyton spun on his heel and stalked off down the draw where the horses were feeding. Molly watched him go, then shrugged to herself. He could dish it out, but he certainly couldn't take it.

Nearly an hour had passed when Peyton trudged back to the camp and hunkered down beside the fire to warm his hands. He did not look into the pot.

Molly stirred the contents of the coffeepot with a stick, then poured him a cupful.

"When you get to Texas, Mr. Lewis, what are your intentions? What do you really want out of life?"

He studied her in the pale daylight, surprised by the true intelligence that shone in the depths of her dark eyes as she gazed at him. He pondered that phenomenon and came to the conclusion that, for a woman who thought so little of herself that she would sell what should have been the most precious gift that she could bestow upon a man, Molly Klinner was full of unexpected revelations. In that respect, however, Peyton would have been astounded at how mistaken he was: once, four years ago, Molly Klinner had given her heart, soul, and body to a man—and had asked for absolutely nothing in return.

"I intend to buy land and raise cattle, Miss Klinner. Now that the war's over, there'll be a big market for beef."

Observing her face for reaction to his comment, he saw genuine interest, and without his being aware of it, the sight pleased him. Peyton swallowed a sip of the scalding coffee. "This nation is on the brink of an era of progress such as no country on earth has ever witnessed. There'll be no limit to what a man with a little foresight and guts can accomplish. I'll start with the cattle industry because Texas is full of cattle. But the truth is, I'll do, buy, or sell whatever it takes to become successful. Someday I will own property from one end of Texas to the other. I intend to be a wealthy man, Miss Klinner . . . a man worthy of respect."

Molly was bothered by Peyton's final statement, and she

nearly blurted out that she had known many a wealthy man who was most certainly not worthy of respect. Respect was earned, not purchased. Instead, she said nothing, and allowed herself to be caught up in his enthusiasm. Grinning beautifully at Peyton, she clapped her hands in appreciative applause.

"That was a fine and wonderful speech, Mr. Lewis." Then her smile faded, to be replaced by a look that was a rarity on her young face: awe—the pure, old-fashioned, heart-accelerating, scary kind that is filled with wonder mingled with veneration and dread. Suddenly she was powerfully stricken with a deep regard and a raging desire to be a part of Peyton Lewis's dream, to help him build it into a reality.

Molly ducked her head and busied herself with the meat in the skillet, thankful for the strong aroma of fried pork that wafted through the frigid air as though it were a living thing that gobbled up the pure oxygen and left its heavy, pungent odor in its place, for it gave her an excuse to take several deep breaths to try to still the racing of her heart.

Fletcher Rucker groaned and opened his eyes. He lay there a moment, gathering his bearings before attempting to sit up. Clenching his teeth in pain, he drew himself up on his good elbow and peered feverishly at Peyton and Molly.

Molly took the cup of coffee from Peyton and carried it to Rucker. She slipped her arm beneath his shoulders to steady him, then placed the rim of the cup between his lips. Rucker took a sip and swallowed.

Molly placed her palm against his forehead. It was hot to the touch.

"How do you feel, Fletcher?"

"Like I had a huggin' contest with a porcupine—and lost." His voice was a hollow whisper.

She grinned at him. "If you can joke at a time like this, I'd say you are on the mending list."

Peyton squatted beside the fire and turned the meat in the skillet with the stick Molly had used. "We got some salt pork frying, Fletcher. Think you can stomach a little hog meat?"

Rucker lay back and closed his eyes. "I ain't very hungry, Peyton."

Molly playfully ruffled Rucker's hair. "You've got to eat, Fletcher. You've got to keep up your strength."

She touched his forehead again; perspiration chilled her palm—a bad sign. In subzero weather such as this, perspiration could freeze on a person's skin, creating a thin film of ice that lowered the body temperature. The result could be death.

Rucker turned his face away and gazed at the distant horizon. "I told you . . . I ain't hungry."

Molly shrugged. "I was looking forward to feeding you, Fletcher Rucker. But if you're going to play the part of a spoiled brat, you can forget it!"

At least the first part was true, she thought, studying his profile as he looked away from her. She was certainly looking forward to feeding the handsome boy.

Rucker rolled his eyes toward her. "You sure ain't got no qualms about kickin' a man when he's down, have you, ma'am?"

Molly laughed. "Sometimes, Fletcher, kicking a man when he's down is the only way to get him up. Now, are you ready to eat?"

Rucker threw her a sickly grin. "I'll try, Miss Molly."

Peyton stared at Molly. She was an accumulation of improbabilities that somehow appeared to work to everyone's best interest. With a shake of his head, he lifted the skillet off the flames and, using his bowie knife, sliced the meat into thick strips, then into bite-sized portions.

Using her fingers, Molly fished a small piece of meat from the greasy skillet and placed it in Rucker's mouth. With crooning words a mother might have used on a sick infant, she encouraged him to at least try to swallow it.

It took all of Rucker's strength just to chew the tough, over-cooked meat, but he managed to get several bites down before turning his head aside.

Once again, Peyton found himself appraising Molly Klinner with a begrudging admiration for the way she had handled the boy. He had a fleeting impulse to put his praise into words. Instead, he climbed to his feet and walked, for the second time in less than an hour, down the draw to check on the horses.

Molly watched Peyton walk away. She had seen the reluctant

approval in his eyes and had prayed he would voice that regard. When he did not, the smile that had hovered at the corners of her lips faltered, then vanished. She laid the skillet in the coals at the edge of the fire, then turned to Rucker and peeled his clothing down over his shoulder. She removed the bandage and examined the wound. The flesh surrounding around the injury was a multicolored configuration of black, blue, red, and yellow that looked more like a slab of polished marble than human flesh. The punctures were angry and inflamed, especially above his chest where the bullet had exited. The only bright spot in the dismal examination was that the hemorrhaging had stopped.

Molly forced herself to smile at Rucker. "If you think you could stand the pain, Fletcher, I'll heat some water and sponge a little of the dried blood off your chest and back."

She almost wept with pride when the wounded boy bit back his pain and attempted a manly grin, that, in truth, was little more than a weak grimace, and shoved his damaged shoulder more closely to her.

"Do whatever you have to do, ma'am. You'll not hear a peep out of me."

Molly beamed at Rucker, a false show of optimism brought about by her knowledge of gunshot wounds. While his words were brave and well meant, they were just words. Before she was finished, Rucker would make more than a peep.

Molly filled her coffee mug with snow and set it near the fire. As the cup heated, she added more and more snow until the container was filled with boiling water. Then she dipped the hem of her skirt in the steaming liquid and gently blotted the flesh surrounding Rucker's chest puncture. As she applied pressure to his damaged skin, Rucker sucked in his breath, and the muscles around the wound quivered spasmodically.

Involuntarily, Rucker shied away from her, and a moment later, when he looked at her, his eyes were filled with tears of embarrassment. "Sorry, ma'am. I didn't know it would feel like you was stickin' a red-hot poker iron in me."

Steeling himself against the pain, Rucker sat perfectly rigid as Molly again dabbed at the congealed blood, and in spite of the freezing temperature, perspiration beaded his forehead and flowed down his face, where it dripped off his chin like a summer sweat.

Rust-colored water trickled down Rucker's chest and mingled with the sparse blond hair that encircled his navel, and Molly used the tail of her coat to blot it away.

"How long have you known Mr. Lewis, Fletcher?" Molly was not prying; she was merely attempting to distract the boy from the agony she knew she was causing. "Peyton is certainly . . . a strange individual, don't you think?"

Rucker nodded his agreement, and when he spoke, it was obvious he was using up his reservoir of willpower just to answer her in a civil manner.

"Why, I've known Peyton all my life, ma'am. Hell . . . Excuse me for cussin', ma'am. Why, heck fire, me an' Peyton are cousins. We grew up together, joined the army together, fought side by side. We rode with Bloody Bill Anderson. An' later with Quantrill."

Molly's hand ceased its movement, and incredulity filled her face. William Anderson was the most feared Confederate guerrilla fighter the Civil War had produced—a cold-blooded leader of men who neither gave quarter nor asked any.

Irony pulled Molly's lips into a half-smile. Had Caleb King known whom Lewis and Rucker had soldiered with, he would never have chanced a shot at them. Molly stifled a laugh. It was poetic justice, because King and his Jayhawkers had been the Union army's less than adequate answer to Confederate raiders like Bloody Bill Anderson and William Quantrill. No, indeed! Caleb King would never have taken a shot at two of Anderson's men—not even in the back.

Rucker was rambling on, his words coming fast, edged with suffering. "Peyton's folks an' mine owned adjoinin' farms in Missouri. In '63, the Yankees came to our neck o' the woods. They killed Peyton's pa an' mine outright, and then carried off our families an' a bunch of neighbors, an' put 'em in prison in an' old dilapidated brick buildin' in Kansas City. While they were in prison, the buildin' collapsed. It killed Bill Anderson's sister, an' injured Cole Younger's cousin an' Frank and Jesse's mom an' sister, an' maimed Bill Anderson's other sister for life."

Rucker sighed, and tears sprang to his eyes. He blinked them away. "It also killed my maw an' Peyton's whole family, his maw an' his baby brother an' sister—they was twins. It was awful."

Molly's stomach had drawn into a tight knot with the telling of Rucker's story. She could feel his pain, his loss, for during the war, she, too, had suffered the forfeiture of someone dear to her. While she detested herself for insisting that he dredge up memories that were best left buried in the past where they belonged, she was also aware that she must keep him talking, not only to take his mind off the pain but because she desperately longed to know more about him—and Peyton.

Dipping the bloody cloth into the hot water, she wrung it out and again applied it to his wound.

"Were you and Mr. Lewis in the army when it happened? You would have been very young, I would imagine."

The pressure of the hot cloth against his shoulder caused Rucker's head to swim with pain, and it took a moment for him to respond.

"Me an' Peyton had gone down into the breaks that day to look for a lost cow. I reckon that's what saved our lives—we was searchin' for a goddamned lost cow. We heard the shootin' comin' from the direction of the house, an' we run back as fast as we could. When we got home there weren't nothin' left. The house an' barns were afire. The stock was gone. The menfolk dead, the women an' children missin' . . . Everything was either dead or gone."

Molly stared into Rucker's face. Her mind reeled back to September 1863, when United States Army Brigadier General Thomas Ewing's Federal troops had marched into Bates County, Missouri. General Ewing's army had been reinforced by the fanatical Kansan "Doc" Jennison and scores of Kansas Jayhawkers bent on looting, burning, and murdering the pro-Confederate civilian population. One of those Jayhawkers had been a big, red-bearded man named Caleb King.

General Ewing's rabble had carried out his notorious Order Number 11. Homes, farms, even entire cities across four western Missouri border counties, including the town where thirteen-year-old Malinda Klinner worked for her board and keep in a brothel, had been burned to the ground—the "Burnt District," where more than twenty thousand innocent civilians had been left either dead or homeless and nearly every man over the age of twelve had been shot on sight. But they had not shot the women . . . no, they had not shot the women.

A nervousness churned unbidden in Molly's stomach as the long-suppressed memory forced its way into her mind. She took a deep breath, pleased that the reaction was merely anxiety, for there had been a time when it would have been true nausea.

It had been a cool, fall-like morning when the Federal army marched into town. The officer in charge had immediately initiated martial law, and the troops had rushed about the streets, entering homes and businesses at will.

Molly recalled vividly the sound of wood splintering, of turning from her scrub board to find the door to the laundry room kicked from its hinges. More curious than afraid, she smiled uncertainly at the dozen Union soldiers who burst into the room. She asked the wrong question: Could she help them?

A burly captain had stepped close, forcing her to retreat until the washtubs brought her up short. She could feel the tepid water that had sloshed from the casks saturating her skirt and dripping onto her bare feet. One of the soldiers remarked that she was so scared she had peed her drawers. Their laughter had infuriated her—another mistake.

Amused by her lack of intimidation, the captain, laughing louder than his men, had calmly drawn his pistol and ordered her to disrobe.

She had refused—her third mistake, because, a moment later, with the muzzle of a cocked revolver pressed against her temple and a dozen bayonet points pricking her skin, Molly hurriedly unbuttoned her blouse. She remembered plainly her determination not to cry.

Rucker, believing the haunted shame that had crept into Molly's face was the product of his and Peyton's miseries, hesitated in his narrative. "I'm sorry for upsettin' you, ma'am. Maybe it's best if I just shut my big mouth."

Molly jerked herself back to the present. "You haven't upset me, Fletcher. Please, I want you to continue." *I need to hear it; I need to know that I am not alone in my suffering. . . .*

Rucker cleared his throat, still not certain if he should proceed. Molly touched his hand reassuringly. "Please go on."

"Well, Miss Molly, me an' Peyton set out walkin'. We walked all the way to Rocheport, Missouri, where Bloody Bill Anderson was in quarters. An' you're right, we was just kids—me, fourteen, an' Peyton, fifteen. But on that trip, Peyton turned sour on the world. Yes, ma'am, Peyton got real quiet."

Interest replaced the melancholy on Molly's face. "I've seen the sour side of him. What was he like before he turned bitter, Fletcher? What kind of person was he?"

Rucker thought about that. What was Peyton like before the war?

"Peyton was more like a big brother to me than a cousin—always lookin' out for me an' all. We had fun back in them days. Hunted an' fished. Peyton was the best rifle shot in the county—won nearly every turkey shoot he entered. He was a hard worker, and he was honest as the day is long . . . wouldn't lie for nobody. He laughed a lot, had lots of friends—they're mostly dead now, killed in the war. . . . Anyway, everybody liked Peyton, even the girls. I reckon, if I had to sum up Peyton back in those days, I'd say he was a real popular boy, a nice person . . . always good to folks.

"But he changed when our families was murdered—we both did, but him more than me. The fun went out of Peyton. He hardly ever laughs anymore, or jokes, or takes folks into his confidence. Won't let 'em get close to him. Like I said, I first noticed the difference on our way to join the army."

While Rucker talked, Molly soaked the cloth, wrung it out, and reapplied it to the wound. As the cloth touched his ravaged flesh, and in spite of his pledge to not make a peep, Rucker shuddered and jerked, and finally moaned aloud. Blinking perspiration from his eyes, he tried to concentrate on the story he was telling.

"When we reached the Confederate camp, Bloody Bill Anderson had already fell out with Quantrill and formed his own brigade. An' when Anderson raided the Yankees in Kansas and

Missouri, why, naturally, Peyton an' me rode with him, along
with Frank and Jesse James, the Todd brothers, Davy Pool, Arch
Clement, the Younger boys, an' . . . well, heck, a whole bunch
of us. . . ."

Rucker's voice was becoming faint, and he looked at her
apologetically. "I'm tired, ma'am. I think I'll just listen to you talk
for a while. . . . Tell me about you, Mrs. King. How'd you come
to be married to a damned backshooter?"

Molly Klinner considered Rucker's request for a long instant. She wished it had been Peyton who had asked that question—but it was not, and all the wishing in the world would not
change that. Molly studied Rucker's haggard face. What should
she tell him? How much could she tell him? That she had been
at the wrong place at the wrong time with the wrong people?
That she had become a female animal fighting with the only
weapons available to her for the simple, God-given right to live?
No, she didn't think so; Rucker was idealistic, a dreamer—and
she had long since given up believing in either of those luxuries.

Perhaps she could reveal part of the truth: before the soldiers came, before Caleb King.

"I'm not Mrs. King, Fletcher. I'm Malinda Klinner, but most
people call me Molly. I, too, was raised in Missouri. My people
were—are—Mennonites. There was a small colony of them in
Laclade County. I'm not certain they are even still there." She
hesitated, reluctant to crack open the door to her innermost
self, to unleash long-suppressed secrets that she had kept locked
inside her for so many years.

"I . . . was twelve years old when the war began. . . ." Molly
faltered, the sound of her voice ringing loud and foreign in her
ears, as though it were not she who had spoken, as though it
were a stranger inside her, a woman who refused to leave the
safe, secure haven where she had rested for so many years, then
suddenly found that she had been coaxed into the bright sunlight of another human being's harsh judgment.

Again, she looked at Rucker. Would he understand if she explained to him that she was one of those unfortunate young girls
who fully matured at an early age, who had the looks, figure,
and mentality of a woman half again her years, who turned the

heads of grown men who should have known better? No, she decided, he would not understand. Oddly, she felt certain that Peyton Lewis would.

Rucker urged her to continue. "I ain't never known no Mennonites, but I heard they were strict, God-fearin' folks."

Molly felt the callous cloak of apathy settle over her like a mantle. She embraced it, indeed, hid beneath it, allowing it to cover her with its strong, protective fibers, affording her the strength to smile saucily at Rucker, while inside, her stomach was a raw knot of nerves.

"They are a God-fearing people, Fletcher, and yes, they are very strict." Molly turned her face away, for the nervous knot in her stomach had climbed to her throat. Yes, the Mennonites were very strict, especially where their women were concerned. "Intolerance" best described their sternness—and no leniency at all when it came to fornication. She had learned that lesson the hard way.

Molly took a deep breath and laughed brightly, a sound that carried a false, lighthearted lilt that any man, except one whose senses were dulled by physical pain, would have recognized instantly.

"As you probably know, Fletcher, it's against the Mennonite religion to fight in war." Rucker nodded, and she continued. "I was in love with a boy who was eighteen years old. One night in early March, 1862, he begged me to slip out and meet him. So, like many young girls who fancy themselves in love, I did just that. He told me that he intended to run away, to join the Union army. I, of course, was totally stricken to think of him leaving, yet I was excited that he confided in me. . . . I felt very mature. I pleaded with him to marry me and take me with him, but he refused, promising that we would wed when he came home on furlough, so . . . I gave my fiancé a going-away present, and . . . he left me with one."

"What was it?"

Molly frowned with impatience, unable to believe Rucker could be so naive. Then, seeing that he truly did not understand, she grinned crookedly at him. "Why, I was expecting, of course."

Rucker stared at her through feverish eyes, and for a moment she was afraid he still did not grasp her meaning. He nodded. "It happens, ma'am."

Rucker watched her through troubled eyes, uncomfortable with her revelation. The only unmarried girl he had ever known who had found herself in the family way had been unable to face her disgrace, and had hanged herself in her father's barn loft.

"What happened after he left for the war, Miss Molly?"

Molly shrugged. "When it became obvious that I was carrying, the whole settlement . . . well, let's just say, things changed. In the eyes of the elders, I was a true soiled dove. They called me a Jezebel, a harlot . . . those were the nice names they called me. They sent me to the fields to 'work the Devil out of me.' " She laughed. It was a harsh sound. "They made sure that I would be too tired in the evenings to even think about temptation."

Rucker's colorless face turned indignant. "Evidently them fool elders didn't know much about nothin'."

Molly raised her eyebrows in question, and Rucker grinned boyishly at her. "Why, Miss Molly, anybody with any sense a-tall knows that the only way to avoid temptation is to yield to it before it sets in!"

Molly blotted the beads of sweat that had formed on Rucker's forehead. "I don't believe the elders would find that amusing, Fletcher . . . and I think we should let you rest."

Rucker did, indeed, long to close his tired eyes and sleep, but he was much too caught up in Molly's story to stop now.

"If you was . . . in the family way"—his forehead wrinkled from the labor of attempting a coherent thought—"what . . . where . . . aw, hell . . ." He was fighting an overwhelming desire to give way and drift into a stupor. "What happened to your baby?"

For an instant Molly's eyes glistened with tears before hardening into a flintlike brittleness. "In my fifth month, Fletcher, I fell from a hay wagon. Three days later I miscarried."

Rucker blinked in an effort to focus on Molly's face. It was becoming more difficult by the moment. Even his voice was a slur. "I'm real sorry, Miss Molly."

She shook her head. "Don't be. It was the best thing that could have happened."

Rucker's eyes glazed and his lids drooped. "You can't mean that, ma'am."

She sighed, wishing he would let go and drift into unconsciousness. "It's not important, Fletcher."

Rucker took her hand and squeezed it with considerably more strength than she had expected, but his voice was barely a whisper.

"Important comes in two sizes, Miss Molly—yours an' mine. Right now, mine's bigger than yours. I might die without ever hearin' the rest of your story . . . an' I don't want to go to hell an' have to get the rest of the yarn from the Devil. You know how he lies."

Molly exhaled, and her shoulders sagged; he was not going to let it lie.

"My lover was wounded at a battle in Arkansas . . . a place called Pea Ridge. He got home a week after I fell from the wagon. I . . . I think he would have done right by me, but the elders told him I would never be able to bear any more children . . . that I would be worthless as a mother, a wife . . . a woman. They said I would be nothing but a burden on a husband and the community." She laughed. It was a mirthless sound that lay heavy on his ears. "The ironic part of the story, Fletcher, is that he came home with one leg missing at the hip. He was half a man. . . ." Her voice became softly bitter and drifted on the cold breeze like goose down, lightly caressing everything it touched but settling on nothing. "But I wasn't even half a woman. Not to him. Not to them."

Molly blinked as though coming out of a trance, and her voice strengthened with a stubborn reserve. "They were wrong not to let him visit me while I lay abed . . . or to at least acknowledge the death of our unborn child." She glanced down at her abdomen, and her eyes misted. They were wrong, the elders—and her parents—wrong about many things, but most especially about her not bearing any more children. "And they were wrong about another thing. I was a good, God-fearing girl.

I loved that boy with all my heart, and would have made him a good wife . . . a good mother for his children."

Again Molly looked away. Again her eyes misted. She had stolen away not long after, had merely shoved her scant belongings and a few scraps of food into a linen sack and walked into the night. The closest town was ten miles west.

It had been easy once she reached the city. She had simply told folks that she was sixteen years old, and that her parents had died of colic.

Mr. Oller, proprietor of the general merchandise store, upon learning that the quiet, pretty orphan girl could read, write, and do sums, offered her a job as a clerk, and with his wife's approval moved her into a small alcove above the store.

Throughout July, August, and September, the arrangement worked very well. Molly opened the store in the mornings and closed it in the evenings. People talked about how lucky Mr. Oller was to have such a nice, polite, smart girl working for him. She attended church on the Sabbath with the Ollers, and took Sunday dinner with them. During the week, she waited on customers and eventually began keeping the books, for Mr. Oller, although a sharp businessman, could barely read or write. In the evenings, she would eat a meager meal in her room—usually leftovers that Mrs. Oller prepared and deducted from her wages—then sit for hours at the window in her tiny alcove, watching the street below, where, even at night, commerce flourished. The saloon, two blocks down, did an uproarious business six nights a week. Somewhere further on, though she had never ventured into that section of town—and was aware of it only because the preacher constantly damned it from his pulpit—was something called a house of ill repute, which she had thought meant a place where people with terrible diseases lived—and had wondered why the good women of the church never carried food to them. The answer to her question was not long in coming.

One day in late October, Molly looked up from her bookkeeping to see wagonloads of the elders from her colony draw their teams to a halt at the hitching rail just beyond the store's open double doors. She had been elated, had craned her neck hoping to catch sight of her parents, to tell them how well she was doing, to show them her new dress, the material for which she had purchased with her own wages. And finally she did see them in the last wagon to arrive. But when the men climbed down from their spring seats and marched into the store, looking neither right nor left, moving purposefully to the rear of the building where Mr. Oller was stacking bolts of cloth that had just arrived from St. Louis, her parents sat in their wagon like statues and refused to acknowledge her.

Molly watched with growing concern as the elders spoke in low, intense voices to Mr. Oller, occasionally glancing her way, scowling when they saw her watching them. Then her spirits lifted, for Mr. Oller was nodding at them. They had come to take her home! Her heart soared. She missed her mother and father, longed with all her heart to be with them, to be their daughter once again. Then the elders were filing past her, not one glancing in her direction, and a moment later, Mr. Oller called her to the back of the store.

Even now, nearly four years later, she could hear his voice plainly: "Malinda, I want you out of this establishment within the hour—and there will be no wages for this week's work."

Molly was stricken with disbelief. Discharged? She? Where would she go? What would she do? She turned and gazed out the large front window at her mother and father as they backed their wagon into the street and turned east toward the colony. There had been no redemption in their eyes as they glanced at her one last time; there never would be.

Molly turned to Mr. Oller, and the misery in her young face touched him. Taking a deep breath, he exhaled through his nose. "I'm sorry, Malinda. But those Mennonites are fine customers. Without them coming in to trade with me, why, I'd have to close my doors."

When Molly merely stared at him, color crept into his cheeks and his voice rose. "I said I'm sorry, but business is business. Furthermore, you lied to me. You're only twelve years old, and you've already birthed a bastard. . . ."

Molly turned and fled for the door. But she heard plainly his parting phrase: "You should be working in the house of ill repute!"

Everything changed. No one would hire her. The church shunned her; people who a week before had praised her work ethic turned their heads when she passed them on the street. Finally, cold, tired, and starving, she took Mr. Oller's advice and approached the house of ill repute.

If the middle-aged madam who answered the knock was surprised to find a bedraggled, unkempt young girl standing at her door, she was no less astounded than Molly, who could only stare at the woman's painted face and sheer undergarments.

The madam burst out laughing. "Haven't you ever seen a whore before?"

Molly blushed. So this was a house of ill repute. She felt very foolish. "No, ma'am. I've read about them in the Bible, but I've never seen one. You are very pretty."

"Pretty? Me? Mercy, child, I still love to hear it. Come in out of the cold and let me have a look at you."

The woman escorted the wide-eyed girl through a parlor more elegant than any Molly had ever imagined to a small kitchen at the rear of the house. Seating Molly at a table, the madam introduced herself as Stella Kirby. Then she bade her Chinese cook, Mr. Ling, to find something for Molly to eat.

Molly was amazed when the Chinaman set a plate piled with several delicacies, one of which was a thick slice of broiled chicken, before her. Yet, as starved as she was, she bowed her head and said grace.

Stella, who was a good judge of character, appraised Molly through troubled eyes. There was no overlooking the good breeding in the girl, nor her manners and poise—and she was educated. So why was she there? A job? That might be interesting, because without a doubt, the girl would be a seductive little vixen with the right training and encouragement.

"How old are you, girl? And why did you knock on my door?"

"My name is Malinda Klinner." Molly hesitated. Should she

tell Stella the truth? Yes. She had lied to Mr. Oller, and it had cost her her job. "I'm twelve years old, Miss Kirby. I . . . need a place to stay. I'm a good worker. Why, there isn't a lazy bone in my body!"

Stella stifled a smile. "What kind of employment are you seeking, Malinda?"

Molly forked a piece of chicken into her mouth and chewed vigorously. "I can sweep, and clean, and keep books. I can also cook, but not nearly as well as Mr. Ling."

She smiled around the chicken. "Mr. Ling, would you teach me to cook like this?"

Although she was only being truthful, Molly had just made her first friend among the hired help, for Ling bobbed his head happily and fairly beamed at the girl.

Stella raised her eyebrows. Molly had a nice way of handling people, and that was important in her line of work. "What I need, Malinda, is a girl who can wash frilly dresses and lacy underwear, someone who can iron and sew a fine stitch. Someone who can please women whose job is giving pleasure. It's not as easy as it sounds, my dear."

"I can do those things, Miss Kirby. I'll please them good, I promise."

Stella smiled, liking Molly's fresh, young enthusiasm. The girl was a welcome change. "I'm sure you will, Malinda. Now, if you're finished eating, let me introduce you to the girls you will be working for. And, let me warn you, they are particular about their finery."

Molly laughed at the thought of a woman being so vain as to be concerned about her pantaloons. It was a pure, heady sound that Stella Kirby found enticing. Someday, perhaps when Malinda turned fourteen, she could begin really earning her keep. It was a thought.

So Malinda Klinner, age twelve, became the laundress at Madam Kirby's bordello; and by the time Christmas arrived, she was an indispensable fixture among the girls. They called her Molly, complaining that "Malinda" was much too sophisticated a name for someone working in a whorehouse.

The months sped by for Molly, until that cool morning in September 1863, when she heard the sound of splintering wood. . . .

Molly felt Peyton's presence even before she looked up. He walked to the fire and squatted on his heels. Using his hunting knife, he speared the remaining portion of the meat and stuffed it into his mouth.

Molly watched him out of the corner of her eye. If he was curious about her conversation with Rucker, he did not show it. Well, his lack of interest was his loss. Still, she was disappointed.

Molly finished cleansing Rucker's wounds and sprinkled them with sulfur. "You're a lucky boy, Fletcher. That forty-four Henry usually leaves a bigger, messier hole." It was a lie, but she felt Fletcher needed a few words of encouragement after the depressing story she had just told—or perhaps it was she who did.

Rucker was hanging on to consciousness by a thread, and it took a moment for him to respond. When he did, it was barely audible. "It's like I told Peyton, Miss Molly. If I'd really been lucky, Caleb King would have shot him instead of me."

Molly glanced sideways at Peyton, thinking Rucker had no idea how close that was to the truth. Caleb King had intended to shoot Peyton first, but when he could not get a clear shot because of Peyton's horse, he turned the rifle on Rucker. She kept that information to herself, and laid her palm against Rucker's forehead. It was still burning.

Molly made a snowball, then flattened it to a patty, and laid it across Rucker's brow. Then, dumping the bloody water out of the coffee mug, she rinsed the cup with scalding coffee and refilled it.

She offered the cup to Peyton. "The horses all right?"

Peyton cupped his cold hands around the tin mug, feeling its heat penetrate his stiff fingers all the way to the bones. "They're still alive."

Lifting the cup to his lips, he took a thirsty draw, watching Rucker all the while. "Is Fletcher going to be in any condition to travel today?"

"He's burning with fever, Mr. Lewis. It would be better to

wait at least another day or two before we attempt to move him."

She wondered why she called Peyton "Mr. Lewis," instead of his given name. She had no trouble addressing Rucker as "Fletcher," but it was different with Peyton; he was not the kind of person with whom one could assume a familiarity.

Peyton raised his face and squinted at the silver-gray outline of the sphere that hung in the heavy, low-lying, gun-metal sky and judged it to be nearly ten o'clock in the morning. The day was half gone.

"We don't have a day or two, Miss Klinner." Peyton was thinking of the posse that was certain to be following; and to make matters worse, sooner or later someone was bound to find Caleb King's body.

Peyton walked to Fletcher and knelt down beside him. "How you feelin', cousin?"

Rucker opened his eyes and smiled at Peyton. The grin did not quite come off.

"Some better, Peyton." Rucker rolled his head sideways and gazed at Molly. "A month of nursin' don't equal an hour of sweetheartin', Peyton . . . an' Miss Molly sure is good at sweet-heartin'. She's the tenderest an' finest little thing I've met since we left home to go to war."

Molly watched Peyton expectantly, wondering if he would tell Rucker she had offered herself to him last night. Suddenly she was angry: at Peyton for thinking so little of her, at Rucker for thinking so much of her.

"I'm not a sweetheart, Fletcher! Nor am I a tender little thing." Molly smiled acidly at Peyton. "Go ahead, Mr. Lewis. Tell Fletcher what I am. I'm sure you're just dying to enlighten him as to the truth about Molly Klinner."

Peyton's face filled with disgust. "What you are, or are not, Miss Klinner, is none of my business."

Rucker frowned at Peyton. "You got somethin' stuck in your craw, Peyton? Somethin' concernin' Miss Molly?"

Peyton glanced accusingly at Molly. "Nothing to get excited about, Fletcher. But the truth is, she's one of the reasons you're wounded. She's one of the reasons we're not already halfway to Texas."

Molly's mouth dropped into a rounded *O* of astonishment. Indeed, if the truth was known, she was very probably the only reason they were on their way to Texas! What astounded her most, however, was the fact that not one word of her explanation concerning Caleb King had affected Peyton Lewis in the least. He must certainly be an incredible imbecile.

Peyton drew Rucker to a sitting position. "Can you make it to your feet, Fletcher? Are you able to ride?"

Every plane of Rucker's young features was shadowed with pain, and his normally healthy skin had taken on a pasty gray tone that fairly screamed of fatigue and loss of blood. "You might have to tie me on, Peyton, but I'll stay in the saddle."

Molly sucked in her breath; they were both imbeciles! Rucker's sickness aside, if Peyton would but take the time to notice the sky, he would see that any evidence of the sun had vanished into clouds so low they were touching the treetops; and any fool who even halfway understood the elements would read that as a bad sign. But no, Peyton Lewis was too caught up in his wants and his needs to notice—or hear—the important things.

Molly's hands tightened into fists, and she fought to control a temper that longed to unleash a tongue-lashing such as Peyton Lewis had never experienced.

"I think, Mr. Lewis, it would be the worst sort of folly to move Fletcher." When Peyton did not respond, her patience snapped. "If you insist upon moving him, then I suggest we return to the soddie and wait for better traveling weather." She jabbed a finger at the sky. "Those are snow clouds, Mr. Lewis, and they are hanging low and heavy. And if it's as bad a blizzard as I believe it will be, we certainly don't want to be caught without shelter."

A faint smile curved Peyton's lips. "We're riding on, Miss Klinner. But you're free to go any direction you damn well please."

Molly pierced him with a glare as cold and unrelenting as the snow-covered terrain. She could learn to hate this man. She raised her eyebrows. "Only a guilty man or a buffoon runs when no one is chasing him, Mr. Lewis. In your case, however, I'm beginning to think you are both."

Seven

The storm hit at noon. It came out of the north with a ferocity that drove the horses' chins to their chests and plastered their tails against their rumps.

The three riders pulled their hat brims low and turned up their collars. They rode with their hands drawn into their coat sleeves, their shoulders hunched against stinging, biting snowflakes that attacked every vulnerable portion of exposed skin and seemed to penetrate the threadbare fabric of their clothing like a million tiny knives.

Molly shouted something to Peyton, but the gale whipped the words away as though she had not spoken. She edged her horse closer until her knee brushed against his.

"I can't tell which way we're traveling!" Her face was only inches from his, yet she was not certain he had heard her until he nodded that he understood. Molly pointed ahead. "If we are still heading west, we might have a chance. Caleb King once told me of a Butterfield stagecoach station that was twenty miles west of the soddie. But he never took me there, so I have no idea where it is."

Peyton peered into the blinding wall of snow. He was well aware that locating one small stagecoach station in the middle of a snowstorm such as this would be more difficult than looking for a diamond on a frozen pond. It dawned on him that perhaps Molly Klinner had been right about him on both counts: he was definitely a guilty man, but was he also a fool? He had never thought so before, but now he was not so certain.

Reining his horse around, Peyton rode to Rucker, who was ten yards behind, and shouted to him that they were going to try for a stagecoach station Miss Klinner had heard about.

If Rucker heard the exchange he made no indication, and Peyton decided against attempting to outshout the raging storm. At this point it made little difference whether Rucker knew their intentions or not—and if they failed to find the stagecoach depot, it made no difference at all.

Four hours and five miles later, with night closing in, which, due to the reflection of the snow against the low-hanging clouds, amounted to little more than a dimming of the grayness, their horses suddenly floundered belly deep in a snowdrift. As the animals struggled to climb out of the basin, their hooves rang against solid ice, an indication that they were crossing a frozen stream.

Squinting against the pelting sleet, Peyton saw on the far bank above the creek a small depression that had been created by the uprooting of an ancient tree. The trunk and limbs had long since either rotted away or been used to fuel the fires of other travelers, leaving a hollowed-out crater below the root mound that appeared to be two feet deep by three feet wide. The slight bowl offered a windbreak from the deadly blizzard that howled all around them like a fiend from the netherworld.

Gazing around him, Peyton spied several small bushes so spindly that they would hardly serve as adequate kindling to light a fire, much less fuel one for twelve hours in subzero weather.

Although Peyton was less than elated with the find, he was well aware that even those scant sources of protection against the elements might possibly be the single determining factor that separated their lives from certain death.

Peyton spurred his floundering mount out of the creek bed and up the incline to the depression under the roots and dismounted. As he began raking the snow from beneath the mound, he was surprised to find Molly Klinner on her knees working industriously beside him. In minutes, they had cleared a pocket in the snow some five feet across and three feet deep.

Peyton retrieved his blanket roll from his saddle and draped it from the top of the roots to the foot of the pit they had dug, creating the roof of a makeshift lean-to that was nearly four feet tall at its apex. Molly's rifle served as a tent pole to counter the accumulating weight of the heavily falling snow that was pelting the cover as though it knew its purpose and resented its presence.

Molly quickly spread her's and Rucker's bedroll in the cleared depression beneath the canopy, then ran to help Peyton lift Rucker from the saddle and carry him to the shelter.

Snow had already covered the roof by the time Peyton and Molly dragged Rucker inside and wrapped him in his blanket. Peyton crawled from the chamber and made his way to the creek bank, where he gathered an armload of twigs from a spindly bush. When he retraced his steps to the campsite, he could barely see the trail he had just made.

In spite of his and Molly's efforts to enclose the sides of the structure, an icy wind whipped through the open space under the edge of the blanket, extinguishing Peyton's every attempt to keep a lucifer lighted long enough to ignite the kindling.

As a last resort, Molly stretched her body full length along the edge of the enclosure to act as a shield against the piercing blasts of air. Her threadbare overcoat and thin woolen dress did little to dispel the penetrating cold that seeped into the small of her back and caused her abdomen to ache as though some unseen hand had driven wedges of ice beneath her skin. She visualized the child inside her drawing into a tight knot, and she wondered if unborn babies shivered from the cold. Molly clenched her teeth to stifle the moan of misery that came unannounced to her lips.

Peyton struck a lucifer; it sputtered feebly, then burst into full flame.

Molly held her breath as he carefully laid the match beneath the kindling. She closed her eyes. "Please, God, I've never asked you for much . . ." The twigs burst into flame. "Amen!"

The instant the fire was sufficiently strong to withstand the occasional blast of wind that whipped through the crack beneath the blanket, Molly crawled close to the flame and chafed her aching hands. Feeling the circulation return to her fingers, she filled the coffeepot with snow and set it near the fire.

While Molly huddled over the flame, determined to absorb every particle of escaping heat, Peyton crawled out of the shelter to attend to the horses.

The animals stood in a dejected huddle as sleet and snow plastered their shaggy coats to their bodies and the raging wind whipped their manes and tails as though they were ships' sails that had been ripped loose from their booms and gaffs.

Peyton slipped the horses' bridle bits and loosened their saddle girths and cinches, but chose to leave the saddles, bridles, and blankets in place; they were scant protection from the blizzard, but they were better than nothing.

Peyton left the animals where they stood and made his way down the creek, breaking off branches for fuel as he went. When he finally crawled beneath the shelter, it was growing dark outside. He laid the bundle of twigs beside the fire and thrust his hands over the flames.

Molly offered him a half-filled mug of lukewarm coffee, her eyes taking in the pitifully small pile of sticks. "Is that enough kindling to last the night?"

Peyton gulped down the drink and handed her the empty cup. He refused to meet her eyes.

Molly had her answer.

Molly poured the remaining coffee into the cup and took a sip, again eyeing the small stack of wood. If those few pitiful sticks were their total fuel supply for the night, their chances of surviving until daylight was . . . "We'll make it."

She was surprised to hear herself speak. She looked at Peyton, and her lips drew into a half-smile. "Even if we have to sleep three deep, we'll make it." Then she laughed, a strange and unexpected sound in the unearthly quiet that came with nightfall. "If we sleep three deep . . . I want the bottom!"

Peyton was not amused. In fact, her attempt at cheerfulness annoyed him, and he wondered if she had the remotest idea how truly life-threatening their predicament was. He doubted it.

Molly's smile faded. "You're a real stick-in-the-mud, Mr. Lewis. Do you know that?"

Peyton fed a handful of sticks into the fire and watched with a begrudging tolerance as the flames licked greedily at the scant fuel. He was forced to cut an opening in the overhead blanket so the smoke could escape, and each time the wind blasted down through the ventilation hole and whipped the flames into a frenzy he gritted his teeth, aware that their meager supply of life-supporting warmth was being uncontrollably wasted. It was as though the elements absolutely refused to give up their quest to destroy them.

When twilight slipped into full darkness, they lost all track of time, and Peyton was so miserly with their meager supply of fuel that at several intervals during the following hours, Molly feared he had waited too long to add another stick to the fire. On each occasion, however, Peyton somehow managed to revive the embers and rekindle the flame. Finally, he laid the last spindly twig on the coals.

Molly stared hard at the dancing flames, mentally willing the stick to burn slowly. All too shortly, only a few coals glowed in the darkness. Molly shivered, and her teeth chattered as the cold marched in as though it were a victorious army that had finally overpowered a weakening enemy, like the cold steel of a bayonet—a feeling she knew well, the cold forced its way deep into her body as though it had waited patiently for the kill, and now its time had come.

Peyton was startled when Molly plunged into her gunny-sack and began throwing utensils and what little foodstuff they retained hither and yon. When she pulled out her Bible and clasped it to her breast, he fully expected her to begin reading the Scriptures, as would most folks who are aware that death is imminent. Instead, she carefully tore out the pages that recorded her family heritage, then handed the remainder of the book to him. "Burn it."

When Peyton searched her face with a questioning gaze, Molly folded the pages she had torn out and slipped them into her coat pocket. "I couldn't very well read the Scriptures if I were frozen stiff, could I, Mr. Lewis?"

Peyton ripped a page from the Bible and held its ragged edge to a live coal. A moment later, the brittle paper burst into flames; a moment later it was gone.

Page by page, the book diminished until all that was left were the aged leather covers. Then they, too, were ashes.

As the intense cold again seeped into the dugout, Peyton pulled his greatcoat collar more tightly about his neck and brought his arms up across his chest, his fingers tucked beneath his armpits. Molly huddled into herself and shivered with violent spasms that left her even more weakened because of the very energy spent in the act of shuddering.

With an oath at his own stupidity, Peyton jerked upright and began unbuttoning his greatcoat. When his numbed fingers refused to negotiate the buttonholes, he clutched the coat by its lapels and ripped it open.

Molly watched Peyton's display in wonder. Surely he did not intend to play the gentleman and offer the coat to her? Of all the absurd things! She was fully prepared to refuse his generosity when he ran his hand inside the garment and withdrew his Spiller and Burr revolver.

Molly's heart skipped a beat. "What do you intend to do with that?" A very real fear welled up inside her; she had heard stories of snowbound, freezing people who murdered their companions for their food and clothing. With a cry of rage, she flung herself against him and pummeled his face with her small fists.

Peyton dropped the pistol and knocked her hands aside. Catching her shoulders, he shook her savagely. "Has the cold driven you loony?"

Molly fought hard to twist from his grasp, but his fingers were like steel bands where they encircled her arms. "If you think you can shoot me without a fight, you're the one who's loony!"

Peyton glared into her face, and words of denial formed on his lips. Then his mouth snapped shut with a firmness that all but shouted that she was not worth an explanation. Pushing her from him, he fished his clasp knife from his trouser pocket, leaned close to the feeble light cast by the dimming coals, and attempted to open the blade.

Molly drew herself to a sitting position with her back braced staunchly against the wall of the dugout. Judging the distance from her heavy work shoe to the top of his bent head, she lifted her skirts up over her knees and slowly cocked her leg until her knee was pressed tightly against her breast.

Peyton squinted at her in the darkness. "Can you open this knife? My hands are so numb they're useless." He could barely see the outline of her raised foot, and for a moment her intent evaded him. His lips drew into a thin line. "If you kick me, Miss Klinner, I'll break your leg." It was a soft-spoken promise.

Molly kept her foot raised. "What do you intend to do with that knife?"

Peyton took a deep breath and let it slide between his teeth. *She is crazy.*

"When I pulled my pistol, you assumed I was going to shoot you, and you hit me in the mouth. I took out my knife and you immediately believe I am going to stab you, so you prepare to kick me." He frowned at her. "Is it any wonder that I'm reluctant to travel with you, Miss Klinner? Upon occasion, you act totally demented."

Molly lowered her foot. "All I am asking, Mr. Lewis, is for you to explain your actions."

"I shouldn't have to explain anything to you, Miss Klinner. But just this once, I will. When I was in the army, an old soldier told me that a man could make a tent of his blanket and stay alive in the coldest of weather with nothing more than the heat from a solitary candle."

Well, that answer is as clear as mud. Molly took the knife from him and attempted to open the blade. To her dismay, her fingers were as cold and ineffectual as his, and after struggling with the clasp for what seemed an eternity, frustration brought a whorehouse word to her lips. She swallowed it, then wondered why.

"Is it really important that we open this knife, Mr. Lewis? Why do we need it?"

"Are you demented, for Christ's sake? I just explained all that to you. The fire's down to ashes. There's no wood. And we've burned your Bible. It's six, maybe eight hours till daylight and we're already losing our senses."

"But what good is this knife?" She looked at him as though being demented came in two sexes. "We've no candles, nor wicks to trim if we had them. And you will freeze in two minutes if you venture outside to cut more branches."

"If we can get the blade open, Miss Klinner, I intend to use it as a screwdriver to take apart the butt strap of this pistol." He snatched up the revolver and shook it in her face. "These walnut handles are oil saturated. They'll burn slow . . . like a candle!" He glared at her. "But first we've got to open the goddamned knife, and my hands are frozen!"

Molly studied him pensively as though she were struggling for an answer to a personal question known only to her, a question concerning him.

"I know a way to warm your hands, Mr. Lewis." She lay back and opened her legs. Holding his eyes with hers, she took his hands and guided them beneath her skirt and placed his palms on the flesh of her inner thighs. The shock of his icy hands on her sensitive flesh took away her breath.

If Peyton was startled by her gesture, he was even more shocked when he realized she wore neither petticoats nor pantaloons. Surprised or not, when he felt the heat of her flesh seeping into his fingers, he pressed his hands even more firmly against her skin.

Molly closed her legs around his fingers, gritting her teeth against the deep, cold ache that spread upward through her abdomen.

"It's a good thing I wasn't entertaining any romantic notions, Mr. Lewis."

Peyton scowled at her. Even though he appreciated her willingness to sacrifice her modesty to warm his hands, he was embarrassed and infuriated by her open acknowledgment of it.

"You really don't give a damn, do you?"

Molly was taken aback by the question. "You mean about letting you touch my legs?" When he did not answer, anger sent splotches of color into her pasty white cheeks. Raising herself to her elbows, she looked directly into his face. "Not when it means the difference between life and death, Mr. Lewis. I accepted that truth long ago."

When he did not reply, she kicked his hands away and snatched her skirt down over her knees. "And I'll tell you something else, Mr. Lewis! If you ever touch my body again, it will cost you—in gold!"

In spite of himself, Peyton grinned at the asininity of her comment. "I didn't ask to put my hands between your legs, Miss Klinner. And even if I had, I wouldn't pay you one red cent because I can't feel one darned thing!"

For a long moment she stared sullenly into his face. Then she dropped her head back and laughed delightedly.

"I don't believe we're as close to freezing to death as we think we are, Mr. Lewis. When people are on the verge of freezing to death, their senses become dull and sluggish, and they grow drowsy and incoherent. They certainly don't fight and yell at each other."

Peyton shrugged. "The very fact that I hollered at you, Miss Klinner, proves that my senses are dull and unwitting. If I wasn't freezing to death, I'd have quietly told you to go to hell."

Molly laughed again. "Your hands aren't the only thing that's cold about you, Mr. Lewis—you pious son of a bitch." She guided his hands again to her thighs. "Do you find me offensive because you think I'm a prostitute? Or is it that you've something against me personally?"

Peyton shook his head. "I don't even know you, lady."

"Well," she smiled wolfishly at him, "if it's because you think I'm easy, Mr. Lewis, let me remind you of something: if I were a prim and proper little lady, your hands would be frozen off by now with no chance at all of opening that knife. And another thing." She was heating up again. "The only difference between a girl selling her charms for enough money to make a new start and a man robbing a bank for enough money to make a new start is that . . . what she does isn't against the law."

Several minutes passed before Peyton's hands began the tingling, needle-pricking sensation that indicates increased circulation. Then two things occurred: the pain that accompanies nerve stimulation snapped his teeth together in an agonizing clench, and he slowly became conscious of the smoothness of her inner thighs and the soft texture of her pubic hair.

He blushed, thankful for the darkened interior that hid his embarrassment. The few professional women he had bedded had shaved their bodies, especially the pubic region, in an effort to eliminate body lice and vermin; so the very act of touching Molly Klinner thus seemed somehow overly personal and intimate.

Molly was aware that his sense of touch was returning. Even had she not felt it in the heat of his fingers, she would have known it by his sudden refusal to make eye contact with her.

His childishness reminded her of an old saying: "Never trust a man who can look a pretty woman in the eye." She wondered why that particular bit of philosophy had popped into her head. The truth was she had never believed the saying, nor did she particularly like or trust men who did not have enough confidence to challenge her gaze. Yet she trusted Peyton Lewis and had since the first moment she saw him.

Peyton withdrew his hands and massaged them briskly. When he reached for the knife, Molly's fingers were frozen stiffly around its handle. As gently as possible, he pried them apart, experiencing a stab of shame each time he forced one open, because in his heart he knew that if the situation were reversed, he would never have allowed Molly Klinner to touch his person— not even to save his life. When the knife came free, Peyton quickly thumbed open the blade and attempted to insert its point into the screw slot on the pistol's butt strap. In the darkness, the blade missed the slot and slipped off the metal strap. He felt the blade plunge into his hand, and immediately a warm, sticky substance trickled down his palm and dripped from his fingers. He held the pistol aloft and squinted at its butt plate in the darkness, turning it first this way, then that. "Try to revive a live ember from that pile of ashes, Miss Klinner. I can't see a darned thing!"

Molly crawled to the fire pit and blew gently on the ashes. One tiny glow showed in the bed of coals. Terrified that the spark would die, she withdrew the pages she had salvaged from the Bible, her only link to her ancestry, her family, her past. For an instant she hesitated, holding not only her own but more importantly her unborn child's genealogy in the palm of her hands—and now that she was preparing to start one of her own, family, past and present, was very important to her. She looked at Peyton. He was waiting. With a sigh that was lost on him, Molly touched the edge of a page to the live ember.

Molly's heart hammered as the paper merely curled up and smoldered. To burn her bloodlines to stay alive was in itself a difficult feat; to waste it was unacceptable. She squinched her eyes shut. "Please, God, one more time . . . please help us." Suddenly, the page burst into flames. Molly glanced aloft, an expression of awe on her face.

Turning the screw was more difficult than Peyton expected, and Molly was compelled to forfeit a second page, and then a third. As sheet upon sheet turned to ashes and Peyton still had not loosened the screw, Molly hesitated before adding her last treasured leaf to the embers.

"Perhaps we should try a different pistol, Mr. Lewis." She ran her hand into her overcoat pocket and withdrew the Bacon and Company pistol.

Peyton snatched the pistol from her and examined its handles. Unlike his heavy revolver, whose grips were held in place by a metal butt strap and machine screw, the Bacon's light, two-piece handles were secured by a small brass screw that passed through both pieces of wood from the side and was made tight by an inleted steel nut.

As Peyton began turning the screw, Molly fed the last of her ancestral record into the fire. Even though unscrewing the handles was a quick process, by the time they slipped free, the page was nearly gone.

Peyton hurriedly laid the wood on the fire, then watched helplessly as the flame died. He dropped to all fours and blew gently on the ashes; a coal flared in the darkness, then settled into a winking ember that grew more feeble by the second. Peyton's shoulders sagged in defeat.

Had he glanced at Molly Klinner and been able to observe her face in the darkness, to see into the depths of her intricate mind, he would have been astounded at the indecision that

warred with her common sense concerning a five-dollar bill that
was tucked into the inside headband of her hat. She was sickeningly aware that a person—especially a woman—who was totally
destitute of currency was one of the most vulnerable human beings on earth. In a society that demanded immediate payment
for goods delivered, the five dollars made her a woman of means.
Without it . . . Reluctantly, she shoved the paper money into Peyton's hand.

When Peyton once again had a flame going and the pistol
handles were burning nicely, he looked up at Molly's sour face
and wondered what kind of woman would unhesitatingly watch
her ancestry go up in smoke, yet balk at burning paper money.
Had he inquired, Molly would have told him that the five dollars,
as paltry a sum as it was, represented as large a fortune to her as
his five thousand dollars in gold did to him.

Instead of asking, Peyton merely frowned his displeasure at
what he considered a woman whose values ran counter to his, for
the five-dollar bill would have been the first thing he burned.

"Don't pout so, Miss Klinner. You couldn't very well spend
the money 'if you were frozen stiff.' "

Molly tilted her head sideways and studied Peyton in the
dim light. "I've heard it said, Mr. Lewis, that imitation is the sin-
cerest form of flattery. If that is true, sir, then I suggest that you
stop wasting your breath—and what little fire we have left—and
get busy on those other handles."

When Peyton fished two additional revolvers from his saddlebags and began stripping them of their grips, Molly crawled
to Rucker and searched his coat and trouser pockets for anything that would burn.

"Good Lord!" Molly withdrew four sidearms from various
hideouts in Rucker's clothing. "You boys are a walking arsenal!"

Peyton took the weapons from her. "Not really, Miss Klinner.
We only carry three or four revolvers each. Bloody Bill Anderson
carried six or more. In fact, he had six on his person when he
was killed."

Peyton shoved Rucker's ivory-handled Confederate Shawx
and McLanahan revolver into his waistband, and immediately
began removing the grips of two large Walker model Colts. They

were old revolvers and required more time and effort to disassemble. The .32-caliber five-shot pocket pistol with very small grips he laid aside.

Molly pointed to the Henry repeating rifle. "You can burn that, too."

Peyton eyed the polished rifle stock. It would burn long and it would burn hot. He shook his head. If they survived the night, chances were they would need the long shooting range the rifle offered more than the handguns, because game on the prairie was nearly always a great distance away, requiring a heavy-caliber weapon.

Outside, the wind howled like a banshee, as though it were outraged anew by the life-saving warmth that was slowly forcing the cold from the confines of the enclosed depression in the snow.

Molly settled back and watched the tiny flame languidly. She was not warm, but at least her teeth had ceased chattering.

Peyton turned the charred pieces of walnut in the fire, coaxing every last bit of warmth from the fuel. When that pair of handles had burned down to ashes, he laid the second set on the coals.

He looked at Molly. "When the last set is burned, win, lose, or draw, we'll push on." He added silently, *There's no point in sitting here waiting for death.*

Molly snuggled deeper into her coat. "We can still burn the rifle stock . . . and our saddletrees . . . and your saddlebags . . ."

Peyton waved her suggestion aside. He did not want to burn the rifle, and his and Rucker's saddletrees were bone, not wood. And the saddlebags! Irony pulled his lips into a tight line. He had robbed a bank, and for all practical purposes was a rich man. Now, less than four days later, he was snowbound on the Kansas prairie with a young whore he did not want, a wounded cousin he could not help, and a raging storm that he could not stop, one that, in all likelihood, would freeze them to death. And come spring, some fool would find their bones—and ten thousand dollars in gold—and become instantly wealthy without having suffered one whit. Justice be damned.

Peyton wondered what Molly would think of that. He

glanced over at her. Her eyes were closed, and her chin rested on her chest. Her breathing was soft and regular.

"She's asleep!" His words sounded loud in the silence of the small enclosure, and he was totally unaware of the disappointment that edged them. Apprehension nagged at his memory as he gazed at her, something he could not quite recall, something important. Then it hit him. She had stated it earlier: "When people are on the verge of freezing to death, they grow drowsy . . ."

"Wake up!" He crawled over and grasped Molly's shoulders, then shook her savagely.

Molly moaned incoherently, but did not open her eyes.

Peyton backhanded her across her mouth. "Wake up, damn you!"

"Let me sleep." Molly attempted to push him away. "I'm having the best dream . . ."

Peyton shook her again, snapping her head back and forth.

Molly's eyes popped open. "All right! I'm awake . . . I'm awake."

Peyton peered closely at her, but in the dim light he could not tell if her eyes were focused. He had heard people talk in their sleep, and he had seen people die with their eyes open.

"See if Rucker's still alive." When Molly did not move, Peyton slapped her hard across the face with his open palm. The blow nearly toppled her over.

"I'm awake." There was a very real anger in Molly's voice this time. She crawled to Rucker and shook him gently. Rucker cursed, then asked for a drink of water. Peyton took his canteen from an inside coat pocket and handed it to her.

Molly fumbled unsuccessfully with the cork stopper for several seconds, then raised the canteen to her lips and pulled the cork with her teeth.

"Can we heat this?" She shook the container; the icy slush rasped against its pewter sides. "There's no coffee left, but a warm liquid, even plain water, would do us all some good."

Peyton wedged the spout of the canteen between the exposed mainspring and the backstrap of one of the handleless revolvers and held the canteen over the flames.

When they had drunk the canteen empty, Molly snuggled deeper into her overcoat. "You really spoiled a good dream a few minutes ago, Mr. Lewis." She sighed unhappily, and her lower lip puffed out in a pout. "I don't have many good dreams."

"It might have been your last."

"It might have been worth it."

"I doubt it."

Molly smashed her fist against his lips.

Peyton stared at her.

"That's just in case you're wrong." She sat back in satisfaction as a thin trickle of blood wound its way down his chin. "You didn't wake me up because you were afraid I was going to die. You woke me up because you were afraid Rucker and I would die, and you would be left all alone." She eyed him angrily. "That's it, isn't it? It wasn't that you cared about us! You just didn't want to be left to die by yourself."

Peyton wiped the blood from his chin with the back of his hand. "There's a certain amount of truth to that, I suppose."

Molly leaned toward him, her eyes flashing in the dim light. "I wasn't dying, Mr. Lewis, I was sleeping."

He shrugged. "You said that drowsiness is common when a person is freezing to death."

"Drowsiness is also common when a person is totally exhausted!"

He grinned at her and wondered if she intended to hit him again. To his surprise, she laughed also, then snuggled down against Rucker and put her arms around him. "I'm going to sleep, Mr. Lewis."

Peyton added another set of handles to the fire. When Molly's eyelashes dropped onto her cheeks and did not rise, he adjusted Rucker's blanket so that a portion of it covered her body. She was right; he did feel very much alone with both her and Rucker asleep. He settled down beside the fire and stared into the flames. *No*, he thought, *that's not true. I feel very much alone because she is asleep.*

Eight

Peyton laid the last pair of handles on the flame and reached for the Henry rifle that acted as their tent pole. When he removed the weapon, the ceiling, weighted by more than a foot of heavy, wet snow, sagged down around his ears, and smoke from the flaming pistol grips swirled about his head. He coughed and quickly returned the rifle to its former position.

Fanning the smoke toward the ventilation hole he had cut in the overhead blanket, Peyton ran his arm through the opening to remove any blockage that might be stifling their draft. As the smoke raced for the newly opened flue, Peyton gazed at Molly Klinner and wondered if she had been able to recapture the wonderful dream he had interrupted. He sighed. She looked peaceful, snuggled against Rucker as though they were longtime lovers. He considered crawling in beside them, aware that without a fire none of them would last two more hours. It would be an easy death, a drifting death, into oblivion, into nothingness. Then the truth hit him, and he bolted upright. He could see Molly! He could see her plainly!

Peyton threw back a corner of the blanket roof. Full daylight washed through the enclosure. He raised the edge of the blanket higher until he could see the horses. They were huddled close together just as he had left them the evening before. They looked wretched—and beautiful.

Peyton shook Molly awake. When her eyes opened and she assured him she was alive and well, he left her where she lay and crawled outside. The intense cold seared his skin, but he did not care. Bowing his head against the wind, he waded through waist-deep snowdrifts to the horses. Like icing on a cake, fourteen inches of new snow lay atop the saddle seats. Peyton raised the stiff leather fenders and tightened the cinches.

As Peyton worked, he gazed across the prairie in search of a landmark, but there was nothing, not even the outline of the shallow stream that ran beside the camp.

Molly crawled from beneath the blanket and stood erect. She stretched, blinked, and rubbed her eyes. The wind whipped her hair across her face; she did not bother to brush it aside. "Lovely morning."

Peyton drew his hands up into his overcoat sleeves and balled his fingers into fists to warm them. "How's Fletcher?"

"He's alive."

"Get him up. We're movin' out."

Peyton caught his horse by the bridge of its nose and attempted to force the bridle bit into its mouth. The animal locked its jaws and tried to rear; the movement lifted Peyton off the ground and dumped him into a snowbank.

Molly shook her head at him. Why did he insist on being such an ass?

"If you warm the bits a little with your hands, Mr. Lewis, the horses might accept them easier."

Peyton ignored her. When he tried to force the bit a second time, with the same result, she shrugged. "Suit yourself. You always do, anyway."

With deadly intent and brute force, Peyton worked the bit between the horse's teeth and quickly adjusted its bridle. He glared triumphantly at Molly, but she had already turned away and was in the process of uncovering the camp. When she rolled back the blanket roof, she found Rucker awake with his blanket pulled tightly up under his chin.

"Well, Fletcher." She grinned impishly at him. "You got to sleep with me for free last night."

When Rucker made no effort to rise, she knelt down beside him and slipped an arm under his shoulders. "Come on, Fletcher, you've got to get up. Mr. High-and-Mighty has laid down the law. We're moving on."

With Molly's help, Rucker stumbled to his feet and stood wobbling like a newborn foal as Peyton led his horse over. It took both of them to get Rucker into the saddle.

"Tie me down, Peyton." Rucker's eyes were bloodshot, and he reeled drunkenly in the saddle. Molly steadied him, then guided his feet into the stirrups.

Peyton studied the icy terrain. It would be a dangerous compromise, lashing Rucker to his saddle. Should Rucker's horse fall, and that was a very real possibility . . . Peyton looked up at Rucker, noticing that the boy was so weak he could barely grip the saddle horn. Peyton shook out his lariat.

Molly slipped her foot into her stirrup and attempted to raise herself into her saddle. Her head spun, and her breath came in short, urgent gasps as though she had been running. Sinking back into the snow, she leaned heavily against her horse for support.

Peyton walked over to her. "You all right? You look a little peaked."

Molly grasped the saddle horn and again lifted her foot to the stirrup. "I'm all right. Just tired, I suppose." But she knew that was not true. She was pregnant, and the past two days had taken their toll on her endurance, her nerves, even her sanity.

Peyton gave her a leg up and held her steady while she settled herself into the saddle. With seemingly little effort, he trudged back through the snow to where his horse waited. Even though a reluctant admiration sparked in Molly's eyes, she could not help but resent his strength, his willpower, or whatever it was that kept him going.

"What about you, Mr. Lewis? Don't you ever get tired? Don't you ever want to just lay down and quit?"

Peyton lifted himself into the saddle, and for the briefest instant, when he turned toward her, he could not hide the haggard weariness that etched hard lines into his young face. Then it was gone, replaced by the cold, unreadable look he normally wore.

"You better hope not, Miss Klinner."

Peyton urged his horse forward, into that wide expanse of prairie that seemed to stretch on forever.

Well, Molly mused, watching Peyton struggle to maintain his balance as his horse crow-hopped through snowdrifts that came nearly to its chest, *at least I know he's as tired as Rucker and me.*

As Molly reined her horse and Rucker's into the trail Peyton had just broken, she wondered why Peyton's show of weakness left her suddenly longing to take him to her breast and comfort him. She shook her head. *I am losing my mind.*

All that morning, they pushed their horses with only minimal rest periods. In many of the flat places, the Kansas prairie winds had swept away much of the snow, and the traveling was easier— not better, just easier. They rode three in a line, without conversation, seeing neither house nor person nor any warm-blooded creature save themselves. It was not only depressing, it was scary, as though they were the only living beings who inhabited this cold, white planet.

When they stopped for their noon breather, they sat their horses like so much baggage, slumped in the saddle, too weary to dismount.

Peyton dug into his saddlebags and found a cloth sack that contained a handful of stale, hard jerky. Dividing the strands into three equal shares, he passed them around.

When they moved on, Molly took the lead. Her horse struggled valiantly to keep its footing as it plowed through the unbroken snow, but Molly knew the poor animal would not last the day. Peyton followed behind her, and Rucker brought up the rear.

It was a bone-weary cavalcade that inched its way across the great expanse of frozen Kansas plains. To make matters worse, another storm was building in the east.

Two hours later, Peyton urged his horse up beside Molly.

Her mount was laboring heavily, its breath coming in short, quick gasps that sounded like a wood rasp being drawn across a pine board. It was only a matter of time, he knew, before the animal collapsed. He had to shout to be heard above the roaring wind. "Drop back behind Rucker!" When she hesitated, he pointed to her horse, shook his head, then pointed to the rear.

Molly nodded and allowed his and Rucker's horses to forge ahead. Even then, with Peyton breaking the trail, her horse lagged behind, barely able to hold up its head.

The storm hit them without warning, pelting their exposed skin with snow and sleet until it was raw, forcing them to bow their heads to protect their eyes, which was a self-defeating action if they were to locate the stagecoach station.

Peyton halted his mount and let Rucker draw abreast of him. He raised the brim of his hat just enough to see Rucker's face, then leaned close to the boy and shouted into the gale: "If we don't find that stagecoach station in the next half hour, I'm for killing the horses, skinning them out, and stretching their hides between their carcasses for a shelter. At least we'll be out of the blizzard and have plenty of warm meat to eat."

When Rucker did not answer, Peyton peered more closely at him. The boy was either asleep or dead. Peyton rode back to where Molly's horse had come to a standstill some twenty yards away and repeated his decision.

Molly nodded her head that she understood, then cupped her hands around her mouth. "You might as well do it now, Mr. Lewis. My horse is all but dead anyway."

Indeed, her horse stood humpback, its chin touching the snow. The steam of its breath, like pistol shots, came fast and irregular.

Molly eased herself out of the saddle and sank to her hips in a heavy, wet snowdrift. She was vaguely aware that the icy granules felt warm against the skin of her unprotected legs. With unfeeling hands, she uncinched her saddle and let it slide off the horse's back to fall where it might. She was beyond caring.

Peyton drew Rucker's ivory-handled revolver from beneath his greatcoat and attempted to thumb back the hammer. He had no sensation of touch. Using both hands, he cocked the pistol.

When he leveled the revolver at Molly's horse, the wind died abruptly and the countryside became as still as a grave, as though nature waited with bated breath for him to accomplish his grisly deed. He aimed at the horse's head.

The shot was earth-shattering in the stillness. Molly's horse sank to its knees, then fell heavily onto its side and lay there quivering. Steam rose from its body as though it were a smoldering ember.

Beneath the animal's head, the snow turned pink, an ever widening stain that reminded Peyton of sunrise creeping gradually across a still land.

As the horse kicked its death throes, Molly dragged her saddle well away from the animal and slumped down on the frigid leather seat. She buried her face in her hands and took several deep breaths. The stale jerky she had eaten lay nauseatingly heavy on her empty stomach, reminding her of the morning-sick days she had endured not so many weeks before. Scooping up a handful of snow, Molly crammed it into her mouth to try to curb the churning in her stomach. A moment later, she retched up everything.

Peyton uncinched his saddle and dragged it and the saddlebags from his horse's back onto his shoulder. He labored through the snow to where Molly sat and dropped his gear next to her.

He returned to his horse and patted its neck affectionately. The animal had proven a steady and trustworthy companion to him for the past three years; it had bottom; it was no quitter.

Steeling himself, Peyton put the muzzle of the pistol against the horse's head and pulled the trigger.

The shot, even though it was a muffled blast, sounded loud in the stillness. The horse dropped as though all four feet had been snatched from beneath it.

Without so much as a second glance at his dead mount, Peyton walked to Rucker's horse, which stood waiting patiently, as though it, too, knew its time had come. Peyton worked at the stiff knots that lashed Rucker's feet to his stirrups. He had just gripped Rucker's arm in an effort to drag the boy out of the saddle when a shout sounded behind him. Peyton snatched his pistol from his waistband and wheeled about to find three men making their way through the drifts toward him. Dropping to one knee, he sighted down his pistol barrel at the lead man. Then he eased the hammer of his pistol to half-cock and climbed to his feet. The stagecoach depot stood in plain sight not two hundred yards beyond the men.

Molly stumbled to her feet as the men rushed toward her. Laughing and crying at the same time, she turned to Peyton, who was staring at the two horses he had just shot. She sobered, and her heart went out to him. She took a faltering step toward him.

"You didn't kill them needlessly, Mr. Lewis. You had no way of knowing the station was there."

"I should have looked. It was in plain view; all I had to do was look."

Without waiting for Molly to join him, Peyton waded past her as though she had ceased to exist, and trudged through the snow to meet the men.

Before the group was halfway to the station house, the storm attacked them with a raging passion, as if it were bent on making up for its moment of silence. Peyton, leading Rucker's horse, stopped and visually searched the prairie they had vacated only moments before. Try as he might, he could not locate the bodies of the horses he had shot. They were gone, obliterated by a wall of snowflakes so white and dense that they might have been a giant bedsheet draped over a clothesline, a fabric that could not be penetrated by the human eye.

Molly, having stopped beside him, laid her hand on his arm. "Scary, isn't it? How close we came to missing the station." She patted his arm affectionately. "Somebody is watching over us, Mr. Lewis. In spite of you being a bank robber and me being a shamed woman, somebody likes us."

While the three men from the Butterfield depot escorted Molly and Rucker inside the building, Peyton led the boy's exhausted mount to a long, low pole barn that housed fresh horses for incoming stagecoaches. Down the middle of the stable was a walkway with four stalls fronting each side. The place smelled of hay, horse manure, and harness leather.

Peyton scrutinized the barn's interior, searching out any nook or cranny that he might use to hide the gold-laden saddlebags. There were none.

Walking the horse to an empty stall, he dragged the heavy bags from behind the cantle and stacked them beside the stable door.

Turning Rucker's horse into the stall, he forked hay into its manger and, as a precaution, should he be forced to make a run for it, he walked down the main aisle, appraising the six coach horses that comprised the relief team. They were large animals, half Percheron, half saddle stock, bred for speed yet possessed with the strength and endurance necessary to pull a heavy Butterfield stagecoach. Two gaited horses were also present, but neither of the animals was nearly so fine as the cavalry horse he had shot.

Peyton stepped out of the barn and surveyed the depot. It was a long, low, log structure, with a roofed porch that shaded the front of the building. If there was any smoke rising from the chimney, it was lost in the blizzard. Still, the place certainly looked inviting.

When Peyton entered the station house, he was surprised to find the main chamber warmed by a dry-laid stone fireplace where logs blazed with a cheerfulness that belied the deadly storm outside. Two small, glass-paned windows enhanced the warm, pleasant feeling, expelling the dreary gloom that was an integral part of most cabins and soddies.

Peyton walked to the hearth and removed his hat and greatcoat. Hanging them on a peg beside the chimney, he thrust his hands toward the flames. From the corner of his eye, he examined the room. Two of the three men who had assisted in their rescue were sitting on long slab benches that flanked a heavy wooden trestle table that acted as the depot's dining area, gambling casino, and, upon occasion, a lectern for a circuit riding judge or a pilgrim preacher. The men watched Peyton with open interest.

His gaze moved beyond them to the far end of the chamber, where a bar that also served as the stagecoach ticket counter sported several whiskey bottles and a mixed assortment of shot glasses.

Molly's voice echoed from an adjoining alcove, and Peyton cut his eyes in that direction. The door to what Peyton assumed was the bedchamber was ajar, and he could make out Rucker lying atop a makeshift bed. He could see neither Molly nor the person to whom she was speaking. That bothered him.

As Peyton started toward the bedchamber, one of the men at the trestle table, a tall, thin, elderly man, with an iron-gray mustache that matched his shaggy, shoulder-length hair, climbed to his feet.

"Sorry about your horses, son, but if you hadn't of shot 'em when you did, why, we'd never of knowed you were out there."

Peyton hesitated, then inclined his head to the man in acknowledgment. When he again turned toward the bedchamber, the second man at the table, rawboned, red-faced, and weak-looking in a mean way, hailed Peyton and flung his hand toward the bar.

"Pour yourself a shot of liquid heat an' meander on over here, mister. We been sittin' out this storm for three days, an' we're just plain wore out a-listenin' to our own tall tales."

The gray-haired man scowled at his companion. "Now, Herman, if there's any invitin' done, I'll do it. You keep that in mind."

Something in the way the older man had taken charge of the younger one caught Peyton's attention. Changing direction, Peyton walked to the bar, where he picked up a half-empty whiskey bottle. He ignored the dirty shot glasses and tilted the bottle to his lips.

The old man motioned toward a black iron kettle hanging from a swing crane in the fireplace. "There's grub in that there pot. An' you'll find a tin plate or two 'hind the bar. Help yourself."

Peyton heaped two plates with a thick stew that looked and smelled like wild game and dried vegetables. He left one plate on the hearth and carried the other to the adjoining room, where

Molly was bent over Rucker, tucking a heavy quilt beneath his chin.

The station agent, a hard, grizzled man who appeared capable of handling any circumstance, stood beside the bed holding a dishpan half full of rust-colored water and a blood-soaked cloth.

Peyton ignored the man and handed the plate of stew to Molly, who eyed the contents dubiously and wondered if the food would lie on her stomach. She indicated the agent with a nod of her head.

"Meet Charlie French, Mr. Lewis. Charlie and I cleaned Fletcher's wounds and put fresh dressings on them. Charlie says that Fletcher will be as good as new in a week or two."

Peyton stepped aside as French carried the dishpan out the door. The moment the man was gone, he turned to Molly. "Did French ask any questions?"

She shook her head. "He helped clean and bandage the wound, but he didn't pry and I didn't offer."

Molly spooned a bit of stew into her mouth and chewed it slowly, praying that the food would stay down. To take her mind off her nausea, she studied Peyton closely, noting that, for the first time since she had met him, he had removed his hat and greatcoat. Molly was surprised to find Peyton as spare and lanky as Rucker, but she was unprepared for the broad width of his shoulders, the flatness of his stomach, and the way his muscles rippled beneath a shirt which was at the least two sizes too small for him. Understanding softened her gaze for, like him, she had had no new clothing since the second year of the war. She forced her gaze to his black, unkempt hair, which hung an inch or two below his collar. It gave him a wild, savage look. His checkered shirt was threadbare and faded, and his gray woolen trousers, shiny at the inseam from living in the saddle, were nearly worn through at the knees where they disappeared into the tops of badly scuffed cavalry boots. Only his weapons, the bone-handled bowie knife and Rucker's Shawx and McLanahan revolver, appeared well cared for. Somehow, she found that reassuring.

"What are you going to tell them?" She cut her eyes to the men in the adjoining room.

"Nothing."

Molly stared pensively after him as he headed for the door. *You are wrong, Mr. Lewis. You'll tell them something, rest assured.*

Peyton walked to the hearth and squatted down with his back to the wall so he would have an unobstructed view of French at the counter and the two men at the table. He ate his stew slowly, watchfully.

French left the bar and walked to the table. After refilling the whiskey glasses of the two men, he ambled to where Peyton sat and offered him the bottle. When Peyton refused, French hunkered down before him with his back to the men at the table. "I've seen that Henry rifle that woman brung in here, Lewis. It belongs to Caleb King."

Peyton laid his spoon on his plate, then slipped his hand around the ivory handles of Rucker's pistol.

French saw the move and shook his head. "I ain't lookin' for trouble, mister, but I ain't sidesteppin' it, neither. King's a bad man to have as an enemy. I don't want him comin' in here lookin' for a fight."

"He won't."

French's gaze was level. "You certain?"

Peyton resumed eating.

A flicker of a smile touched French's lips. "Fair fight?"

Peyton's expressionless eyes climbed to French's face. "Whether a fight's fair or not, Mr. French, depends on who's left standing when it's over."

French shrugged. "Makes sense to me."

Peyton reached into his pocket and withdrew a twenty-dollar gold piece. "We'll be staying until the weather breaks, Mr. French."

French took the coin and climbed to his feet. He gazed down at Peyton. "I never did like Caleb King." Pocketing the money, he headed toward the bar, being careful to keep his hands in plain sight as he walked behind the counter and set the whiskey bottle on the shelf. He had already decided he would rather face two like Caleb King than one like the young man seated at the hearth. It was not that Lewis had the look of a killer about him. No, it was something infinitely more dangerous: Lewis had the look of a man who would kill a killer.

Peyton finished the stew and laid the plate on the hearth. He studied the two men at the table. Had they, too, recognized King's rifle?

Molly joined him at the hearth, the plate she carried hardly touched. She set it on the mantel.

Peyton flicked his eyes toward the table. "Have you ever seen either of those men before?"

Molly did not look at them. "No, I've never seen them before. Why?"

"French recognized King's rifle. They might have also."

"How do you know Charlie recognized the rifle?"

"He said so."

"What did you tell him?"

"I told him King wouldn't be needing it."

Molly's eyes met his, and he saw approval there. "That's all he needs to know." She picked up their plates and sauntered toward the bar.

Peyton walked to the small frosted-paned window and peered out at the prairie. Nightfall was but minutes away, and the wind whipping across the flats was stirring the snow with such violence that it was impossible to tell if the blizzard was raging or had abated.

The gray-haired man at the table pushed himself to his feet. He was in his late fifties, with a deeply grooved, weather-burned face and an easy stance that was erect yet slightly stoop-shouldered, as though he had spent much of his life on horseback. He walked to the window where Peyton stood, and there was a sharp intensity in his eyes that belied the friendliness of his voice when he extended his hand. "Daniel Sloan."

Peyton ignored the hand; nor did he acknowledge the name. When he turned again to the window without speaking, Sloan's face took on a wary look.

"It's mighty poor weather for travelin'. You folks just passin' through?"

Lawman! The certainty of it set Peyton's nerves on edge,

and he had to fight to control his voice as he turned back to Sloan and eyed the man levelly. "We're headed to the Indian Nation. Oklahoma."

Sloan pursed his lips as though it was the answer he was expecting. With a shrewdness in his eyes that suggested a suspicious nature, he pushed his face close to Peyton's. "I'm curious about how your friend got shot."

Peyton worked hard to keep his actions neutral, but his words, when he spoke, were edged with a threat. "You might do well to mind your own business, Mr. Sloan."

Sloan dropped his head back and peered down his nose at Peyton, assessing him a second time.

"It is my business, son. I'm the sheriff of Franklin County, which is what you're standin' in right now." With a slow, precise movement that could not be misinterpreted, Sloan opened his coat and withdrew his pipe and tobacco from a vest pocket, making sure Peyton saw the badge pinned to the watch chain that dissected his chest.

Peyton's heart pounded. He watched the sheriff's face, knowing that a man's eyes often said things that his actions did not. "My cousin was bushwhacked three days ago, Sheriff. Caleb King did the shooting."

Sloan struck a lucifer and applied it to the pipe. He took a long pull at the stem, then blew a trail of smoke toward the ceiling.

"When the snow lets up, I reckon I'll mosey down to Caleb King's soddie and talk with him for a spell."

"You do that, Sheriff." Peyton turned again to the window and stared at the terrain.

Sloan walked to the bar, where Molly leaned casually on the counter. She had overheard enough of the conversation to know who approached her. She waited for the sheriff to begin.

Sloan took another draw on his pipe, then exhaled slowly while watching her face. "I can't talk to that boy, ma'am. He's real edgy, and edgy folks do unnecessary things—like shootin' a man who's jest tryin' to do his job."

Molly shrugged, and her eyes narrowed until her long

lashes were nearly touching, neatly concealing her gaze from his scrutiny. "That sounds like a personal problem, Sheriff."

Sloan nodded at Molly, thinking that she was as tough as Lewis. Maybe tougher.

"I reckon it is, missy. Did he kill Caleb King?"

Molly grinned at Sheriff Sloan, taking in his eyes, his nose, his mouth, studying him, considering the question, how to answer. "If Mr. Lewis says he did, Sheriff, he did. If he said he didn't, Sheriff, he didn't."

Sloan took another draw from his pipe. Yes, sir, tough people, these. He sighed; since the war, Kansas was full of them. "Did King bushwhack that boy in yonder?"

Molly could answer that question truthfully. "Yes, Sheriff, Caleb King shot Fletcher Rucker in the back. You can look at the wound."

Sloan again pursed his lips, causing his mustache to turn down at the corners. Back-shooting sounded like something King would do. "King still live over in Johnson County?"

Molly nodded.

The sheriff knocked the ashes from his pipe into the palm of his hand. "Then it's out of my jurisdiction." He raised his bushy eyebrows at her. "You folks ain't killed nobody in Franklin County, have you?"

Molly shook her head.

Sloan tipped his hat to her, then crossed the room to Peyton, who had watched the exchange with growing apprehension.

Sloan scrutinized Peyton carefully, aware that he was treading on dangerous ground, mindful to keep the animosity he felt out of his voice. "Mister, I've got somethin' to say, an' you can do with it as you will."

Peyton's hand inched toward the five-shot revolver tucked in his waistband.

The sheriff saw the motion, and for an instant his voice faltered. Then he went on, determined to say his piece, unable not to. "The woman says you haven't broke any laws in Franklin County, an' I believe her. So you can get your hand away from that pistol because I don't meddle in things that happen outside my jurisdiction. However, if she's lyin', you'll have me to deal with."

Peyton moved his hand away from the gun, and Sloan visibly relaxed, his eyes twinkling as he gazed at Peyton. They were almost friendly. Almost. "Son, I want to pass along a word of wisdom. You can take it or leave it." He glanced out the same window through which Peyton had been peering. "A man who constantly watches the horizon has more on his mind than seein' the sights. It makes a sheriff wonder. . . ."

Sloan walked back to the table and eased himself down beside his companion.

Molly caught Peyton's eyes and held them. A smile touched her lips; it spoke of conspiracy, something personal between just the two of them. When Peyton did not return the gesture, she spun on her heel and stepped into the room where Rucker lay.

Nine

Peyton was beginning to believe there might be some truth to Rucker's claim: "An hour of sweetheartin' equals a month of nursin'." With Molly Klinner watching over the boy like a mother hen, clucking over this, purring over that, Rucker had improved remarkably in the four days they had been at the station.

Molly had also, when not attending to Rucker's wounds, taken on the responsibilities of cook, barmaid, and listening companion to the snowbound men. She had quickly become a favorite of everyone at the station, especially Charlie French, who laughingly offered her a full-time job.

Rucker proposed marriage to Molly daily and Molly declined daily, whispering to him that a jail cell for bank robbers was not her idea of a honeymoon cottage.

Peyton watched Molly from afar, noting with an amused half-smile how she twisted the men, including Sheriff Sloan, around her finger and worked them like puppets to gain their friendship and confidence. Well, that was fine with him, because this was as far as she was going in his company.

February 24, 1866

On the fifth day, the snow stopped, and on the sixth morning, the sun rose in all its splendor, its bright rays penetrating the greasy windowpanes to cut like a knife through layers of tobacco smoke that twisted and turned in the small room like banners hanging in a gentle breeze.

For what seemed like the hundredth time, Peyton walked to the window and gazed out at the blue sky and the vast expanse of dazzling, snow-covered brilliance. He squinted against the near-blinding glare and scanned the horizon as far as the narrow window would allow, searching for the westbound stagecoach that Charlie French promised would arrive the moment the weather broke.

No stagecoach. Nothing. Peyton fidgeted, anxious to be away from Sheriff Sloan, who seemed bent on watching him like a hawk.

Molly moved up behind Peyton and peered over his shoulder at the vivid blue sky. The sight, unobstructed by snow clouds, perked her spirits. "It's beautiful, isn't it? The sky?"

When Peyton did not answer, Molly sighed with disappointment. "You might as well relax, Mr. Lewis. Fletcher won't be able to travel for another week. And besides, no stagecoach driver who knows his business would be foolish enough to try to shepherd a rig through snow that's axle deep."

Peyton continued to stare out the window. "So now you're an expert on stagecoaches as well as a . . ." He let the words trail off, wishing he had kept his mouth shut, wondering why she could bait him so easily. Molly smiled at his vexation, enjoying it.

"Being a what, Mr. Lewis?" Her taunt twisted the knife of his discomfort a little deeper. "What was it you were about to call me?"

Peyton gazed out the window a moment longer, then turned and walked to the bar.

Molly watched him pour a tumblerful of whiskey and down it in one gulp. He poured another. Anger welled up inside her. She was sick to death of his half sentences and innuendos. If he had something to say, he should say it. Say it plainly!

She crossed the room in angry steps and caught his arm. "Mr. Lewis, I resent your—"

Peyton jerked his arm free with such venom that Molly stood with her mouth open, shocked speechless.

Peyton saw hurt and humiliation replace the surprise on the girl's face, and a touch of shame, the first he had experienced in a long while, piqued his conscience. "All I was going to say, Miss Klinner, was that obviously you know stagecoaches as well as . . . you know men."

Peyton brushed past Molly and strode to the table where the sheriff, his companion Herman—who, as it turned out, was Sheriff Sloan's prisoner—and French were playing poker. Peyton dropped down on the bench and told them to deal him in. As he shuffled his cards, he wished again he had said nothing to Molly. Hell, the minute Rucker could travel, he was leaving, so why didn't he just steer clear of the woman until they could go their separate ways? What she did with her life was her business, and he, an outlaw himself, had no right to judge her—most especially no right to judge her.

Peyton divided the cards into suits and studied them without seeing them.

Molly walked to Rucker's room as casually as her screaming nerves would permit, for at that precise moment she detested all men in general and Peyton Lewis in particular.

When she entered the room, Rucker rose on one elbow and grinned at her. "I'm jest plumb tired of bein' cooped up in here, Miss Molly. How about movin' me out to the big room?"

Molly's patience was stretched to the breaking point. "Stop your whining, Fletcher. I'm in no mood to listen to it."

Rucker lay back, stunned.

Molly flopped down on the foot of Rucker's bed. "What makes Peyton Lewis such an asshole? I want to know!"

Rucker stared at her, his mouth agape, for he had never heard her curse; indeed, did not approve of women who swore. "Why would you say such a thing, Miss Molly? Peyton's plumb straitlaced an' respectful when it comes to women. Why, when we was bivouacked near a town, he hardly never went with us to the whor . . ." Rucker blushed and squirmed deeper into his blankets. "He stayed in camp most nights when we were soldierin'."

Molly waved Rucker's statement aside. Yet, like he, she, too, wondered why she would say such a thing about a man she hardly knew. Why was it so important to her to understand Peyton Lewis? The question nagged at her, and she attempted to reason it out. Was it because she never allowed a man to get close to her? She had slept with men, yes, but never had she allowed them to trespass that invisible barrier which would bind her securely to their souls as she had with Peyton Lewis. She had offered him sex, yes, but she had offered him something many times more fulfilling, more precious—she had offered him an opportunity to come inside her through her heart instead of her body. Was he not aware that it was a thousand times more difficult to consummate true friendship, with its many facets and complexities, than to merely go through the motions of fulfilling the immediate needs of a lustful man? She sighed. That was an understatement.

"I don't give a fiddlee-damn about the number of women Peyton has slept with, Fletcher. I want him to trust me. To talk to me. To . . . like me . . . just a little."

So caught up was she in her search for answers that she did not see the anguish her words had brought to the boy's face.

Rucker lay quiet, observing her. "Why, Miss Molly, I thought you knew that you've got all that with me. . . ."

Molly looked into Rucker's eyes. She would be lying if she pretended surprise, so she did not. Since that first night when she had ministered to his wounds and brought him a measure of comfort, Fletcher Rucker had fancied himself in love with her. It was nothing new to her, that reaction. She had experienced it with many a lonely man or sick lad. Unlike most of the men to whom she offered her affections or medical expertise, however, she was truly fond of Fletcher Rucker, so she chose her answer to his declaration of love very carefully.

"Yes, Fletcher." She smiled crookedly at him, softening her words. "I know I have all that with you. But you are a rolling stone—here today, gone tomorrow. That's the way it is with you devil-may-care boys."

Rucker caught her hand and brought it to his lips. "A stone

quits rollin', Miss Molly, when it finds the kind of moss it wants to gather."

Molly sighed and disengaged her fingers, wondering what had changed her. All the men she had ever known were like Fletcher Rucker, wanderers and drifters, or married with families—and that had been all right. Why, then, was she all of a sudden thinking in terms of a permanent relationship? It was because she had had no say in the matter; that decision had been made by Caleb King.

"Thank you for the offer, Fletcher." She bent and kissed his forehead, surprised that she was actually flattered by his candid overture. "But it just wouldn't work. You're a friend. A true friend." *But I don't need a friend; I need someone with stability, roots, intelligence, social standing—permanence.* There was that word again: permanence.

Molly wondered why, when she thought of permanence, her mind automatically conjured up Peyton Lewis. Because he was all those things she longed for. It was as simple as that. Also she knew that someday he would be a power among men and that she wanted—no, she intended—to play a part, however small or insignificant, in his climb to the top.

Sometime or another, in the past few days, though Molly knew not when, Peyton Lewis had become her sole possible claim to respectability; and deep down inside, the part of her that was not soiled needed that stamp of social approval and acceptance, craved it badly.

Molly almost laughed aloud when she realized she was dabbling in two worlds that were not compatible; there was no such thing as a virgin whore. Even more ridiculous was her foolish belief that a man could respect a woman for her honesty, decency, and integrity when he was perfectly aware that men had purchased her most intimate charms for a given sum of money.

Yet respect was what she yearned for from Peyton Lewis. No, that was not true; respect was what she would demand from Peyton Lewis. Her face blanched. Demands! Who was she to be making demands? If Peyton were to learn that he was traveling with a pregnant woman, a rain barrel filled with demands would be to no avail. He would leave her. It was that simple.

When Molly became aware that Rucker had once again taken her hand and was vowing fervently that he wanted to be more than just her friend, she expertly steered the conversation in a different direction. "Did you help Mr. Lewis rob the bank, Fletcher? I bet that was exciting. Like I told Mr. Lewis, you fellows will be Southern heroes . . . probably be written about in history books."

Molly's praise had the effect on Rucker she had expected. His chest swelled with pride, reminding her of a bantam rooster that had just topped a dominicker hen and was strutting his stuff. Rucker blushed boyishly and fingered the bedcovers, refusing to meet her eyes. "Why, heck, Miss Molly, when there's heroin' to be done, somebody has to hold the horses. That's all I did. Frank an' Jesse an' Peyton did the robbin'."

Rucker launched into his version of the holdup, and Molly had to suppress a smile, for he had suddenly forgotten all about being madly in love with her.

Throughout the day, the more Molly Klinner considered Peyton Lewis's arrogance, the more angry she became, until at midnight, after the others had retired to their sleeping places, which were nothing more than bedrolls spread on the floor of the main room, she walked to the bar and filled her coffee mug with whiskey.

She never drank alcohol. In fact, she abhorred any substance that dulled her wits. She had learned early in life that her mind, not her body, was the one true element on which she must depend for survival. Tonight, however, she was not fighting for survival. Tonight she was safe. Tonight she could allow herself the luxury of anger—and whiskey—and she intended to make the most of both.

Molly raised the mug to her lips, then tilted it toward the ceiling. When she removed the cup, it was empty. The raw alcohol exploded in her head with a volcanic eruption; water overflowed from her eyes as though it were lava, and her breath, trapped in her throat, burst from her lips in a fit of coughing that doubled her over. Straightening, she caught the whiskey bottle by its neck and walked unsteadily to the fireplace. The embers had died down to coals that pulsated from bright red to dim to bright again, giving one, especially a girl fast becoming intoxicated, the impression of living, breathing, vital organs that had been ripped from a body and scattered aimlessly across the floor of the firebox.

Molly shuddered, wishing she would not think such thoughts. It was the whiskey. It was dulling her wits as she knew it would.

The coals sputtered and popped, then flared into a blue-green flame that lit the area near the firebox. Molly's hand tightened on the bottle, for Peyton Lewis, who had pitched his blanket beside the hearth, had raised himself to one elbow and was watching her intently. A glint of perplexed amusement filled his face that even the deep shadows could not hide.

An unaccustomed bitterness that was, indeed, the product of the alcohol she had consumed prompted Molly to walk unsteadily to where Peyton lay and stare down at him with open contempt.

"I jus' want you t' know, Mr. Lewis"—she tried hard not to slur her words, but it was a wasted effort—"I think you are nothin' but a hypocrite. You seem to b'lieve it's perfectly fine for you to use a gun t' make a new start in life, but you sneer at me for usin' my body for the same purpose."

Molly glared drunkenly at him, wanting desperately to slap away the annoyance that suddenly filled his face.

"An' 'nother thing, Mr. Lewis, when I take a man's money, I give 'im somethin' worthwhile in r'turn—I don' steal it!" Self-satisfaction that bordered on smugness twisted Molly's normally pleasant lips into a tight, ugly smile that was even more unbecoming because of the accentuated shadows that danced and fluttered across the angular planes of her gaunt face.

Peyton sighed through his teeth. "Miss Klinner, I was a bank robber for only five minutes out of what I hope will be a long, productive life." He raised his eyebrows. "How long will you be a whore?" He pillowed his head on his forearm and closed his eyes.

Molly's lower lip trembled, then her face hardened.

"I'm jus' like you, Mr. Lewis. I'll pros'itute myself for as long as it takes." She leaned down and planted a sloppy kiss on his lips. "Are we so diff'rent, Mr. Lewis? I think not!"

Peyton wiped his mouth on the back of his hand and fought down the urge to slap her sober. "It's a lot easier to stand the smell of whiskey, Miss Klinner, than to listen to it. You're drunk. I suggest you get back to your blankets and sleep it off."

Molly laughed and took a long pull from the bottle. She hiccuped, then leaned close to his ear. "The diff'rence b'tween drunks an' fools, Mr. Lewis, is that drunks sober up!"

Peyton rolled onto his side, showing her his back, and closed his eyes. He was tired. Tired of the snow, tired of being nervous about the sheriff, and most especially tired of her.

Ten

At two o'clock in the afternoon, eight days after Peyton shot the horses, a westbound stagecoach, amid a cacophony of screeching wheels, snapping trace chains, jingling harness, and a driver cursing his six windblown horses, came to a sliding halt in front of Charlie French's station.

French snatched his overcoat from a peg near the door and hurried outside, bellowing a welcome to John H. Wright, the driver, who, bundled from head to toe in a heavy, hair-side-in buffalo-hide coat, climbed stiffly down over the front wheel of the coach and dropped into six inches of slush that blanketed the ground.

French caught John Wright's hand and pumped it firmly, thrilled that the road was finally open to travel.

"How was your trip, John? Any trouble crossin' the Des Cygnes?"

Wright looked past French to the four men and a woman who had followed the agent out of the station. He knew the sheriff, but the others were strangers. He eyed Peyton and Rucker with interest, especially Rucker, who carried his arm in a sling. His gaze passed on to Herman, then to Sheriff Sloan, and finally to Molly, who, judging by the way she hovered near the two young men, must surely have been in their company.

Wright turned to French, but he watched Peyton and Rucker, who stood casually beside the station house door, returning his assessment. "The run was mean, Charlie. Yes, sir. A damned mean run. Crossed the Cygnes River without no trouble. But all the way from Kansas City, the snow's been nigh on belly deep on a seventeen-hand horse. An' the wind cuts like a Comanche scalpin' knife. Hell, my mouth's so cold and chapped, I couldn't even pucker enough to blow my bugle to let you know I was arrivin'."

With one last look at Peyton and Rucker, Wright walked to the wheel team of coach horses and began unhooking the trace chains from the doubletrees.

The sheriff, with Molly and Herman one step behind, splashed through the slush to the Butterfield stage, where a young woman had stepped down from the coach and was picking her way gingerly through the icy water toward the station house. She was followed by a man wearing an unbuttoned overcoat that revealed a business suit beneath. He had the paleness of skin and weakness of stature that suggested he might have been a store clerk, or a custodian, or possibly a lawyer.

Peyton paid the woman a passing glance, his attention on the man who had quickly made his way to the rear of the stage, where an oversized trunk was lashed to the coach's boot. The man drew back the leather boot cover, and inspected the lashings of the chest to be certain they were secure.

Rucker edged to Peyton's side and tipped his head toward John Wright, who had moved to the lead team. "I don't like the look that driver gave us, Peyton. He acted like he knew us. Where's my pistols? I can't find 'em anywhere."

"They're in our saddlebags in the barn."

"All of 'em?"

"All but your ivory-handled revolver and my five-shot Colt. I'm carrying them."

Rucker frowned, feeling the first stirrings of doubt and unease concerning the bank robbery, which, until now, he had considered a lark. It was possible someone had recognized him at the bank; suppose they had posted a reward with his description on it! Rucker shifted his feet uneasily.

"Well, I'd sure breathe a heap easier if one of them pistols was in my holster, Peyton. Suppose that driver tries to arrest us?"

Peyton shook his head. He had seen that spooked look on Rucker's face before, and was well aware that when his cousin became nervous or excited, he was apt to shoot without thinking—which was why Jesse James had delegated the horse-holding to Rucker during the robbery.

"I'm keeping the guns, Fletcher. At least until your arm's in good enough shape to use one accurately."

"How come the rest of our guns are at the barn?"

"They haven't got any grips on them."

Rucker groaned. "I thought I'd dreamed you were burnin' our pistol handles—" He stopped in midsentence and gawked owlishly at the young woman whom Molly Klinner was ushering up the walkway.

"My God, Peyton! That girl with Miss Molly is beautiful. Jest plumb beautiful. I believe I'm fallin' head-over-heels in love again. Reckon she's travelin' alone?"

Peyton cut his eyes to his cousin, wondering if he should be disgusted or amused.

"You fall in love with every pretty woman you see, Fletcher. One of these days, some girl is going to let you chase her until she catches you. You're going to get caught in some girl's loop, and her daddy's going to come after you with a shotgun."

"I mean it this time, Peyton, I swear I do! That's the girl I'm goin' to marry. You can bet on it."

Peyton's eyes traveled to the woman. She was indeed striking. Small and slender, yet regal in her bearing, she carried herself with an elegant grace that spoke of wealth and position. The small hat perched saucily atop her coiffured dark hair was adorned with a long, curved pheasant feather that perfectly accented her tailored, charcoal-gray, floor-length traveling habit, the hemline of which she had daintily lifted above her expensive, low-heeled pumps to ensure that the ankle-deep slush would not ruin the fabric. Even the coach blanket offhandedly draped about her shoulders was of superior design and weave.

Indeed, the woman's entire wardrobe, worn with such casual disinterest, boasted a glaring contrast to the battered wide-brimmed felt hat, shapeless topcoat, and heavy woolen dress that Molly Klinner sported. To add insult to injury and underscore their differences even more, the oversized, nondescript tracks of Molly's scuffed, hard-leather brogans, when compared to the dainty imprints left by the expensive slippers of the eastern woman, were a comical mockery.

To make matters worse, as the two women drew near, Peyton heard Molly barraging the young woman with questions concerning the latest clothing fashions in the world beyond the Kansas plains. Peyton almost laughed aloud. Less than two weeks ago, Molly Klinner was burning the pages of her ancestral record to stay alive; now she was asking enthusiastically about what the women in the East were wearing, as if it were truly important.

A slight smile raised the corners of Peyton's mouth as he appraised Molly Klinner from head to toe, for he could not help but think that it mattered little what the latest eastern fashions were. The sad truth of it was—and he unintentionally spoke the thought aloud—"You can't make a silk purse out of a sow's ear."

The woman, a girl, actually, who, now that she was close, appeared to be no more than sixteen years of age, raised her eyes to Peyton's, and in their depths was a certain glint that let him know that, even though it had only been a murmured phrase, she had heard his comment plainly. Her gaze, which held his for a long, unwavering second, was neither friendly nor hostile, merely interested.

Peyton tipped the brim of his hat to her as she passed, and he wondered where she had spent the last four years—obviously someplace in the North or East, where the War Between the States had not reached. Unlike Molly Klinner's gaunt features, which reflected a mixture of malnutrition, loneliness, neglect, and wistfulness, the girl's face was young, alive, unblemished by either time or life—like the faces of the young women he had known before the war.

Shifting his attention away from the woman, he evaluated the man who was splashing through the slush, his cheeks cherry red and pumping like a bellows as he puffed his way toward the depot door. The man was shifty-eyed and soft, in a feminine sort of way, and there were no bulges in his coat pockets to indicate that he might be carrying a concealed sidearm.

The man stopped beside Peyton and thrust out his hand. "William Beecher's the name, sir. I'm from St. Louis. I'm a drummer, yes, sir, a real, live, traveling salesman who's going to make his fortune in Texas."

Peyton ignored William Beecher and swung his surveillance to the sheriff, who, along with Herman, was assisting John Wright, the stagecoach driver, as he herded his six winded horses toward the barn. The sheriff and Wright had their heads together in close conversation.

William Beecher dropped his hand and self-consciously walked into the station house.

French, who had followed Beecher up the walk, stopped beside Peyton, and he, too, watched the three men and the team of horses disappear into the barn. From the corner of his mouth, French told Peyton he had overheard John Wright tell the sheriff that a bank in Liberty, Missouri, had been robbed about two weeks ago. "Wright swears it was a broad-daylight holdup by a bunch of young toughs who were probably ex–Confederate cavalrymen." French swung his gaze to Peyton. "Wright mentioned that the gang got away with nearly sixty thousand dollars in gold." He took Peyton's twenty-dollar gold piece from his trouser pocket and turned it over in his fingers. "Lawmen all over the country, everywhere the telegraph reaches, are lookin' for men with twenty-dollar gold pieces to spend. Men ridin' fine-blooded cavalry horses . . . like the one you shot . . . like the one in my stable." He raised his eyes to Peyton, and there was a thoughtful twinkle in them. "I believe if I was a travelin' man with a pocket full of twenty dollar gold pieces, I'd sell my horse an' go by stagecoach. . . ."

Peyton stared off across the plains. He had not taken into consideration that in 1861, the Western Union Telegraph Company had completed its transcontinental line tying New York City to San Francisco, California. Had they run lines into Kansas, Oklahoma, and Texas? If so, then what the stagecoach driver had said about the gold coins and horses altered his plans drastically, for he had intended to purchase Rucker a horse from French and head cross-country for Texas the moment the sheriff and Herman took their leave.

"Mr. French, would you suppose, if you were inclined to do so, that Fletcher's horse would be worth returning that gold piece to me and throwing in the stagecoach fare . . . say, from here to Texas?"

Rucker's mouth dropped open. "Now, wait just a doggone minute, Peyton. That's my favorite horse! Why, that's a Tennessee plantation horse worth at least forty dollars!"

Peyton ignored Rucker. "Well, Mr. French, have we got a trade?"

French thought for a moment, then flipped the gold piece to Peyton.

"I reckon Rucker's horse should jest about cover the price of three tickets 'tween here an' the Red River. An' speakin' of Texas, you're in luck, Lewis. John Wright told me the Butterfield line hired him to deliver that brand-new coach he's drivin' to the company's territorial agent in Dallas." French nodded appreciatively. "Yes, sir, you're in luck. It's a straight-through run, with John Wright hisself handlin' the ribbons all the way to Texas, an' they ain't a better driver in the whole danged country than John Wright. I'd say the three of you made out like road agents on this deal." He laughed at his own wit, but Peyton merely stepped off the porch and walked toward the barn.

A few feet out, Peyton stopped and looked over his shoulder at the agent. "We'll only need two tickets to Texas, Mr. French. The woman won't be accompanying us."

French scowled, aware that Molly Klinner believed she would be traveling to Texas with Peyton and Rucker. He started to protest Peyton's decision, but Peyton turned on his heel and continued on toward the barn.

Rucker grimaced from the strain on his shoulder as he took long strides in an effort to keep abreast of Peyton.

"We ain't goin' to just up an' leave Miss Molly, are we, Peyton?"

"Yes."

"Now, by God, Peyton!" Rucker caught Peyton's arm and spun him around. "Molly helped us—"

Peyton jerked his arm free and walked on.

"We owe her somethin', Peyton." Rucker clutched Peyton's arm again.

Peyton stopped and stared deep into Rucker's eyes. "We don't owe her anything, Fletcher . . . and that's twice you've put your hands on me."

Rucker had known Peyton Lewis all his life, and he was well aware that Peyton never allowed anyone to touch him in anger, not even kinfolk. Self-consciously, he removed his hand.

"I think you're wrong about leaving her here, *Mr.* Lewis."

Peyton threw a quick look at the barn, and a sigh slipped between his teeth. At any other time, he would have been open to discussion on the subject of Molly Klinner. At present, however, something far more important than her going or not going to Texas with them was in the making, because, if Peyton's suspicions were correct, the sheriff was in that barn investigating the contents of their saddlebags. He said as much to Rucker, then hastened his step toward the barn.

Rucker's head swiveled to the open doorway of the barn. Instinctively, he swept back his coattail and reached for his pistol. His holster was empty.

"Damn it, Peyton, give me a gun!"

Peyton ignored him.

When they entered the building, the sheriff and John Wright were at the far end of the aisle harnessing a fresh team of horses. The excited animals stamped and twisted, anxious to be away from their confining stalls and on the open road.

Peyton felt much the same; he had been cooped up indoors too long. Texas awaited, and every delay, whether it be inclement weather, poor traveling conditions, or unexpected disruptions, such as the wounding of Rucker or the sudden appearance of Molly Klinner, was to him as agonizing as being confined in a barn stall.

Peyton's eyes cut immediately to the corner where he had stored the saddlebags, and his heart palpitated, for the bags were open, and Peyton's only change of clothing, which normally lay atop the gold, was strewn across the floor.

Herman looked up from his pilfering, and the look on his face was that of a child caught with his hand in the candy jar.

Peyton crossed the space between them in three strides. The straight-from-the-shoulder fist that smashed against Herman's chin sent the man crashing against the barn wall with such impact that it shook the entire building. Peyton followed up with a hard left to Herman's midsection that doubled the man over, then a roundhouse right to Herman's temple that dropped the prisoner onto the hard-packed dirt floor.

Rucker bounded to Herman and aimed an off-balance kick at the man's jaw. Rucker's ice-encrusted boot sole caromed off Herman's forehead and sent the boy crashing into the wall. White-hot spasms of pain seared through Rucker's upper body, and spots swam before his eyes.

Herman bellowed for the sheriff, his voice ringing louder and louder.

Rucker grasped his wounded shoulder and danced excitedly from one foot to the other in pain and panic.

"Hit Herman in his goddamned mouth, Peyton! Mash his mouth before the sheriff hears him!"

Peyton jabbed a quick, powerful blow to Herman's lips that drove the man's head back at such an angle that for an instant Peyton thought he might have snapped his spine. A moment later, however, Herman was on his feet again, squealing like a castrated pig and attempting to put as much distance as possible between himself and Peyton.

The sheriff and John Wright had abandoned the horses and were trotting down the aisle toward them.

Rucker ran to the edge of the stall and peered down the aisleway. "Hit him again, Peyton! Knock him out! Knock him out, quick!"

When Rucker stepped in front of Sheriff Sloan, intending to slow the lawman up long enough for Peyton to knock Herman unconscious, the sheriff stiff-armed Rucker out of his way, caught Peyton by his coat collar, and flung him away from the prisoner.

"What in hell's name is goin' on here?" Sloan's eyes darted

from Peyton to Herman, who had sunk to his knees, his hands covering his bloody mouth.

Sloan squatted beside Herman and attempted to pry the man's hands away from his mangled lips. Herman held fast. The sheriff settled back on his haunches and scowled at his prisoner.

"Damn it, Herman, how can I tell if he knocked out your teeth if I can't see inside your mouth?"

When Herman reluctantly removed his hands, the sheriff caught his jaw in his fist and twisted the man's head first one way, then the other, which brought another howl of pain from the prisoner. Sloan nodded in satisfaction.

"Well, Herman, your jaw ain't broke."

Rucker took a belligerent stance and jabbed his finger at Herman. "It's a damned shame if it ain't! We caught the thievin' bastard pilferin' our belongin's."

Sheriff Sloan tipped his head back and squinted up at Rucker. "I told him to do that, Fletcher. I wanted to know what you boys are carrying in them bags. They 'pear to be mighty full, seein' as how they belong to a couple of slick-seated former *Confederate* soldiers."

Peyton walked to the saddlebags and closed the flaps. "What we're carrying is none of your business, Sheriff."

Sloan climbed to his feet and faced Peyton squarely. "John Wright claims there was a robbery in Liberty, Missouri, two weeks ago. A young man was murdered. Murder is every lawman's business, sonny boy."

Peyton slipped his hand inside his greatcoat and tightened his fingers around the handle of the five-shot revolver. The trigger was icy to his touch, as cold as death.

Rucker thrust out his chin. "We ain't killed nobody in Missouri, Sheriff. Hell, Caleb King shot me in Kansas."

Sloan ignored Rucker. "What's in those saddlebags, Lewis?"

"We've got guns in those bags, Sheriff." Out of the corner of his eye, Peyton saw John Wright move off to one side of the aisle and point the double-barreled shotgun that lay in the crook of his arm toward Rucker. Peyton shifted his body so that the teamster was in his line of fire. If a shooting was inevitable, his first shot would be aimed at Wright.

Sloan looked at Herman for confirmation of Peyton's claim, but before the man could answer, Peyton told the sheriff that there was also a little money in the bags, and a clean change of shirts and socks; nothing to get excited about.

"How much money?" The sheriff's hand cautiously brushed aside his coattail to reveal the worn walnut grips of a Remington revolver, and it was plain by his actions and stance that he expected trouble and would meet it head-on.

Peyton turned his body so the sheriff could not see him remove the five-shot pistol from his waistband and point it through his greatcoat at Wright's midsection. He eased back its hammer.

"We've got enough money to start a new life, Sheriff, but not enough to take one."

Indecision played across Sheriff Sloan's face, and Peyton could almost hear him mentally weighing the consequences should he choose to force the issue.

Finally, the sheriff shook his head. "I'd like to believe you, son, but you have something in them saddlebags that Caleb King wanted bad enough to shoot a man in the back. What is it, Lewis? Your share of the money taken from the Liberty bank?"

Peyton went dead inside, the way he always felt when going into battle. He watched Sloan's every move, down to the breath he was taking. If the sheriff so much as blinked, Peyton intended to shoot Wright and then him.

"Caleb King shot Fletcher Rucker in the back because of me, Sheriff."

All eyes whipped to Molly Klinner, who stood silhouetted in the bright sunlight that streamed through the barn's doorway. She was standing hipshot, relaxed, with the butt of Caleb King's rifle resting easy against her thigh. The Henry's muzzle was pointed directly at Daniel Sloan.

"Caleb King shot at both Lewis and Rucker . . . because I was leaving with him." Molly tilted her head to indicate Peyton, then stepped out of the glare of the sun and into the dimness of the building.

"I was Caleb King's woman, Sheriff. . . ." She walked slowly toward the lawman, her rifle barrel steady, and Peyton had to admit to himself that Molly Klinner, in her floppy hat, frayed topcoat, and oversize brogans, when attached physically to that deadly rifle, appeared much more formidable than she would had she been dressed in a fancy eastern traveling habit and dainty shoes. Indeed, Molly Klinner was no sow's ear at that moment! She was going on: "And you know as well as I, Sheriff, Caleb King never willingly gave up anything he owned."

Sheriff Sloan scowled at Molly. This was a fine kettle of fish. She was lying, he knew that, but she was also offering him a way out of what would be a down-and-dirty shoot-out—one he was not certain he could win.

Molly's voice, as she continued, was low and unhurried, as though she was unaware that violence could erupt at any moment. "Caleb King was a killer and a robber, Sheriff. If you were to dig behind his soddie, you would find several bodies buried there."

Sloan's scowl deepened. Things were becoming more confusing by the minute, and he wondered if that were her intent.

"What bodies, Miss Klinner? What are you talking about?"

"Travelers mostly. Sometimes his friends . . . if they had something Caleb coveted. King didn't care who he murdered, Sheriff—he enjoyed killing."

Herman raised himself to a sitting position. Now that the tension of a shoot-out had abated, bravado, encouraged by the memory of a saddlebag full of gold, prompted him to speak out.

"She's lying, Sheriff. She knows about the—"

Rucker kicked Herman in the abdomen, cutting the man off in midsentence. Herman's eyes bulged, and he slumped to the ground, gasping for breath like a fish out of water.

Rucker glowered at the sheriff. "Ain't no criminal goin' to call Miss Molly a liar, Sheriff."

When Rucker drew back his foot to kick Herman again, Sloan pointed a hard, bony finger at him. "Damn it, Rucker! You get yourself over there by Lewis and stay there."

Sloan turned to Molly, and irritation drew his mustache tight around the corners of his mouth.

"Start at the beginning, Miss Klinner, and tell me what went on out there at King's soddie."

Molly told Sloan simply and to the point about the murders

and burials behind the dugout. She explained that the money in Peyton's saddlebags belonged to her.

"Caleb King came home one night about a year ago and buried that money behind the stove, Sheriff. He did not tell me where he got it, and I certainly did not ask. But it's mine now . . . and I intend to keep it. It's my new beginning."

Sloan's frown deepened. Her story sounded authentic. Still, Lewis and Rucker were guilty of something, of that he was certain.

Molly watched Sloan closely. When she saw the glimmer of doubt in his eyes, she smiled demurely. "Surely, Daniel, you wouldn't begrudge a girl a new start in life?"

Sheriff Sloan's shoulders sagged, and he sighed audibly, his breath ruffling the ends of his shaggy mustache. For a split instant Molly was sorry for him. Sloan had suddenly become a tired old man, beaten by his inability to question a woman's honesty and integrity. Molly inwardly cursed herself for her part in the assassination of Sloan's character, and she promised herself that never again would she be a party to destroying a fine lawman like Sheriff Daniel Sloan—not to save Peyton, nor Fletcher . . . not even herself.

Sloan turned to Wright. "Harness your team and get rollin', John. I want these three out of my bailiwick by sundown."

Wright grinned at Molly. He, too, wondered if she was lying, but, either way, she had averted certain bloodshed, part of which might have been his, and he was obliged to her. His look said as much. Wright eased the hammers down on his muzzle-loading shotgun and hurried up the aisle to the horses.

Herman lowered himself on a nail keg and crossed his ankle over his knee. "I'm in bad need of a doctor, Sheriff."

Sloan cuffed Herman an open-handed blow to the side of the head, then turned to Peyton. "Be on that coach when it leaves, Lewis." His eyes swiveled to Molly and Rucker. "All of you."

Tipping his hat to Molly, he walked out of the barn and headed for the station house.

Peyton stuffed his clothes into the saddlebags and, gripping his saddle by the horn, swung the rig to his shoulder. Stepping out of the barn into the sunlight, he tilted his hat to shade his face, then stomped off through the melting slush toward the stagecoach some thirty yards distant.

Molly walked to the barn door and leaned casually against the jamb. She watched Peyton climb up on the hub of the rear wheel and throw his saddle over the guard rail that formed the luggage rack on the roof of the vehicle. She told herself that she had not expected his praise for deterring the shooting, but she knew that was not true. She had expected something, surely she must; otherwise why would his silent disregard for her actions leave her with such an aching in her breast?

Rucker walked up beside Molly and slipped his arm around her shoulder. "I'll be glad to get away from here, Molly. Sheriff Sloan's goin' to keep proddin' Peyton till Peyton shoots him."

"French told me Mr. Lewis intends to leave without me, Fletcher. Why would he do that?" Molly's question was edged with pain.

"Peyton's got a burr under his saddle concerning you, Miss Molly. He thinks you're bad luck or somethin'."

"What I told the sheriff was the truth, Fletcher. I want a new beginning. A new life. I intend to go to Texas whether Mr. Lewis likes it or not."

Molly watched Peyton climb down from the coach and splash through the slush toward her. He looked tall and menacing, yet somehow magnificent in a dark and brooding way. "I'm falling in love with him." The realization astounded her, for she had not experienced the sensation of truly loving a man since she was twelve years old. She was not at all certain she enjoyed the feeling.

Rucker doffed his hat and stared at her. Now it all made sense to him, her spurning his proposals of matrimony: she was in love with Peyton!

Rucker cleared his throat and shifted his weight uncomfortably. "That might be a mistake, Miss Molly. Peyton ain't never been in love with nobody. . . ."

But Molly did not hear him, so caught up was she in her newly discovered disadvantage—for to her that was exactly what it was.

Peyton walked past Molly and hoisted Rucker's saddle to

his shoulder. As he headed for the door, he was forced to step aside to allow Wright and his six skittish horses to pass. The animals rolled their eyes at him and pranced sideways, their breath steaming, their harness jingling.

Molly shrugged off Rucker's arm and edged up beside Peyton, being careful that the fourteen-hundred-pound horses did not crush her against the barn wall.

"In spite of what the sheriff said about all of us being on that coach when it pulls out, Mr. Lewis, I know you intend to go on without me."

She had not expected a denial, so she was not disappointed when Peyton walked out of the barn and followed the horses toward the coach. Still, he could have said *something*.

Molly ran out into the sunlight and cupped her hand around her mouth so her voice would carry. "I won't be left behind, Mr. Lewis. I just want you to know that! I'll be on that stagecoach even if I have to ride in the boot."

Rucker, who had relaxed against the doorjamb, shook his head at Molly. So she was in love with Peyton. Astounding!

Tears of rage welled up in Molly's eyes, and she angrily knuckled them away. "He makes me mad enough to bite nails, Fletcher."

Rucker shrugged his shoulders, recalling the incident in the church with Jesse James. "He makes everybody mad sooner or later, Miss Molly."

Molly marched into the barn and flung her saddle over her shoulder as Peyton had done. Raising her ragged skirt out of the slush with the hand that held the Henry rifle, she tromped off through the icy muck toward the stagecoach.

Herman, sitting on the keg where the sheriff had left him, raised his battered face to Rucker. One eye was swollen shut, and his nose was still pumping blood.

"I hope Lewis leaves that woman here. Hell, I'm goin' to need some nursin' like she give to you, Fletcher, when you was sick." The man laughed; it had a nasty ring.

Rucker glared dangerously at the prisoner. "You've got a dirty mouth on you, Herman. I should have kicked your head off when I had the chance. I might do it anyway."

Herman scoffed at Rucker's empty threat. "I didn't mean no offense, Fletcher. By damn! You an' Lewis sure are a touchy pair."

"We don't take kindly to fools who try to get us arrested, Herman. You're lucky Peyton only mashed your mouth. It's a natural wonder he didn't just up an' shoot you an' be done with it."

Herman shrugged. "Hell, Fletcher. The sheriff told me to look in them saddlebags."

Rucker waved Herman's excuse aside. "You didn't have to tell him what was in there! Where's all this 'honor among thieves' stuff I keep hearin' about?"

"Honor among thieves?" Herman scowled at Rucker as though he were daft. "They're fixin' to lock me up, Rucker. An' it ain't no fun bein' locked up alone. I jest wanted you boys for company . . . practice my card playin', things like that."

"You lunatic! Don't you know there ain't no such thing as practicin' gettin' hung!"

"They don't hang bank robbers, Fletcher."

"Maybe not. But Jesse James killed that boy in Liberty, an' they sure as hell hang men for killin' people."

Herman wiped a trickle of blood from his split lips. "I ain't never heard of nobody named Jesse James."

"Well, you will. He's goin' to rob the bank at Lexington, Missouri, in a few months. Fact is, after I get Peyton an' Miss Molly safely to Texas, I'm thinkin' of headin' back to Missouri an' givin' Jesse a hand . . . but that ain't none of your never-mind, Herman. You'd best keep your mouth shut 'bout what you saw in them saddlebags."

When Herman did not answer, Rucker caught the man's coat collar in his good hand and shook the prisoner fiercely. "You listenin' to me, Herman?"

Herman nodded that he was.

Rucker walked to the barn door. "They're fixin' to board the stagecoach, Herman. You want me to give you a hand back to the station house?"

Herman shook his head and settled himself more comfortably on the nail keg. "Nope, I believe I'll just sit right here an' make the sheriff walk back down here an' get me."

"Well, now, that ain't very respectful, Herman. What did you do to make Sheriff Sloan arrest you in the first place?"

"Oh, I stole a few horses. . . ."

Rucker's mouth fell open; horse thieves were considered the scum of the earth, even by fellow criminals.

"You mean to sit there an' tell me I been standin' here jawin' with a miserable, low-down horse thief? I ought to kill you myself, Herman!"

Herman reared back on the nail keg and cackled like a hen that had just laid an egg.

Rucker stomped out of the barn and marched toward the stagecoach, where Molly and Peyton were in heated conversation.

Molly, controlling her anger by the thinnest of threads, peered up at Peyton, standing on the hub of the rear wheel.

"If you absolutely refuse to allow me the luxury of accompanying you to Texas, Mr. Lewis, then purchase a ticket for me and I shall catch the next stagecoach that happens by. You owe me the price of a horse, Mr. Lewis. You shot mine, remember?"

Peyton wished Molly would lower her voice. The eastern woman was standing just outside the station house door, and, judging by the way she was observing him and Molly, it was obvious she could plainly hear Molly's angry dialogue. Furthermore, Molly Klinner was well aware he had shot her horse to save her life. Hell, she had even approved of it, so why the show of temper now?

Peyton hefted Rucker's saddle onto the stagecoach roof. "Would you have rather I shot you and saved the horse, Miss Klinner?"

"Don't try to be amusing, Mr. Lewis. If someone poured your entire sense of humor into a thimble, it wouldn't cover the bottom."

Molly flung her saddle into the ankle-deep slush and pointed a grimy finger at him. "I saved your neck a few minutes ago, Mr. Lewis. Sheriff Sloan is no fool. He's very much aware of what's in your saddlebags. He just didn't want bullets flying around that barn with me in there . . . and he's too much of a gentleman to call a woman a liar. I was depending on that." Molly was heating up, much like she had the night of the blizzard. "And you're an idiot, Mr. Lewis, if you believe you can outshoot Sheriff Sloan. He would have shot you dead, and don't you ever think he wouldn't!"

The corner of Peyton's lips twisted into the slightest hint of a smile, and his cool gray eyes mocked her. "You just might have saved Sloan's life, Miss Klinner. That thought never occurred to you, did it?"

"You are such a pompous ass, Mr. Lewis. Sheriff Sloan knew you had that gun in your hand. But that wouldn't have stopped him from shooting you. And if he had missed, the stagecoach driver would have got you—and buckshot leaves an ugly corpse, Mr. Lewis."

Peyton dropped down off the wheel hub and picked up Molly's saddle. Flinging it over the luggage rack and onto the roof, he strode off toward the stage station to retrieve their blankets and personal gear.

Molly opened her mouth to continue her argument, but the words caught in her throat. Was he telling her to get into the coach? Was he taking her with him?

A radiant smile lighted her face, and had Peyton glanced over his shoulder he would have been astounded by the transformation. Molly Klinner was lovely.

As it was, however, only the eastern woman witnessed the metamorphosis, and she was not in the least surprised by it. The girl shifted her attention to Peyton, and she wondered why he could not see something so obvious. The woman worshiped him.

When Peyton drew near, she offered him her small, gloved hand. "I'm Gabrielle Johnson. I understand, sir, that we will be traveling companions." Her eyes were so clear and green they reminded Peyton of a dew-covered magnolia leaf.

Peyton ignored her outstretched hand and instead touched the brim of his hat. "Nice to make your acquaintance, ma'am."

Gabrielle Johnson laughed delightedly. "Oh, yes, I forgot. Southern men don't shake hands with women, do they, Mr. Lewis?"

Peyton brushed past her and entered the station. He gathered up his and Rucker's bedrolls, then made his way to the corner where Molly's blanket lay neatly folded. He gazed down at the thin, ragged piece of cloth, and again found himself comparing Molly Klinner to Gabrielle Johnson. Not surprisingly, Molly Klinner came up lacking in all respects.

Eleven

The stagecoach was ten long days out of French's station, yet it had covered only ninety short miles due to the hazardous road conditions and the fact that it stopped periodically to pick up or drop off travelers who had been stranded at various depots along the route. Indeed, it appeared that the entire Midwest had been brought to a standstill by the snowstorms.

Inside the coach, Peyton, Molly, Rucker, and the salesman were cramped shoulder to shoulder on the thinly padded leather seat that ran the width of the coach. Facing them from across the narrow aisle was the northern girl, Gabrielle Johnson. To her right was a heavyset man named Joseph Robertson, who boasted of owning a bank in Austin, Texas, and to her left were two Union cavalry officers, Captain Sam Cramer and Lieutenant Theodore Pendleton. The three men had boarded the coach at a depot on the banks of the Neosho River, some sixty miles west of French's station.

The weather had taken a turn for the better, and only the north slopes and deeply shaded nooks and crannies showed isolated patches of dingy, bluish-white snow. In spite of the warmth of the sun, the cramped interior of the coach was as cold as an icehouse—and with the side curtains down, it was nearly as dark.

The above-freezing temperatures brought a midday thaw, which usually occurred from ten o'clock in the morning until two o'clock in the afternoon. During that four- or five-hour melting period, the Kansas mud clung to the iron tire rims and spokes like plaster to a wall, growing bigger and heavier with each revolution of the wheel.

With growing frequency, as the thaw penetrated deeper and deeper into the earth, the sticky gumbo would bring the heavy Butterfield to a standstill, and the male passengers were obliged to climb out of the coach and spend twenty to thirty minutes using muck ladles, which were paddlelike boards kept in the coach boot, to scrape the accumulation of mud from the rims, spokes, and hubs. As though that were not enough harassment, intermittently the coach bottomed out in a particularly deep hole or rut, and the men had no choice but to lay their shoulders to the wheels and lift the stage onto more solid ground.

John Wright's schedule, because of obstacles such as chuckholes, washed-out gullies, hidden rocks, and deep mud, dropped further and further behind, until, from sheer necessity, Wright designated a man to walk ahead of the coach so it might avoid the deeper ruts that could splinter an axle, snap a coupling pole, or shake the spokes loose in a wheel.

During those times, John Wright, up on the box, cracked his whip and shouted encouragement to the horses, and wished he was driving an eight-horse team.

In truth, while everyone appreciated the warmth of the long-awaited thaw, by early afternoon they were so disgusted with their slow progress that they found themselves looking forward to the drop in temperature that would again freeze the mud as hard as cobblestones so that Wright could coax his six-horse team into covering four or five miles an hour instead of the one or sometimes two that they progressed during the sunny part of the day. Either way, it was a sad comparison to the eight to ten miles an hour a coach normally achieved in the summer months when the roads were dry and cushioned with dust.

High noon, on the twelfth day of travel, found the coach at a standstill with Rucker and Peyton raking muck from the iron tire and spokes of the right rear wheel. From under his hat brim,

Rucker appraised the two cavalry officers who were working the smaller front wheel.

"I'm gettin' plumb fed up with those two blue-bellies, Peyton." Rucker weighed the muck-raker in his good hand as though it were a shillelagh. "Have you noticed how they never speak to us? They only talk to the women . . . kinda like we wasn't even present."

Peyton ladled a wad of mud from the wheel hub and dumped it beside the coach. He hesitated in his work, and he, too, studied the soldiers. He had fought men such as they, had defeated them, and in turn had been defeated by them. Perhaps they had a right to hold former Confederate soldiers in contempt, but Rucker was correct: it was getting more and more difficult to ignore their unspoken insults.

Peyton grinned mockingly at Rucker. "What do you suggest we do, Fletcher? Cut their throats or shoot them?"

Molly, having overheard the threat, raised the window curtain of the coach and peered down at Peyton.

"Every time you get near decent people, Mr. Lewis, you look for trouble." Lines of concern etched her brow. "I should think, under the circumstances, you would try to avoid drawing attention to yourself."

Peyton scowled up at Molly, but she had already dropped the curtain into place, and a moment later, he heard Gabrielle Johnson ask her a question.

Try as he might, Peyton could not make out the gist of the girl's inquiry. When Molly answered, he did not bother to listen to her reply. He wondered about that. Why was he more concerned with Gabrielle Johnson's question than with Molly Klinner's answer? Because he trusted Molly Klinner—he did not particularly like her, but he certainly trusted her. No one—not the sheriff at French's station, or Gabrielle Johnson, or anyone inside the coach—would glean one word of information from Molly Klinner that she did not intend to divulge.

That truth comforted Peyton, which, in turn, irritated him because without her knowledge or intent, Molly Klinner possessed the power to set his mind at ease.

Rucker frowned at Peyton. "Did one of us marry Miss Molly

in the past day or so? She sure does sound like a naggin' wife."

"We might as well have." Peyton found a measure of fulfillment in the fact that Molly Klinner's interference in his and Rucker's business had finally made an impact on the boy. He considered reminding Rucker that he had suggested leaving Molly at French's stage station, but his sense of fair play cried out against such pettiness.

Rucker glanced wistfully at the curtained window. "Molly's as pretty as she can be, but Miss Johnson is just plumb beautiful, ain't she, Peyton?"

Peyton also peered at the window, annoyed by Rucker's declaration, because any idiot knew that most women were as pretty as they could be. Also, he wished Rucker would stop talking freely about Molly Klinner and Gabrielle Johnson, for he and Rucker had been reared as gentlemen, and gentlemen did not publicly discuss a lady's virtues—especially when the lady in question could very likely hear their every spoken word.

Peyton raked a glob of mud from the wheel and dumped it on the ground. Rucker was mistaken, anyway. Molly Klinner was not nearly as pretty as she could be. Her hair needed washing and combing. Her face needed scrubbing. Her clothes were deplorable. And those brogans . . .

Rucker stopped raking mud and scraped the ooze off his paddle onto the tire rim. "I believe you ought to marry Miss Molly, Peyton. She's in love with you."

Peyton jumped to his feet. Rucker was a genuine fool. He was worse than that. He was a dangerous fool. Peyton thrust his ear close to the curtained window, listening intently for any sign that might indicate the women had heard Rucker's comment. For a long moment, the interior of the coach was as silent as a bubble—just before it pops—and Peyton's pulse accelerated to match the anger and humiliation that heated his face.

Not a sound emanated from the coach's interior. Peyton snatched off his hat and laid his head more closely against the leather window curtain. The seconds ticked past. Then he heard the murmur of a feminine voice and answering laughter, neither of which indicated the women had overheard Rucker's comment.

As Peyton bent again to the wheel, his thoughts drifted back to that first night when Molly Klinner had ridden into his camp—the night she had made her profession known and had so brazenly offered her sexual favors to him. Peyton took a deep breath and let it slide through his teeth. Molly Klinner in love with him? Marry her? Why, Fletcher Rucker must be out of his mind to suggest such a thing!

Peyton pointed his muck ladle at Rucker. "If you ever say something that stupid again, Fletcher, I'll stomp a mud hole in your ass!"

When the coach finally rocked into motion and they were once again traveling west, conversation between the tired, muddy, male passengers was limited to an infrequent question or indifferent answer.

Peyton, with one shoulder against the wall of the coach and the drummer pressed against his other, passed the time between breakdowns by mentally structuring his future ranch, seeing it evolve in his mind's eye as though it were already a reality. Cattle. Thousands of cattle. His cattle. The East was clamoring for beef, and a few men with foresight, nerve, and stamina would reap the wealth of that clamoring. He intended to be one of them.

Peyton became aware that Lieutenant Pendleton, sitting across the aisle, had asked him a question. He leaned forward in an attempt to see the young officer's face in the darkened interior. "Did you say something to me, Lieutenant?"

Pendleton was in his midtwenties, but somehow he seemed more Rucker's age, in a juvenile sort of way. When he spoke, his voice boasted the clipped, nasal twang of the northeastern seaboard, a sound that naturally grated on a Southerner's ears. "I asked you, Lewis, what army you served with during the war?"

Peyton settled back against the thin padding of the upholstered seat and contemplated his answer. He resented being questioned by a Union officer, especially one who, judging by the crisp newness of his uniform, had not been in the army long enough to have seen either action or service. Probably the son of a Washington politician. The thought nettled Peyton, because the open wound of the Southern defeat was still too raw to allow casual conversation with the victors—especially one who had never tasted blood, or smelled his own fear.

"I fought for Jefferson Davis, Lieutenant." Peyton tipped his hat down over his eyes, ending the conversation.

The lieutenant glanced at the other passengers, embarrassed by Peyton's quiet yet obvious dismissal. His question had merely been a lead-in so he could boast the fact that he and Captain Cramer, seated on his right, were on their way to Texas to join Major General George Armstrong Custer's Second Cavalry Division, billeted at Austin. So Peyton's open disrespect pricked not only his newly acquired professional vanity but his personal conceit as well.

Turning to Gabrielle Johnson seated on his left, Lieutenant Pendleton spoke loudly enough for all to hear. "The captain and I are en route to enlist in the Second Cavalry, under George Custer, the 'boy general.' "

The tone of his voice implied that he was personally acquainted with Custer. Seeing that he had captured Gabrielle Johnson's attention, the lieutenant grinned at the girl, then looked toward the captain, including his superior in the conversation.

"General Custer is a hero of the late war and has stated publicly that he intends to be the greatest Indian fighter who ever lived. Captain Cramer and I can't wait to get a few redskins in our sights. Why, it will be a thrilling experience."

"How magnificent!" Gabrielle Johnson laid her gloved hand on the lieutenant's arm. "I am en route to visit my very best friend in the world, Lieutenant Pendleton. Her name is Elizabeth . . . Libby." She hesitated, then smiled coyly at the young officer. "I mean, sir, her name is Mrs. Autie Custer. Autie is what we who know him call the 'boy general.' "

Lieutenant Pendleton's face drained; only a chosen few who knew Custer intimately referred to him by his wife's pet name.

Gabrielle could not suppress the urge to twist the knife of humiliation a little deeper.

"I am looking forward, Lieutenant, to an extended holiday in Texas. Libby, the general's wife, invited my former traveling companion and myself to lodge with her in the general's spacious home. Libby and I were next-door neighbors in Monroe, Michigan. We have been friends since childhood. If it had not been for Libby, my life in Monroe would have been quite colorless."

As the coach bumped and rattled down the trace, Gabrielle told them that Monroe was a small, quiet, unexciting town, and that Autie Custer's courtship of Libby, because of his thirst for "Old Demon Rum," had created quite a stir throughout the community.

"I was really surprised when Libby agreed to wed Autie. He was such a rake, not at all like the young men of Monroe."

She went on to relate that she had one brother, twelve years her senior; that her father was an attorney and a close associate of Judge Daniel Bacon, Libby's father; that Libby had been like an older sister to her ever since she could remember; and that she had led the sheltered, nondescript life of a small-town debutante. Her coming-out party, just a few weeks before, had been a celebrated affair, but had left her yearning for something different in her drab life, something exciting, more meaningful— thus, her trip to Texas!

She bored them, all except Molly, with her detailed account of choosing just the right wardrobe for the venture west. She hoped that she had chosen wisely? She batted her eyes at Pendleton, awaiting confirmation. The young Union officer assured her that, indeed, she had.

Gabrielle did not tell them of the tantrum she had thrown that had forced her parents to agree to her cross-country trip to visit Libby, nor of the catfight she had had in a St. Louis hotel room when her forty-year-old aunt, Martha Hataway, who was acting as chaperone, became ill with a touch of food poisoning and insisted they return to Michigan. The result had been that Gabrielle had put her aunt on a train home—and for the first time in her young life had found herself totally free. It was a heady sensation, even scary at times, but she cherished each and every minute of it. She did, however, voice the fact that she was thrilled with the West and how terribly exciting it was to be "on her own."

Exciting, indeed! Molly Klinner stared at Gabrielle Johnson and found herself questioning the girl's common sense. Any fool knew that since the end of the war the country was crawling with homeless former soldiers, carpetbaggers, riffraff, freed blacks, fortune hunters, and outlaws who had no real destination in life or purpose for existing. Southwestern America was ten times more dangerous today than it was just a year ago, especially for a woman traveling alone. Where was the girl's mind? A proper young lady never traveled unchaperoned—unless she was a spoiled brat rebelling against parental authority, which seemed quite probable in Gabrielle's case. Also, Gabrielle had, with obvious and deliberate purpose, embarrassed the young lieutenant quite unnecessarily and most cruelly. Why would she be so unkind?

Molly had a deep-burning suspicion the girl had cheerfully sacrificed the lieutenant's self-esteem in order to accomplish her real purpose, which was simply name- and status-dropping. Did Gabrielle Johnson actually believe that anyone in the coach other than the lieutenant could be impressed so easily? Molly smiled to herself. If that was truly her reason, then Gabrielle had wasted her breath; for she, Molly Klinner, could very certainly enlighten the young woman as to the true character of the high-ranking officers of the Union army.

Lieutenant Pendleton sought safer ground and shifted his attention across the aisle to Rucker, who was riding beside Molly. He prodded Rucker with the toe of his boot. "How about you, fellow? Were you a Reb, too?"

Rucker kicked the soldier's foot away. "I'm still a Reb, an' if you touch me again, Pendleton, I'll loosen a few of your teeth."

The young lieutenant, raw from the sting of Gabrielle Johnson's rebuff, saw the opportunity to reassert his authority. "You lost the war, mister. You'd do well to keep that in mind when addressing a United States cavalry officer."

Gabrielle's hand tightened on the lieutenant's arm, but her

words were directed to Rucker. "This trip has been unpleasant enough, gentlemen, without our making it worse by starting unnecessary trouble."

Rucker grinned boyishly at the girl. "Why, this here lieutenant an' captain have been lookin' for trouble ever since they boarded this Butterfield, ma'am. All I aim to do is oblige 'em."

Captain Cramer, who had thus far kept silent, leaned around Pendleton and looked hard at Rucker. "You talk big for a man with one arm, Rucker. But that's not surprising, because that's all you Rebs were—big talk."

Molly felt Rucker stiffen beside her, and her gaze swiveled to Peyton. She fully expected him to champion his semi-invalid cousin, but Peyton sat with his head resting against the coach wall, hat over his eyes, seemingly asleep. Molly's eyes flicked back to Rucker, who appeared to be mentally gauging the distance between his fist and the officer's face. She nudged Rucker with her knee, a signal to keep quiet.

Rucker ignored Molly, and leaned toward the captain. "Seein' as how they ain't but two of you blue-bellies, Cramer, the fact that I have one arm in a sling makes us about even, I reckon."

Molly's eyes jumped again to Peyton. He had raised the brim of his hat and was studying Rucker with concerned impatience. A sigh escaped his slightly parted lips, and with deliberate casualness, he straightened in his seat. Molly's stomach tightened into a nervous flutter of dread as it always did when violence was but a breath away.

"Miss Johnson." Molly smiled sweetly at the young woman across the aisle. "I'm sure this gentleman"—she rolled her eyes toward William Beecher, the drummer, who sat between her and Peyton—"would be delighted to change seats with you. I believe you'll find this side of the coach more comfortable than your present position."

Gabrielle frowned at Molly's odd suggestion. "I'm not sure I understand, Miss Klinner."

Molly indicated Captain Cramer with a nod of her head. "I'm afraid that Captain Cramer has said all he can say for free.

His next few words will cost him dearly . . . and if I were you, Miss Johnson, I believe I'd rather be sitting on the Southern side of the stagecoach."

Cramer leaned forward and scrutinized Molly's face in the dim light. "I've seen you somewhere before, Miss Klinner. I just can't remember where or when . . . but I know I've seen you. I never forget a face."

Molly stared pensively at him. "I don't think so, Captain." Then recognition hit her with such force that it twisted her stomach into a knot and threatened to send what little food she had eaten that morning to her throat. Her fingers drew into talons.

She knew the man, remembered him well. As though it were happening that very instant, she could feel his heavy bulk, pinning her naked buttocks to the cold, hard, washroom floor, invading her, pounding her, defiling her. Bile rose in her throat, suffocating her. And it took every ounce of her self-control to quell a compelling rage to fling herself at him and rip out his vile, black heart.

Cramer nodded at her, his words slow and measured. "Yes, ma'am, I've seen you someplace. . . ."

Rucker, unaware of the murderous force building in Molly, unwittingly gave her the necessary moment it took to come to grips with the situation. "If you're callin' Miss Molly a liar, Cramer, you're askin' for a passel of trouble, an' it's startin' right here, right now, with me!"

Joseph Robertson, the banker seated next to Gabrielle Johnson, gaped first at Rucker, then at Cramer. "Now, wait just a minute! This has gone far enough!" He quickly rapped the head of his cane against the ceiling of the coach to gain John Wright's attention. "Stop this coach, driver! Stop it this instant!"

John Wright slammed his foot against the brake pole and locked the rear wheels. He whipsawed the bridle reins with such force that the bits cut cruelly into the horses' mouths, the animals went to their haunches, and the stagecoach came to such a screeching halt that the unsuspecting passengers were thrown from their seats.

Wright scrambled nimbly down over the front wheel as though he were a man half his age and snatched open the door.

"Whoever's hollerin' like a Comanche in there better have a durn good reason to cause me to mistreat my horses."

The banker climbed hastily out of the coach and jumped to the ground. "There's going to be a fight in there!"

Wright's face turned livid. When he spoke, his voice was low and deadly. "You made me abuse them fine horses because a couple of passengers are havin' a disagreement?"

The banker cleared his throat nervously. "They were about to come to fisticuffs . . . maybe even shoot each other."

Captain Cramer scowled at Wright. "Climb back on your box, driver. This is none of your affair. Me and my lieutenant just decided that we're tired of riding with these two stinking Rebels, that's all."

John Wright settled back on his run-down bootheels, and his squinted eyes became even more slitted. "Anything that happens in this Butterfield is my business, soldier boy." His gaze shifted to Peyton and Rucker. "An' they ain't goin' to be no fist-fightin' in my coach, not with women present, there ain't. An' there sure as heck ain't goin' to be no pistol shootin', period! Why, you might hit one of my horses!"

Wright reassessed the men in the coach. They were belligerent, had been cooped up too long, too closely packed, and he realized that no matter what he said, a fight was inevitable. He sighed through his teeth; they might as well get it out of their systems.

"Well, boys, they's one thing for certain: you can't tell how good a man or a watermelon is till you thump 'em. So if this here problem can't wait till we get to the next change station, why, jest pile right out o' there an' thump one another."

Captain Cramer threw a quizzical look toward Peyton. "Are you in this, or are you going to play it smart and stay out of it?" The captain's voice carried the conviction of superiority found only in one with little experience at judging an enemy.

Peyton silently appraised the man, finding him too thick through the middle to be a seasoned field veteran, too arrogant to be a line officer, and too pasty-faced to be a cavalryman. The captain had to be a professional garrison soldier, whom no fighting man respected.

"Well?" Captain Cramer leaned forward in his seat. "Are you in it, or are you out of it?"

"I *am* it." Peyton climbed to his feet and stepped to the door.

Rucker shot upright, forced to stand stoop-shouldered because of the low coach ceiling. He pointed his finger at Peyton. "Now, wait just a minute, Peyton. This is my fight. I started it."

Peyton cut Rucker a look of such unbridled contempt that Rucker's mouth snapped shut, and he settled back in his seat like a naughty child who had been chastised.

Molly slipped her arm through Rucker's. "Keep still, Fletcher. If you get into a fight and open that wound, gangrene might set in." *Furthermore, if Peyton is as salty as you say he is, he might just kill Captain Cramer and save me the trouble.*

Gabrielle Johnson smiled ardently at Peyton. "Bravo! You are a true gentleman, Mr. Lewis, to champion Mr. Rucker, who is in no shape to defend himself. I like that in a man."

Molly was amazed to see color creep into Peyton's cheeks, and, by his return smile, it was obvious he enjoyed the young woman's approval. A flicker of uncertainty—the embryo of jealously—drew Molly's eyebrows together in thought; perhaps this fight between the North and the South wasn't limited to just one sex. She evaluated Gabrielle anew.

When the lieutenant started for the coach door, Cramer, annoyed by Gabrielle Johnson's insinuation that he and Pendleton had attacked an invalid, ordered the junior officer back into his seat. Then, with a cavalier gesture, Cramer bowed to the women, but spoke to Pendleton. "We can't have these good ladies thinking the United States Army would gang up on these poor, feeble Rebels, Lieutenant. So, as your ranking officer, it is my duty—and privilege—to dispose of this incident without further delay."

Tipping his hat to Gabrielle, and with a jeering smile for Peyton, he inclined his head toward the coach door. "After you, sir."

Peyton caught the doorframe and swung lightly to the ground. With deft movements, he shucked off his greatcoat and cast it from him. His hat followed.

John Wright leaned against the rear wheel of the coach and

grinned at Peyton, exposing a gaping row of broken, tobacco-stained teeth. He liked a good fight, had been in plenty of them himself, and, unless he missed his guess, Lewis would prove to be a tough adversary.

Wright switched his appraisal to the burly captain who filled the doorway of the coach. The man looked able—and mean—and Wright knew that in rough-and-tumble fights where men had been known to get an ear bitten off or an eye gouged out, meanness had its advantages.

The captain climbed slowly and deliberately out of the coach and stepped into the ankle-deep mud. When he turned to face Peyton, a million shooting stars exploded behind his eyes, and he sat down heavily in the mud, his legs thrust out before him, his shoulders slumped against the fold-out coach step. In the middle of his forehead, a gash two inches long and a quarter of an inch wide welled with blood that overflowed into his eyebrows, then trickled down both sides of his nose to drip like ruby-colored raindrops onto the deep blue fabric of his Federal army tunic.

Molly bit her lip to suppress the urge to shout out encouragement to Peyton to go on and not stop, to beat the man slowly and methodically to death, to make him cry out in pain and fear. She longed to look down into his tormented face and laugh—just the way he had done when . . .

Lieutenant Pendleton was halfway out of the coach before Molly noticed the pistol in his hand. She shouted for Peyton to beware, causing him to look up just as the lieutenant lashed out with his pistol barrel. The cold metal raked Peyton's cheek and spun him in his tracks, and before he could regain his balance, Pendleton had thumbed back the pistol hammer and pointed the gun at his head.

Molly was already at the doorway, prepared to do she knew not what—something—anything—when John Wright's bull-whip snaked out and coiled itself around the lieutenant's neck. In less time than it takes a reptile to strike, the lieutenant found himself flat on his back in the mud alongside the captain. With a flick of Wright's wrist, the whip fell free.

Molly settled weak-kneed into her seat. She glanced at those around her, but they appeared to be mesmerized by the events taking place outside the coach. Placing her hand against her breast in an effort to slow the wild palpitations of her heart, she closed her eyes and emitted a long sigh of relief.

Lieutenant Pendleton clawed at his throat and emitted loud wheezing noises as he choked and sputtered and attempted to suck in great gulps of air.

Wright began coiling his whip into loose circles. "Soldier boy, I could have snapped your spine jest as easy as I pinched your windpipe. You might keep that in mind if you still feel up to reachin' for your sidearm. I don't allow no shootin' around my coach. I *thought* I made that clear."

Wright squatted down beside the lieutenant and tilted the young officer's chin up so he could inspect his throat. "Didn't even break the hide. You'll be good as new before you can say Jack Sprat."

The lieutenant staggered to his feet and leaned heavily against the coach's wheel. He hawked and spit, and hawked again.

Wright pounded Pendleton's back, a good-natured grin splitting his weathered face from side to side. "I know jest what you need, Lieutenant. You need air, lots of fresh air . . . an' Cap'n Cramer needs some, too." Wright prodded the captain with his boot toe, and the man looked up at him through unfocused eyes. "Can you get up, Cap'n? Or have you taken root an' growed to that spot?"

"I can get up." Cramer made two wobbly attempts to rise before he gained his feet, and even then he was forced to lean against the coach for support.

Wright spit a stream of amber toward the lieutenant's boot that struck the ground an inch from the toe. "Well, boys, let's see if you fightin' men got enough strength left to climb to the top of that coach. Lots of air up there. Yes, sir, lots of air . . . an' it's as fresh as a green buffalo chip."

Captain Cramer fished a checkered bandanna from his jumper pocket and applied it to his lacerated forehead. "My face needs attending to, driver . . . It probably needs stitches."

John Wright peered at the gash, then cackled cheerfully.

"That little scratch? Why, that ain't nothin'! Hell, I seen a man kicked by a mule oncet; laid his head open like a whore with clap. He didn't have no stitches, an' he's still alive an' kickin', so I 'spect you'll live till we get to the Wichita depot . . . which ain't goin' to be no time soon if we don't get movin'."

He jerked his chin toward the top of the coach. "Hit the roof, boys. You're ridin' the wind."

Still laughing, John Wright climbed to the box and kicked loose the brake. A moment later his whip snapped like a gunshot six inches above the ears of the lead team, and the coach was rolling.

As the coach lurched into motion, Peyton heard one of the soldiers complain to John Wright that they would freeze to death riding on top. Although he could not hear Wright's response, he guessed that it was less than sympathetic, and he laughed under his breath. It was poetic justice: the Yankee officers were riding on top in the frigid wind because they refused to ride inside with former Rebels. Where would they ride, he wondered, if Wright were to confide in them, as he had done with him during one of their layovers, that he had served in the Confederate army as an ambulance driver under the command of General A. P. Hill?

Gabrielle Johnson stared at Peyton in open admiration. She had never witnessed violence up close, and it had left her flushed with a mysterious, smoldering excitement that began in the bedrock of her belly and spread like liquid heat to the tips of her nipples. It was an agitating sensation that caused her to squirm uncomfortably on the hard coach seat. When she became aware that Molly Klinner was observing her display of erotic arousal, the girl blushed guiltily and looked away.

Molly was stunned. She had worked with women who became sexually stimulated by physical violence, and while she personally experienced no sensual thrill in watching two men maim one another, she understood the natural excitement it induced in certain female spectators. Usually, however, it was most prevalent when the woman was the reason for the dispute—or the prize.

Molly glanced obliquely at Peyton to see if he was aware of

the effect his fight had on Gabrielle. She watched him for several moments before deciding that he was ignorant of the woman's stimulation. That knowledge pleased her. Leaning around the drummer, she touched Peyton's arm. "Your cheek is bleeding, Mr. Lewis. May I . . . ?" Without awaiting his permission, she blotted the cut on his face with her coat sleeve. Surprisingly, Peyton blessed her with a rare smile of thanks—and that insignificant act also pleased her.

Joseph Robertson cleared his throat and tapped Peyton's knee with his cane. "You knocked that soldier's block off, Lewis." The banker shuddered with an affected grimace that was intended to promote camaraderie. "Yes, sir! You flattened him like a pancake. Did you hurt your hand?"

Rucker guffawed. "Peyton didn't hit that captain with his fist, Mr. Robertson. He just slapped a little hide off his head with a pair of brass knuckles."

Peyton groaned under his breath. Would Rucker never learn to keep his mouth shut?

William Beecher, the drummer, threw Peyton a look filled with disgust and stated that he had once seen a man killed with brass knuckles; Congress should pass a resolution outlawing the weapon.

Rucker did not like the traveling salesmen, had no time for milksops such as William Beecher, always wanting to pass laws that protected the cowards of the world and hamstrung the courageous. He frowned defensively at Beecher.

"I reckon a big businessman like you, Bill, would rather break your hand in a fistfight than break somebody's jaw. Well, not me an' Peyton! No, sir. We don't fight for fun. We fight to win!"

Gabrielle Johnson's face fell. "Am I to understand, Mr. Lewis, that you struck Captain Cramer with a brass apparatus of some kind and did not use your fist?"

Peyton ignored her.

A frown of disapproval flickered across Gabrielle's face. "Is that gentlemanly, sir?"

Molly settled back in her seat and pursed her lips, waiting for Peyton to explain himself out of that one.

Peyton smiled awkwardly at the girl. "No, Miss Johnson, I don't suppose it's gentlemanly."

Rucker, concerned with Gabrielle's perception of the fight, attempted to explain. "When you deal with scalawags like that army captain and his lieutenant, Miss Johnson, you do whatever it takes to win. 'Cause if'n you don't, that son of a gun will tear your arm off an' beat you to death with it! You saw Lieutenant Pendleton, officer and gentleman that he is, pull his pistol on Peyton when Peyton's back was turned. Why, ma'am, bein' a gentleman in a free-for-all fight will leave a fellow laying in the mud . . . dead."

Gabrielle's hand fluttered to her throat. She had not expected such a heated attack. To make matters worse, Molly Klinner was laughing at her.

Gabrielle straightened in her seat and worked hard to regain her composure.

"I assume by your amusement, Miss Klinner, you find all this violence commonplace? Obviously you are on familiar terms with cruelty and barbarity."

Molly laughed delightedly. Why, Gabrielle Johnson was no woman at all. She was just a little girl in a woman's clothes who did not have a clue about real life.

"Not at all, Miss Johnson. In fact"—Molly lanced Gabrielle with a calculated gaze—"I get absolutely no *thrill* out of violence whatsoever."

When Gabrielle Johnson flushed with embarrassment, Molly smiled her small victory, then decided to confound the flustered girl even more. "Nor do I approve of brass knuckles, Miss Johnson, and I will readily admit that I was surprised when Mr. Lewis chose that particular means to defend himself. I rather thought he would shoot the captain and be done with it."

Gabrielle turned an ashen face to Peyton Lewis; she was close to tears. "Would you have shot Captain Cramer, Mr. Lewis?"

Peyton exhaled. Molly Klinner was intentionally provoking the girl. Why? What possible good could it do to upset the young lady even more than she was already?

Rucker took the silent moment as an opportunity to jump back in the discussion. "I'll answer that question, Miss Johnson.

John Wright don't allow no shootin' around his coach, an' it's a good thing, too, 'cause if it hadn't been for that, Peyton would have shot the captain where he sat."

Peyton groaned under his breath. With a look that commanded Molly and Rucker to drop the subject, he tilted his hat down over his eyes and lay back against the padded backrest. Try as he might, however, he could not clear his mind of the mysterious animosity that seemed to have developed between the two women.

They had traveled only a mile or so when Rucker leaned around Molly and tapped Peyton's shoulder. "Miss Molly was right, Peyton. There might have been shootin' back there if John Wright hadn't meddled."

Peyton tipped his head back and peered at Rucker from beneath his hat brim. "So?"

"You've got all the pistols! Hell, I feel plumb naked." Rucker grinned sheepishly across the aisle at Gabrielle. "Beg pardon for the cussin', ma'am." Gabrielle inclined her head to indicate that the apology was accepted.

Molly, still amused by her discovery concerning Gabrielle, laughed at the girl's implied modesty. Her smile vanished and her face paled, however, as a sudden notion forced its way to the forefront of her thoughts: suppose Gabrielle's pretentious ignorance concerning men and violence might actually be genuine? Could the girl really be one of those pampered young socialites who had been shielded from the real world and its daily vulgarities?

Molly shifted uneasily on her seat, not liking that thought, for if that were true, then she, Molly Klinner, must reevaluate her first impression, because Gabrielle was not merely a lovely female traveling alone, she was a genuine lady from the "good side of town"—the kind of person society referred to as a "chaste woman." Molly sank back in her seat and closed her eyes. Suddenly she felt very much the whore.

Peyton unbuttoned his coat and drew Rucker's ivory-handled pistol from his holster. When he leaned across the drummer to surrender the gun to Rucker, the stagecoach hit a rut, and Peyton's hand brushed Molly Klinner's breast.

Molly looked quickly across the aisle to see if Gabrielle had witnessed the encounter.

The young woman dropped her eyes and blushed modestly, embarrassed for Molly.

Peyton murmured an apology, and Molly, emulating Gabrielle's downcast eyes, worked hard to create the same high color that her rival across the aisle had achieved.

After several unsuccessful attempts, Molly gave up her endeavor to conjure up a blush, because in truth, Peyton's touch, no matter how personal, was welcome—and she really did not care who knew it. Raising her eyes boldly to Gabrielle, she gave the girl her best I-don't-give-a-damn grin, but the genuine shock and disappointment on Gabrielle's face elicited the very reaction that Molly had tried unsuccessfully to achieve. Only then did she blush—and it was real.

Peyton sat back in his seat, and a frown creased his forehead. He had seen Molly Klinner's devil-take-all grin that changed so quickly to very real embarrassment, and he was puzzled. On the one hand, Molly Klinner appeared to go to great lengths to be crude and shameful, to encourage one's contempt and disapproval. On the other hand, she was loyal, honest, and courageous—and occasionally even shy.

As Peyton worked through his perplexing analysis of Molly Klinner, he became aware that Gabrielle Johnson had spoken to him, not because he heard her question but because he felt the intensity of her presence. "Did you say something to me, ma'am?"

Gabrielle's expression was a curious mixture of anxiety and trepidation, as though she were attempting to understand something alien to her concept of right and wrong, and needed assistance in reaching a conclusion.

"It bothers me a great deal, Mr. Lewis, that you would actually have shot Captain Cramer."

When Peyton merely stared at her, Gabrielle wrung her hands nervously. "I know you commented, sir, that you didn't care to discuss it, but I . . . I am trying to understand the people

out here in the West . . . for, you see, Mr. Lewis, shootings are a
rare occurrence where I grew up. I . . . I've never witnessed one."

That she was from Monroe, Michigan, Peyton knew; and by
her own words he had gathered that the town was well organized
and probably had a fine police force and that the law frowned
upon people who carried sidearms for the purpose of shooting
each other over something as trivial as an insult. Sighing, he
tipped his hat down over his eyes. "No, Miss Johnson. I wouldn't
have shot anyone."

Molly felt the emptiness that accompanies acute disappointment fill her chest. It was evident that Peyton was protecting the northern woman's sensitivities, shielding her from reality,
permitting her to continue her misconception of the goodness
of mankind—of Peyton Lewis in particular—but it was a lie!
Molly felt her face grow hot with anger. Not because of Peyton's
sympathy for Gabrielle Johnson, but because he had not demon-
strated that same protective sentiment toward her. She longed to
slap his face. If he assumed that he was doing Gabrielle a favor
by avoiding the truth, he was mistaken, because the day would
surely come when she would be forced to accept the West for
what it was—or leave it. There could be no middle ground or
fence straddling once they reached Texas.

Rucker leaned back in his seat and guffawed. "Peyton's fun-
nin' you, Miss Johnson. He'd 'a shot that blue-belly dead before
you could whistle 'Dixie.' " Gripping the Shawx and McLanahan revolver as though it were a long-lost friend, he dropped his
head back and studied the coach ceiling. The urge to send a
round through the roof in hopes of hitting one of the Yankees
was nearly overpowering. Wouldn't they be surprised! Grinning
at the thought, he slipped the pistol into its holster.

Gabrielle Johnson's pale lips drew into a startled "Oh." She
gazed big-eyed at Peyton, who had given up all pretext of catching a catnap, and spread her hands apologetically. "The reason
I asked Mr. Lewis the question, Mr. Rucker, is so that, should
something of this sort arise again, I won't have to be *told* to move
out of the line of fire." A hint of a smile dimpled her cheeks, and
she stabbed Molly with a calculated stare before again turning
her gaze to Peyton. "I've so much to learn about the West. It ab-

solutely horrifies me . . . but I'm sure you will enlighten me, won't you, Mr. Lewis?"

Molly's grin vanished, replaced by a reassessment of Gabrielle Johnson. She had been right about the girl all along; she was not nearly so guileless as her young, innocent face and modest blushes would lead one to believe.

Molly's eyes narrowed. Just how dangerous was Gabrielle? She was beautiful, in a dainty fashion, educated, wealthy, and very probably had a sensuous body beneath all those skirts, petticoats, and whalebone stays. And she appeared to be a childishly dependent, a trait that men seemed unable to resist.

Peyton considered the question Gabrielle had asked: would he enlighten her about the West? Her request, to a private person such as he, bordered on invasion of privacy. Crossing his ankle over his knee, he settled against the backrest. "What is it about the West that you want to know, Miss Johnson?"

Gabrielle was delighted by Peyton's interest and answered quickly. "My trip to Texas is two fold Mr. Lewis. I am traveling to Austin, not only to visit Libbie, but to spend some time with my brother, Paul. He is adjunct to the general, and I have only seen him once since the war ended. I would like to know something about Texas and its people before I arrive there." She cut her eyes to Molly. "I would rather not learn my lessons the hard way. It could be embarrassing to Paul . . . and possibly harm his career."

Rucker palmed his hat to the back of his head. "Well, now, Miss Gabrielle, that's fine an' dandy. Me an' Peyton can sure tell you all you want to know about Texas. But the best part is you'll be in Austin. An' me an' Peyton are fixin' to start a ranch down around Houston. Why, they're only a hop, skip, an' jump apart. We'll be neighbors."

Gabrielle smiled demurely at Rucker, wishing Peyton had answered. "I sincerely hope so."

Molly smirked and settled herself more comfortably on her seat. "Houston is two hundred miles from Austin, Fletcher." A faint smile drew up the corners of her mouth, and she cocked her head at Gabrielle. "That's a long hop, skip, and jump for someone wearing a hooped skirt, Miss Johnson."

Twelve

At two o'clock in the morning, amid the blast of John Wright's bugle, the stagecoach rolled into Wichita, Kansas.

If the passengers were expecting Wichita to be a town, or even a community, they were sadly disappointed. Wichita was an adobe way station in the middle of a vast expanse of more of the same nothingness that they had been crossing for the past week. Even the cloak of absolute darkness, the product of clouds covering the thin sliver of a new moon, could not dispel the gloom that surrounded the isolated soddie; and the anemic light that fought its way through the station's small, parchment-covered window offered little more than an invitation to come in out of the cold.

The station agent, a stout man made even more portly by his heavy woolen kapote, threw open the stagecoach door and bellowed a hearty welcome that grated on the nerves of the sleepy passengers.

John Wright bounded down from the box and trotted directly to the privy behind the station, leaving the two soldiers to climb unassisted from the roof. Their movements were slow and clumsy due to the freezing fifteen-mile ride they had endured since having been ordered to the top. They rubbed their hands and stamped their feet and watched the passengers descend from the coach. They had a job to do.

Joseph Robertson was the first person out of the Butterfield, followed by William Beecher, then Gabrielle Johnson, whom the two businessmen ushered across the area in front of the building, a labyrinth of frozen ruts made by stagecoaches and freight wagons prior to the big snow.

Rucker climbed down and blinked, yawned, and wondered how long he had slept. An hour? Two hours? Not enough.

Peyton stepped to the ground, then turned to help Molly out of the coach. She ignored his outstretched hand and clambered down unassisted, then picked her way gingerly across the uneven ground until she reached the rear of the stagecoach, where her gunnysack and rifle were stored in the boot.

Piqued by Molly's rebuff, Peyton slung his saddlebags across his shoulder and started toward the muted light that streamed from the open door of the station house. As he made his way across the frozen ruts, Captain Cramer and Lieutenant Pendleton stepped out of the darkness and blocked his path.

Cramer planted himself firmly on widespread legs and informed Peyton that they had some unfinished business that demanded immediate attention. His voice carried on the icy breeze as though he had used a megaphone.

Rucker, already halfway to the station and all but tasting the hot food, good whiskey, and a chance to become better acquainted with Gabrielle, heard the captain's command and stopped to peer over his shoulder toward the coach. Although he could barely see the three men through the darkness, he had no problem recognizing the belligerent stance of the two soldiers. Taking a deep breath, he released it slowly through his teeth, it felt warm against his face in the frigid night air. The sight of Gabrielle, chatting amiably with Robertson and Beecher as they hurried up the path to the depot, brought another sigh to his lips. This was not a good time for a showdown.

Peyton dropped the saddlebags to the ground and unbuttoned his greatcoat, drawing it back for quick access to the handle of the five-shot Colt that was shoved into his waistband. He wished the two soldiers would just go on about their business, just

let their differences lie. He did not want to fight them again—
but no force on earth could have pried that admission from him.

Rucker stepped to Peyton's side. His overcoat hung open,
revealing the fact that his good hand already gripped his pistol
handle. He was wide awake now, eager to get this problem finished, wishing there was more light so he could see the soldiers
plainly, could pick a target to shoot at, such as a button on a
tunic. "Are these boys still lookin' to get their ears pinned back,
Peyton?"

As it always did when Peyton faced death, time had stopped
for him. Breathing had stopped. Living had stopped. His death's-
head stare at the two men, and the quiet words that followed,
pierced the darkness like a fatal blow. "Kill Pendleton, Fletcher.
I'll kill Cramer."

The two officers, who had been so self-assured the moment
before, heard Peyton's death sentence, and their breath came in
bursts, like gunshots. They scowled at each other, neither man
accepting the blame for their predicament, for the arrival of
Rucker had not only cost them the advantage in numbers, but
the sight of his cutaway holster—the type gunmen wore for instant access to their weapons—left them sickeningly aware they
would be forced to open the flaps of their military-style holsters
before they could draw their weapons—and that slight delay
could mean the difference between life and death.

Gabrielle stopped on the threshold of the station-house
door and turned to see if Peyton was following. Darkness engulfed the coach, rendering it all but invisible, and it took a moment for her to absorb the full impact of the drama unfolding
not fifty feet away. Her breath caught; men were actually preparing to shoot each other. The danger was suddenly real to her—
not like the romantic exchange in the stagecoach when she had
chided Peyton about shooting the soldier. At that time, the
prospect of gunplay had been exciting, even thrilling. This was
different; it was terrifying.

Gabrielle was aware of the morbid curiosity that held her
spellbound, yet she was enthralled by it, mesmerized, powerless
to turn away; and she found herself reluctant to even blink for

fear she might miss that split instant when souls were traded for pride.

It was eerie to her, the way the light that filtered through the open door of the depot washed the station-house yard in a sickly glow and appeared to focus its full illumination on Peyton Lewis, for she could see his face plainly, so still, so devoid of emotion, so cold. Her heart fluttered wildly in her chest, for it was obvious that Peyton possessed that certainty of the inevitable that assures special individuals a spot in the winner's circle no matter what the odds.

William Beecher, standing beside Gabrielle, took one look at the men who were squared off for battle and stampeded through the station-house door, sweeping the entranced girl before him.

In spite of Gabrielle's rage at being manhandled from her vantage point, Beecher slammed the door and leaned heavily against it.

Gabrielle raced to the window, but the thin, translucent square of rawhide nailed over the opening was impenetrable, and she could see nothing. Then it was too late; a shot shattered the stillness.

In less than a heartbeat, Gabrielle crossed the room and threw herself on Beecher with a vengeance that staggered the man. She pummeled his face with her fists, she kicked his shins, and when he backed away to avoid her raking fingernails, she wrenched open the door and ran with her heart in her throat into the yard.

Gabrielle Johnson drew up short. The four men who faced each other in the darkness were rigid silhouettes, standing as though they were made of ice, frozen in time, afraid to breathe, to break eye contact with one another, to look away for the instant it would take to see who had fired the shot that had kicked up a geyser of icy dirt between them.

Molly Klinner stepped away from the rear of the coach and levered another round into the Henry repeating rifle. "I'll shoot the first man who blinks." Her voice was icier than the frigid air that engulfed them.

The rifle, with the light from the open door dancing off the brass receiver, was indeed menacing as she walked toward the men. It was her face, however, as she gazed bitterly at the four, that held Gabrielle's attention, because Molly Klinner, at that moment, was even more dangerous than the rifle she carried.

Molly pointed the weapon at the captain, then the lieutenant. The desire to shoot Cramer was like a hunger that demanded to be fed, that, if not sated, would turn inward and devour her. Moaning like a caged animal that had smelled blood just beyond the bars, she fought to overcome the demon that had sprung to life inside her heart since having recognized the man. Little by little, her common sense prevailed. She was surprised at the calmness of her voice when she addressed the soldiers.

"You two simpletons need shooting, there's no doubt about that . . . but not by these two bigger morons." She indicated Peyton and Rucker with a sweep of the rifle barrel. "They haven't got the rest of their lives to waste running from the Federal army for killing fools like you . . . and neither do I. But they haven't thought that through yet, because they never think—not when their precious Southern honor is at stake. But they will think of it, like they think of everything else . . . after it's too late."

Peyton and Rucker exchanged irritated glances. That she was very probably right was beside the point; that she had interfered in their business was inexcusable.

Molly eyed Cramer with open disgust. "My advice to you, mister, is to smile and walk away. You can look tough when you are out of sight." She turned and stumbled across the frozen ruts into the darkness. They watched her go, too stunned to move.

Captain Cramer stared after Molly. Why had she singled him out? Again, he had the nagging sensation he had seen her before . . . but where? The memory was fleeting, a haunting suspicion of something in his past—something important.

Peyton buttoned his coat, then he, too, gazed off into the darkness where Molly had fled. Damn her! All she had accomplished was to postpone the inevitable.

Rucker palmed his hat to the back of his head. "Well, what in the hell do you make of Miss Molly?"

Without answering, Peyton stomped off toward the depot where Gabrielle Johnson waited beside the door.

John Wright, who had watched the incident through a crack in the privy door, hooked up his breeches and made his way into the darkness where Molly had disappeared. He found her huddled dejectedly on a windswept knoll a hundred yards beyond the coach. He hunkered down beside her and stared off into the night as she was doing.

After a long interval, he laid his hand on her shoulder. "What you did was a right admirable thing, Miss Molly. But it was wrong."

Molly nodded in agreement. "I know it was a mistake. But those two dunces I'm traveling with make me so damned mad. . . . Peyton Lewis is my chance at a decent life, John. He might be my only chance. I won't stand idly by and allow his childish pride to destroy his future . . . or mine."

It did not occur to John Wright that he was being hypocritical when he shook his head and continued his lecture. "That ain't a good enough reason to go an' meddle in somethin' that don't concern you, Molly. An' I can tell you for certain, they ain't no man worth his salt goin' to stand still for a woman doin' that."

Molly raised her chin stubbornly with every intention of telling Wright to stay out of *her* business; that *she* considered it reason enough, and that was what mattered. But the words died on her lips, for she knew he was right. She had deliberately breached that forbidden line in the scheme of male/female relations, and in so doing, she had shamed Peyton Lewis and pushed him even further beyond her reach. Molly sighed with the realization that for every giant step forward she was taking two backward; she was getting nowhere in a hurry. Still, she believed she had done the right thing, and if need be, she would do it again, because, when all was said and done, she would pay the price for her actions—she and she alone.

Molly laughed shakily and gazed up at John Wright. The

tears, frozen on her long lashes, caused them to droop heavily over her eyes, lending her an exotic look that would have excited a younger man. "The only mistake I made, John, was not shooting all four of them."

They sat like that for a long while, quiet, each enjoying the other's presence. Then Molly stood up and squared her shoulders. She slipped her hand through the crook of Wright's arm and held it tightly.

"Thank you for coming to find me, John. Shall we go to supper?"

John Wright, wishing he was forty years younger, walked proudly beside Molly Klinner as they made their way toward the dim light that seeped from the soddie, a light that held no warmth for her, no invitation.

When they neared the stagecoach, Wright disengaged Molly's hand and encouraged her to proceed on to the station while he unhitched his team. The tired horses stamped and blew, impatient to be unharnessed.

As Wright unhooked the wheel team, he watched Molly Klinner walk up the path toward the depot. It was certain that she had stopped a killing, yet, like Lewis and Rucker, he believed she had been wrong to intervene. Still, what she had done took raw nerve and courage, and he liked that quality in a person, man or woman.

Wright absently patted the off horse's rump. "There goes a damn fine woman, but that Lewis boy has blinders on his bridle an' can't see her for shit!"

Wright chuckled to himself, thinking the good thing about talking to his horse was that it couldn't argue back.

When Molly stepped into the room, Peyton was laying a log on the fire that blazed merrily in the large stick-and-wattle fireplace. Sparks swirled and danced like summer fireflies before darting up the chimney, and the heat that surged throughout the room stung her chapped face.

Leaning her rifle against the wall, she walked to the hand-hewn table, where the male passengers, seated on a long slab bench, were eating from tin plates filled with something that looked like barbecued goat mixed with Hungarian goulash.

Molly picked up an empty tin and ladled a spoonful of the concoction from a three-legged iron pot onto the edge of her plate. No one spoke as she slumped tiredly down on the bench, but from the corner of her eye she saw that Captain Cramer was again appraising her with that singular look one has when he or she cannot quite remember something meaningful.

Molly spooned a small helping of food into her mouth; it tasted awful, as though it had been simmering for weeks. She cut her eyes to Gabrielle Johnson, who stood alone at the ticket counter, which Molly thought odd until she noticed a second plate of food on the counter beside the girl. She guessed the extra plate was for Peyton, who was warming his hands at the fire-place. She wondered if he was aware that Gabrielle intended that he join her.

Rucker, having been to the privy, kicked the depot door shut behind him, and walked to the counter where Gabrielle was nibbling at her food. Without a word, he elbowed up beside her and began wolfing down the food she had prepared for Peyton.

Molly ducked her head and took another bite of stew to keep from laughing outright as the girl, taken aback by Rucker's unexpected presence, glared at him with distaste and marched to the iron pot to fill another plate.

Molly watched with amused interest as Gabrielle crossed the room to the hearth and extended the plate to Peyton. She fully expected him to decline the girl's offer as he had hers on nu-merous occasions when she had made such overtures.

Molly's chest constricted, and her heart nearly stopped. Not only did Peyton accept Gabrielle's simple proposal, but he ap-peared to be taken aback by it.

Peyton rose to his feet and offered Gabrielle his seat on the hearth. The young woman smiled her thanks, shrugged off her cloak, and hung it on a peg beside Peyton's. Making an issue of smoothing out her traveling habit and tugging her long skirt down over the toes of her shoes, she sat down primly on the edge of the stone hearth.

Molly bridled anew at Gabrielle's seemingly endless acts of virtue. Had she ever been that pure and innocent? A sigh slipped between her teeth. Yes, she had twice been that modest: the first time she had gotten her period, and the night she had given herself to the boy she loved.

Molly looked again at Gabrielle Johnson. This time, however, she assessed the younger woman for what she was—competition. Her eyes narrowed enviously as she noted that the girl's expensive traveling habit lent just the right accent to her trim figure and flat midriff—a waistline so tiny that a man could span it with his hands.

Unconsciously, Molly gathered her shabby overcoat more securely around her thickening abdomen. Unlike Gabrielle, who openly flaunted her lithe figure, Molly had not removed her coat since having met Peyton Lewis. She longed to do so now, to shed her clothes and stand before him nude and say, Look at me! I have . . . I had a good figure before . . . She touched her abdomen and wished for the first time since conception that she was not pregnant. The thought horrified her. She wanted this baby more than life itself.

Disgusted with herself for even allowing such a thought to surface, Molly caught up her plate and stalked to the counter where Rucker ate alone. "Can I join you?"

Without waiting for a reply, Molly slammed her plate down beside his and forked a portion of foul-tasting stew into her mouth. She chewed slowly, thoughtfully.

A moment later, her face took on a sly countenance. "Why don't you take Gabrielle Johnson to the barn loft and teach her about the birds and the bees, Fletcher?"

Rucker cut his eyes to Molly. They were bloodshot, and his breath reeked of whiskey. "She's not that kind of woman."

Molly glared at him and swallowed the food. "Don't kid yourself, Fletcher. We are all 'that kind of woman' when the right man comes along."

"Bullshit."

"It's true."

"Go eat with Peyton."

"Miss Johnson beat me to it."

"Don't come cryin' to me."

"I'm not crying, Fletcher!" She could feel an angry heat

surging into her cheeks, but she did not care. She had reached the end of her patience concerning men. "I was just trying to do you a favor, Fletcher."

"Bullshit."

"Bullshit yourself! I know you are sweet on Gabrielle. Everyone knows it. So don't deny it."

Rucker glared at her. "What do you want, Miss Molly?"

"I want you to have what you want, Fletcher. But you are going to have to fight for her. You'll have to win her, Fletcher."

"I don't see you fightin' to 'win' Peyton."

Molly's hand crept to her abdomen. "I . . . I can't. Not right now." *But my day will come, you can bet on it.*

"Get away from me, Molly."

Molly was startled by Rucker's reaction. She attempted to smile beguilingly at him, then thought better of it. A voice clamored in her mind, shouting for her to tell Rucker the truth. She squinched her eyes closed. "The reason I can't fight for Peyton . . . is because I am pregnant, Fletcher."

She watched Rucker expectantly, searching his face for a reaction. There was none. *He is becoming more like Peyton every day,* she decided, not at all certain she liked that kind of hardness in him. When his silence dragged on, Molly tried a different tack and grinned playfully at him. "You are not going to get *real quiet* like Peyton did, are you?"

"Maybe. It worked for him. First you . . . and now her."

"Don't do it, Fletcher."

"Why not?"

"Because you are a nice, happy-go-lucky boy"—she smiled at him—"and I like you the way you are."

"Nice boys come in last, Miss Molly."

Molly sighed. "I know that, Fletcher." *Why does it work just the opposite with girls?*

Rucker drunkenly caught up a bottle, poured a double shot into a tin cup, and held it aloft. "Here's to motherhood . . . an' Gen'ral John Bell Hood . . . an' Robin Hood." He downed the double shot in one gulp.

Molly retraced her steps to the dining table and slumped down on the rough wooden bench. Dropping her head into her

hands, she wished she had kept her mouth shut about her pregnancy. Rucker would probably tell Peyton, and that would be
the end; no decent man ever looked seriously at a woman with
a bastard child. She laughed caustically: had there ever been a
beginning?

Captain Cramer, who had been conversing with the banker
and the salesman, excused himself and walked around the table
until he was beside Molly. Bending down, he pressed his lips
close to her ear. "Where have we met, Miss Klinner?" He studied
her profile, his foul breath warm against her cheek. "I know I've
seen you before."

"You've said that several times, Captain. Is there a point you
wish to make?"

"I never forget a face, Miss Klinner." When she did not answer, Cramer shrugged his shoulders and stood erect. "It'll come
to me." With one last look at Molly, he walked to the bar where
Rucker was nursing another glass of whiskey and offered to buy
the boy a drink.

Molly watched the two from under her lashes, surprised
when Rucker held out his cup for the captain to fill. Alarm
caused her to jerk erect on the bench. Surely Fletcher was not
drunk enough to drink with his enemy? Not an hour ago, they
were preparing to shoot each other!

Molly's hand trembled as she raised her coffee mug to her
lips. Questions raced through her mind. Would Rucker tell the
captain about her past? About Caleb King? About the baby she
carried? *Oh, God,* she thought, near panic, *why did I tell Rucker
anything?*

Molly jumped to her feet, fully intending to interrupt their
conversation. Before she was halfway across the room, Rucker
took the cup the captain had just filled and poured it down
the front of the officer's tunic. Then, grinning tightly at the
man, his hand on his pistol butt, Rucker shoved Cramer from
him. "Drinkin' with a dead man is bad luck an' a waste of
good whiskey. An' that's what you are, Captain Cramer: a walkin'
dead man."

Cramer's face mottled with rage, and for an instant it was

plain that he considered bracing the boy. Finally, with a look that promised he would deal with Rucker later, he turned on his heel and rejoined his three companions, and Molly heard him tell them that Rucker was nothing but Southern white trash.

Molly raised her eyebrows and sauntered to the captain. "I would be careful what I say behind Fletcher's back, Captain. You can cut your throat with a sharp tongue."

She walked back to the bench and plopped down on it. She tried to concentrate on her food, but as though he were a magnet, her eyes were drawn again to Peyton Lewis. She noted that he appeared younger in the soft light of the fireplace, almost boyish, like Rucker. She pondered that. Then it hit her: he was relaxed, totally at ease. It was the first time she had seen him unguarded since having met him.

Peyton set his empty plate aside, rested his shoulders against the wall, and watched Gabrielle nibble at her food. He rarely engaged in small talk, was not good at it, but Gabrielle reminded him of the only good times in his life, and he longed to recapture that mood, if only for a moment. "Were you close to your brother when you were a child, Miss Johnson?"

Gabrielle patted her mouth with a handkerchief, her brow furrowed in concentration. "Oh, yes. Of course, he was a lot older than me, and very protective, but I adored him. I was so proud of him when he joined the cavalry at the beginning of the war. He looked so dashing in his uniform. He and Autie Custer were classmates at West Point. They went through much of the war together. Paul was best man at Autie and Libby's wedding. I was bridesmaid. As to the war, I know very little. One could say I was sheltered . . . and I suppose I was. I did accompany Libby once or twice when she visited Autie in New York. It was exciting, but . . . I was only fourteen, a silly little girl."

Gabrielle laughed, a lovely sound in a room that was totally devoid of beauty. "Tell me about you, Peyton. Tell me about the war and what you've been doing since Appomattox Courthouse."

Peyton grimaced. He did not want to discuss the war or his actions since. His eyes slid to the saddlebags lying alongside his bedroll in the corner next to the hearth. Shifting uncomfortably, he changed the subject. "I believe you'll be pleased with Texas, Miss Johnson . . . if you can stand the heat, drought, and loneliness."

Gabrielle scooted closer to him, and when she gazed into his face, a deep warmth smoldered in her eyes. She was well aware that Peyton Lewis shared very little of himself with others, but she was determined to get inside of him, one way or another. "Very well, Mr. Lewis. If you won't tell me about yourself, then tell me about Texas."

Molly watched Gabrielle with interest. An underlying mockery in the girl's speech and actions strongly suggested that even though she pretended naïveté, she was well versed in the art of utilizing her feminine wiles to manipulate men. Thought lines appeared between Molly's eyes: Gabrielle Johnson was so accomplished in her subterfuge that only another woman would recognize it for what it was. A hint of respect for the girl crossed Molly's face, then was replaced by a touch of doubt as she scrutinized the impressionable young woman again: Gabrielle knew nothing of the complexities of men. Molly pursed her lips. Could spite or envy be impairing her judgment? Molly watched as Gabrielle edged closer to Peyton and laid her hand on his arm.

"Please elaborate, Mr. Lewis . . . Peyton. I would truly enjoy hearing about Texas."

Molly's throat constricted, and her fingers balled into fists. No, she was not wrong about Gabrielle Johnson—not even a little bit!

Peyton spread his hands as though he did not know where to begin. "Well, ma'am, it gets hot enough in Texas in the summer to fry an egg on a flat rock. And when folks talk about a six-inch rain in west Texas, they're talking about one drop every six inches. And unlike Monroe, Michigan, Miss Johnson, a crowd in Texas is three people—two, if they're strangers."

Gabrielle raised her eyebrows in mock severity. "It's that bad? My goodness, I don't know how I shall ever survive!"

The amused twinkle in Gabrielle Johnson's eye caused Peyton to laugh. "The truth is, Miss Johnson, Texas is worse than that. There's rattlesnakes, and buffalo, and Indians . . ."

"If it's that awful, Mr. Lewis, why in the world do people want to live there?"

"Because it's new, it's wild, untamed; a place where a person can become something—or nothing—according to one's own merits."

He looked levelly at her. "Even though Texas is a state, Miss Johnson, your Federal government in Washington City is many miles away. And law and order, the kind you're accustomed to, is nothing but words written on pieces of paper and stored in some building in Washington. They mean nothing out here."

Gabrielle studied him intently, hearing in her mind his words, "your Federal government."

She pouted prettily. "You sound very accusing, Peyton."

When he did not answer, she raised her eyebrows. "My brother and General Custer will ensure law and order, sir. And as for the Indians you spoke of, why, Autie Custer holds them in the utmost contempt." She touched his arm and laughed merrily. "The Union army is invincible, Peyton. You Southerners should know that by now."

"Only a staunch Unionist believes that, Miss Johnson."

Again her delicate eyebrows arched. This time there was no mirth in her face. "Then I am a staunch Unionist, Peyton, because I truly believe that General Custer and my brother know what they are talking about where Indians are concerned. We were victorious over *your* Confederate army—and *you* certainly fought with more than bows and arrows!"

Peyton studied the young woman closely. She was very honest with her answers. Such honesty would not serve her well in Texas.

"Most Texans would disagree with you about both the Indians and the Confederacy, Miss Johnson. That could pose a very real problem for you when you reach Austin."

Gabrielle thought about that. "I suppose it could present a problem of sorts, but . . . I suppose it depends upon whether or not . . ." Her voice trailed off.

"Depends on what?"

She could see the very real interest in his eyes, and she shrugged indifferently. "I suppose it would depend upon whether or not *your* Texans can and will accept their defeat by *my* Federal army."

Peyton observed Gabrielle with grudging admiration and more than a little concern. She would not allow anyone to push her around, that much was obvious. The question was: would she have the wisdom to know when to speak, and when not to?

Peyton measured his words. "The South wasn't defeated, Miss Johnson. We weren't even whipped. We were beaten. There's a difference."

Gabrielle had the sensation that Peyton's cool gray eyes were probing into the very depths of her soul. It made her uncomfortable. Breaking visual contact with him, she turned her head toward the flames that danced in the fireplace. "If you say so, Mr. Lewis."

Peyton settled back against the wall. He had not been aware that he had pushed his face to within inches of hers. The realization left him impatient with himself. He had unsuspectingly allowed this snip of a girl to neatly and deviously nettle him into a box where any further dispute on his part concerning the South's surrender would appear trite, foolish, and defensive.

He sighed. Perhaps the entire debate had been trite and foolish from its conception. The only people who would disagree with her were die-hard Confederates, and while Peyton did not consider himself a die-hard, he found it downright galling to be outmaneuvered by a young Northern woman who knew nothing of the world outside of Monroe, Michigan.

A half-smile turned up a corner of his mouth as it dawned on him that his superior attitude toward Gabrielle Johnson, his eagerness to underestimate the people above the Mason-Dixon Line—especially its women—was the very same arrogant sentiment that Southerners reserved for the world in general, and that blind impudence had played a major role in the Union army's victory over the Confederacy, just as it had in *her* triumph over him.

Peyton laughed aloud at his discovery and was about to voice his conjecture to Gabrielle when the front door suddenly opened and John Wright, followed by Lawson, the station attendant, stepped hurriedly into the room and motioned for Peyton to join him.

When Peyton approached Wright, the driver turned his back to the people at the table and spoke in hushed tones that could not be overheard.

"We got a problem, Lewis. Lawson here says the Comanches are hittin' the stagecoaches hot 'n' heavy down around the Texas-Oklahoma border. They burned a coach three weeks ago. Killed several passengers. He says that we're the first stage that's come through headin' west since the snow, an' he figures there might be trouble."

Lawson shifted his quid of tobacco to his other cheek and spit a stream of amber expertly over Gabrielle's shoulder and into the fire. He smiled apologetically at the girl as she scrambled hurriedly to the far end of the hearth and examined her clothing for spots of spittle, then turned his attention again to Peyton. "Ain't no 'might be' to it, Lewis. It's just a matter of where an' when they hit you. The Oklahoma Territory is wide open since the war. Every sort of riffraff has moved in there, and they're all mad as hell. The Indians are mad because the United States took their land away from them for fightin' for the South. The ex-slaves are mad because the government didn't give Oklahoma to them. An' both Northern an' Southern white trash are just plain mad on general principle. It's plumb dangerous down there, an' that's the truth of it in a nutshell."

John Wright shifted his weight uneasily. "An' that brings us to the big question, Peyton. Should we lay over here at Wichita for a spell an' wait for an army escort, or do we try our luck, an' maybe pay the consequences?" He settled back on his heels and looked Peyton in the eye. "The decision is up to you folks, Lewis. I suggest we call a meetin' and vote on it."

Peyton glanced over his shoulder at Gabrielle. She was watching the flames in the fireplace and had obviously not heard a word concerning the possible dangers that awaited them. He turned to the other travelers. Molly Klinner was the only one in the group who had paid the least attention to the men at the door; she was studying them inquisitively, as though she had heard the conversation and was awaiting an answer. Robertson and Beecher were eating again, and Cramer and Pendleton were at the bar, drinking steadily. Rucker had taken his bottle to the far end of the dinner table and was drowning his sorrows alone.

Of the seven people Peyton had just assessed for the purpose of defending the stagecoach should the need arise, he discounted the banker and drummer as unknown factors and eliminated the women as noncombatants. That left five trained fighters, all military or former military men, to confront whatever dangers awaited them beyond the Kansas border. Five men who knew how to use a gun. Against what? Comanches? Apaches? Former slaves? Angry whites? Peyton weighed the odds, then took a deep breath. "I'm for going on."

John Wright nodded. "I figured you'd vote that way. Now, let's see what the rest of 'em think."

Wright walked to the table and rapped loudly on its pine planking with the leaded butt of his bullwhip. When he had the travelers' attention, he described the situation, leaving out nothing. He appraised their faces, seeing shock, fear, and indecision.

"You folks call the shots. If you vote to stay, we stay. If you vote to go . . ." Wright shrugged.

Joseph Robertson rose heavily to his full height, his pudgy face lined with concern. "We have no choice, Mr. Wright. We cannot—no, we must not!—jeopardize the lives of these fair ladies. For their sake, I vote that we wait for an escort."

William Beecher concurred with Robertson, stressing the futility of taking unnecessary risks. Surprisingly, the soldiers, in spite of their brave talk about fighting Indians, cast their lot with the banker and the drummer, bringing the count to four against traveling on, to three, Peyton, Rucker, and John Wright, in favor.

Joseph Robertson grinned his relief. "It's settled. We wait for an escort."

Molly, who had listened silently while the vote was taken, jumped to her feet and eyed Robertson contemptuously. "I'm one of those lady passengers you spoke of not jeopardizing, Mr. Robertson. And if you're voting against pressing on for my sake, then it's no contest. I'm for taking the chance." She stepped back and crossed her arms over her breasts.

Robertson raised his chin arrogantly. "Women have no voice in this decision, Miss Klinner."

Molly's face was incredulous. "Why do I not? You said yourself, sir, that your opinion was based on your belief that to go on would jeopardize the lives of us 'fair ladies.' That makes Miss Johnson and me very real factors in this decision." Her heated gaze penetrated each man at the table and lingered pointedly on the captain and lieutenant. "You two were certainly anxious to shoot someone a little while ago. Well, you just might get your chance. Furthermore"—she turned to John Wright—"I'll not have Mr. Butterfield shut down his stagecoach line because of me, nor will I be the reason for certain individuals' cowardliness!"

Captain Cramer, still smarting from Rucker's challenge a few minutes earlier, scowled his displeasure at Molly. "Now, see here, Miss Klinner, just because we understand and appreciate the danger of attempting to journey through the Oklahoma Indian country unescorted . . . well, it most certainly is no sign of cowardice. And I resent—"

Molly spun toward the man. "Resent and be damned, Captain!"

Joseph Robertson waved Molly into silence, then turned to Gabrielle Johnson. "If Miss Klinner's vote counts, then that makes the tally a tie, four to four. The final decision, therefore, must lie with this grand young lady." All eyes were riveted on Gabrielle, and Robertson smiled cunningly to himself. Gabrielle was eastern bred, and he was certain that a lady of quality would not jeopardize her life, or the lives of others, merely to save a few days' travel. Still, there was the remote possibility that she did not fully grasp the danger they faced. "Indians, Miss Johnson, especially those in the Oklahoma nation, are notorious for their cruelty, especially toward white women. They do all manner of deplorable things to females—unspeakable behavior to their bodies."

Gabrielle's hand fluttered to her throat, and her eyes grew

as round as saucers. She looked quickly to Peyton for confirmation.

Peyton eyed the banker coldly. "You've made your point, Mr. Robertson."

Robertson, aware of the young woman's vulnerability, ignored Peyton's warning and pushed his advantage. "The savages have no morals, Miss Johnson. They make white women their slaves, force them to bear red children. They even——"

Peyton took a quick step forward and backhanded Robertson across the face. The impact sounded like a gunshot. Robertson staggered sideways and crashed against the table. When the man drew himself erect, Peyton's hand gripped the butt of his revolver, and the deadly calm of cold rage that filled his face frightened Gabrielle even more than had the banker's descriptive tale. Swinging her eyes to Rucker, she silently pleaded for his intervention. Rucker looked away. She turned to Molly, who simply raised her eyebrows, offering nothing but a silent challenge. Balling her fingers into tight fists, her nails cutting into her palms, Gabrielle faced the four men who had voted no.

"If the Oklahoma Territory is as dangerous as you imply, gentlemen, then I wholeheartedly suggest that you wait for an escort. I, however, am expected in Texas."

Gabrielle was the picture of eloquence as she laid her hand on John Wright's arm. "Shall we board the coach, sir . . . now?"

John Wright cackled aloud. "Sorry, ma'am, but nighttime running lights on a stagecoach this close to the Oklahoma Territory would be a beacon to disaster. We'll leave at first light."

Stunned by her own impulsive outburst, Gabrielle's knees suddenly turned to sand, and she sank down onto the wooden bench. What had prompted her to say such a thing? It was madness to venture on! She raised her face imploringly to Peyton with the intention of recanting her proposal, but he had walked to the far end of the room and was spreading his bedroll. Her eyes swiveled accusingly to Molly Klinner, who was gathering up the soiled plates and eating utensils and carrying them to the dishpan behind the counter. Bitterness turned Gabrielle's lips into an ugly line. *It's because of you! You make me say and do things— crazy things! God, I detest you!*

Gabrielle attempted to force the unladylike declaration from her mind as being beneath her, but, as though it was stronger than she, the undeniable truth refused to be blinked away. She did indeed loathe Molly Klinner. The woman stirred something deep and primitive within her, a facet of her inner self she did not even know existed. For never in her young life had she experienced such a potent drive to compete for the eye of a man she did not love, a compelling intent to win him at all costs, and a wild desire to possess him completely.

Gabrielle became aware that Molly was returning her gaze, and it startled her, for Molly's lips were pursed, her face thoughtful as though she were reading her mind.

Molly walked to the door and caught up her rifle. As she passed Gabrielle on her way to her bedroll, she smiled challengingly at the girl. "We'll see what you're made of when the time comes, Miss Johnson. And, believe me, the time will come."

Gabrielle's green eyes flashed defiantly. "I already have a very good idea of what you are made of, Miss Klinner."

Molly laughed delightedly. "I've never tried to hide what I am, Miss Johnson. Can you say the same?"

Thirteen

They crossed into Oklahoma Territory four days after leaving Wichita, just as the sun fought its way over an opaque skyline that refused to release its hold on the night. The terrain, as it swam through the hazy mist of predawn to become the stark reality of morning, showed little change from the Kansas country they had just traversed. Plains swept to the horizon with an occasional plateau pushing up out of the flats like a parlor table whose coarse linen coverlet fell in rumpled pleats to the floor. Other than that, it was the same nothingness, dotted now and then with the bleached bones of buffalo or a longhorn cow.

Peyton and Rucker, having elected to ride shotgun for John Wright, sat atop the coach and watched the birth of the new day through slitted eyes, alert to every shadow, every movement.

Inside the stagecoach, it was a totally different atmosphere. In spite of the fact that they had stopped each night at full dark and rested until just before false dawn, it was plain by their demeanor that not one of the passengers had more than cat-napped since leaving Wichita.

The four male passengers, except for an occasional groan or curse, rode in surly silence, a muteness born of having revealed their cowardliness in the presence of the gentler sex—and then blaming that sex for their own inadequacies. The women sat primly hostile beside each other, trying hard not to allow body contact, failing each time the coach jarred into a rut or over a rock, which was frequent. Neither of them had spoken to the other in four long days.

As the morning light began fingering its way into the gloomy interior of the coach, Molly Klinner unbuckled a side curtain and rolled it up. Frigid air rushed against her face and stung her cheeks as the barely risen sun washed the countryside with a clean stillness that promised a cloudless, pristine day.

Molly leaned closer to the opening and breathed deeply, welcoming the relief that the cold, fresh breeze brought as it flushed away the odor of stale cigar smoke, food scraps, and soured bodies that was one's constant companion in a closed stagecoach.

A smile dimpled the corners of Molly's lips as the cobwebs of sleepiness evaporated from her mind. She wished she was riding on top with Peyton and Rucker so she could enjoy the entire panorama, feel the wind in her hair, taste the sun.

Settling back against the upholstery, Molly thought about her future—or lack of one. Until she had met Peyton Lewis, her foremost consideration had been to get out of Kansas, away from everything connected with Caleb King. She had done that. Now what? She had no money, no property . . . just the clothes on her back, a Henry rifle, and a new life in her womb.

Not much of a start. Still, she was better off than some. She had her face and her body, and both were young, healthy, and pretty . . . or would be in another two months, after the baby was born.

That thought brought a frown to Molly's face. Physically, she felt fine, just as she had the first time she had become pregnant, wonderfully healthy, vigorous, full of life—two lives. Caleb King's child. Caleb King—a thief, a robber, a murderer, a pimp, and she was carrying his baby. *Only the good die young. The bad live forever.* She shuddered and wished she had not said that, not even to herself.

Molly turned her attention again to the landscape. It lay fallow with winter, but, like her, it, too, would bring forth new life, and no matter the amount of ugliness, suffering, and death that preceded it, that new life would be fresh, clean, beautiful—and welcomed. She must remember that. Yes, she must never allow herself to forget that new life should always be welcomed. Molly smiled contentedly, and the frown lines between her eyes disappeared.

Gabrielle Johnson was intrigued with the internal war that was changing the landscape of Molly Klinner's face as though it were a battleground. She could only imagine what must be going through Molly's mind to cause the kaleidoscope of sensations that rushed across the woman's features. First there was very real appreciation as she gazed out at the sunrise, but that sentiment quickly gave way to bitterness, which was eventually replaced with fear, then confusion, which was transformed into what appeared to be forgiveness, then lastly, the serenity of acceptance.

Gabrielle's breath caught, and her eyes narrowed in thought, for never had she seen a face more animated, more full of life, more beautiful. She winced. Stirrings of the same hostility toward Molly she had experienced that night in Wichita rose up in her like bile, bitter and offensive.

Surely I can't be jealous of her! Gabrielle's slitted scrutiny took in every detail of Molly Klinner's drab clothing, dirty hands and broken fingernails, and the dull, unkempt hair beneath her floppy, wide-brimmed hat. No! She was definitely not jealous of Molly Klinner.

Gabrielle released her pent-up breath and sat back on the coach seat, chiding herself for being apprehensive when there was no justification.

Molly's unkempt appearance, utterly disgusting to Gabrielle, also brought up a very real dilemma that the girl found herself bandying around in her mind. What *did* people in the wilds—no, not people; she had long since come to the conclusion that men, especially during the winter, seldom bathed—what did women in the wilds do when it came to personal cleanliness?

Gabrielle squirmed self-consciously on her seat. Her last long, hot bath—in a real tub—had been in Topeka, Kansas, more than three weeks ago. Since then, at the outlying stagecoach depots where they had laid over for a night or were snowed in for a day or two, if there was a room that afforded privacy, she had demanded a tub of hot water, which usually turned out to be a wooden or tin pail that she could barely get her feet into.

It would have astounded Gabrielle had she known that the majority of the women on the prairie felt fortunate if they were afforded the luxury of a partial bath once a week, many times with the same water in which they had done the laundry.

Even more appalling to the city girl would have been the toilette of frontier women, their use of a coarse, skin-chapping lye soap which they rendered from animal tallow—a far cry from the perfumed, exotic soaps and lotions to which her pampered skin was accustomed.

Again she appraised Molly, and her delicate nostrils quivered. Surely there was nothing more offensive than a slovenly woman, and Molly Klinner was certainly that!

As the coach rumbled on, Gabrielle's aversion to Molly Klinner persisted until she became so disgusted by the uninvited sensation that she longed to reach out and slap her face. "What are your intentions once we reach Texas, *Miss* Klinner?" Gabrielle blanched, appalled by the maliciousness of her own voice, for it was so unlike her to speak callously to a person.

Molly turned and looked directly at the girl, surprised, not by the tone but by the question itself, for she had just been contemplating those very thoughts about her future with little success. She answered Gabrielle truthfully. "Why, I really don't know, Miss Johnson."

Had they been alone, Molly might very well have explained her predicament. She needed a woman to confide in. The baby had moved that morning, and it was a grand feeling—one to be shared with a friend, a loved one, Peyton Lewis. But he had no idea she was even pregnant. And that axiom bothered her more than she cared to admit. If Rucker were to mention it to him, what would he do? What would he think? Well, she had made her bed and now she would lie in it. With a sigh, she returned her gaze to the passing countryside. The sun was a foot above the horizon, yet patches of mist clung to the low places as though they had seized a tight handhold on the upward-reaching branches and tentacles of the bushes and shrubs that grew there and refused to let go. Or could it be the other way around? Could it be the foliage that fought so hard to keep its grip on darkness? If so, why? Why did the tentacles not let go of the mist and enjoy the sun to its fullest? *It's because all living things are alike,* Molly determined. *They would rather be cloaked in a misery with which they are familiar than face the unknown that comes with a pristine dawn. Not me! I'm ready for the new day. I ache for it.* Molly raised her eyes to the sun, and her lips moved ever so slightly. "Let it come." It was more a demand than a plea.

Peyton searched every nook and cranny of the plains as far as he could see. He scanned the horizon, then the low places. The sun glistened off the bleached skull of a longhorn cow. Skeletons of cattle were becoming more frequent the closer they got to Texas. Something moved. Peyton's eyes were riveted to the spot, and his hand tightened on the stock of Molly's rifle.

He saw it again, a flash of gray among the purple shadows. He squinted at the spot. A moment later, a coyote trotted to the top of a barren knoll and raised its nose to the wind. It was a forlorn creature, alone. It sniffed in all four directions before trotting down the incline to disappear into the brush.

Peyton settled back on the seat and shifted his attention to the other side of the road; there were no hidden enemies where a coyote was hunting.

Rucker, sitting between Peyton and John Wright, straightened from his comfortable slouch and peered over the horses' heads, his gaze intent on the road far in advance. "Something's up ahead . . . can't tell what."

Peyton squinted into the cold wind. His eyes watered. Two miles ahead, he saw a speck by the roadside, but, like Rucker, he could not make it out. Wiping his eyes with his coat sleeve, he peered again. It was still too distant to see plainly.

John Wright laughed at the two. "I don't know how you boys have stayed alive as long as you have. If'n it's true that a sharp eye is the mother of good luck, then you fellers must'a been aborted, 'cause that's a man you're lookin' at out yonder. An' he's afoot."

Rucker hooted and slapped his knee in mirth. "You'd have

to have spyglasses for eyes to make out what that is, John. Why, it ain't nothin' but a dot—a little dot."

Wright spit a stream of tobacco juice onto the wagon tongue between the wheel horses. "When you sit up on this perch as long as I have, Fletcher, you get t' where you know what somethin' is jest by the way it moves. That ain't no horse. It ain't no buffalo. It ain't no longhorn. An' it sure as hell ain't no Injun. Now, what's that leave?"

Rucker looked startled. "Why, lots of things."

Peyton slipped the lever of Molly's rifle and checked the breech to make sure there was a shell chambered. He had no idea what awaited them, but whatever it was, he did not intend to be caught unawares.

When they were still half a mile from what was indeed a man standing beside the road, John Wright slapped the reins hard on the horses' backs. "It's a nigger! Look sharp, boys, there may be a passel of 'em hidin' in the brush!"

Wright unlimbered his whip and snaked it out over the lead team with a loud crack. The six horses stampeded into their collars, and the stagecoach lurched into greater speed. Again the whip exploded, then again, and again.

Peyton and Rucker braced their feet against the footboard and grabbed the edge of their seats as Wright whipped the horses into an all-out run.

Above the thundering hooves, jingling traces, and rumbling of the coach, John Wright yelled to Peyton that since the war had ended, freed slaves had been banding together and attacking travelers crossing the Oklahoma Territory.

Wright spit a stream of amber over his shoulder, and the wind whipped it away. "They make out like they're Indians, but they ain't. They're niggers. An' lots of times, they put one man out on the road, an' when folks stop t' help him, the others attack an' butcher 'em. So we ain't takin' no chances. I intend t' roll by that pickaninny so fast he'll think this coach is a tumbleweed stuck to a horse's ass!"

As the coach rumbled past, the Negro threw his hand up in a salute.

Peyton gave him a quick once-over, then riveted his attention to the surrounding countryside, searching for anything out of the ordinary. There was nothing. Twisting on his seat, he glanced back across the top of the luggage rack.

The man waved again, then slipped his hands into slits sewn into his coat to serve as pockets. He appeared small and despondent as he trudged back into the road and began once again following that narrow ribbon of dual ruts that dissected the vast expanse of prairie—the only indication of human presence in the entire godforsaken country.

Peyton leaned close to John Wright and tapped him on his shoulder. "Pull up, John!"

John Wright wrapped the reins around his forearms and drew back mightily, sawing the bits to bring the runaways under control. At the same instant, he braced his foot against the brake pole and threw his weight into it. The brakes squealed their protest. As the coach drew to a halt, Wright leaned around Rucker, who was riding in the middle, and the look on his face spoke volumes. "What in hell did you want t' stop for, Lewis? We're a sittin' duck out here!"

Peyton quickly scanned both sides of the road. Nothing moved, not a jackrabbit, not a coyote, not even an eagle in the sky. He pointed back the way they had come. "That man needs a ride, John."

Wright stood up on the footboard and peered over the rear of the coach at the solitary figure a half-mile back. Someone inside the vehicle began pounding on the ceiling, and Wright yelled for them to pipe down.

Peyton flung out his hand in a gesture that took in the desolate landscape as far as the eye could see. "That's a mighty big country out there to leave a man afoot in, John."

Wright cut his eyes to Rucker. "Well, what do you think? I know you're jest itchin' t' add your two cents' worth to this conversation."

Rucker grinned at Wright. "Long as you put that darky downwind from me, I ain't got no problem with pickin' him up. He can ride in the boot."

Wright pointed his whip handle at Rucker. "Fletcher, you're plumb used t' your own stink. Fact is, you need t' get downwind

of yourself. You're about as ripe as a skint 'possum on a July day.
I expect if that feller had to smell you for the next twenty miles,
he'd consider it a favor t' ride in the boot!" Wright snatched off
his hat and waved for the Negro to hurry.

Joseph Robertson, the banker, flung back the window curtain and rapped on the side of the coach with his cane. "What's
going on here, Wright? First you drive like a wild man. Then you
stop in the middle of nowhere. I'm telling you right now, your su-
periors will hear about this. . . ." His voice trailed off as the Negro
trotted past the coach and paused at the front wheel to catch his
breath.

The black man appeared to be in his early to midforties, of
medium height and slender build. His skin in the morning sun
glistened like a piece of polished mahogany, and his hair, more
wavy than kinky, was long and streaked with gray. He wore a
ragged army overcoat and faded Union trousers that stopped
just above a pair of badly scuffed brogans with rawhide laces.
His coat clung tight against his chest, and a badly soiled, rolled
canvas blanket crossed over his shoulder, the ends tied together
under his arm. A haversack, worn on his right side, sagged no-
ticeably as though something heavy was housed there.

John Wright spit a stream of tobacco juice that spattered
on the front wheel rim next to the Negro's hand. The man did
not flinch.

"Where you headed, Uncle?"

The Negro doffed his slouch hat and grinned up at the
three men on the box. "Home, mista' driver. I'm headed home."

"An' jest where might that be?"

"Texas, mista' driver." The Negro covered his heart with his
hat. "The great state of Texas."

Wright scratched his chin thoughtfully. "You got enuff
money to pay your fare on this here Butterfield?"

The black man grinned and rolled his eyes. "All I can afford
is what I been a-ridin'." He raised a worn-out army brogan and
shook it at John Wright. "Ol' shanks' mare!"

"That's what I figured." John Wright's eyes slid skeptically to
Peyton.

The black man saw the look and knew that his chance for a ride was slipping away. He walked quickly to the wheel horse and patted its rump.

"Howsomever, mista' driver, I'm a right fine hand with hoss-flesh. I shore would be tickled plumb pink t' help with yore stock. P'haps I could work out my fare?"

John Wright bellowed out a loud guffaw; he liked the man's sense of humor. "For a Texas boy, you're downright ignorant. You know damned good'n well they ain't a driver in the world who would allow a stranger near his team, much less a nigger stranger! You're goin' to have t' do better'n that."

The black man settled back on his heels and grinned up at John Wright. "What 'bout this here stagecoach? It's goin' t' need a passel of mud knocked off'n it by the time it arrives in Texas. It's a-goin' t' need spit an' polish, 'cause I know they ain't no real, sho'-nuff driver in the world who would want folks t' see him a-drivin' a hog-wallowin', pig-rootin' piece of Butterfield such as this'n. Why, t' tell you the truth, mista' driver, I ain't jest plumb certain I want t' soil my duds a-ridin' on this coach!"

John Wright reared back and hooted. Rucker guffawed and punched Wright in the ribs. Even Peyton grinned.

Joseph Robertson, who had found nothing humorous in the exchange, told the passengers that as a businessman carrying a sum of money, he thought it an absolute disgrace that a stagecoach would stop in such dangerous country to pick up a wayward nigger. A disgrace! He would see to it that the Butterfield executives were enlightened.

Captain Cramer climbed out of the coach and walked to the front wheel. He looked the black man over with open hostility, then raised his face to the driver. "Now, see here, John, fare or no fare, this *boy* ain't riding in that stagecoach. Why, we have white female passengers in there!"

Rucker leaned around the driver and scowled down at the captain. "Well, if that don't beat all! You Yankees freed 'em, but now you're too good to ride with 'em!"

With a muttered oath, Rucker climbed onto the roof of the coach, and with a wave of his hand indicated the space on the seat he had just vacated. "Just climb right up here, Uncle. You can ride in my spot."

John Wright's face was a question mark as he turned to Peyton. "Is Rucker always this wishy-washy? He changes his mind quicker'n an Injun changes camps. Not five minutes ago, he was layin' down the law that this nigger would have to ride downwind from him. Now here he is offerin' him his seat."

Wright shook his head and unlimbered his whip in preparation of leave-taking. "Beats all I ever heard tell of."

The captain spun on his heel and reentered the coach, slamming the door in the process.

The Negro scrambled nimbly up over the wheel, and made his way across the footboard of the box to the vacant space. He tipped his hat to Rucker. "You, sir, is a gentleman an' a scholar."

Wright popped his whip, and the coach jerked into motion.

The Negro grinned over at Peyton. "This sho'-nuff beats walkin'. I done walked and walked till my feet ain't nothin' but nubbins."

Peyton evaluated the man again, finding him older than the forty years he had first guessed. Also, he was of mixed blood, probably Mexican or Indian. Maybe both. Whatever his heritage, it created a curious blend.

Although Peyton made it a habit not to meddle in another man's business, he was curious as to what a lone Negro was doing on the open prairie, and where he had come from. Their lives might depend on the answer. Peyton tried a tactful approach. "How far does a person have to walk, Uncle, before his feet are worn down to nubbins?"

The Negro contemplated for a long moment, and Peyton could see his lips moving as he mentally calculated his answer.

"I reckon I've walked nigh ont' two, maybe three thousand miles, boss. I done walked more in the last year than I walked in my whole life all put t'gether!"

"You're from the East?"

The man laughed, his teeth startlingly white against his dark skin. "Naw, sir! I'm a Texan!"

Rucker, holding on to the iron rail that formed the luggage

rack, leaned toward the man. "What Peyton is trying to find out is whereabouts you are comin' from, Uncle."

"Well . . ." The Negro grew evasive as he looked over his shoulder at Rucker. "I been with Mista' Lincoln's army."

Rucker dropped his head back and hooted. "A damned Yankee nigger from Texas! I've seen it all. There ain't nothin' left in the world that will surprise me after this!"

The Negro laughed with Rucker, but Peyton saw the man quickly gauge the distance from the box to the ground as though he were contemplating jumping from the coach.

Peyton grinned at the man. "We're not going to throw you off just because you fought for the North."

The Negro relaxed. "Much obliged, boss. I've been nigh onto a year a-crossin' Southern country, an' I had t' walk mighty light ever' step of the way. Folks is in a terrible humor since the war."

Wright cut his eye to the Negro. "If you're a Texan, then what were you doin' fightin' for the North? An' don't give me none of that slave hogwash, 'cause I can tell you ain't never wore no fetters."

The Negro laughed easily. "Well, sir, mista' driver, now that's a natural fact. I ain't never been no slave."

He told them he had been in a prison in Galveston, Texas, when the Northern army blockaded the seaport and garrisoned the town. "They offered me an' all them other niggers our freedom. They figgered that 'cause it were Southerners what locked us up, we naturally had a bone t' pick with 'em, so they give us a choice of joinin' the Union army or else. . . ." He spread his hands in a futile gesture. "Now, tell me, mista' driver, what would you have done?"

When Wright did not answer, the man continued with less enthusiasm. "They put us on a boat an' floated us up t' the state of New York. We was 'signed to General U. S. Grant's army, an' when we got there, he put us t' diggin' trenches, an' latrines, an' crappers for the soldiers—same stuff we did in prison. An' when the war was over, General Grant, he turned us loose up in Virginia, an' tolt us we was free. So, I set out a-walkin'. Been a-walkin' an' a-workin' my way t'ward Texas ever since."

Wright pursed his tobacco-stained lips and peered owlishly at the man. "Well, you didn't actually fight for the North. Never carried a gun or nothin'?"

"Naw, sir!" The Negro shook his head emphatically, then settled back and released an exaggerated sigh. "Lordy, mercy! It sure feels good t' be a-ridin' t'ward Texas."

Wright cracked his whip, and the horses stepped up their pace. The next stagecoach station was still ten miles ahead.

As they rolled deeper into Oklahoma, the weather warmed, the mud dried, and the terrain changed gradually into rolling prairies and gentle hills covered with blackjack and post oak thickets. It was a welcome transformation after the miles of Kansas plains. With every turn of the wheel, however, they were nervously aware that the coach was moving further into hostile country.

Peyton and Rucker spent their daylight hours perched on the coach top scrutinizing the countryside while the driver concentrated on the road and the horses, and they spent their nights, along with the other white male passengers, standing guard duty. They could not afford to drop their vigilance for an instant.

Each morning, when the stagecoach was boarded for the day's run, the black man, Ben, with no last name he could remember, would climb to the roof of the coach and go immediately to sleep.

Ben's unconcerned slumber irritated Rucker, who, after three days of watching and wondering, finally shook the black man awake. "Uncle, how can you sleep at a time like this? How come you ain't worried about bein' attacked by Indians? Do you know somethin' we don't?"

Ben flashed his perpetual grin. "Well, Mista' Rucker, I probably know a whole heap 'bout most things that you ain't learnt yet, 'cause I'm quite a sum older'n you. They's one thing, howsomever, that I learnt when I was jest a pickaninny. . . ." The coach hit a rut, and Ben clutched at the seat to keep from being thrown against the driver. When the coach righted itself, Ben released his breath.

"As I was sayin', I learnt long ago that worryin' 'bout somethin' a feller ain't got no control over is like ridin' a rockin' horse: it's a whole lot of work an' it ain't goin' t' git you no place!"

Drawing his hat down over his eyes, Ben made himself comfortable. He contemplated telling Rucker the truth, that he patrolled their night camps from dark to dawn and slept during the daylight hours. He decided, however, that were they to know that he was slipping about in the darkness, it just might make them more nervous than they already were.

Rucker settled down onto the roof of the swaying coach and mulled over Ben's words. There was a lot of truth in what the man had said . . . or at least it sounded like the truth.

Rucker drew the makings from his shirt pocket and built himself a cigarette. Cupping his hands around the paper cylinder to ward off the wind, he struck a lucifer with his thumbnail and sucked the tobacco into life. He smoked and studied the sleeping Negro.

Ben's seemingly nonchalant attitude toward life irked Rucker, especially when the man began to snore loudly, as he did most mornings.

"Just like a nigger!" Rucker scanned the terrain in all directions before his eyes came again to Ben. "Let somebody else do all the work while he sleeps."

Rucker took a long draw on the cigarette, then flipped it away and watched it hit the ground and lie there smoldering.

Ben came instantly awake. "Mista' Rucker, if'n I'd known yo' was goin' t' throw that butt away so soon, I'd ast yo' for dubs on it."

Rucker frowned; the man was, without a doubt, the most brazen black person he had ever encountered. Fishing the makings from his pocket, he handed them to Ben. Rucker returned his gaze to the countryside, contenting himself with the fact that Ben would only be traveling with them as far as the first way station in Texas, which, if his calculations were correct, should not be over two hundred miles ahead. Rockin' horses? Hell, he hadn't seen a rockin' horse since he was three years old—an' a three-year-old didn't have no business goin' nowhere nohow! He scowled at Ben with disgust.

Fourteen

In spite of their foreboding and apprehension, and due to fine traveling conditions where they could average six miles per hour, the journey across the Oklahoma Territory was accomplished without major incident. They crossed the Arkansas River, the Black Bear, the Cimarron, the Little Canadian, and finally the Canadian itself, where an enterprising Cherokee had built a ferry.

At the stagecoach depots, those that were still manned, they changed teams, ate and rested, and listened to the latest news about marauding Indians, who had slowed down their attacks on travelers because the spring thaws had arrived and most of the tribes were migrating to their seasonal hunting grounds.

On the cool and windy afternoon of April 3, they rounded a bend in the road that proved to be the summit of a long, slow, half-mile decline that culminated at a muddy river perhaps two hundred feet across at its widest point. John Wright brought the coach to a halt on the hill's crest and studied the stream.

"Well, boys, there she is, the mighty Red River. An we're in luck, 'cause she don't 'pear to be over hub deep—which is a mite unusual for this time o' the year." He pointed with his whip handle. "Over yonder is Texas."

They sat in silence and took in the rolling sweep of Texas beyond the Red. The desolate country seemed to stretch on forever until it merged and became one with the horizon.

Peyton felt a curious excitement rush through his being. A new world awaited him on the other side of that river, a future as limitless as the vast countryside spread out before him.

John Wright stood up in the box and carefully surveyed the banks of the ford where the road entered the stream. He spoke his thoughts aloud. "Injuns likes to surprise folks in the middle of a river, gents. Hit 'em when they're movin' slow an' ain't got no cover . . . like we'll be doin' when we cross the Red." He turned to Peyton. "You mind scoutin' those bottoms 'round the ford while we sit here an' let the horses blow a spell?"

Peyton climbed down over the wheel and dropped to the ground. Ben started down also, but John Wright caught him by his coat collar and drew him back into his seat. Wright's eyes held a hint of suspicion as he searched Ben's face. "Where do you reckon' you're goin', Uncle?"

Ben studied John Wright for a long moment. "The truth is, mista' driver, I'm a fair han' at readin' sign. So I 'sumed I might mosey on down there with boss Lewis an' take me a look-see."

Wright shook his head. "You jest sit up here on this box an' keep me company."

Ben nodded and settled back into his seat. He took no offense at the driver's thinly veiled warning; John Wright was a careful, suspicious man.

Rucker, who was still atop the coach, retrieved four handleless pistols from their saddlebags and dropped them over the side of the coach to Peyton.

Peyton opened the coach door. Ignoring the questions of the male passengers, he presented one of the pistols to Molly and his small five-shot revolver to Gabrielle, who, with a bewildered expression, handled the weapon gingerly, then laid it on the seat beside her.

Peyton inspected the cylinders of the remaining revolvers to ensure that the percussion caps were secure, then slipped them into his trouser pockets and picked up Molly's rifle. With the weapon lying easy in the crook of his arm, he walked down the hill toward the stream, scanning the trees along the riverbank, the shadows beneath the shrubs and underbrush, searching for horizontal lines that would denote the backs of horses. He saw nothing out of the ordinary.

Peyton approached the river cautiously, listening for a murmur of voices, the snort of a horse, the stamping of a hoof. Hearing nothing, he scanned the stream in both directions, then slowly and methodically scouted the bank for several hundred feet. Other than the tracks of the wild animals that watered there, not one hoof- or footprint was evident. Peyton walked into the open road and lifted the rifle over his head.

John Wright cracked his whip, and the coach rolled noisily down the incline. At the ford, Wright brought the horses to a halt. "See anything?"

Peyton, waiting at the water's edge, shook his head.

Rucker nudged Wright in his ribs. "Gettin' kind'a jumpy in your ol' age, ain't you, John? If Peyton says the crossin' is clear, it's clear."

"If'n you live t' be as old as me, Fletcher—which is doubt-ful—you'll learn that a smart man never takes it for granted that a wolf is shore-nuff dead till it's been skint out an his hide is salted down. So regardless of what Lewis says, when we go into that water, you boys keep a sharp eye on both them riverbanks. You get my drift?"

Rucker rolled his eyes at Ben, but he nodded that he did, in-deed, understand.

As the coach splashed into the stream, Peyton jumped onto the boot and seated himself on the drummer's trunk so he could watch their back trail. In midstream, with the water nearly hub deep, Wright drew the stage to a standstill for the purpose of soaking the wooden wheels' spokes and rims. As the minutes ticked by, he nervously scanned the Texas side of the river, ex-pecting to see a band of savages appear at any moment.

Rucker leaned out over the coach's side and watched the water swirl sluggishly around the hubs. "You ain't afraid them iron-tired bobbins are goin' to fall apart, are you, John? Hell, they're brand-new!"

The driver wished Rucker would keep his voice down, but

he knew the boy would not shut up until his curiosity was slaked.

"Them wooden spokes an' rims has shrunk a mite since we left French's station, an' that's a natural fact. Truth is, Fletcher, there ain't a driver in the country who would cross a stream of water without stoppin' to swell his wheels—especially on a new coach."

Ben nodded at Wright and peered nervously up and down the river. "They's a passel of truth in what you said, Mista' John. But ol' Gabe Bridger, he oncet tolt me when me an' a company o' trappers was runnin' from the Blackfeet and wanted t' stop an' rest, ol' Gabe sez, 'Boys, it ain't no time t' enjoy a smoke when you're a-sittin' on an open keg of powder!' "

John Wright glowered testily at Ben, not liking the rebuff, no matter how cleverly it was executed. "Uncle, they's one thing for certain: every jackass thinks he has horse sense, includin' old Gabe. Truth is, howsomever, it weren't Bridger who made that statement. It were Kit Carson."

Ben shook his head. "'Now, I don't mean t' be d'sputin' your word, Mista' John, but—"

Rucker, tired of their dialogue, stood up on the toeboard and peered in all directions. "You gents are a little skittish, ain't you? There ain't an Indian in a hundred miles of here."

Wright and Ben ignored Rucker and continued their argument, right up to the moment that the coach came out of the water and rolled onto Texas soil. Then both men emitted a sigh of relief. Not because they had reached Texas, but because they both knew the ford had been an excellent place for an ambush—too good—and the very fact that they had crossed the river without incident bothered them. Without a doubt, the Indians knew of their presence. So where were they?

As the horses heaved the cumbersome stagecoach onto dry ground, Peyton climbed to the roof and stood erect, sweeping the terrain in all directions, for, like Ben and Wright, he felt that the crossing had been too easy.

Captain Cramer opened the coach door and leaned out far enough to see John Wright sitting on his perch. "Pull up, driver. We need to stretch our legs a bit. Call of nature, an' all that . . ."

Wright leaned over the edge of the coach and glared down at the man. "Get back inside, you damned fool. If there's Indians watchin', an' I'm danged certain there is, we need to keep 'em wonderin' how many guns are inside this coach!" He looked over at Ben. "They're watchin'. I can feel 'em."

Ben shook his head, careful not to dispute John Wright's word again but certain that the driver needed his expert opinion. "Naw, Mista' John, they done been here an' gone. Somethin' drew 'em away. But they'll be back, an' when they find our tracks, you can d'pend on it that they'll commence huntin' us."

Wright pointed his finger at Ben. "Now, you jest shut up that kind of talk, Uncle. You'll scare them women half to death a-talkin' like that—an' you ain't seen nothin' till you see a pair of spooked women totin' guns!"

A minute later, however, Wright halted the coach amid a copse of cottonwood trees, "jest to give the horses a breather."

Ben laughed to himself as he climbed down from the perch. *White folk sure are a strange an' proudful lot. Wouldn't take a nigger's word for nothin', without makin' it appear to be their idea.*

The passengers piled out of the coach and scattered in pairs in search of a spot where they could relax with a degree of privacy.

Molly stood guard while Gabrielle performed her toilet. She fingered the heavy Colt revolver that Peyton had given her and wondered if the weapon would function properly without handles. She prayed it would not be necessary to find out.

When Gabrielle had straightened her skirts and made herself presentable, Molly offered her the pistol. The young woman eyed the weapon with distaste.

"I abhor firearms, Miss Klinner, and it saddens me that you people in the West seem to have such little regard for one another's welfare that you feel compelled to go armed."

Gabrielle was a constant source of surprise to Molly, and it showed on her face. Welfare indeed! "All I am asking, Gabrielle, is that you hold the gun while I make water. And the fact of the matter is, people in the West go armed because they hold one another's welfare in *high* regard."

Gabrielle Johnson caught up her skirts and rushed back the way they had come.

Molly watched her go, perplexed by the girl's absolute refusal to form any semblance of a bond with her. After all, they were the only women present amid a host of males, and they needed one another—if only for feminine reasons. Molly laid the pistol on the ground and hiked up her skirt.

Rucker caught Molly as she came out of the thicket. He blushed and stammered and finally removed his hat. Molly braced herself for a proposition.

Rucker looked at his boots, then nervously kicked at a stone. "I been thinkin' about what you said at the Wichita station, Miss Molly, an' . . . well, the truth is, I ain't got no idea how to court Miss Johnson . . . to win her favor. I was hopin' you might enlighten me."

Molly suppressed the urge to laugh aloud. Rucker wasn't asking for sex, he was asking for help. A sudden sympathy for the boy caused her to reach out and touch his hand.

"You are a fine, warm-hearted man, Fletcher, with a lot to offer a woman." Molly hesitated, wondering what she should tell him. Playing matchmaker was a new role for her. Haltingly she told Rucker what she thought most women looked for in a man. She finished with: "My advice, Fletcher, would be to talk to the girl. Some men talk because they have something to say, while others talk because they have to say something. Be the one with something to say, Fletcher."

Rucker donned his hat and grinned at her, assuring her he would try to remember all she had told him. As he struck off in a fast walk toward the coach in search of Gabrielle Johnson, Molly called to him, and he turned toward her.

"One more thing, Fletcher"—she smiled at him—"a little heroing every now and then never hurts a man's chances."

As Fletcher hastened away, Molly studied him thoughtfully. How would she have reacted had Fletcher made a sexual overture toward her? He was most definitely a handsome boy, and she liked him. She pursed her lips with uncertainty. Her past cried out, "yes, yes!" but the decent side of her—which had been surfacing quite often of late—shouted just as loudly in the negative.

Molly was the last to return to the coach, and John Wright complained to Ben that women were a nuisance, with their long dresses and petticoats and pantaloons. "Why, it ain't nothin' but a damned wonder them women don't piss all over theirselves afore they get all that foofaraw up an' then down!"

Ben was not listening; he was studying the skyline to the north, where black clouds were piling up on the horizon. "You reckon we ought t' be more concerned with them women's petticoats an' pantaloons than them there thunderheads over yonder, Mista' John?" He pointed across the broken countryside at a distant rainstorm that was rolling toward them like a herd of stampeding buffalo.

Wright cursed under his breath and slapped the reins against the horses' backs. "Get up! Get up there!" Then, as though he were passing the time of day, he turned a jaundiced eye to Ben. "I reckon we might ought t' mosey on over t' the way station without any further delay."

The truth was, John Wright had an innate fear of being caught in the open when jagged bolts of lightning dropped out of the sky like long serrated knife blades and plunged like liquid heat into the earth's belly, and he was especially nervous when he was perched atop a metal-laden stagecoach that could very easily act as a conduit for the fireballs.

Ben looked dubiously at the thunderstorm marching toward them. "I don't b'lieve I'd spare the whip none on this run, Mista' John."

Wright cracked his whip, and the horses leaned into their breast straps and collars. Another flick of his wrist sent the lash snaking out to sting the rump of the left-hand lead horse. The team broke into a brisk canter.

Rucker clambered down from the roof onto the seat beside Ben and braced his feet against the toeboard, and Peyton caught a good handhold on the luggage rail. A Butterfield pulled by six horses at full gallop was no easy ride.

Inside the coach, the thinly cushioned upholstery did little to absorb the jolts, bangs, and bumps of an iron-tired, stiff-sprung stagecoach at full speed. The passengers were propelled from one side of the interior to the other, and occasionally, because of a particularly severe shock, they were flung into the air to crash heavily against the seats or floorboard or one another.

After one such impact, the banker, unable to regain his balance, pawed at Gabrielle Johnson for support.

The young woman secured her hat to her head with one hand and disengaged the banker's arm from around her shoulder with the other. Her eyes penetrated the man, a very real threat that sent him scurrying for something more substantial to hang on to.

Molly laughed delightedly. It was a race they would never forget, one which they would boast about to their grandchildren: the day they tried to outrun the stormy wrath of God.

The coach careened on two wheels, then crashed down with a jolt that unseated the passengers and sent Molly Klinner crashing to the floorboard. As she scrambled to climb back onto the bench, a pain laced through the small of her back and spread like liquid fire to her pelvic region. The sudden realization that such a beating could very well bring on a miscarriage brought a cry of genuine terror to her throat. She clutched at the window rail for support.

The wall of rain hit the coach like a tidal wave, and lightning split the sky like a giant chopping ax. The interior of the coach grew as dark as night, adding a new terror to those inside. A bolt of lightning struck the earth not a hundred yards behind them, and the resounding clap of thunder sent the horses into a panic that nearly overturned the coach. Chaos prevailed.

It was a freezing winter storm that pelted those riding the top like liquid ice. In a matter of seconds, they were soaked to the skin, their lips blue with cold, their teeth chattering. The raindrops pulverized the road, turning it into a treacherous quagmire that sucked the strength from the powerful coach horses.

John Wright reluctantly drew the team to a walk. He wiped the rain out of his eyes, then winced as another bolt of lightning ripped into the earth a quarter of a mile to his left. He hunkered down on the seat, thankful that the depot was only another mile or so away. He envisioned a warm and dry room with hot food and coffee, and maybe even a hand or two of poker while they sat out the storm.

Wright lifted his brass bugle and blew into the rain. The sound was drowned out by a thunderclap that jarred the earth like an explosion, followed by a jagged spear of lightning that split the sky from zenith to horizon.

Wright blew another blast on his bugle, then grinned at Rucker. "That ought to let ol' Clete know we're a-comin'. He'll be plumb tickled to see us."

A gust of wind turned Rucker's hat brim up in front, exposing his face to the downpour. He squinted into the rain. "Hell, John! In this rain, the lead horses would have had a hard time hearin' that squeak you just blew."

Rucker elbowed Ben in the ribs, then laughed uproariously as John Wright puffed out his cheeks and blew a resonant note on his bugle.

Wright regarded Rucker peevishly. "I reckon he, by God, heard that!"

Now that the coach had slowed to a crawl, those inside the vehicle settled back into their seats and nursed their aches and bruises. Curses and moans came from every quarter, so no one paid the least attention to Molly Klinner when she turned her face to the wall, took her bottom lip between her teeth, and wept aloud as an unbearable pain surged through her abdomen from backbone to navel. The baby was moving—too much!

Molly laid her head against the backrest and forced her mind to concentrate on the way station they were approaching. Once they were safely inside the building, she would find a place with privacy and examine herself for hemorrhage. Her abdomen convulsed again, and she bit her lip harder. A salty, metallic taste soured her mouth.

Gabrielle watched Molly Klinner with interest. The woman was gripping the edge of the window so tightly that her fingers were bloodless, and her face was drawn and pinched with pain.

A smile turned up the corners of Gabrielle's lips. Perhaps Molly Klinner wasn't so brave and courageous after all? Perhaps her heroics had been nothing more than an attempt to capture

Peyton Lewis's attention? With the intent of upsetting Molly even more, Gabrielle touched her arm. "Are you quite all right, Miss Klinner? You don't look well at all."

Not trusting her voice for fear that it would betray her near panic, Molly nodded that she was fine. She sighed deeply, wanting nothing more than to arrive at the station and lie down to rest. Every muscle in her body quivered from the physical strain of attempting to protect her unborn child during the hectic run of the past five miles. She shuddered, thinking back to that day four years ago when she fell from the hay wagon. The pain in her abdomen after the fall was the same as now. Molly trembled even more violently; she would not survive a second miscarriage. She would not want to.

Molly turned her face away from Gabrielle and listened to the rain pelting the top and sides of the coach. Since her earliest memories, the drumming of raindrops on a rooftop or windowpane had had a lulling effect on her. She closed her eyes tightly and willed herself to concentrate on the downpour. Again John Wright piped a shrill blast on his bugle. It was a welcome sound to Molly because it meant they were nearing the station.

The bugling cut off in the middle of a note, and the silence, as Wright drew the horses to a standstill, was ear shattering. Even the rain seemed suddenly mute.

Molly tore open the side curtain and peered into the downpour. She could see nothing. Snatching off her hat, she forced her face through the narrow window. Pelting raindrops pounded her eyes closed, and when they opened, she wished to God they had not. A quarter of a mile away, a smoldering pile of charred debris hissed and popped in the driving storm.

Captain Cramer, with Lieutenant Pendleton right behind him, were the first men out of the coach. The unexpected sight brought them up short. Cramer eyed the ruins in disbelief. "For Christ's sake, there's nothing left. Nothing."

Molly dropped the window curtain into place. For a long moment she sat unmoving. Then, clutching her churning stomach, she climbed out of the coach and joined Cramer and Pendleton.

Joseph Robertson crawled out behind her and stared in

shock and horror at the scene. His chubby features drew into a mask of unforgiving accusation. "This is your doing, Miss Klinner, yours and Miss Johnson's. You two just had to push on. . . ." His gaze leaped to Gabrielle Johnson, who stood just inside the open door of the coach. "If it hadn't been for your vote, we wouldn't be here!"

"Shut up!" Molly's eyes were ablaze in her pale face. Droplets of rain clung to her eyelashes. She knuckled them away. Water streamed down her cheeks and dripped off her chin. "We're alive, Mr. Robertson—you, me, all of us! But the poor souls who worked that station aren't. They're dead . . . or worse. So you just shut your big mouth!"

Gabrielle gathered her cloak tightly about her shoulders and climbed out of the coach. Her singular vote to break the tie had been a proud moment in her life, something she had viewed as romantically courageous. Now that she was faced with the reality of that decision, her sentimental idealism dissipated like the smoke from the burned-out station, replaced by a fear so intense that it was actually nauseating. Icy rivulets of rainwater streamed down her neck into the V between her breasts. She could not have cared less; indeed, she welcomed the discomfort.

Molly, squinting against the downpour, raised her gaze to the top of the coach where Peyton stood on widespread legs, stonelike, as he evaluated the buildings that had been laid to waste in any direction one cared to look.

"Could it have been lightning, Mr. Lewis?" Even as Molly voiced the question, she knew in her heart that it had not been the elements.

Peyton gazed down at Molly. He had heard the banker vent his fear and frustration on her, and for her sake he wished it had been lightning. It was not; all the wishing in the world would not change that fact. He shook his head at her.

Gabrielle clung to the rear wheel of the coach as though she was afraid that if she released her hold on the iron tire, her knees would buckle and she would swoon. Although she did not fully understand or appreciate the enormity of what had transpired at the station, she knew it was a disaster—and the very sight of it sickened her.

Molly splashed through the ankle-deep mud and caught the girl's arm. "Are you ill, Miss Johnson?"

Gabrielle nodded. She covered her mouth with her hand as though she could physically hold back the bile that was rising in her throat.

Molly quickly ushered Gabrielle to the rear of the coach where they would be out of sight of the men and held the girl's shoulders as she bent at the waist and retched—again and again.

The four male passengers had already boarded the stage by the time Molly and Gabrielle climbed inside. Neither the army officers nor the businessmen so much as glanced at the two women, and a cold, accusing silence filled the coach.

The slow, steady crawl of the stagecoach as it moved toward the ravaged station reminded Molly of a funeral procession treading solemnly toward an open grave. She responded to the depressing thought by crossing her arms over her breasts and clasping herself in a tight embrace. She wished she would stop having such morbid notions.

Fifteen

When the stagecoach rolled to a halt in the way-station yard, there was not a solitary living soul, neither man nor beast, for as far as the eye could see. The absolute silence that shrouded the place was demoralizing, as though the hush were a wake for a funeral that had happened eons ago when the world was uninhabited by living organisms. Yet, if one listened hard enough, one could still hear the Indian war cries in the wind; if one looked long enough, one could see, with every crack of lightning that lit the sky, the flaming arrows speeding toward the depot; and if one stood still long enough, one could feel, with each roll of thunder, the churning of scores of unshod ponies' hooves charging toward the station house.

John Wright surveyed the destruction. It was worse close up. He turned to Ben. "Any idee how long ago they hit here?"

"Two, three days, maybe more."

Rucker stood up on the coach roof and scanned the smoldering ruins. The destruction appeared more recent than two or three days ago. "What makes you so certain, Uncle?"

"We would've seen the smoke on the horizon, Mista' Fletcher."

They knew Ben was right. Portions of the log house and barn still popped and sizzled, but the main fire had burned itself out before the rainstorm.

Peyton, Rucker, and Ben climbed down and, together with Cramer and the men from inside the coach, waded through the hock-deep mud to the charred ruins. The stench of burned wood, wet ashes, and charred flesh would have been overpowering had it not been downwind of the coach. Even with the breeze blowing in the opposite direction, when they approached the collapsed building, they were forced to press bandannas over their mouths to stifle the reeking fetidness.

Rucker reached out with his boot and nudged a blackened timber that protruded from the wreckage. It collapsed in on itself. "How many people do you reckon are underneath that heap?"

Captain Cramer eyed the rubble skeptically. The charred roof beams and timbers that had not fallen in appeared to be nothing more than a teetering pile of refuse that the slightest prodding would send crashing down on anyone foolish enough to venture near. Squatting down, he peered beneath the jumbled timbers. "If there's a body under there, I say we leave it be. It's too dangerous to try to dig down through a hodgepodge such as that. One of us might get hurt or killed."

Peyton walked to the rubble and caught hold of a blackened timber. Laying his shoulder against it, he dragged it from the building.

"If there are bodies under there, we're going to find them—and we are going to bury them." He turned to John Wright. "Can we unhitch one of the horses and use it to drag some of these bigger timbers free?"

Rucker groaned under his breath. Much as he hated to admit it, he agreed with Captain Cramer; it would be better to wait for dry weather, or at least for a sunny day, to investigate the destruction. However, if Peyton's mind was set on moving those timbers, he would do the job alone, if necessary. Rucker walked forward and took hold of a timber.

It was a surly group of men who lent their backs to the task of harnessing the coach horse to the slippery, blackened beams and dragging them out of the building. The downpour hampered their every move as if it took a personal delight in creating the most hazardous working conditions imaginable. To make matters worse, the lower portion of the log wall was still intact, forcing the workers to remove the debris through the opening that had been the front doorway.

Within minutes, the men were stained from head to toe with an ebony paste of watery ash and soot that burned their exposed skin like acid and saturated their clothing so thoroughly that even the protected flesh of their bodies, arms, and legs was dyed a blue-gray tint that would later refuse to be washed away, short of scrubbing the top layer of skin until it was raw.

The two soldiers worked with a passion, as though they were set on redeeming their manhood. The drummer and the banker, however, toiled listlessly, complaining the entire while as though physical labor was beneath their dignity.

Molly, who watched from the shelter of the coach, found herself viewing the banker and drummer through eyes filled with contempt. She had seen their type on many occasions at Miss Kirby's brothel. They belonged in the same category as the upright gentleman who visited a whore on Saturday night, then escorted his wife to church on Sunday morning and "amened" the loudest each time the preacher damned adulterers and fornicators.

Molly turned her attention to Gabrielle Johnson. The girl was mortified, and it showed in her every move and expression. Molly wondered why she was not elated by the young woman's trepidation. Why did she not experience a certain smugness of superiority? She felt neither of those sensations. Instead, she found herself pitying Gabrielle, for being out of her element, for her refusal to cope with it. "Welcome to the real West, Miss Johnson."

Gabrielle plucked at her skirt with nervous hands, balling the damp fabric into wads and then smoothing them out. Her lips trembled, and she looked frantically at Molly.

"Mr. Robertson tried to tell us it would be like this, Miss Klinner! He tried to warn us. . . ." Tears glistened on her pale cheeks. "We should have listened to him. We should have heeded his foreboding."

Molly laid her cheek tiredly against the leather upholstery and closed her eyes. She wished the girl would take heart and show a little fortitude. "If we had waited until it was safe to travel to Texas, Miss Johnson, or until Texas was safe for those who live there, none of us would have seen Texas in this lifetime."

"What good did it do us to come to Texas if we can't enjoy living here? I don't want to be afraid every day of my life. That's no way to live!"

Molly opened her eyes, surprised by the girl's remark. "Quite the contrary, Miss Johnson. It makes life very much worth living—each and every moment of each and every day."

Gabrielle slumped down into her seat, looking very much defeated. "For people like you perhaps, but I'm not like you. I am used to something better, something more genteel, more civilized. . . ."

Molly was suddenly impatient with her. What had happened to all that talk of excitement, all her grand ideas of being on her own, of seeing new country, new people?

"If I felt the way you do, Gabrielle, I would catch the first stagecoach that's eastbound and go back to where I came from, where life is safe and secure, where every tomorrow is like yesterday. I'd go back to Monroe, Michigan."

Gabrielle's face shattered, and she began to weep in earnest. "I am a coward, Miss Klinner. I don't want to be . . . but I cannot help it. I am so scared."

Molly was taken aback. Candor was not what she had anticipated. She had expected false bravado and insincere courage from the girl. She had gotten the truth. A flicker of admiration stirred in Molly's breast, for she had not lied to anyone since that day so long ago when she told Mr. Oller she was sixteen years old—and had paid a horrible price. As a result, she respected truth above all other human qualities.

Sympathy for Gabrielle softened Molly's face. She was prepared to confide to her that she was not alone in her fear, that they were all terrified, even the men. But Gabrielle's stinging retort, "I'm not like you" and the words "genteel" and "civilized" flashed through Molly's mind, causing the flame of empathy she had felt moments before to turn to ashes as cold and bitter as those of the burned-out station.

The banker opened the door and climbed into the coach. His clothes reeked of wet wood ashes, and water pooled on the floorboards around his muddy shoes. "We found a body. They're digging the grave now. The poor man was mutilated and scalped . . . a ghastly thing. Absolutely horrible."

Gabrielle pressed her fist against her mouth and closed her eyes tightly as though she might swoon.

Molly's head snapped toward the man. "We don't want to hear about it, Mr. Robertson. In fact, I would think you would be out there assisting them with the burying."

The banker settled heavily onto the seat. "They've got hands enough. I shouldn't even have been out there in the first place." He frowned at Gabrielle with tight-lipped implication. "I didn't vote for this. . . ."

Gabrielle withdrew her hand from her mouth and straightened. "Perhaps I am to blame for your being here, sir, but I am not to blame for your shortcomings. Furthermore, you are dripping water on my clothing."

Molly's eyebrows shot up in surprise, and she laughed appreciatively. Gabrielle had said it all—had said it nicely!

Robertson shifted his bulk toward Molly and fished a cigar from his vest pocket. "If you think it's so blasted funny, Miss Klinner, why don't *you* venture out into the rain and help them bury that body?"

Settling back in his seat, he struck a lucifer. A moment later the coach was filled with a heavy, pungent layer of smoke. Robertson eyed Molly from head to toe, then blew a stream of smoke toward the ceiling. "A good drenching wouldn't do you any harm, madam—and I'd bet a pretty penny you can't even remember the last time you touched soap and water!"

Molly recoiled as though she had been physically struck. She had given little thought to her appearance in months. Personal cleanliness had been a vanity that meant less than nothing to Caleb King, and water on the prairie had the same value as blood—it was too precious to squander on something as trivial as a bath. Not that she hadn't tried to bathe in the beginning, when he had first taken her to the soddie. She had washed her dress and mended it, then climbed into the rain barrel with a bar of lye soap and scrubbed herself clean. Caleb King had found her there, and had beaten her bloody with a leather saddle girth. From that day on, if and when Molly bathed, it was with leftover water in the dishpan. As time went by, she had ceased to bathe or care.

Molly looked questioningly at Gabrielle, praying that Robertson was exaggerating her condition. The girl dropped her eyes and blushed her embarrassment, not for Molly but for herself, for it had been she who had broached the subject to the banker not fifty miles back. Now she was sorry she had, for she would never have been so unkind as to have voiced her complaints openly for Molly to hear.

Molly lifted her chin. "My personal appearance is none of your business, sir, and you are a clod for mentioning it." Even to her, the words rang weak with uncertainty.

Robertson sucked his cigar, enjoying her discomfort. "We have to ride with you, Miss Klinner." He flicked an ash onto the floor. "So I believe that makes it my business. Furthermore, I'm not the only one who's complaining." He scowled pointedly at Gabrielle.

If Robertson had expected Molly to draw herself into a fetal position and wail out her humiliation, he was sorely mistaken. Molly's lips drew into a determined line, and a slow-burning anger smoldered in the depths of her eyes like live coals. Raising her heavy Colt revolver, she pointed it directly between his eyes. "Then don't ride in the same stagecoach with me, you miserable son of a bitch. In fact, I suggest you get out now!"

Surprise caused the cigar to slip from Robertson's open mouth. As it tumbled down his vest, sparks showered onto the lap of his trousers. With a howl, he sprang erect and beat at the embers that smoldered into the wet fabric of his suit. Pointing an accusing finger at Molly, he opened his mouth to protest. Molly cocked the pistol. Whatever choice words he had intended were swallowed, and he scrambled quickly out the door into the downpour.

Gabrielle Johnson, refusing to meet Molly's eyes, reached over and laid her hand on the coach door. Should she leave also? No, that would not be necessary. Robertson had not called her by name, so Molly was unaware that it was she who had complained. Quietly, she closed the coach door.

Molly laid the pistol beside her and collapsed back onto the seat. Robertson's comment reeled through her mind. How did she look? She had not so much as seen her reflection in a looking glass since Miss Kirby was killed and her house burned. Suddenly Molly longed to curl up in the darkest corner of the coach and . . . do what? For a moment she could not define the sensation that churned in her breast. Then it hit her. She wanted to do exactly what the banker had expected her to do—weep with embarrassment and shame—for all at once, it became abundantly clear to her that when one is forced to live with an animal for three long years, one becomes like an animal.

When had she stopped caring? When had she, as a person, ceased to matter? From somewhere distant, beyond her mind's realm, Molly heard the sound of the downpour—nature's bathhouse—and she ached to rip the soiled clothing from her body and stand naked in the drenching rain, and glory in the knowledge that the cold, life-giving water was cleansing her of everything she had become. Raising the side curtain, she peered into the rain and mouthed a silent vow: "When I get home, I will never again be dirty. Never!"

Molly dropped the window curtain into place and faced Gabrielle Johnson. Her eyes were dry.

Fifty yards beyond the burned-out ruins, the men stood in the downpour and lowered the body of the station agent into the shallow grave they had scooped out with mud ladles. There was not so much as a blanket for a coffin nor a sheet for a shroud.

They raked the mud into the pit, and Peyton fetched a piece of scorched timber from the rubble and drove it into the ground to mark the spot. The men removed their hats and bowed their rain-plastered heads. No one spoke.

Peyton looked at the muddy mound that marked the man's

final resting place and wondered if the agent had a family. Strange that he should suddenly bring up the question of family. He had deliberately erased that word from his vocabulary on August 14, 1863, when his mother and the twins had, like the man they had just buried, died violent, unnecessary deaths.

Peyton looked at the men around him. "Does anyone know if the agent has kinfolk, someone we could notify?"

William Beecher waved Peyton's question aside. "Forget about his family, Lewis, and think about us. What are we going to do now?"

Peyton's fingers balled into tight fists, and flashes of blinding light burst behind his eyelids as the drummer's words—"forget about his family"—raged through his brain. Suddenly it was 1863 all over again, when someone, perhaps a group such as this, had stood around the graves of his family and scoffed at the idea of notifying him, indeed, had made no effort to contact him at all, not then, not ever. He had read about his family's deaths weeks later, in a Kansas City newspaper.

A wave of white-hot hatred washed over Peyton, drowning all other emotions. Without his even being aware of his actions, his fist, sounding like a crack of lightning, exploded against William Beecher's chin. The man fell flat on his back, spread-eagle in the mud. Had it not been for the rain pelting his upturned face, Beecher would undoubtedly have been rendered unconscious.

Peyton, indifferent to the anger, fear, and surprise that filled the faces of the men around him, challenged each of them with a deadly stare. "I asked you people if the hostler had a family."

John Wright, wondering what had come over Peyton, shrugged. "That weren't ol' Clete we buried. It was a young feller who I ain't never seen before. I'll notify the company, an' they'll make the necessary inquiries."

Beecher pushed himself to a sitting position and squinted up at Peyton. "You're loony, Lewis. You should be locked away from normal people."

Peyton stared at the distant hills, barely visible through the downpour. Perhaps he *was* crazy. He had lost control a moment ago, but only he, Peyton Lewis, was aware of how truly dangerous that unguarded instant had been. He had wanted to kill William Beecher.

Joseph Robertson assisted Beecher to his feet and scraped the mud from the man's soiled clothing. "You've ruined Bill Beecher's suit, Lewis, and probably fractured his jaw! Damn you! You and them stupid women got us into this dilemma. Now, instead of trying to get us out of it, all you seem capable of doing is beating up an innocent man."

Rucker slipped his wounded arm out of its sling and shook his fist under the banker's nose. "Peyton ain't the only one who can whip ass around here, Robertson. One more word out of you an' I'll give you a 'stupid' fat lip."

John Wright stepped between Rucker and Robertson, but it was Peyton he regarded warily. "Call off your dogs, boys. Fightin' amongst ourselves ain't helpin' our dilemma. An' Robertson's right; we ought to be tryin' to figure out what to do next." When Peyton nodded his agreement, Wright summarized his thoughts: "We know three things for certain. We know the Injuns was here; we know they didn't cross the Red River at that ford five miles back; an' we know they're sure as hell still out there somewheres." He gestured toward the west with a sweep of his hand. "They're probably sittin' out this storm in a sheltered ravine 'tween here an' Gainesville, which, as I recollect, is nigh onto twelve, maybe fifteen miles due south of here."

"Fifteen miles!" Beecher brushed his rain-drenched hair off his forehead with a muddy hand and peered in the direction John Wright had indicated. "There's no way we can cross fifteen miles of open country and not be seen by Indians. I demand that we hurry back across the river to the closest way station and wait for an escort."

John Wright nodded passively. "That's a practical suggestion. But there's somethin' else to consider while we're considerin'." He looked each man in the eye to be certain he had their attention. "Those folks at Gainesville may not know the Injuns are already out in force. I'd sure hate t' think those good people might be caught by surprise, like this here station was. . . ." His voice trailed off pointedly.

Beecher shifted his feet uncomfortably; they made sucking

sounds in the mud. He looked away, unable to meet Wright's gaze. "I still say it's suicide to go on, John."

Joseph Robertson agreed: "Why should we put our lives in peril to warn a town of an Indian attack that may never take place . . . or may have already happened? For all we know, the savages may have burned Gainesville to the ground."

Ben stepped forward and doffed his hat. The rain plastered his thick, wavy hair to his skull. "Mista' John, I don't hardly b'lieve there'll be no goin' back. After a rain like this un, that river'll be stagecoach deep. I b'lieve, howsomever, I see a way out o' this here dilemma. If'n yo' would loan me one o' your hosses, I'd make a sojourn down the road a piece an' see if I could pick up a remnant of a track or maybe a sign or two that would tell us which way that war party was headin'."

Wright pursed his lips, considering Ben's proposal. He shook his head, and the look he shot Ben was peppered with skepticism. "Ain't goin' to be no tracks or signs after this rain, an I ain't lettin' none of my horses out of my sight. Truth is, I'm still somewhat suspicious of you, Uncle. No offense, but I am."

Ben grinned at Wright. "I don't take no offense in that, Mista' John. I'm kind o' like that myself. I learnt a long time ago, a man can't trust women, tenderfoots, an' strangers. So I can't hardly find fault with yo' fo' not trustin' yo' hosses to a nigger. Naw, sir, I can't."

Wright thumbed rainwater from the end of his nose and wiped his hand on his sopping coat. "My sentiments exactly, Uncle."

Ben held up his hand. "Howsomever, Mista' John, that great mountain man, Hugh Glass, oncet tolt me, 'Before yo' go into a canyon, Ben, know how yo'll get out!' Well, sir, I'd say we was at the mouth of a canyon."

Ben justified his argument by pointing out that it was absolutely pertinent they know for certain which way the Indians were traveling. If they were moving south toward Gainesville, then the town should be warned; if they were riding north toward the Oklahoma Territory, then the stagecoach could travel on to Gainesville at its leisure.

Captain Cramer listened with interest to Ben's conjecture.

The part about searching for signs made sense. The trouble with the scenario was that it had been proposed by the wrong man, and he, as a senior military officer of the United States Army, intended to rectify that oversight immediately. Drawing himself to full height, he squared his shoulders. "I'm absolutely against turning this nigger loose with one of our horses. Hell, John, he might just up and make a run for it—then where would we be? I'll commandeer a horse and scout out that war party myself."

Wright scowled at the captain. "I don't recall you or your army ownin' any shares in the Butterfield stagecoach line, Cramer. So I don't reckon you'll be *commandeerin'* any of these here horses an' goin' no place."

Rucker was running out of patience. To him, it seemed the height of stupidity for grown men to be standing in a downpour arguing about horses. "Whatever the hell you gents aim to do, hop to it! This jawin' ain't dryin' me out none, an' my shot-up arm is startin' to ache, an' my—"

John Wright glared at Rucker. "Pipe down, for Christ's sake! A man can't hear himself think with you a-jabberin' like a guinea hen!"

Peyton agreed with Rucker; they had wasted enough time in useless conversation. He nodded to Ben. "If you were to make an educated guess, Uncle, where would you say those Indians are right now?"

"I s'pect, boss, them Comanches has pitched camp in an arroyo some five miles t' the west . . . but that ain't fo' certain. They could jest as easy be camped in the middle o' the road."

The word "Comanches" caught John Wright's attention. He had fought Comanches on two occasions and did not want to do it a third time; they were very probably the most bloodthirsty group of savages on the North American continent. "What makes you think them Injuns were Comanche, Uncle?"

Ben walked to the ruin, where scores of arrows jutted from the collapsed timbers. Breaking one off at the head, he returned to the group and pointed to rings painted on the shaft. "The markin's on this here arra is Comanche—which is good an' bad."

John Wright thought Ben had taken leave of his senses, and said so.

Ben merely nodded his agreement with Wright's assessment, then went on as though the man had not spoken. "The good part is that the Comanche don't like wet weather; it stretches their sinew bowstrings. So when it's rainin', they go t' ground an' hole up like a badger. The bad part is, it means they're more'n likely still around here some'rs close . . . an' they prob'ly got scouts out watchin' our every move."

Rucker scoffed at Ben's notion about bows and arrows. "Why, any fool knows Indians have guns, Uncle, an' probably plenty of 'em."

Ben shook his head. "Naw, Mista' Fletcher. I'd say from the number o' arras stickin' in things 'round here that this p'ticular war party ain't got nothin' much but ol'-time weapons—bows an' arras an' spears, an' maybe a wore-out trade musket or two. Unless, o' course, they was some weapons here at the station."

Captain Cramer was growing angrier by the minute. How dare this uppity black man speak and act as though he were an expert on savages! "How do you know it was a war party, nigger? And what makes you so sure this wasn't a small band of Shawnee or Chickasaw out hunting buffalo?"

Ben heard the sarcasm in the captain's voice, and it annoyed him. He had already pointed out the markings on the arrow shaft. He studied the man, undecided as to how he should answer. Finally he shrugged. "It's a sho'-nuff war party, Cap'n, sir, an' a big one at that. I can tell by a passel o' things. . . ."

Cramer's face twisted into a sneer. "Just how in hell can you tell this wasn't a hunting party? Speak up, boy!"

Ben wished that he had said nothing. He shuffled his feet, shrugged, and stared at the ground. He was well aware of the possible consequences should he, a black man, make a fool of a white army officer. He had witnessed such an exchange during his sojourn in the Federal Army. The black soldier had been hanged.

Ben glanced at the faces that surrounded him. They, too, were awaiting his answer; they were not friendly. "Well, mista' cap'n, sir. If'n it had been a huntin' party, it would have had women an' chillun with it. A Injun man, he don't do no skinnin' an' butcherin'; he lets the womenfolk do that. Naw, sir. Injuns never go on a big hunt without they have their womenfolk along." Ben shook his head to emphasize his point.

It chafed Cramer's professional pride that an illiterate black man should have more knowledge of Indians than he, so he continued to press Ben for information as he searched for an opportunity to show him up for the fool he surely must be. "What makes you so certain there weren't any squaws with this party?"

Ben glanced at Peyton, imploring him to intervene, but Peyton gazed back at him without expression. He, too, was curious about Ben's belief that it was a full-fledged war party.

Ben sighed, unsure of how he should proceed. "The gentleman we done buried was shot plumb full o' arras, an' he was scalped. If'n there had been women along, that po' man would'a been skint out an' butchered like a hog. Why, there wouldn't even been 'nuff o' him left fo' us t' bury. Naw, mista' cap'n, sir, it weren't no huntin' party 'cause . . . well, the truth is, there ain't nothin' t' hunt down here in this part o' Texas this time o' year. The buffalo done moved west fo' the winter an' ain't returned yet."

Lieutenant Pendleton, embarrassed by his captain's refusal to admit his total ignorance of the West, attempted to come to his superior's rescue. "Could it have been a horse-stealing foray that attacked this station, Uncle? The relief horses for the coach are gone. Hell, it was probably just a bunch of Cherokee or Pawnee out of Oklahoma looking for livestock."

When Ben remained silent, the captain saw that as a good sign and immediately took the offensive. "The lieutenant's right, ain't he, nigger? You've been lying all along. It was nothing but a band of Cherokee horse thieves."

Ben's hands trembled as he struggled to control the mounting resentment that threatened to send him clawing for the captain's throat. He willed himself to meet the man's eyes.

"Naw, sir, mista' cap'n, sir. If'n it had been Cherokee or Creek, or any o' them tame tribes of the Five Civilized Nations, they wouldn't have burnt that stagecoach in yonder barn." Ben

pointed at the remains of the burned-out building where the
skeletal frame of a coach could be seen. "They'd o' stole that
coach an' made a wagon out'n it. An' before yo' ast if'n it could
have been Apaches, the answer is naw, sir, it weren't them neither. If'n it had been Apaches, they'd o' took that agent alive an'
burnt him over a slow fire for three or four days. It was Comanche, no doubt 'bout it."

Ben turned abruptly to John Wright and asked if he could
speak to him in private. The others watched as Ben led the driver a short distance away, then leaned close to his ear and spoke
rapidly. When they walked back to the group, John Wright had
a gleam of amusement in his eye.

"I've decided t' cut loose a horse an' send Uncle Ben out t'
scout around an' see which way them Comanche went. The rest
of us will stay put till he gets back."

Peyton appraised Ben anew. The man was a constant surprise, and most assuredly a master at argument to have per-
suaded a hard crust like John Wright to relinquish one of his
precious horses. Still, Peyton was reluctant to simply dispatch
Ben, an unknown entity whom they had picked up on the roadside, to spy out an enemy.

"Cut out two horses, John. I'll ride along with Uncle Ben."

Ben shot Peyton a look that plainly accused him of unnecessary concern. "If'n it's all the same t' yo', boss, I would p'fer t'
do my scoutin' alone. Yo' can trust me."

A half-smile touched Peyton's lips. "But I don't."

Captain Cramer, still bristling from his verbal trouncing by
Ben, sided quickly with Peyton. "Lewis is right! We don't know
this man from Adam's off ox! Hell, he might even have an al-
liance with the Comanches."

Ben's patience was wearing thin, and it showed in the frown
that creased his forehead as he challenged the grim-faced white
men surrounding him. "I ain't got no—whatever that word
was—with no Comanche!" He considered informing them that
he did not trust white folks any more than they trusted black
people; that a search for hostile Indians should be done by a
professional tracker; and that, unless he missed his guess, these
greenhorns, with the exception of John Wright, would actually

hamper his ability to find the Comanche—or worse yet, get him killed in the offing. He said nothing.

Peyton glanced at the overcast sky and wondered how many hours of daylight were left; not many, he would guess. He struck out in a fast walk toward the stagecoach to cut the two lead horses out of the team and get them saddled.

John Wright fell in beside him, and as they walked, he informed Peyton that the coach and its passengers were his first priority, and, in his estimation, he needed his best pistol and rifle shooters and coolest heads to protect the women and the coach. Without waiting for Peyton's opinion, Wright turned and shouted for Rucker to get a horse saddled and accompany Ben on his sojourn.

Rucker groaned and swiveled his gaze to the stagecoach, where Gabrielle and Molly were sitting out the storm. A frown dented his forehead, for when they made night camp, he had intended to talk with Miss Johnson about her stay in Austin. Rucker sighed through his teeth. John Wright sure as hell had thrown a chock into that wheel.

When Rucker sloshed off through the mud to unhitch the team, Wright instructed Peyton to advise Rucker to keep a close eye on Ben. "I jest ain't real certain about that nigger yet, Lewis. No, sir. Not real certain."

When Ben ambled past, John Wright fell in beside him, and together they headed for the coach. He peered at Ben out of the corner of his eye. "Uncle, I didn't want to say nothin' in front of those other folks, but that weren't Hugh Glass who made that statement 'bout goin' into a canyon; it was Kit Carson."

Peyton waded through the quagmire to the coach, where Rucker had already stripped the harness from a horse, thrown his saddle onto the animal, and was pulling the cinch tight. Peyton told him what Wright had said about Ben, then added that they would wait twenty-four hours for him to return. If he wasn't back by then, they would take their chances and head toward Gainesville—and pray that the town was still standing.

Rucker slammed his knee into the horse's belly, knocking the wind from its diaphragm. Before the animal could take another deep breath, he had the cinch drawn and tied. He looked across the horse's back and watched Ben break the other lead horse out of its harness. The idea of going off with a black man into a wild and unknown countryside did not sit well with him, and he certainly did not like the part of Peyton's speech about being out in the wilds for twenty-four hours. Lastly, he did not like leaving Gabrielle Johnson alone with no one to protect her.

Rucker, in a temper, ran his hand angrily down the horse's flank to gauge the tightness of the cinch. The animal shied away from him, and Rucker yanked him back into control. "These goddamned animals ain't worth a shit, Peyton. They're plumb nervous about the weather an' tuckered out to boot. I sure as shootin' hope we don't have to run 'em, 'cause if we do, me an' Ben's goin' to be in a pickle."

Peyton patted the horse's neck, then gave Rucker a leg up. "Kill them if you have to, Fletcher. Just find out where those Comanches are, and get back here in one piece."

Rucker rode the horse up next to the coach. "Miss Molly, Miss Johnson, are you in there?" When Molly cracked the blind, Rucker bent low and peered past her into the darkened interior, hoping to catch a glimpse of Gabrielle. He longed to watch her eyes when he told her he was riding ahead to scout for Indians. Why, she would probably think he was a hero, just like Molly had told him to be.

Disappointed because he could not see Gabrielle, Rucker straightened in the saddle. "They're sendin' me out to scout for Injuns, an' I was wonderin', Miss Molly, if you would mind if I borrowed your Henry rifle?"

Molly watched Rucker from the dark interior of a coach that had suddenly become a refuge for her. Ten minutes ago, nothing on earth would have stopped her from jumping to the ground and giving him a grand send-off hug. Now, all she longed to do was to be alone with her thoughts, to sort out this new, humiliating discovery about herself.

She looked at Gabrielle, huddled on the far side of the seat, and dropped her voice. "Why don't you step outside and give Fletcher a good-luck kiss? It's what he wants, you know."

Gabrielle shook her head. "I don't kiss strange men, Miss Klinner, and certainly not someone as wild and unruly . . . and unsophisticated as Fletcher Rucker."

Molly looked quickly at Rucker, hoping he had not heard the girl's reply. His young, anxious face indicated that he had not. "Take the gun, Fletcher . . . and come back safely."

Rucker leaned from the saddle and again peered into the stage. He wished Gabrielle would at least acknowledge his presence—or his leaving.

After a long, embarrassing interval, Rucker pivoted the horse and rode to the rear of the coach, where he caught up Molly's rifle. Twisting in the saddle, he gazed one last time at the window, hoping that Gabrielle would raise the curtain. It did not so much as flutter.

Rucker spurred the horse into a hard canter. Ben was already two hundred yards ahead on the road toward Gainesville.

John Wright snatched off his hat and slammed it angrily against his leg. "Don't be runnin' that horse, Fletcher! It's worn out!"

Rucker rode on as though he had not heard.

Wright shook his head at the boy's inconsideration, then walked hump-shouldered against the rain to the rear of the coach, where he unlashed the leather boot cover and shoved aside the drummer's heavy trunk in search of the wooden crate that each stagecoach carried for emergencies. He lifted the box to his shoulder and struck out hurriedly for the only building still standing; a tall, split-log shed, open on both ends so that a stagecoach could be driven into it, repaired or unloaded, and driven out. Somehow it had been spared from total destruction.

Wright chose a spot in the middle of the building to set up camp. Using sticks and debris gathered from a corner of the room the rain had not penetrated, he struck a lucifer and in short order had a fire blazing. He pried the lid off the wooden crate and lifted out a battered coffeepot, which he carried to the back doorway and filled to the brim with water that poured from the shake-shingle eaves.

When he turned again to the fire, Molly Klinner was there.

She had taken a frying pan from the box and was attempting to grease its interior with an unwieldy four-pound slab of salt pork. She kept her eyes on the skillet when he approached. "I could do this much easier, John, if I could simply slice off a small piece of the fat."

Wright heard the dull tonelessness in her voice. Why had she avoided looking at him? Hell, Molly Klinner was usually a happy-go-lucky person not prone to mood swings or self-pity. Handing her his bone-handled skinning knife, he cocked his head to one side and squinted at her through his bushy eyebrows. Something was certainly amiss; the girl kneeling before him was not at all the steadfast young woman who had stopped a gun battle not only at French's station but also at the Wichita depot. Indeed, Molly Klinner was the only passenger of the lot, besides Peyton Lewis, whom he could depend upon to be the same person day in and day out.

Molly sliced a strip of fat from the bacon and rubbed its grease into the pan. From habit, she wiped the knife blade on her skirt. Realizing that such acts were what had triggered the banker's remarks regarding her slovenliness, she snatched up her skirt and inspected the rancid stain.

When she realized John Wright was watching her, she smoothed out her skirt and busied herself with the skillet, carefully avoiding his eyes.

It dawned on Wright that Molly's odd behavior appeared to be the product of a deep humiliation. He scanned the room for the culprit, but they were alone in the shed. Wright scowled at Molly; surely he was not her problem? If that were true, then he was disappointed in her. Hell, he was old enough to be her grandfather. Wright stood up and walked to the doorway of the shed, which faced the coach. No one was in sight. "Where's the other passengers, Molly?"

"They're in the coach, John. All but Mr. Lewis. I think he's out at the corral."

"Well, if they think they're stayin' dry in that coach, they're whistlin' in the wind. The roof on that Butterfield leaks worse than this shed."

He turned and pierced her with a hard stare. "You want to tell me why you're uncomfortable bein' in here alone with me, Molly?"

Molly shifted uneasily under his penetrating gaze. She liked and trusted John Wright, but not enough to confide in him that she had left the stagecoach because, for the first time in her life, she was ashamed of her person and attire. No, she would not endow him with that information. "I don't think staying dry has anything to do with their preferring to stay in the coach, John."

Wright squinted at the coach. It stood forlorn in its solipsism, with water pouring in sheets down its sides. "What's eatin' at their craw?"

Molly fidgeted, and changed the subject. "You wouldn't happen to have a mirror in that crate, would you, John?" She pointed at the wooden box of emergency supplies.

Wright's face took on an owlish look of surprise. "A mirror? You mean one of them lookin'-glass things that women use to primp with?"

Molly nodded.

"Naw, missy, I sure ain't. I ain't never knowed nobody who needed one. Years ago we traded 'em to the Injuns, but we never used 'em. Why, to tell the truth, I ain't never rightly hankered to see what I resembled."

Molly was disappointed, more so than she would have admitted. For nearly three long years, she, like John Wright, had not considered her appearance important—until today. Now, all of a sudden, it was the most compelling factor in her life.

Wright set the coffeepot at the edge of the flames. "Why don't you see if'n that eastern woman has got one o' them lookin' glasses?"

Molly shook her head. "I don't even want her to know I inquired about one."

Wright shrugged. The intricacies of the female mind were out of his realm. "What's a lookin' glass got t' do with them folks who are holed up in the coach?"

"I suppose it's because I pulled a gun on that fat banker a while ago . . ."

John Wright squatted down beside her. "Why'd you pull a gun on Robertson, Molly?"

When she looked into his eyes, she was startled by the very real concern that was plainly visible in his gaze, and she knew without a doubt if she so much as hinted that the banker had insulted her, John Wright would consider himself honor-bound to defend her reputation and would in all probability horsewhip the man. She almost laughed at the word "reputation." What reputation? If only John knew the truth.

Molly was suddenly miserable and wished she could retract her statement, but it was too late; Wright was demanding an answer. She grinned sheepishly at him and told him a portion of the truth.

"Robertson made a casual remark about my . . . dirty clothes . . . and it upset me, John. I just wanted to see for myself what kind of shape I was in. That's why I asked about a mirror."

Wright settled back on his haunches and studied Molly from head to toe. "Well, you're somewhat soiled, an' that's a natural fact." His honest scrutiny brought a quick blush to her cheeks. She was not "somewhat soiled"; she was somewhat filthy! But Wright was going on: "An' while I ain't never seen one, mind you, I recollect a minin' feller who told me once that the finest diamonds in the world is found in mudbanks. Yes, ma'am, them beautiful gems is hid 'neath a layer of mud an' clay."

Molly flinched at his comparison, and Wright shook his head irritably. "Durn it, Molly, you're the diamond, not the mud! All you got to do is wipe that film of wet dust of'n you an' everybody will see the sparkle."

Molly shook her head woefully. "I'm no diamond, John."

For the first time in his sixty-odd years, John Wright wished he were an educated man. Not once during that long, unpretentious duration had a woman ever needed his expertise. Now that one had called on him, he most certainly did not want to let her down because of his ignorance. Wright chose his words carefully.

"Miss Molly, a snake-bit man is afeared of a rope. Now, I ain't got no notion why, but I'd say somebody done snake-bit you concernin' your looks. But they's one thing for certain: we ain't never goin' to know if'n you're a diamond 'less'n you wash off the mud!"

"There's nothing under there, John, nothing that sparkles, anyway."

"Well, you had me some kind o' fooled. I never took you for no yeller-bellied quitter."

"I'm no yellow-bellied quitter, John. You just don't understand. . . ."

Wright waved her dejection aside. "I don't know much about women an' ain't never claimed to. But I do know somethin' about prime horseflesh, an' when you git right down to the brass tacks of it, one of God's critters is purty much like another. Anyhow, like I was sayin', I've seen some mighty intelligent folks overlook some fine horseflesh 'cause the critter was starved half to death an' uncurried." He studied her critically. "It 'pears to me, young lady, that all you need is a bite o' food an' a little combin' out."

Wright stood up and stretched the kinks out of his muscles. "Speakin' of horseflesh, I've got some that needs attendin' to." He struck out through the downpour toward the coach, where the horses stood miserably in their traces, waiting to be unhitched.

Molly ran to the edge of the shed. "Do you want some help with the horses, John?"

He hunched his shoulders against the downpour and waved her back into the building.

Molly sighed. She wished she had thanked him for his kindness, but she had not. As she turned back into the shed, she noticed the stream of water that rushed from the eaves. What was it John Wright had said about a diamond—about washing off the mud?

Molly cupped her hands under the runoff and splashed the icy water over her face. It took her breath away. Again she drenched her face. Then again and again. With all her rinsing, however, her skin still felt grimy to her touch.

Molly scooped up a handful of gritty mud and scrubbed her hands beneath the stream. When she examined them, to her disappointment, she found that in spite of the industrious scouring that left her skin nearly raw, an accumulation of dirt and grease was still embedded in her pores and under her fingernails.

Molly's hand flew to her cheek. Was her face equally abhorrent?

When she walked to the fire and squatted on her heels to dry her hands over the flames, she thought about the past years with Caleb King and wondered what day, what hour, what minute, she had ceased to care about herself. She pondered that, aware that a person reached the bottom of the pit of depravity when he or she lost that final thread of personal pride and dignity. Yet she, and she alone, had allowed that to happen, so gradually that she had not even noticed. *Yes, that's how it works . . . like a creeping shadow, so slow and easy and silent that you don't even realize that daylight is gone until it's too dark to see.*

Sixteen

Rucker and Ben topped a hill two miles west of the burned-out station and drew their horses to a halt. A long valley spread out before them, and they studied it carefully, especially the shadowed places where the driving rain and mist cloaked the area in a shroud that was visually impenetrable. They looked for movement, for horses, for a fire. There was nothing.

Rucker twisted in the saddle and surveyed their back trail. The stagecoach and the pile of rubble that had once been the station house were lost in the mist. Rain pelted the nape of his neck and funneled down his spine. He shivered and pulled his hat brim lower. He wondered how Gabrielle Johnson was faring, and wished he was there to watch over her. That was a new sensation for him, feeling protective of a woman. He enjoyed the feeling.

He cut his eyes to Ben, blaming him for his being out on the prairie in the driving rain, instead of with Gabrielle in the warmth of a campfire.

Rucker cupped his hands around his mouth so he could be heard above the storm. "What'd you say to John Wright to make him change his mind about the horses, Uncle?"

Ben crossed his hands over his saddle horn. He had been

waiting for that question. He leaned toward Rucker. "All I tolt him, Mista' Fletcher, was that them Injuns knowed where we was, but we didn't rightly knowed where they was. So they had the 'vantage. An' I reminded him that while I . . . yo' an' me was out scoutin' t' find out where them Injuns was, his hosses would be restin', an that four fresh hosses pullin' a stagecoach could cover more ground 'n a hurry than six wore-out ones. An' then, too, I 'splained to him that if'n he had t' make a run for it, he better feed them passengers, 'cause there mightn't be another chance t' eat for quite a spell. But what done changed his mind was when I tolt him that Gov'nor Sam Houston once tolt me, he sez, 'Ben, don't yo' never 'proach no longhorn bull from the front, no long-eared mule from the rear . . . or a fool from any d'rection!"

Ben grinned at Rucker. "I tolt Mista' John that I knowed he weren't no longhorn, or no mule, but I weren't too sure 'bout that there third thing. . . ."

Rucker threw up his hands in resignation. "All right, that's enough! You sure are mouthy, Ben. No wonder John Wright sent you out here. He probably did it just t' get some peace of mind."

Ben laughed good-naturedly. "Might be some truth t' that, Mista' Fletcher. But yo' have t' admit, it's better for yo' an' me t' be out here 'stead o' them two soldier boys, 'cause they 'bout filled that 'fool' part Gov'nor Houston was speakin' o' t' the brim, don't yo' 'gree?"

Rucker sobered, not certain he liked Ben talking that way about white men—even if they were Yankees. He studied the terrain that stretched out before them. The rain was falling in heavy sheets that traveled diagonally across the landscape, obliterating nearly everything in sight. Ben had been right when he told the men at the station that on miserable days such as this, the Indians holed up. Hell, this was the kind of day anybody with any sense ought to hole up.

"You really think the Comanche are between us an' Gainesville, Ben?" When Ben nodded, Rucker frowned at him. "What makes you so confounded certain them Indians didn't jest up an' hightail it out of the country, like Lieutenant Pendleton said?"

Ben wiped rainwater off the bridge of his nose, then drew his hat brim lower over his forehead in an attempt to shield his eyes from the crosswinds. "Them Comanche are 'tween here an' Gainesville, take my word fo' it, Mista' Fletcher. Course, there's the chance they's already burnt Gainesville t' the ground." He shrugged indifferently. "Like I tolt Mista' John, we need t' know somethin' fo' certain." He grinned at Rucker. "I don't hanker fo' yo' white folks t' get this ol' nigger's ass staked out on top o' no anthill 'cause of your natural ignorance. Mista' Fletcher, we *got* t' know p'cisely where them Injuns is at."

Rucker touched a spur to his horse's flank and started down the slope. He had only gone a short distance when he drew rein and peered over his shoulder at Ben, who was following a short distance behind. "Do you carry a gun, Uncle?"

Ben patted his heavy haversack. "That's a mighty foolish question t' ask a Texican, Mista' Fletcher."

Rucker stared pointedly at Ben. "Foolish, Uncle, would be us gettin' into a shootin' ruckus with them redskins—an' then findin' out you didn't have a shooter!"

Ben laughed and nodded his agreement. "I got me a fine Walker's Colt with three extra cylinders loaded full round, Mista' Fletcher." Again he patted his haversack.

Rucker raised his eyebrows in surprise. A Walker Colt was supposedly the heaviest, largest revolver that Sam Colt manufactured, weighing more than four and a half pounds. Most men preferred a lighter, smaller sidearm, but if Ben enjoyed carrying a hand cannon, that was his business. Rucker touched his heel to his horse's flank, and trotted the animal down the incline.

Molly looked up from the coffeepot that was just beginning to boil and watched Gabrielle enter the shed. The young woman stopped just inside the doorway and removed her dripping traveling cloak. She looked miserable; her pert little hat was drenched and sat askew on her head. The pheasant feather drooped down across her eyes and clung to her cheek, mingling with the dark ringlets that hung limply against the sides of her face. Her expensive suit, in spite of the protective cloak, clung damply to her body, and the hem of her skirt, where it had dragged in the mud, molded itself to her legs in an unladylike fashion that left little to the imagination. Her pumps were ruined beyond redemption.

Molly knew she should feel dreadful because of the girl's misfortune, but, in truth, she did not. In fact, she experienced a certain perverse satisfaction in Gabrielle's disheveled, muddy appearance, and she wondered what Peyton would think of her fashionable attire now.

Gabrielle saw the spark of pleasure that lit Molly's eyes and glared her resentment through dripping lashes. "If you had mentioned that you were leaving the coach to do the cooking, Miss Klinner, I would have joined you. I assure you, I do at least know how to cook. Furthermore, I do not appreciate your leaving me alone in that coach with all those men. A lady would have been more sensitive."

Molly picked up John Wright's knife and offered it to the girl. "Slice the meat."

With expert motions, Gabrielle began slicing off thick slabs of pork and laying them neatly in the skillet. Catching movement from the corner of her eye, she glanced up to see Peyton Lewis and John Wright, with the four coach horses in tow, heading for the pole corral just beyond the open end of the shed. Her breath caught in her throat, and her pulse quickened. Even muddy, bedraggled, and unshaven, Peyton Lewis was more desirable, both physically and mentally, than any of the dashing young cadets to whom she had been introduced while visiting her brother at the U.S. Military Academy at West Point.

Gabrielle did not understand her erotic reaction to Peyton Lewis. Indeed, the sensation of desire that ran rampant through her body when he was near was a new experience for her.

Gabrielle set the skillet at the edge of the fire, then watched Molly mix a concoction of sourdough that she referred to as "hardtack."

"Will Mr. Lewis make a good husband once he settles down?"

Molly was taken aback by Gabrielle's unexpected question, and it took her a moment to collect her thoughts. "Why, I doubt if Peyton Lewis will ever settle down, Gabrielle. At least, not until he's so old and worn out that he will be of no earthly use to a woman—and then he will probably demand to be waited on hand and foot."

Gabrielle walked to the doorway and leaned against the upright. A gust of cold, wet wind whipped through the opening and plastered her hair across her face. She brushed it aside, and crossed her arms over her breasts. Peyton and Wright were turning the horses into the corral and closing the pole gate. "Is he a mean person, do you think?"

Molly looked at the woman. "Peyton?"

Gabrielle nodded. "He struck Captain Cramer with a pair of brass knuckles. He could have killed the poor man. . . . And he knocked William Beecher down for no reason."

"If Peyton had intended to kill the captain, he would have. And as for Beecher, I'd like to slap the pantywaist myself. No, Gabrielle, Peyton isn't mean. But he's certainly nobody to fool with. If you try to shove him around, he'll hurt you, but he's not mean."

Molly considered telling Gabrielle about Caleb King. Oh, yes, Caleb King had been a mean person. He had enjoyed making people suffer; he had thrived on other people's pain . . . especially her pain.

Gabrielle's eyes flashed mockingly at Molly. "Are you certain you're not saying that just because you are in love with him?"

Molly stared at the girl. "That's not true!"

"It is true and you know it. What you seem to ignore, however—and it's obvious to everyone except you, Miss Klinner—is that Peyton Lewis does not return your interest in the least." Gabrielle pursed her lips as she waited for Molly Klinner to defend herself.

When Molly merely shrugged and busied herself with stirring the coffee to settle the grounds, Gabrielle's mouth drew into a determined line. She decided to try another tack.

"Fletcher Rucker, however, is different matter entirely, Miss Klinner. He simpers after you like a lovesick schoolboy."

Molly nearly laughed outright at the girl's asinine statement—not because Fletcher Rucker had transferred his romantic inclinations to Gabrielle days ago, but because she was on steady ground now that the conversation had swung away from Peyton Lewis.

Molly poured an inch of coffee into the bottom of a cup and viewed it critically. Not satisfied with the strength of the brew, she poured it back into the pot and added more beans. As she set the pot on the coals, she watched Gabrielle from beneath her lashes. "A woman could do a lot worse than Fletcher Rucker, Gabrielle."

A flicker of annoyance crossed Gabrielle's face. She was aware she had somehow lost her advantage, but being too young and immature to reverse her avenue of attack and sally from a different direction, she blundered on: "Then why won't you accept what you can have and stop lusting after someone who is beyond your grasp? Why not expend your energies on a man who obviously entertains thoughts for you?"

"Miss Johnson, men don't have *thoughts* about women until they're at least forty years old. Before then, all they have are *feelings*. Fletcher Rucker is a fine boy, and I like him very much, but were he to have any interest in me—which he does not—it would be purely physical, because, the truth is, Gabrielle, Fletcher Rucker has simply been without . . . a woman too long."

Gabrielle was startled. Never had she heard a woman speak so candidly about men and sex, not even her mother during the few "womanly" discussions they had shared. "Perhaps men are that way toward you, Miss Klinner, purely . . . carnal, but Peyton isn't that way at all. He is a gentleman!"

Gabrielle's absurd defense of Peyton Lewis sent such a rush of resentment through Molly that she glared at the girl with unbridled contempt. What did Gabrielle Johnson, an eastern gentlewoman who had never before been west of the Missouri River, know about men like Peyton Lewis or Fletcher Rucker—men who sometimes went for month upon month never speaking to a woman, much less touching one?

"Miss Johnson, it might interest you to know that Peyton Lewis is a man—nothing more, nothing less. When he and I were snowed in one night, about a month and a half ago, Peyton put his hand between my thighs. I . . . I had to kick him away. Furthermore, Peyton Lewis shot a man named Caleb King right before my eyes. The man died."

It was a partial lie, of course, but Molly could not have cared less as she watched Gabrielle's face for her reaction. Sweet revenge dimpled her cheeks when the young woman's hand fluttered to her throat and her eyes grew round as saucers. "I don't believe you." The girl's voice was but a whisper and held no conviction. "Only a moment ago, you said that Peyton was not a mean person. Now you're implying that he is a murderer and a . . . a . . ."

Molly wondered if Gabrielle was actually going to swoon. "You can always ask him yourself . . ." She hesitated as her gaze moved beyond Gabrielle to the cookfire, where the skillet of greasy meat had burst into flames. "But in the meantime, Gabrielle, you're burning the meat."

With a cry, Gabrielle snatched the frying pan out of the fire and held it at arm's length. Heat and smoke swirled about the girl's head, forcing her to turn her face aside to catch her breath. Blackened vapors billowed toward the shed's ceiling and fanned out along the rafters in search of an opening in the roof where they could escape.

Heat-induced tears filled the girl's eyes and overflowed down her cheeks. She blinked several times to clear her vision, and when she did, to add insult to injury, Peyton Lewis and John Wright were standing in the entrance to the shed watching her.

Gabrielle stamped her foot in childish frustration and burst into genuine tears, for the sad truth was that she had not exaggerated her ability to cook. Fine cuisine was one of her most prized accomplishments.

John Wright, who had never seen a grown woman break down and weep like a child, pushed his hat to the back of his head and scratched his thinning hair. He wondered what in tarnation had gotten into the two women. First it was Molly Klinner and her problem with her looks; now it was Gabrielle Johnson and some burned victuals. Vexation drew his eyebrows together.

"Folks burn grub all the time, Miss Johnson. Why, I have a

time or two my own self." When the girl cried even harder, Wright's patience snapped. "Well, now, there ain't no need to bawl like a calf what's lost its mama, for Christ's sake!"

Peyton strode to the girl and grasped the skillet by its handle. The touch of his cold hand on her flushed fingers sent a thrill through her that made her stomach tingle. Then she remembered what Molly Klinner said about his hands having been between her thighs, and she released the handle as though it had scorched her palms.

When Peyton carried the smoldering skillet to the edge of the overhang, Gabrielle fully expected him to dump its contents on the ground. Instead, he held the pan under the stream of rainwater for an instant, then returned it to the fire.

Suddenly she felt the need to explain. "Miss Klinner and I were conversing, and . . . and I got carried away. . . . I forgot about the meat. I'm sorry. It won't happen again."

John Wright cut a plug from a twist of tobacco and fingered it into his mouth. After a long moment of chewing vigorously, he spit a stream of amber into the fire and wiped his mouth with the back of his hand. "No harm done, missy, but I'd be a bit more careful next time. That's all the meat we got."

Wright tipped his hat to Gabrielle, sauntered out of the shed, and splashed his way through the mud toward the stagecoach.

Had John Wright spit his amber in Gabrielle Johnson's face, she would not have resented it more than she did his thinly veiled chastisement. When Wright reached the coach and opened its door, she sneered in his direction.

"Mr. Wright is a very indelicate and rude old man. I didn't burn the meat on purpose."

Molly considered allowing Gabrielle's comment to pass unchallenged. The more she thought about it, however, the more she resented it.

"No, Miss Johnson." Molly filled a coffee cup to its brim and handed it to the girl. "John Wright isn't indelicate—or rude. It's just that, like most old salts from the West, he has little tolerance for foolish mistakes. Out here in Texas, a simple error in judgment can cost a person his life . . . or worse, it can cost someone else their life. John wasn't being insolent or discourteous. He was merely offering a crusty warning to a tenderfoot who doesn't know any better. You could learn a lot if you would listen to him."

Gabrielle doubted that an uneducated man such as John Wright could teach her one thing of importance, and for Molly Klinner to even suggest such a thing was a direct insult to her intelligence. Angrily, she handed the untasted coffee back to Molly, then wiped her hand on the sleeve of her jacket.

"I told Mr. Wright that I didn't burn the meat on purpose . . . and you know that is the truth, Miss Klinner."

Molly took the cup and drank thirstily. Obviously the girl had chosen to ignore her explanation, so she tried again. "It won't make any difference to a starving person, Gabrielle, whether their hunger is intentional or not. It will be just as real and just as deadly either way."

Gabrielle turned her back on Molly and walked to the shed door, where she stared into the rain. How dare Molly Klinner preach to her!

Peyton squatted beside Molly and stirred the meat in the skillet. The pork sizzled and popped. "You're being a bit harsh on Miss Johnson, aren't you, Molly? She didn't do any real harm. The meat's still edible."

Molly sat back on her heels and studied him through half-closed eyes, surprised, not by the haste in which he came to Gabriel's defense but that he came to her defense at all. "There's no real harm done this time, Mr. Lewis. But what about the next time?"

When he did not answer, she shrugged and took another sip of coffee. "If you want to pamper Miss Johnson, be my guest . . . but in my opinion, she's already spoiled worse than that scorched meat you are trying so hard to salvage."

Peyton removed his hat and ran his hand through his wet hair. It must be that time of the month, he decided—for them both! He dumped the contents of the skillet onto a tin plate and walked to the far end of the shed, away from the women. Turning his back to them, he hunkered on his heels and wolfed down the scorched food as though it were good.

Molly Klinner and Gabrielle Johnson's eyes met and locked, each blaming the other for her childishness. Neither wavered nor blinked—nor were they a pretty sight.

Seventeen

Rucker and Ben urged their horses off the hill and into the mist-enshrouded valley. Thunder rolled, lightning flashed, and rain pelted them like buckshot, drowning out all other sights and sounds, rendering their quest to locate the Comanche war party all but impossible—especially when that entity had no intention of being discovered.

When they reached the valley floor, it was as though they were riding deeper and deeper into a large silver-gray pool of water that had no substance. The mist swirled and eddied around the horses' legs, but it was without the buoyancy or undercurrent normally associated with a river or lake.

The effect was ghostly, and the short hairs on Rucker's neck rose. Twisting in the saddle, he gazed at Ben, who was riding a little behind and to the right of his mount, for he, like Peyton, put a lot of stock in reading a man's eyes, especially a stranger who bore watching—and Ben was a stranger.

Ben's face was sallow and pinched, his eyes never still, as he, too, scrutinized the area. He grinned nervously at Rucker and muttered that it was like riding into the valley of death. Rucker wished Ben had not voiced that thought aloud.

As they penetrated deeper into the mist, Rucker tightened his grip on Molly's rifle, and his thumb crept up to rest on the hammer. He was becoming more uneasy by the minute, for even though the rain had slackened to a drizzle, the fog thickened with each step of their horses, and Ben, who was now two horse lengths to the side, was nearly invisible in the silent gloom. Rucker gazed over his shoulder at the hill they had just descended. It was entirely lost in the fog. Indeed, not one landmark was visible in any direction.

Ben rode on, unhurried, as though he knew exactly where he was going. That possibility—that Ben knew exactly where he was going—lay like a deadweight on Rucker's stomach.

Rucker edged his horse up beside Ben, so close that their stirrups touched. The muzzle of Molly's rifle rested only inches from Ben's chest, a subtle promise to the Negro that if he proved to be a false prophet, vengeance would not be the Lord's. Rucker would shoot him out of the saddle.

They rode like that for an hour, and the only sounds that broke the eerie silence were the raindrops on their hats and the occasional ring of the horses' iron-shod hooves when they struck a stone.

Finally Rucker's nerves got the best of him, and he lifted his hand, drawing them to a halt. "You've traveled this country before, Uncle. When was it, an' what was you doin' here?"

Ben studied Rucker from beneath his soggy hat brim. He knew the boy was edgy, and rightfully so. By the same token, he had learned at an early age not to divulge any more information than was necessary to a white man, even a friendly one.

Ben considered his words carefully. When he spoke, it was without his perpetual grin. "I hunted this here section o' Texas a time or two when I was jest a boy, Mista' Fletcher."

Rucker studied Ben's face in the waning light for a clue to the man's age and identity. How long ago was it that Ben "was just a boy"? Hell, chances were, when Ben was "just a boy," there weren't a half-dozen white people in Texas! As to his genealogy? Ben's lips were as thick as a Negro's, but his nose was aquiline. His hair was long, more wavy than kinky, and his skin, wrinkled with age, was a deep mahogany with a satin finish that shone with blue highlights. Rucker shook his head. Ben could be darn near any nationality he chose, except white American.

Giving Rucker every opportunity to shoot him but determined not to be buffaloed by the boy, Ben nudged his horse forward and entered a stand of jack pines that grew so dense he and Rucker were forced to worm their way single file down a narrow game trail that was more a suggestion of a path than an actual passageway.

Water dripped constantly from tree branches to splash soundlessly on the pine needle carpet beneath, which only added to both men's apprehension.

Ben's nerves tingled, stretched nearly to the breaking point, and with every step the horses took, he expected to feel Rucker's bullet smash into his back. He made up his mind that at the next wide place in the trail, he and Rucker were going to reach an understanding, one way or the other.

They rounded a bend in the trail and found themselves at the edge of a small clearing, where a spring bubbled up out of the earth and spilled along a narrow defile for ten yards before disappearing back into the ground.

Rucker stiffened in the saddle, and his heart skipped a beat. Facing him from across a campfire near the spring were a dozen Indians with antiquated flintlock trade guns at their shoulders. All twelve muzzles appeared to be pointing directly at him.

The red men were young, in their late teens. They wore slouch hats with turkey feathers in their bands. They sported all manner and color of faded cloth coats and trousers, and all wore moccasins; they were a motley, mean-looking group who, from the expressions on their faces, were ready to do battle, with or without a reason.

Icy raindrops fell from an overhanging tree branch and funneled their way down Rucker's collar. He did not notice.

Ben raised his right hand and addressed the Indians in both sign language and a singsong dialect with which Rucker was unfamiliar. The Indians responded in kind, and Rucker looked at Ben for a translation.

Ben's reply was soft and careful. "They's Cherokee, Mista' Fletcher, raggedy-assed Cherokee on a huntin' foray."

After fifteen minutes of intense exchange between Ben and the Cherokee, one of the Indians stepped forward and gestured toward Rucker's rifle.

Ben's face remained impassive, displaying none of the apprehension that had dampened his armpits to the point that his fear rose like heat waves to assail his senses with the stench of his own fright. After a long pause, Ben shook his head, and the young Indian's mouth drew into an ugly slash. The boy rattled off another line of singsong and again pointed at the Henry rifle.

Rucker understood that the rifle was the center of the conversation, and his frustration increased. "You better tell me what's goin' on here, Uncle." He slowly drew the hammer of the Henry rifle to full cock.

"Easy, Mista' Fletcher. Jest be real easy. We're in a peck o' trouble."

The Indians saw Rucker cock his rifle and immediately palmed back the hammers of their smoothbore trade guns. It was a standoff, with each party facing the other in indecision. The silence stretched thin, the tension grew taut, and Rucker's patience took a downward swing.

Ben sensed Rucker's mood and spoke to the boy from the corner of his mouth. "Mista' Fletcher, they's got the drop on us. I suggest that yo' an' me haul our freight on out'n here. Let's do it real casual . . . like we wasn't even noticin' it our own selves."

In slow motion, the two men edged their horses around and walked them back into the pines. When they had ridden two hundred yards, Ben drew up and removed his hat, then wiped his face with his sleeve. "That was a close shave, Mista' Fletcher."

Rucker wondered how much of the moisture that beaded Ben's face was rainwater, because he felt wet all over—and it wasn't from the weather. He looked over his shoulder at their back trail. It was clear.

"I thought you said you knew this country, Uncle. Obviously, you didn't remember that campsite . . . an' a mistake like that could've gotten us killed!"

Ben shrugged and tugged his hat back into place. "Ol' age sometimes makes a man a stranger in his own country, Mista' Fletcher."

"Just how old are you, Uncle? And for that matter, jest who in the hell are you? It's time I got a few straight answers."

"I don't rightly know how ol' I am, Mista' Fletcher. I figure I must be 'tween sixty an' seventy years ol'. I can 'member a long ways back . . . prob'ly 'round the turn o' the century when t'weren't hardly nothin' but Spaniards an' Injuns in Texas. But as to how ol' I actually am . . . well, I jest ain't for certain. Howsomever, whilst we are talkin' 'bout ol' age, they's a sayin' 'mongst us Texicans: 'When a man's too ol' t' set a bad example, he hands out good advice.' An' my advice is for us t' put some distance 'tween us an' them Cherokee."

Ben nudged his horse into motion, and Rucker fell in behind him.

The rain had stopped, but the mist had thickened to the point they could see only an arm's length in any direction. A quarter of a mile later, Ben turned onto a side trail that wound through the pines below the Indian camp.

They traveled silently for the better part of an hour before Ben turned again to Rucker and told him his mother had been a slave on a plantation in Louisiana owned by a French aristocrat. His father had been an Apache warrior with a band that attacked the plantation and overran the Frenchman and his family.

"My pappy captured my mama and carried her back t' Texas with 'im. My mama taught me t' speak French, an' my pappy taught me Spanish an' several Injun dialects. An' ol' Jim Beckworth, that nigger mountain man, taught me English."

Ben grinned sheepishly. "I can speak 'bout every language they is, but I can't read or write my own name."

Rucker nodded his understanding. The fact that Ben was illiterate did not surprise him, for he had never known a Negro who could read or write. He knew several, however, who could speak more than one language, and he attributed that phenomenon to the widespread belief that black people could mimic anything they saw or heard.

Rucker waited for Ben to go on with the story, and when Ben hesitated, Rucker prodded him. "You told us that day we picked you up that the Federal soldiers busted you out of a Texas prison. What were you doin' in prison in the first place?"

"Well, Mista' Fletcher, many a thing a man does is judged right or wrong accordin' t' the time an' the place he does it."

Ben leaned low over his horse's neck and ducked under an overhanging tree limb, and Rucker waited impatiently for a wide place in the trail, then rode up beside him. "So? What were you doin' in jail?"

"Mista' Fletcher." Ben twisted in the saddle and looked Rucker in the eye. "Next t' hoss rustlin', I reckon curiosity gets more men shot than any other thing."

Rucker shifted the rifle barrel so that it was pointed at Ben's chest. "When I ride with a man, Uncle, I want t' know what makes him tick. I ain't got no hankerin' t' pry into your personal life or t' be judgmental, but I sure as hell aim t' know who you are an' what you're about."

Ben sighed and peered at Rucker as though he were only half bright. "Mista' Fletcher, yo' know as well as me that yo're plumb lost out here. Yo' ain't got no idea where yo' are or what direction yo're headin' in. Now, we both got sense enuff t' know a man don't shoot the only person who knows the trail . . . so yo' might's well put that rifle away."

Rucker's mouth quirked into a crooked grin, and he cocked the rifle.

Ben stared sullenly at his saddle horn. He did not actually believe Rucker would shoot him, but then again, he was not certain that he wouldn't. "I went t' the penitent'ry 'cause I shot a man. He was foolin' with my woman. . . . I caught 'em t'gether an' I shot him."

"Did you kill him?"

"Naw, but I tried real hard."

"What became of your wife?"

"She ran off with the son of a bitch when he got strong enuff t' travel."

Rucker contemplated that: He had known a man or two who shot someone because he caught him with his wife, but not one of them had so much as been arrested, much less locked away in a prison.

"Sendin' a man to the pen seems a bit harsh for shootin' a feller who's ridin' another man's saddle, Uncle. You sure you told me everything?"

"That's 'bout the sum of it, Mista' Fletcher."

They touched heels to their horses and rode on, ducking under wet foliage when possible, riding through it when not.

A mile further on, Rucker, concerned that the Indians might follow them, craned his neck around and studied their backtrail. "Were those Indians we rode up on part of the band that burned the stage depot?"

Ben laughed silently. "Them Injuns back there was Chero-kee. Prob'ly wasn't a huntin' party a'tall. They was prob'ly on a hoss-stealin' foray, an' a puny one at that. Cherokee are civilized Injuns, Mista' Fletcher. The ones what burnt the station was Co-manche, an' there ain't nothin' civilized 'bout 'em . . . nothin' a'tall. Never will be."

"Well, if those Cherokee were civilized, why didn't we ask them a few questions instead of crawlin' out of there with our tails between our legs?"

"The only diff'rence 'tween a civilized Injun an' a uncivi-lized Injun, Mista' Fletcher, is that the uncivilized Injun is pre-dictable: you dang well know he's goin' t' try an' kill you. An' jest knowin' it makes life a heap less complicated."

They lapsed into silence and rode on, each absorbed in his own thoughts. The shadows were closing in as evening marched nearer. The fresh scent of pine beneath the overhanging branches became a heady intoxicant, held close as it was by the heavy, rain-saturated air.

Fletcher breathed deeply. Oddly, the purity of the forest after the rain reminded him of Gabrielle Johnson. He pondered that and decided it must be because, unlike most of the women he had dealt with since becoming a man, Gabrielle was pure and sweet—a real lady. He wondered if she was thinking about him.

As daylight ebbed, Ben searched for a campsite, anyplace

that would offer shelter from the rain and at the same time conceal a small fire. He selected a tiny clearing amid a thicket of post oaks, thankful that the trees had managed to retain a goodly number of last year's leaves because when the fog lifted, the foliage would dissipate the campfire's smoke while shielding its light from unwanted scrutiny.

In the few minutes it took Ben to unsaddle the horses, Rucker searched for firewood, anything dry enough to burn. He kindled a small pile of pine branches taken from the underside of a blow-down, then squatted beside the flames and chafed his cold hands.

The heat of the fire relaxed Rucker, and for the first time since the end of the war, he admitted to himself that he was utterly exhausted. He longed to do nothing more than hunker in the warmth of the fire and stare into its lambent flames until they put him to sleep.

Ben knelt down on the other side of the fire and peeled off his blanket roll and overcoat, exposing a dingy gray pullover shirt tucked into the waistband of heavy woolen army trousers. He was lean, rawboned and narrow of shoulder, yet, when he moved to lay the coat aside, Rucker could see the ripple of wiry muscles that bespoke strength and agility in a sound body.

Ben kneaded his hands over the flames while appraising the darkening woods around them. As though he were a wolf sniffing the wind in search of a scent, he turned his face to the four points of the compass. A moment later, he climbed to his feet. "B'lieve I'll ease out yonder an' see if I can rustle us up some grub, Mista' Fletcher."

Even though they had not eaten since the previous day and Rucker felt as though his stomach were gnawing a hole in his backbone, he shook his head. It was too dangerous to chance a shot, and he said as much. Why, for all they knew, the war party they had been chasing might be camped just over the next hill.

Ben laughed and picked up a rock the size of his fist. "I was full grown b'fore I ever saw a firearm, Mista' Fletcher, but my family never did go hungry." It was not braggadocio.

Ben weighed the rock in his hand, then discarded it. He selected another, then another, and dropped them into his trouser pockets. He slipped silently out of the campsite, and a moment later blended obscurely into the evening shadows.

Rucker wondered at Ben's animal-like behavior. Must be the Apache in him, he mused, as he set to work cutting limbs from a nearby sapling to build a T-shaped framework near the fire. Spreading Ben's coat over the structure to dry, he built a second frame.

Settling again beside the fire, Rucker draped his blanket loosely around his shoulders and was instantly asleep.

Molly nibbled at the food on her plate. She knew she must eat to keep up her strength, but the truth was, she was nauseated and had been since the jarring ride to the station. The turbulent five-mile stagecoach race from the Red River, combined with the disappointment of finding the expected haven of rest and re-freshment burned to the ground and the attendant murdered, had been almost too much for her to bear. On top of that, the unpleasantness with the banker, and Gabrielle, and Peyton, had upset her more than she would have believed. She glanced at the people around her: the banker and drummer were eating, and the soldiers were making preparations to bed down for the night. John Wright was taking inventory of their remaining food sup-plies, and Peyton was sipping his last cup of coffee before taking the first shift of guard duty. Gabrielle, however, was watching Molly moodily, as though something had been left unsaid. Molly sneered at the girl, a warning for her to mind her own business.

Gabrielle raised her chin defiantly, then drew her cloak more tightly about her shoulders and walked out of the shed into the sodden darkness.

Molly set her plate aside and picked up her tin of coffee. The brew was thick and bitter. Her eyes filled with tears. She blinked them away. What was wrong with her? She never cried. Never! Yet lately it just happened, unexpected, unwanted, at the worst possible moments—like now—when it was important that she and the rest of the passengers be strong for each other.

As if that were not enough, in the last few days she had begun to swell. Her feet were cramped in her brogans where before they had been loose to the point she had been forced to line them with paper. And her hands were puffed and stiff. The most unwanted change, however, was her abdomen; it seemed to be a thing detached from her body. It moved; it ached; and lately, it had decided to expand as it pleased.

While these were all the incredible experiences she associated with pregnancy, they left Molly despondent and irritable—and, for the first time since she was twelve years old and had watched her parents drive away from Mr. Oller's store, she longed for her mother. The very idea that she, Molly Klinner, needed the mother whom she had learned to hate caused her to laugh and cry simultaneously, for she was heartbreakingly aware that if her mother or father had been present that very moment, neither of them would have held out a hand to comfort their daughter, any more than they had the first time Molly had become pregnant.

Molly climbed awkwardly to her feet and stumbled to the far end of the shed, where she cupped her hands under the trickling stream of water that fell from the overhang. She splashed the icy liquid over her face, and prayed no one would be able to tell that she had been crying.

Gabrielle stood thirty yards beyond the shed and gazed into the darkness that engulfed her, thankful that the night diminished her perception of distance and reality, for the ugly rubble of the station house, although only one hundred yards distant, was invisible, as was the gravesite just beyond. Even the prairie, which she knew stretched on forever, was reduced to the abbreviated span of her night vision—and, unlike the daytime when she felt small and insignificant, here, now, in this restricted universe, she had the sensation of being all powerful, invulnerable. Then she thought of tomorrow—daylight, reality—and she shivered uncontrollably, not from the cold, but because once again she would be forced to face the West and the people who inhabited it, both of which she was fast learning to detest. Her shoulders slumped. Texas was not supposed to be like this, lonely, desolate, and dangerous. Elizabeth Custer, in her letters, had promised beauty, entertainment, and the adoration of all the young unmarried officers on the post. Elizabeth had also assured her that the general had subdued *all* the hostile Indian tribes in Texas.

Gabrielle turned toward the shed, where the glow of the cookfire illuminated the structure's open doorway as though it were a theater stage. The light beckoned, warm and inviting, and she hastily walked toward it. Ten yards from the shed, she stopped in the darkness beyond the reach of firelight to adjust her soggy clothing and make herself presentable. As she straightened her skirt, she noticed Molly Klinner standing in the opening, silhouetted against the firelight. Molly was posed, as though a sculptor had hung a white sheet behind a block of ebony and then carved Molly's body in infinite detail so that every curve and indent of her figure was accented in sharp, conspicuous contrast.

Gabrielle's hands froze on her skirts as the indisputable truth of Molly's physical condition hit her like a slap across the face. *She's pregnant. Molly Klinner is pregnant!* Then came the inevitable question, and with it, the obvious answer. A great rage welled up in Gabrielle, directed not at Peyton Lewis, who most certainly must be the father, but at Molly Klinner, who had made the statement not more than an hour ago that "Peyton put his hands between my thighs . . . I had to kick him away."

It was now perfectly clear to Gabrielle why Molly Klinner was so possessive about Peyton Lewis, why she acted as though she knew something about him that no one else did. It was obvious, by the reverse curve in Molly's spine and the swell of her abdomen, that Peyton Lewis had put something between Molly Klinner's thighs that she did not kick away.

Gabrielle clutched the material of her skirt so tightly that her knuckles whitened and her fingernails cut into the fabric. Raising herself to her full height, her head held high, she marched past Molly, straight to the fire where Peyton was finishing a cup of coffee. "I wish I were a swearing woman, Mr. Lewis! I would make your ears burn."

Peyton studied her over the rim of his cup. "You talking to me?"

Gabrielle's eyes seared his face. "I think Miss Klinner is ill."

Peyton glanced at the entrance of the shed, where Molly

stood gazing off into the night. The planes and angles of her face, wet with the water she had splashed over it, glistened in the firelight like polished alabaster. Perhaps Miss Johnson was right. Molly had certainly been acting unusual since having arrived at the station—subdued, confused, even shy, not at all the arrogant, confident woman with whom he had crossed the prairie. Well, she was not his worry any longer; he had kept his pledge and delivered her to Texas. He looked back at Gabrielle.

"So?"

"I should think you would be concerned with her well-being. After all, it's your . . . responsibility."

Peyton wondered at the girl's ability to jump to conclusions. Since when had Molly Klinner become his responsibility? Still, if Molly was sick . . . He set the coffee cup aside and walked to the end of the shed. Molly was unaware of his presence until he touched her arm. "Are you all right?"

"Leave me alone."

Peyton tightened his grip on her arm and turned her toward him. "If you've got a problem, Miss Klinner, I need to know what it is. The Comanche are still around, and . . . well, we're not out of the woods yet. So, if you're sick or something . . ."

"Mr. Lewis, if I was 'sick or something' I would tell you. But there's nothing wrong with me that a little rest won't cure. Just go on about your business and don't waste your concern on me. I'm a grown woman. I can take care of myself."

When he walked back to the fire, Molly felt more alone than ever. She spun toward him, thinking what a fool she was for not trusting him with the truth.

In that millisecond when Molly Klinner made up her mind to tell Peyton Lewis everything, she felt a massive melancholy fade from her heart. Relieved and excited by the prospect of finally taking him into her confidence, sharing the secret she had so unconditionally safeguarded these past months, Molly started toward him, then stopped in her tracks. Peyton was talking with Gabrielle, shaking his head in answer to a question Molly could not hear—did not need to; for Gabrielle's glower slid sidelong to Molly's protruding stomach, then rose with outrage to weld itself to her face. In that instant, when their eyes locked, the truth she had intended to reveal to Peyton died on her lips. She was too late! Turning again to the runoff, she scrubbed her face and hands with a vengeance, but she knew full well they would never come clean in Peyton's eyes. Not now.

Molly sat alone beside the fire and sipped at her cup of coffee. She was feeling better. The cold water on her face had helped. Her stomach was queasy, but her nerves had calmed. She watched Gabrielle Johnson bathe her face and hands in a skillet of heated water, and idly wondered what kind of soap the girl used. It smelled very nice. She would not ask. No, she would never ask.

She gazed at the men scattered around the fire in slumber. Snores, loud and soft, disturbed the silence of the shed. She observed them with detached indifference. Three months ago, even knowing she was pregnant, Caleb King would have used her to turn a dollar or two from these men. Why didn't she do it herself? The good Lord above knew she needed the money. Money. That was the question. How would she and her baby survive now that they had reached Texas? Gabrielle had asked her that, and she had not answered, because there was no answer.

Molly pondered her alternatives. Thanks to Mr. Oller, she understood the internal workings of a dry goods store, and thanks to Mr. Ling she could cook exotic foods. A general store, or a restaurant, however, cost money. Again, she studied the sleeping men, for she had also learned from observing Stella, and how she ran her house, the intricacies of operating a bordello. Again, the question stole quietly into her thoughts: Why not open her own establishment? All she needed was a bed.

Molly sighed. Who was she trying to fool? She knew exactly why she would not now, or ever become a prostitute: at long last, the choice of whom she slept with was hers and hers alone—and she would choose her mate carefully. Furthermore, she did not now—or ever—want Peyton Lewis to find her in another man's arms. Why not? She mulled that over but failed to come up with an answer, other than the fact that she did not want him to think less of her than he already did—and that was no answer at all.

Looking beyond the doorway into the darkness where Peyton was standing guard, she mused about him. Was he the kind of man she wanted to rear her child . . . her children? She had not considered that possibility. Children, lots of them, with Peyton? The thought brought a shy smile to her lips and a sparkle to her eyes. Yes. A thousand times yes! She was head over heels in love with him—even Gabrielle had that right.

Molly puzzled over Peyton's conversation with Gabrielle. It figured that the girl would not hesitate to inform him that she was pregnant. Why, then, had he merely walked away as though nothing had changed? He had passed within arm's reach without glancing at her and had headed to his guard post. She wished he had said something, anything that would have hinted at his true feelings. She needed to know—must know—what he thought of her now that he knew the truth.

Molly refilled the coffee cup and walked out into the night. When she was far enough from the shed that she would not wake the sleepers, she called his name.

Peyton answered from the deep shadows on the far side of the horse pen.

Molly made her way around the corral. He was farther away than she had imagined, and she was all but panting for breath as she approached him. "I thought you might need a cup of something hot."

Peyton studied her face in the darkness, taken aback by her willingness to venture away from the safety of the shed just to do him a kindness. It was a generous gesture. "A man never knows what to expect out of you, Miss Klinner. You are a mystery."

Molly let her pent-up breath slip between her teeth. If he did not know why she had come, then she had rather he just thank her and be done with it. A mystery, indeed!

She held the cup up to the softer darkness above the skyline and squinted at the steam rising from the coffee. "Some men are so blind, Mr. Lewis, they can't even see through the steam that rises from their coffee cup. I think you are one of those people." She handed the cup to him and walked back the way she had come.

Peyton watched the steam rise from the coffee and wondered what Molly Klinner was talking about. What was he missing? "Molly!" When she stopped and turned her face to him, Peyton saluted her with the cup.

Molly walked on, her stomach cramping again, worse than before. She hastened her pace. Surely she could not be in labor. No, it was too early. She had just recently begun to show. But she was not certain. There had been no real need to keep track of her cycles, not when Caleb King controlled her future. Another pain doubled her over, and she stumbled to her knees, then dropped to her elbows and rested on all fours. Perspiration ran down her face and burned into her eyes. She tried to blink it away.

Her breath came in short, heavy gasps as she struggled to regain her feet. Finally, she stood erect. Her head spun sickeningly, and her knees felt as though they would buckle if she so much as attempted to move her feet. Taking a deep breath, she started again for the shed. Before she had gone ten steps, the world turned upside down, and she felt herself falling. She twisted her body so she would hit on her shoulder.

Pain, so intense it surpassed every other human sensation, ripped through her body, causing her to instinctively draw her knees into a fetal position. She screamed, again and again.

Eighteen

Ben returned to the camp an hour after full darkness. Not waking Rucker, he skinned and dressed the rabbit he had stoned, then skewered it on a green stick over the fire.

The aroma of cooking meat brought Rucker awake with a start. He lay there for a moment, watching the flames sear the meat, then sat up and rubbed his eyes and yawned.

Ben lifted his fire-warmed overcoat off the drying rack and slipped it on his chilled frame. He squatted, Indian fashion, beside the fire and turned the rabbit.

Rucker hawked and spit. His mouth felt as dry as a piece of old harness leather. He reached for the canteen. As he drank, he watched the man out of the corner of his eyes, still concerned about Ben's yarn that a jury sentenced him to life in prison for shooting a man whom he had caught in bed with his wife. That just did not make sense. Corking the canteen, Rucker voiced his misgivings, arguing that no jury in the land would do a thing like that.

Ben sighed. John Wright was correct: Fletcher Rucker would not let a subject rest until he was satisfied that he had heard the whole story. "Mista' Fletcher, you should'a done figured it out. It were a white man who was with my wife."

Rucker sat back on his haunches. He looked as though a thunderclap had burst in his mouth. "Hell, Uncle, you're lucky you even had a trial."

Ben grinned at him. "My sentiments 'xactly."

Rucker mulled that over. The more he thought about it, the more certain he became that Ben was indeed fortunate they had not lynched him on the spot, shooting a white man and all. "Are you sorry you shot him, Uncle?"

"Naw, I can't rightly say I'm tore up 'bout it none."

"Would you do it again?"

"Would I shoot the man?"

Rucker nodded. Ben pursed his lips in thought. "Naw, Mista' Fletcher, I wouldn't. Next time, I'd shoot 'em both."

Rucker's eyebrows shot up; that certainly was not the answer he had expected.

Ben observed Rucker's discomfort, and it annoyed him. If Rucker was concerned for his safety because he had shot a white man, then the boy was a fool. If he had wanted to kill Rucker, he would have done it while he was sleeping.

Ben lifted the rabbit off the flames and handed the carcass to Rucker. "I think we'd best eat a bite, Mista' Fletcher."

Rucker ripped a leg from the rabbit, then passed the remainder of the meat to Ben. "She must have been one heck of a woman."

Ben chuckled. "Some men's wives are angels, Mista' Fletcher. The others are still alive."

They ate in silence, each absorbed in his own thoughts.

When they rolled into their blankets and stretched out beside the fire, Ben pushed himself to one elbow and looked across the flames at Rucker. "Does it bother you, me a-shootin' that white man, Mista' Fletcher?"

"No, it don't."

"Well, somethin' 'bout it is settin' heavy on yo' mind. What is it? What would yo' have done if'n it had been your wife?"

It was a quietly asked question, but Rucker sensed its importance, and he weighed his answer carefully before he replied. Finally, tipping his hat down over his face to ward off the evening dew that was beginning to fall, he released a long, contented sigh. "Uncle, if I caught a darky with my wife, I'd have shot *her.*"

Ben made no response, and a few minutes later, Rucker heard a soft snore from across the fire. Rucker considered the sleeping man. Beneath the outward show of laughing, soft-spoken subservience, Ben was intelligent, innovative, and dangerous. He would bear watching. Rucker eased his pistol out of its holster and gripped it tightly beneath his blanket. Only then did he close his eyes and allow himself the luxury of slumber.

Before Molly's first shriek had begun to subside, Peyton had cast aside the coffee cup and palmed his pistol. He looked quickly to the horses; they were standing quietly, ears pricked toward Molly's cries, but they were not milling or nervous as they would have been if danger stalked nearby.

Peyton glanced at the lighted shed. Nothing moved. He swung his gaze to Molly, but he could not make her out in the darkness. He ran toward her cries, expecting at any moment to see her attacker materialize out of the night, prepared to shoot anything that moved.

Shouts erupted from the shed, and Peyton heard someone rushing toward him. He called out to Molly. She did not answer. He caught movement out of the corner of his eye, something lying in the mud, quivering like an animal in agony. Then she shrieked again.

Peyton dropped to his knees beside her and slipped his arm beneath her shoulders. When he attempted to lift her to a sitting position, she screamed and thrashed her head from side to side.

Peyton withdrew his arm and quickly ran his hand over her body in search of an arrow or lance or tomahawk—anything. He could find nothing. "Are you shot?"

"No." It was a long, drawn-out wail.

"Were you attacked? Did someone knock you down? Damn it, Molly, talk to me."

Molly's lips drew back in a pain-ridden grimace. "Gabrielle Johnson has already 'talked' to you about it!"

"She what?"

"I saw you talking to her. . . ."

"She said you were ill . . . you said you weren't. What's going on here, Molly?"

Molly looked up into his face. Even though it was only inches from hers, she could not make out his features. Could it be that Gabrielle had not told Peyton she was pregnant?

Pain drew Molly's knees more tightly against her chest, and she put the question out of her mind. She was too sick to care.

Peyton shucked off his coat and spread it over her.

John Wright rushed up. "I heard a scream." His gaze took in Molly with Peyton kneeling beside her. He took a quick step backward.

"What's the meaning of this, Lewis? What have you done to Miss Molly?"

Peyton's head snapped up. "I haven't done anything to her, damn you! She fell and can't get up. I think she's badly hurt, but it's too dark to tell. We've got to get her back to the shed."

"Is what he said true, Molly?"

Molly flung her head from side to side, wishing the stupid man would go away and leave her be. "Yes, it's true." It was a rasp. "I fell . . . knocked the breath out of me. . . ."

Wright spun on his heel, and with the promise of returning with the other men, he broke into a fast trot toward the distant firelight.

Molly squinched her eyes shut and attempted to breathe deeply. Instead, she vomited, then vomited again. She was experiencing the same symptoms she had the day she fell from the hay wagon.

Perspiration flooded her face as she raised her eyes to the starless heavens. "Please, God. Not again . . . please."

Concentrating on her breathing, she took a deep breath in and slowly exhaled. Deep breath in, exhale. She reasoned that if she could keep an abundant amount of oxygen flowing to her baby, it would live. It must. In the distance, she could hear the men coming, the suck of running feet in mud, the murmur of excited voices. Deep breath in, exhale.

"Easy," she heard Peyton instruct the men as they lifted her. "Be gentle with her." She liked that.

They lifted Molly onto a blanket and rushed her to the shed.

Peyton waited until they disappeared inside the building before returning to his guard post. Seating himself on the watering trough, he stared into the night and thought about Molly Klinner's insistence that she had slipped in the mud, struck the ground hard, and knocked the breath out of her.

He did not believe that for one moment. Molly was of a lot tougher stock than she appeared, and she was no whiner. The very fact she had fallen and then cried out bothered him more than he cared to admit. She would never have made a sound had she not been suffering terribly.

Peyton's brow furrowed in thought. He could not remember one time during their crossing of the Kansas prairie when she had complained—and those had been the most grueling, ruthless traveling conditions he could ever recall, terrible enough to break a strong man. Yet she had not so much as whimpered.

Peyton twisted on his perch so he could see the shed. How bad was Molly Klinner really hurt? He considered leaving his post just long enough to step over there and inquire as to her condition. Instead, he stood up and walked to the corral. Old habits die hard, especially those formed in military training. He rested his foot on the bottom pole of the fence and leaned his elbows on the top rail. He gazed at the shadowed silhouettes of the horses as they fed from a half-burned haystack, but he was not seeing them; he was seeing a young, courageous woman who had been struck down by an assailant he could not grapple with, could not protect her from . . . because he did not have a clue as to what was wrong with her. He looked toward the shed and wondered what was going on in there.

The men carried Molly into the building and laid her close to the fire. John Wright, who fancied himself a veterinarian because off and on throughout the years he had worked on sick horses, dampened a cloth and dabbed at Molly's face where the skin on her cheek was raw and bruised from her fall. "How are you feelin', Molly?" It was a stupid question and he knew it, but he had to ask.

Molly clutched his arm, her fingers digging into his flesh. "I'm pregnant, John. I'm seven months pregnant and I'm terrified that I've miscarried." Why had she not told Peyton that truth long ago? It had been so easy when John Wright had asked.

Captain Cramer, in the middle of building a cigarette, spun toward Molly. What was that she had said? Flicking away the makings, he walked quickly to Molly and squatted down beside her. Now that his eyes were no longer blinded by the assumption she was a virtuous unmarried lady, the truth that had been skirting the fringes of his memory since he had first boarded the stagecoach in Kansas came rushing back with vivid clarity: this self-same Molly Klinner had been working in a brothel in one of the western Missouri towns his commanding officer, General Thomas Ewing, had ordered burned to the ground in the fall of 1863.

Cramer sank back on his heels, and his breath rushed through his teeth. Incredible! She was older, but she was definitely the same woman.

The captain's eyes narrowed. It was a well-known fact among the officers of Ewing's command that the majority of the females in those towns they razed, especially the young and the beautiful—like Molly Klinner—had not survived their ravishment by the Federal troops. Those women, regardless of their age, marital status, color, virtue—or lack of it—had been used indiscriminately and unmercifully. When the officers had tired of their sport, they passed the women along to the noncommissioned officers, then to the rank-and-file soldiers, and finally to the very dregs of mankind: Charles "Doc" Jennison's band of murdering bushwhackers, known as the Kansas Jayhawkers—of which Caleb King was a hanger-on.

Cramer, irritated at not having recognized Molly earlier, looked quickly at the men around him. "I know this woman! During the war, she was a whore in one of them little no-name towns in Missouri. . . . Why, she must have serviced every man in General Ewing's brigade!"

All eyes were riveted to Molly Klinner. The only sounds in the room were the crackling of the fire and the occasional patter of windblown raindrops on the shed's roof.

Gabrielle Johnson, who had been assisting John Wright with Molly's care, backed slowly away from the litter where the sick woman lay. When she realized she still clutched the cloth Wright had used to sponge Molly's face, she flung it away as though it were tainted with a disease. Her fingers balled into fists, and rage filled her as she glared down at Molly.

"I have been traveling with a . . . pregnant . . . woman of the evening? How dare you! How could you allow me to disgrace myself so!"

Molly pushed herself to her elbows and flung aside the blanket that covered her. Her face was pinched with pain, but her eyes were steady when they locked with those of the captain. In her hand, pointed at his head, was the pistol Peyton had given her.

Captain Cramer rose slowly to his feet and backed away from the litter until he was brought up short by the circle of onlookers.

Cramer held up his hands. "Easy now, Miss Klinner. Just take it easy. I didn't mean no harm. It just came to me all of a sudden who you were . . . and it slipped out. I didn't mean no harm."

The crowd stood in stunned silence, afraid to breathe for fear that Molly Klinner might actually pull the trigger. As though the captain had suddenly developed body odor, the onlookers began melting away until finally he was standing alone.

Molly's voice whipped through the silence as soft as down and as hard as steel.

"Yes, Captain, I was in one of those 'no-name' towns that General Ewing and his rabble—which you mistakenly referred to as an army—burned to the ground. And yes, I was one of the women whom you—and those like you—raped . . . and . . . and did worse things to."

Every eye was on her. Every ear was listening. Anger, disgust, and outright hostility toward the captain played across the faces of the spectators, especially that of John Wright, who, having been a Confederate soldier, considered himself a chivalrous champion of feminine virtue. Even the drummer and the banker appeared sympathetic toward her.

Molly saw none of this. Her unwavering attention was cemented to the captain. "And in spite of every depraved thing that you and those like you did to me, Captain Cramer, I survived."

Cramer gazed anxiously at her, afraid to look away, afraid to move, afraid even to breathe.

The shock on his face caused Molly's eyebrows to rise. "That surprises you, doesn't it? That some of us survived?"

Cramer summoned up his courage and took a threatening step toward her. "This has gone far enough, Miss Klinner. You can't intimidate a captain of the United States Army!"

Molly cocked the pistol; it brought him up short. "Don't waste your breath, Captain. You may not have many left. For you see, sir, unlike you, when you held a gun to my head and your soldiers held me down with their bayonets, I want nothing you have to offer."

The captain froze, his eyes glued to the pistol's muzzle. Perspiration beaded his upper lip. He looked at the men around him. There was not one sympathetic face.

Ironically, it was Gabrielle Johnson who, having spent the duration of the war in Monroe, Michigan, and thus having never heard of General Ewing's notorious Order Number 11 that left western Missouri in ashes, came to Cramer's defense.

"But you were a . . . a *soiled dove* . . . before the army came to your town, Miss Klinner. That puts you in a different light than the chaste women who resided there. And I'm sure Captain Cramer was too much a gentleman to—"

The captain jumped at Gabrielle's thread of reprieve. "That's true, Miss Johnson! The decent women were spared. Miss Klinner was already working in a brothel when we arrived in town."

Molly laughed out loud. It was not a pretty sound.

"Yes, I was working in a brothel, Miss Johnson." The memories rushed back as though it had been yesterday. She recalled plainly that she had been forced to unbutton her blouse, exposing her young, firm breasts to the men in the washroom when Stella Kirby had rushed through the door.

The woman had taken in the situation at a glance, and had approached Captain Cramer boldly. "It's rather early for business, Captain." She mentally counted the soldiers; there were fourteen. "But I believe that I and my five girls can adequately attend to your needs."

She had taken a step closer to Cramer and smiled her invitation. "I am experienced in many ways when it comes to pleasing men, Captain." She dismissed Molly with a wave of her hand. "Molly is only a child, my laundress, my seamstress. She's only thirteen years old. She's not a working girl."

For an instant, Molly believed that Stella had saved her, for Cramer had laughed heartily. Then, with no warning, his hand had shot out and grasped her breast, twisting his fingers savagely into its soft smoothness. Agony had sent her to her knees, and she had screamed. Then she was on her back, her skirt and pantaloons hanging in shreds about her naked thighs and buttocks.

She heard Stella Kirby calling to her as the soldiers dragged her, too, to the floor, warning Molly not to fight them, to give them what they wanted. "Go away, Molly! Go away. Everything will be all right if you just go away."

Molly had not understood what Stella meant by "just go away," and she had fought, and the bayonets had pierced her, and then they had pierced her, one man after another after another.

She heard a blast, and for a moment she believed they had shot her, hoped they had shot her, but when she opened her eyes, she saw Mr. Ling, meat cleaver in hand, sag heavily against the door frame. Another blast sounded and he collapsed in the doorway. Molly turned her head and closed her eyes.

When they finished with her, she lay there on the cold floor and writhed in her own blood, murmuring over and over to herself that she was not dead, that she had beaten them . . . beaten them. They had then dumped the tub of wash water over her, and left her where she lay.

Later, when she could move, refusing to look at Ling, who she knew was dead, she crawled to where Stella Kirby lay spreadeagle near the door leading into the kitchen. The woman's eyes stared sightlessly at the ceiling, and her lip rouge and face paint, which she always applied so carefully, was smeared across her face, causing her to appear pitifully comical.

Molly was unaware that Stella was dead until she touched the woman's cheek and her head lolled to the side, revealing a deep red slash across her throat. Only then did Molly weep, for Stella, in her own rough and sometimes vulgar way, had been kind and generous to her, and always protective of her chastity, even though she was well aware of Molly's background.

As Molly lay there on the filthy floor, bruised, broken, and terrified, her cheek pressed tightly against Stella's cold breast, she was unaware that equally brutal rapes and murders were occurring throughout the town, and that few females over the age of nine or under the age of seventy, no matter their status, were spared the unspeakable horrors.

She could hear women screaming and the dull pop of gunfire, but the sounds seemed far away, remote, not real. She could smell the smoke of burning buildings as the town went up in flames, but even that made no impression on her, until those flames were licking at the very walls of the washroom itself.

She had tried to drag Stella's body from the burning building, and had almost succeeded, when a big man with a red beard and small, piggish eyes had galloped his horse up to her and swung down from the saddle to leer at her nudity as she braved the scorching heat in her effort to pull Stella through the blazing doorway.

Laughing loudly, his breath stinking of cheap whiskey, Caleb King had caught Molly up in his arms and carried her to the middle of the street where the heat was less severe, and there he had taken her. At last Molly understood Stella's warning and let herself "go away." She lay there and felt nothing, not pain or pleasure, nor any emotions whatsoever, not this time or any of the seemingly hundreds of times that followed throughout the next three years. Not with him, nor with any of the men he "rented" her to. She had lain beneath him in the middle of the street, and watched with dull, unemotional eyes as other girls and women were dragged into the street and brutalized.

Molly glared at Gabrielle Johnson. "Believe me, Miss Johnson, you can thank your lucky stars you were not one of those 'decent women' who were *spared!*"

As though they were a four-man jury hearing a case argued before a magistrate, John Wright, Lieutenant Pendleton, Joseph Robertson, and William Beecher shifted their attention to Gabrielle Johnson for her response. They would weigh her reaction to Molly's accusations and the captain's denial, and make their judgment accordingly.

Gabrielle was startled to find them watching her so expectantly. Why were they looking at her so? Then it dawned on her: the unspoken code of masculine chivalry concerning decent women dictated that she, as the only truly virtuous woman present, held Molly Klinner's reputation—and future—in the palm of her hand.

The power to acquit or destroy by one's own whim was a heady intoxicant, and Gabrielle reeled with it, not once considering the consequences that accompanied such responsibility. She rose to the occasion and dramatically and deliberately played a waiting game, drawing out her verdict as long as possible.

The seconds seemed like hours, and with each one, Molly became more distraught until finally she broke with a tide of anger toward Gabrielle Johnson that surprised even herself. "I'll say this in my defense, and only this: the very reason that I am alive today is because of a prostitute. She warned me to give in to them . . . to detach my mind and soul from what was happening to my body—and I finally did. I lived, Miss Johnson, but the pure, chaste women—like you—were not able to mentally detach themselves from the . . . depraved acts they were forced to endure. They died, Miss Johnson. They died horribly!"

Gabrielle arched her eyebrows. "A pure, chaste woman would prefer death, Miss Klinner."

It was over.

Molly wished they would all leave, just go away and let her be. She did not need them. She had never needed them.

Molly let the hammer down on the pistol and laid it aside. Drawing the blanket up over her shoulders, she climbed unsteadily to her feet and walked toward the far end of the shed.

She told herself she would rather spend the remainder of the night in the empty stagecoach than in a room full of sanctimonious hypocrites.

As Molly neared the opening, a burning sensation that felt as though someone had sliced open her abdomen and ripped out her innards seared through her body. She clutched her stomach and dropped to her knees. Perspiration sprang to her forehead and flooded her temples; her eyes went wild, darting here, there, seeing nothing but pain. Then they rolled back into her head, and she collapsed.

Peyton Lewis, having become concerned for Molly Klinner's well-being when no one came to relieve him, had stepped unobserved inside the building just in time to hear the final dialogue between Molly and Gabrielle. He was not stunned or surprised by Gabrielle's closing statement; he was angered by it. What did an eastern woman know about self-preservation during wartime? By her own admission, not a damned thing! If she had, she would have known that while it was true that a chaste woman *might* have wanted to cease to exist, the instinct to live is far stronger than the desire to die, and most women—no matter their social status—would do whatever it took to survive.

Peyton had watched Molly Klinner climb to her feet and start, teetering like a drunkard, for the door. He knew she was going to fall—they all did—but they had just stood there. By the time he had elbowed the men aside and raced to catch her, Molly had collapsed.

Nineteen

Peyton dropped to his knees beside Molly and drew her into the crook of his arm.

"Miss Klinner?" He gently slapped her face. "Molly, can you hear me?"

The men watched Peyton in awkward, embarrassed silence, but Gabrielle Johnson eyed him with hostile contempt.

Peyton ignored them, and again cuffed Molly's face. Her eyelids fluttered open. She tried to focus on the man leaning over her, but her pupils rolled and darted with a will of their own, until, a moment later, her lids closed and did not reopen.

Peyton exhaled, wondering what to do next. She had not recognized him, could not tell him what ailed her. He brushed her damp hair off her forehead. Her skin was wet with perspiration, yet she was cold and clammy to his touch.

Molly clutched her stomach and moaned aloud. She took her bottom lip between her teeth and bit hard. Blood trickled down her chin.

Peyton looked up at the men. "What's wrong with her stomach?"

The onlookers glanced uneasily at one another. They refused to meet his eye. Joseph Robertson cleared his throat as if to speak, then thought better of it. He was—they all were—aware Molly Klinner was traveling with Peyton Lewis, and had been for a long while, and they also knew meddling into a man's personal affairs could fast become a deadly venture, especially when it involved someone as touchy as Peyton Lewis.

Peyton swung his inquiring gaze to Gabrielle. "Would you mind telling me what's wrong with Miss Klinner?"

Unlike the men, her eyes did not waver. "You know very well what Miss Klinner's *problem* is, Mr. Lewis."

"Stop playing puppet on a string with me, Miss Johnson. Something's wrong with her. What the hell is it?"

"She's with child, Mr. Lewis. You should know that better than any of us." Turning abruptly, Gabrielle stalked to the edge of the shed and stared into the darkness.

A wind sprang up and charged past her through the doorway, sending smoke and sparks from the unattended fire billowing about the room. No one noticed. Everyone's attention was on Peyton Lewis as he stared at Molly's abdomen. The bulge was plainly visible.

Peyton was staggered. Why had he not noticed it before? How could a man be with a woman night and day for more than six weeks and not notice that she was with child?

Peyton longed to shake Molly Klinner until her teeth rattled. Instead, he cuffed her again, hard.

Molly's eyelids fluttered and then opened. She was back in the world of awareness; her gaze was clear and focused.

"Why didn't you tell me?"

"Tell you what?"

"About yourself."

Molly forced herself to laugh mockingly at him, displaying a row of teeth that were a dingy pink from the stain of her blood where she had bitten through her lip.

"Tell you about myself? That I worked in a brothel? That Caleb King claimed me as a war prize, then sold me to any man with a nickel in his pocket? That I ran away from him three times, and each time he caught me was worse than the time before? That he broke bones in my body, Mr. Lewis?" She cut her eyes to Gabrielle Johnson. "And yes, I still chose life over death . . . no matter the cost."

Peyton's arms tightened about her. "That's in the past, Molly. We can't change it. What I ask is, why didn't you tell me about the baby?"

Anger surged through her. She owed him no explanation about the child in her womb. Who did he think he was, her husband? She grimaced as another pain cut through her from spine to navel, and in spite of her crossness toward him, she was grateful his arms were tightly around her, for without them to hold her steady, she would have been forced to suffer the humiliation and indignity of groveling in the dirt like some kind of wild beast, and that would have been more unbearable than any suffering she had yet endured.

The cramp subsided, and she relaxed against him. Grudgingly, she admitted to herself that he deserved the truth. He had earned it.

"If I had told you about my condition, you would have insisted that I stay behind . . . and I was determined to have this baby in Texas, far away from my past . . . far away from everyone I had known . . . from anyone who had known me. I wanted my child's first breath to be in a world where he or she had a chance at life . . . the kind of chance you told me about, to become something or nothing, by one's own merits. In Kansas, with Caleb King, there would have been no chance at all."

That was not the whole truth, and Molly knew it. She dropped her gaze from his, afraid he would see into the depths of her soul. She was—and had been from the beginning—aware that she had kept her condition from Peyton because she wanted him to desire her, to find her beautiful, to long for her as she longed for him, and she feared he would not if he had the least inkling she was carrying a child.

It dawned on Molly that others were present; they had heard and seen her every word and gesture, the truth of her feelings toward Peyton Lewis, her hopes for the future for her and the child. Everything.

Suddenly she was angry again—with Peyton for allowing

her to bare a portion, no matter how small, of her inner self to him; with those who watched, for intruding into her privacy; with Gabrielle Johnson, who, by figuring out the truth, had brought Molly's ugly past to light; with all of them who stood so tall and guiltless in their own eyes; but most of all with herself for allowing them—any of them—to attempt to force their standards on her.

Molly pushed herself to her elbows and pinned each of them with a stare charged with contempt. "You saw for yourself, Mr. Lewis, the reaction of these fine, upstanding people when they learned about my past. Why should I have assumed that you would have responded any differently?"

"What did you expect from these folks, Molly, a medal?"

Tears filled her eyes. She angrily knuckled them away. "I expected exactly what I got . . . from all of you."

Another pain hit her like the kick of a mule. She arched her back and twisted in his arms. Her eyes rolled again, and the convulsions became so violent that she nearly wrenched free of his grip. She screamed; it was an awful sound.

Peyton turned to the only person in the group who might have some knowledge of childbearing. "Do you know anything about birthing a baby, Miss Johnson?"

"No."

"You're a woman. You must know something!"

Gabrielle turned her back to him and stared into the night.

Peyton's breath slipped through his clenched teeth. If Gabrielle Johnson were a man, he would have beaten her to a pulp. But she was not a man. Hell, she wasn't much of a woman either. A real woman would not turn her back on someone in labor—if not on the mother's behalf, then at least for the sake of the child.

He forced his gaze away from Gabrielle to the men. They shook their heads.

Molly cried out again, and her body arched until her hips were off the blanket. Her head tossed from side to side, and her breathing accelerated until it was almost a pant. She gazed desperately at Peyton, her eyes begging for help.

He glared at Gabrielle, who had turned and was again

watching him. "I guess it's up to you, Miss Johnson. She's got to have help."

"Then you help her, Mr. Lewis. I would assume, under the circumstances, that's the least you would do for her."

Peyton was furious. That was the second time Gabrielle had insisted that Molly Klinner was his responsibility. Surely she did not believe that he was the father of the child? He swung his gaze to the only man in the group he trusted. To his surprise, John Wright, along with the rest of the men, was scowling accusingly at him.

A denial formed on Peyton's lips. Then his mouth clamped shut. There was nothing to say. Gabrielle Johnson's unspoken charge had been readily embraced as truth.

Peyton settled back on his heels and gazed at the faces staring down at him. He was glad Rucker was not there, for he would have blurted out the truth. They did not deserve the truth. Nor would they get it from him. He turned again to Molly, calm, sure of himself. Using his shirttail as a towel, he dried the sweat on her brow and blotted at the blood on her lips.

Gabrielle Johnson was more bewildered than ever as she watched Peyton patiently bathe Molly Klinner's face. She had been positive he would deny the charge; indeed, she had needed to hear him contradict Molly Klinner's physical evidence. He had not, and his condemning silence left her more shaken and insecure than she had been before she forced the issue.

Molly Klinner, however, was the person most shocked by Peyton's unexpected gallantry. His silence was especially dear to her because, by the very act of not replying, Peyton had flung a direct challenge to the men who, just moments before, had held him in complete contempt for not shouldering his duty as the father of her child. Concern etched her brow, for now that he had thrown his reputation to the wind, she suddenly did not want him to suffer her shame and humiliation.

"Don't let me—or them—do this to you, Peyton. Tell them the truth."

Peyton shook his head, silencing her. Whether or not she realized it, a denial would make little difference. They wanted to believe the worst.

As if to punctuate Peyton's thoughts, John Wright, his face a mask of scorn, walked to the corner where his gear was stored and snatched up his bullwhip. He started across the room toward Peyton.

"I ought to stripe you good, Lewis. I got no time for a man who knocks up a girl an' then don't do the responsible thing by her. None a'tall!"

Gabrielle sucked in her breath. Never had she encountered men such as these: hard men who would turn on a friend as quickly as a foe if said friend committed an act they deemed unworthy; dangerous men who would maim or kill in the name of honor—or dishonor; men who said what they meant, and would die rather than break their word. Nor had she ever before heard such base language uttered in the presence of a lady. Such talk and such men disgusted and embarrassed her, yet she found them both so positively exciting that she longed for them to continue—and that truth about her innermost self mortified her even more than they whom she detested.

Peyton eased Molly down on the blanket, then climbed to his feet. He appraised John Wright levelly. He liked the man, respected him, even felt a certain kinship with him because of the war, but he certainly was not afraid of him.

Peyton laid his hand on his pistol handle. "I'd be careful about threatenin' to take a snake to me, John. Nobody whips me."

John Wright glared at Peyton, unintimidated by the subtle warning. Seconds ticked past, each one a nerve-racking millennium in time. The men near Wright stepped away, and Gabrielle Johnson's throat was suddenly too dry for her to swallow the lump that had formed there. They waited.

John Wright made no move to unlimber his whip. He was well aware Peyton Lewis's statement had been no idle threat. He knew, also, he would have to kill Lewis or be killed by him if he touched him with his lash. Yet he knew it had already gone too far for either of them to back down, for honor, once forfeited, could almost never be reclaimed.

Molly Klinner understood more than any other person in the room what was transpiring right before their eyes. One, perhaps both, of these fine men would die because, according to their code, no man worth his salt could live with the stigma of "coward" attached to his name. And neither of them would admit he was wrong; their masculine pride dictated that much.

With her heart in her throat, Molly drew herself to her feet and stood shakily in front of Peyton. Aware that she was again treading on the thin ice of his male vanity, she confronted the driver: "I am disappointed in you, John. Evidently you have forgotten my conversation with the sheriff at French's station when I told him I had been living with Caleb King." Molly touched her abdomen. "This baby belongs to Caleb King, John, and only God above knows why Mr. Lewis is trying to protect me."

Peyton shot Molly an angry glare that plainly said for her to stay out of his business.

Wright scowled at Molly. Would she never learn? Did she not remember that night in Wichita, Kansas, when he warned her about intruding into men's business? Damn her! Still, she had a point. Now that she had mentioned it, he did recall the confrontation in the barn. But Molly Klinner had stated that she was running away with Peyton Lewis. Wright's eyes narrowed suspiciously. Was she telling the truth, or was she, once again, trying to save Lewis's life?

John Wright's hands tightened on his whip handle. The only thing he knew for certain was that Molly Klinner was no liar. *Shit! I done meddled around an' got tangled in my own spurs.* Spinning on his heel, Wright stomped out of the shed.

For a long interval there was total silence in the room. Each onlooker wondered why Peyton had not simply denounced any relationship with Molly Klinner from the beginning. It would certainly have saved a lot of hard feelings, not to mention a near killing. The release of their pent-up breaths rushed loudly through the room.

Gabrielle Johnson took an involuntary step toward Peyton; she longed with all her heart to rush to him and throw herself into his arms, to tell him how confused she was, to even beg his forgiveness. As Gabrielle took another tentative step toward Peyton, Molly Klinner cried out in pain, and her knees buckled.

Peyton caught her to him and held her against his chest. His eyes searched the faces of the men who watched, seeking one who would step forward and offer Molly Klinner his assistance. Not one man so much as blinked.

Peyton's icy gaze locked on Captain Cramer, and something in Peyton's eyes, or possibly the lack of something that should have been there, caused the short hairs on the captain's neck to stand up in alarm.

Cramer flushed with an anger that stemmed from the fear he was experiencing. "You can't shame *us*, Lewis. We won't touch that woman. . . . Why, she said herself she worked in a brothel. Hell, she might have any manner of disease." When Peyton merely stared at him, the captain became even more belligerent. "She's a whore, Lewis. All I did was tell the truth about Miss Klinner." He drew Gabrielle Johnson in as an ally. "A lady's reputation is at stake here, Lewis. How would it have looked for a fine, cultured lady like Miss Johnson to have arrived in a good Christian town traveling in the company of a known strumpet?"

Cramer had finally made a point everyone could hang their hat on: the men murmured their agreement, and Gabrielle used the same reasoning as an excuse to retreat again to the doorway. And Peyton Lewis, who had never actually hated a man until that precise moment, suddenly was acquainted with a brand-new emotion.

The captain saw it in Peyton's eyes, and something inside him turned to jelly. His face blanched white, and Molly Klinner's words from several days ago echoed in his mind with such clarity that she might as well have just this minute shouted, "Captain Cramer has said all he can say for free; his next few words will cost him dearly."

With an oath, Cramer marched past Gabrielle and headed toward the corral. Lieutenant Pendleton, who had thus far been merely a spectator, excused himself and hastened after the captain, mumbling just loud enough for the men to hear that he and Cramer would stand guard duty for the remainder of the night.

Molly raised her face from where it had rested against Peyton's chest and pressed her lips close to his ear. "Why are you doing this? You don't have to, you know."

Peyton took a breath and exhaled through his teeth. Why did women deem it necessary to question and belittle every decent thing a man did?

"Because you were right a little while ago. Some men *are* too blind to see. . . ."

Before Peyton could explain further, John Wright entered the shed and marched up to Molly. "I'm real sorry about your predicament, Miss Molly, an' I wish I could help you. But birthin' a baby is women's work. Men don't know nothin' about female ailments; we jest naturally don't. Now, if you was gunshot or tomahawked, or dragged by a horse, or gored by a bull, well, that would be different. We know about them kind o' things. But bringin' a baby into the world . . . well, that's a horse of a different color."

Molly waved aside John Wright's apology; excuses were of little importance, especially when Peyton Lewis's explanation of why he took the blame for fathering her child was on the tip of his tongue. *That* was of the utmost importance to her.

Gabrielle's face burned with humiliation as John Wright voiced his regrets concerning male inadequacies with female ailments, especially when he implied that midwifing came naturally to all women. Arching her eyebrows, she voiced aloud to John Wright that he had obviously overlooked the fact that nearly all doctors and nurses were men, and that of all the people present, he should know that better than most, because a while back she had overheard him tell Peyton Lewis he had been an ambulance driver during the war.

John Wright nodded solemnly. "That's a fact, Miss Johnson. I drove for Gen'ral Hill. The only trouble with your argument, however, is that we sawed off arms an' legs an' sewed up people an' cauterized wounds, but with all them afflictions we attended to, not one of them soldiers was fixin' t' have a baby."

"Well, I can assure you, Mr. Wright," Gabrielle said, her words clipped, "the subject of childbirth was certainly not part of the academic curriculum at Mrs. Prichert's school for young ladies in Monroe, Michigan. In fact, our instructors absolutely forbade us to associate in any manner at all with young women who found themselves in such a . . . compromising position."

She blushed and glared at Peyton as though she was still uncertain about his involvement with Molly Klinner.

Another labor pain doubled Molly over, and her screams vibrated off the walls of the small structure.

Peyton lowered Molly onto the blanket, then climbed deliberately to his feet. He crossed the room in three strides, caught Gabrielle by her coat lapels, and raised her to her tiptoes. "I don't give a damn what they taught you at that fancy girls' school, Miss Johnson."

Gabrielle felt the contours of his body pressed tightly against her and the warmth of his breath against her face. In spite of her anger over being manhandled, her body responded and she sagged against him, her face tilted up to his.

Peyton looked into her eyes, missing entirely the meaning behind their half-closed sensuality. "Do something to ease Miss Klinner's pain, Miss Johnson. And do it now!"

Gabrielle attempted to jerk free, but Peyton hauled her even more tightly against him until their faces were only a hairsbreadth apart. Her lips trembled at his nearness, and her breathing ran shallow. "Do what, Mr. Lewis? I have no idea what you expect from me!"

Peyton released Gabrielle, and she backed slowly away from him. Self-consciously she smoothed the fabric of her bodice, which was suddenly too tight across her breasts to allow her to breathe freely. Her hand fluttered to her throat, and she averted her face, terrified he would see or hear her heart racing wildly in her chest.

Peyton paced in short circles, blind to Gabrielle Johnson's personal dilemma. His only concern was Molly Klinner's plight and the fact that he truly believed a woman—any woman—naturally knew and understood how to birth a baby. There had to be something Gabrielle could do! He ran his hand through his hair.

"Think of something, Miss Johnson. At least you could examine her to see if she's passing blood."

Gabrielle was aghast. The heat in her face, brought about by his nearness a moment before, suddenly became a volcanic eruption. "I most certainly will not! I'll not lower myself to view another woman's private parts. It's . . . it's indecent . . . it's humiliating! God! I hate you!"

"Indecent? Humiliating?" Peyton's patience was at the breaking point. He took a threatening step toward her. She retreated. Then, again.

"We're talking about bringing a baby into the world, Miss Johnson. It's a normal female function, for Christ's sake!"

Gabrielle eyed Peyton with a venom that left little question of her sincerity. "You can blaspheme me from now to the Second Coming of our Savior, Mr. Lewis. But I assure you, sir, I will not examine Miss Klinner below the waist! No lady would do that. Nor would a real gentleman ask!"

John Wright, while sympathizing with Peyton's agitation, bridled anew: "Simmer down, Lewis. We've got to help Molly, there ain't no question about that. But threatenin' Miss Johnson an' cussin' won't help Molly one whit."

Peyton was at his wit's end. He had heard nothing John Wright said; he was still watching Gabrielle and wondering what being a lady or a gentleman had to do with birthing a newborn. "One thing you can do, lady, is make Molly more comfortable. You can get some goddamned blankets an' make a real pallet. . . ."

Although Peyton's demand was pointed at Gabrielle Johnson, Joseph Robertson and William Beecher stampeded out of the shed and headed for the stagecoach, where the horse blankets were stored.

John Wright walked to Gabrielle Johnson and laid a fatherly hand on her shoulder. "Maybe you won't touch Miss Klinner below the belt—an' nobody's apt to force you to—but there is somethin' you can do for her."

Gabrielle felt as though the weight of the world was on her shoulders. She wanted nothing more than to just sit down and cry. The entire episode with Peyton Lewis and Molly Klinner had left her nerve-racked and exhausted. She gazed at John Wright with weary disinterest.

"And what is that, sir?"

"You can take some of that sweet-smellin' soap you use and wash Molly's face and hands."

Gabrielle was appalled by Wright's suggestion; she would as soon loan Molly Klinner her underwear as waste even one ounce of her precious lavender bars on a prostitute! "How many times do I have to tell you, Mr. Wright, I'll not touch that woman—not now, not ever!"

Wright pushed his face close to hers, his breath reeking of tobacco. "Ma'am, I put it to you nicely . . . kind'a like a formal request. But it weren't. I want Molly's face washed. Do you get my drift?"

Gabrielle met his gaze steadily. "I'll not be bullied, Mr. Wright, not by Peyton Lewis, and not by you!"

"Well, ma'am, I ain't bullyin' you. I'm jest tryin' to wise you up a bit. Out here in the West, there's an ol' sayin' that goes like this: Stay shy of a man who's all gurgle an' no guts." His leathery face hardened into a grim mask. "So far, Miss Gabrielle, I ain't seen much of nothin' but gurgle out o' you . . . an' I'd like t' think there was more t' you than that."

Gabrielle lifted her chin defiantly. "Has it ever occurred to you, sir, that I am not a westerner? Or a man?" She squared her shoulders, stalked out of the shed, and headed for the stage-coach.

John Wright walked to the door. "If'n you're goin' after that soap, fetch your lookin' glass, too."

Twenty

April 4, 1866　FALSE DAWN

Rucker and Ben were up and riding before full daylight. It had stopped raining, but the traveling was slow. Not only did the mist lie heavy in the chilly air, but the rain-lashed terrain was slippery and treacherous, even for their four-footed steeds.

Ben pointed at the dark silhouette of a hill that rose up out of the fog a mile ahead. "We'll cross the stagecoach road jest the other side o' that ridge. If them Injuns is sho' nuff headed toward Gainesville, like we 'sume they are, we should pick up their tracks along 'bout there."

"How far is Gainesville?"

"Maybe five, six miles south o' here." Ben's eyes were constantly moving, prying into the darkest shadows, searching the most distant hills. Missing nothing.

Rucker studied the southern skyline for smoke or the glow of a fire. "There's a good chance they done burned Gainesville t' the ground, Uncle."

"Naw, Mista' Fletcher, I don't b'lieve so. In my estimation, when they raided that depot back yonder"—pointing with his chin, Ben indicated the way they had come—"them Comanche more'n likely carried off the station agent's entire stock o' drinkin' whiskey. If'n they did, well, sir, they prob'ly went t' roost early that evenin' an' did a heap of celebratin'." Ben grinned at Rucker. "I figure them Comanche spent the last two, three days nursin' big headaches, 'cause they ain't nobody on the face o' this earth who can't hold their liquor worse'n an Injun."

Concern furrowed Rucker's brow. If that were true, then there was a real possibility the Comanches were traveling either to or from Gainesville this very moment. Suddenly he was anxious to reach the road. If the war party was headed toward Gainesville, he wanted to know it; if not, he wanted to know that, too.

Rucker spurred his horse into a canter toward the distant hill. An all-out run was preferable, but he had been a cavalryman much too long to chance a fall that might injure his mount and leave him afoot in hostile territory.

The two riders pushed their horses hard all the way to the top of the knoll, then reined in on the crest to give the animals a blow. The sun broke the horizon and bathed the landscape in a golden glow as though someone had lighted a giant lantern.

Ben pointed toward the Gainesville trace, not a quarter of a mile distant: the tracks of scores of unshod Indian ponies were plainly visible, now that the sun was up.

Again Rucker scanned the southern skyline, the direction in which the town lay. Not a wisp of smoke or fire showed on the gunmetal-gray horizon. A ray of hope surged through him. Perhaps there was still time to warn Gainesville that the Indians were on the warpath. He said as much to Ben, stressing that they should make a run for it by the shortest possible route.

Ben waved Rucker to silence, his attention drawn to the Gainesville road. Something was wrong with the displacement of the mud that the Indian ponies' hooves had churned up. It just did not look right.

"I rec'mend we mosey on down t' that trace an' study them tracks, Mista' Fletcher. Yes, sir, they's times when a body can learn a heap from a passel o' pony tracks."

Rucker considered it a waste of valuable time, but he followed Ben down the incline. When they reached the corridor, its muddy bed was covered with hundreds of fresh imprints, and even Rucker's untrained eye could see that they were not heading toward Gainesville; they were traveling north toward the burned-out station.

Rucker's stomach churned queasily, and he leaned on his saddle horn for support. Although he knew the answer, he voiced the question anyway, in hopes that Ben, in his infinite wisdom, might have read something into the obvious that he, Fletcher Rucker, had missed.

Ben pursed his lips and scratched his chin, then answered Rucker honestly. "Fo' some reason, Mista' Fletcher, them Injuns done decided t' give up on attackin' Gainesville. They's a poss'-bility that they figure on headin' back t' the depot an' waitin' fo' another unsuspectin' stagecoach. Or they might simply have 'nother jug or two o' whiskey buried there. Or . . . heck, Mista' Fletcher, they might jest be goin' home. Like I tolt you, they ain't no figurin' what's in a Injun's mind. One thing's fo' certain, howsomever—they're headed back the way they came, straight fo' our folks. We was s'posed t' keep that from happenin', Mista' Fletcher."

Rucker unbuttoned his coat and drew his ivory-handled revolver from its holster. He turned the cylinder slowly, assuring himself that every priming cap was in place. The Henry rifle was also fully loaded with fifteen rounds. He knew Ben was right. It had been their job to locate the Comanche and report back to the station. Now the Indians were between them. Rucker reached out and laid his hand on Ben's shoulder.

"You're a good man to cross the river with, Uncle, but this is where we part company. You ride on ahead and alert those people at Gainesville as to what's happened."

Ben took a deep breath, pleased by Rucker's compliment concerning crossing the river, because a man only made a statement like that about someone he fully trusted. He shook his head. "I don't mean t' be d'sputin' yo' order, Mista' Fletcher, but if'n yo're figurin' on headin' back t' help them folks at the stage-coach depot, then I'm figurin' on ridin' 'long with yo'."

Rucker palmed his hat to the back of his head. Ben was an exasperating mystery. He pointed to the pony tracks. "There must be a hundred Indians in that war party. Why would you want t' ride back and risk your life for a bunch of people

you don't owe nothin'? Hell, some of those folks even mis-
treated you!"

"Risk my life?" Ben laughed and waved Rucker's comment aside. "Mista' Fletcher, I never risk my life. I learnt a long
time ago that if'n a man was born t' drown, he'll drown on the
desert . . . even if it's dry as a bone."

In one fluid motion, the two men pivoted their horses and
quirted them into a dead run back the way they had come.

Molly lay on her blankets and gazed out the open end of the
shed. The sun, inching its way over the horizon, was lifting the
burdensome gray morning mist off the earth's surface. It appeared to be struggling, fighting every step of the way, as though
it shouldered an enormous weight.

Molly blinked to clear her fuzzy vision, an impairment
brought on as the result of a long night without once having
closed her eyes.

Again she looked at the sun, and she felt as though half
that enormous weight lay upon her abdomen and was squeezing
the life out of her. A jolt of pain ran the length of her body. The
contractions were coming closer together now.

To take her mind off her confinement, she picked up
Gabrielle Johnson's hand mirror and gazed into it for the hundredth time since the girl had brought it to her late last night.

Molly was fascinated by the face that peered back at her.
She did not recognize that woman, had never seen her before.

Molly laid the mirror aside. Three years! Three long, hard
years with Caleb King had certainly made a difference in her. She
was no longer a young, pretty girl. She was a woman . . . a soon-
to-be mother.

Another pain snapped her from her reflection. She dug her
heels into the ground and strained, arching her body, her face
flushed anew with perspiration. It was time. She rolled her head
sideways and glanced wild-eyed in search of Peyton. He was
kneeling beside the fire pit trying to breathe life into the banked
coals.

"Peyton!" He looked up from the fire. His eyes were blood-shot, and he sported a dark stubble of beard that added a forbidding look to his haggard face. To Molly he was beautiful.

"Please help me to the coach. I . . ." She gazed at the sleeping forms of the men scattered around the room, then at Gabrielle, who lay in the shadows near the wall. Even though the girl's eyes appeared to be closed, Molly was certain that she was wide awake and watching.

"I need privacy, Peyton. I think the baby is finally coming . . . and I . . . I don't want those people to see." Tears trickled down her cheeks. "Oh, Peyton."

Peyton lifted Molly into his arms and carried her out into the sunshine. She blinked as the brilliant sphere cleared the horizon. The breeze that cooled the perspiration on her forehead was fresh and sweet. The landscape was clean and sparkling. From somewhere she heard a bird sing. Her baby would be born into a fresh, new world.

Molly nestled her cheek against Peyton's shoulder and sighed with pleasure, the first she had experienced in a long while. She wished she were not in labor, that she could lie there, secure in his arms forever. Then he opened the stagecoach door and positioned her carefully on the leather-covered seat.

She was conscious of an unaccustomed feeling of loss as he disengaged himself and stepped away. In spite of the sun that shafted through the open doorway of the coach, her skin chilled where his body had touched her.

Molly dropped her head down against the thin padding of the bench seat and raised her legs so she could plant her feet firmly against the side panel. The muscles in her legs quivered as another pain, lower this time, drew her knees to her chin. Oblivious to the fact that her skirts slid down over her naked hips, she forced her feet back to the side panel and strained hard.

Peyton closed the door and leaned his head against the stagecoach's rough wooden grain. His mind reeled with the drama being played out inside the coach. Again he heard John Wright's words, "We are out of our element," and he realized how very true they were. He had not even been allowed into the house when his mother had birthed his younger brother and sister.

He stepped away from the stage and spoke to Molly through the closed window curtain. "This is as far as I go, Molly. I'm no midwife . . . and don't intend to start trying to be one now."

Molly stared at the closed door. Did he intend to just walk away and leave her? Surely not! *I need you,* her mind shouted. *I need you now more than ever. . . . I don't want to be alone.* Molly closed her eyes and took a deep breath.

"Then leave! The hard part is over, anyway. Go on; I don't need you."

Before the sound of her voice died away, Peyton was halfway back to the shed, and Molly was alone.

Gabrielle lay curled in her blankets, feigning sleep. She felt Peyton's presence as he stood peering down at her. She assumed he would awaken her and demand that she attend Molly Klinner. Well, she would not! She heard him move away, and she slitted her eyes, studying him through her heavy lashes. He had squatted beside the fire and was poking at the ashes. Disappointment that he had not awakened her drew her lips into a pout. If he would simply ask her nicely, perhaps she would help Molly Klinner—perhaps.

Peyton picked up the pot and poured himself a tin of lukewarm coffee. He took a long pull, then sat back on his heels and, like Molly Klinner had done a few minutes earlier, glanced out the open end of the shed to the distant slope where the sun had bathed the crest in a warm, golden glow. He scowled, wondering where Rucker and Ben were. They should have returned hours ago. He squinted again at the horizon; something was moving on a hilltop a mile or more to the south.

Peyton's breath constricted in his chest. Scores of horsemen in feathered headdresses, shields, and lances topped the rise and began spreading out across the pinnacle. It was an eerie spectacle, silent and scary, like a serpent raising its deadly head and baring its fangs.

"People"—that one word, spoken softly, yet with the impact of a shouted warning, snapped those still wrapped in their blankets wide awake—"you better hit the floor running, because we're in a hell of a mess." They surged to their feet. Their greatest fear had at last become a reality.

John Wright trotted to the open end of the shed and squinted at the hilltop. Even as he watched, the horde of savages, who only moments before had sat their horses like statues silhouetted against the clear blue backdrop of a cloudless sky, began walking their ponies slowly down the slope toward the station. Wright thumbed back the hammers of his double-barreled, muzzle-loading shotgun, checked the percussion caps to be certain they were firmly seated on their nipples, then ran his ramrod down both barrels to tamp the charge of powder and shot.

"Any idee how long they've been there, Peyton?"

"Just arrived, as far as I can tell."

Peyton unbuttoned his greatcoat and tucked its tails behind his pistol handle, leaving the weapon free to quick access, then walked to his saddlebags and began a quick assessment of the available firearms.

Wright peered again at the Indians. "Well, they're movin' now . . . an' they're headed this way!"

Gabrielle sprang to her feet and joined Wright at the doorway, her eyes riveted to the menace that was spreading down the hillside like thick, slow-moving molasses. All the horrible stories she had heard concerning the savage red men were suddenly very real; now they were here, riding leisurely toward her, their dark beady eyes searching for her, their mahogany fingers reaching out to her, their naked bodies ready and waiting for her. She leaned weakly against the shed wall for support, and clutched her blanket more tightly around her bosom.

Joseph Robertson and William Beecher pushed up beside the two, and gawked at the war party, for like Gabrielle Johnson, these were the first hostile Indians they had ever seen—and the sight reduced the two men's knees to water.

William Beecher cast an accusing eye at Gabrielle. "I voted to wait for an escort! Now we're all going to die . . . and it's your fault! Yours and that whore's."

Tears welled up in Gabrielle's eyes. It was not her fault; it was Molly Klinner's fault. If Molly had not challenged her . . . She threw Peyton a hate-filled gaze. *I wanted to impress you! I wanted to prove my courage to you!* She buried her face in her hands and wept.

Peyton closed his saddlebag flaps and climbed to his feet. His eyes, when he swung them to Beecher and Robertson, said plainly that he had listened to all the whining he intended. Walking to the men, he handed each a handleless revolver with two extra cylinders. They accepted the weapons in silence, but the moment Peyton's back was turned, their gaze jumped accusingly to Gabrielle Johnson.

Peyton walked to where John Wright was measuring out powder and shot for his double-barrel. "Get Molly out of that coach, John. She's a sitting duck out there. I'll head out to the corral and see if Cramer and Pendleton are still alive."

The driver struck off through the mud toward the stagecoach fifty yards away. Upon reaching it, he snatched open the door and thrust his head inside.

"Miss Molly . . ." Wright faltered at the sight of her exposed nudity, but only for an instant. "I hate to be bustin' in on you at such an indelicate moment, ma'am, but if'n we don't get you out of here in about two seconds, you're fixin' to have half the Comanche nation lookin' up your dress!"

Molly snatched her skirt down over her knees. Fear replaced the surprise on her face. "Comanches! Are you sure?"

"Sure as shootin'." He caught her arm and drew her toward the door.

"How many are there?"

"Looks like a thousand, but they's probably ain't but a hunnert or so."

Molly's heart skipped a beat. A hundred! A hundred Comanche, the most bloodthirsty and feared Indians on the plains—and she in the throes of labor! *Oh, my God!*

Molly climbed clumsily out of the coach. When she stood erect, her head swam, and she was obliged to lean heavily on John Wright for support as they splashed through the sticky muck toward the shed.

"John!" Molly clutched her abdomen and stumbled to her

knees. "I'm sorry, John. I . . . I can't go on. I'm going to have this baby right here in the mud."

Without missing a stride, John Wright swept Molly into his arms and ran for the shed as fast as his aged legs would carry him.

As Wright carried Molly into the building, she peered over his shoulder at the hill. The Indians were now within three-quarters of a mile of the station, advancing their ponies at a walk. At that distance, she could barely make out their feathered war bonnets, their buffalo-horn helmets, their long lances and bull-hide shields, but to her, even the suggestion of such un-Christian apparel was an unnerving sight. It was meant to be.

Wright set Molly on her feet just inside the door, then hurried off to retrieve his shotgun.

Gabrielle appeared at Molly's side. Her bloodless face resembled a death mask. Even her lips, which were normally a deep, healthy pink, were lost in a visage without contrast.

"We are to blame for our being here, Miss Klinner. You and I . . . and Peyton. And when we all die here today, God will make us answer for what we have done. We will be judged as murderers. We will burn in hell." Her voice was a monotone, as lifeless as her hands and face. She was gripping the five-shot pocket pistol; her knuckles were white and trembling.

Molly discounted Gabrielle's comments as nothing more than the delirium of a terrified person. She could not, however, stop herself from questioning the reasoning behind Peyton's giving the woman the small, easy-to-manage revolver instead of the heavy, cumbersome army Colt that he had pressed on her. Obviously he considered the smaller firearm more ladylike. The thought stabbed her with envy.

Then Molly burst into laughter, and the mere act of tightening her muscles sent her stomach into such a flurry of constrictions that she was forced to grip the doorjamb to keep her knees from buckling. She pressed her forehead against the damp upright and swallowed back the nausea that threatened to drive her to the dirt floor to heave up her insides.

Through the mist of sickness and pain that fogged Molly's

mind, she could hear Gabrielle's voice drone on and on about how she, Peyton, and Molly had fallen from grace, until Molly felt as though she were going to scream. And finally she did, shouting for Gabrielle to shut up, just shut up; that it was neither Gabrielle's nor Peyton's nor her fault they were in this quandary.

"It's our fate, Gabrielle! God sent us here! We are not going to die! If there's any killing done here today, it will be us killing those murderous savages out there—and I assure you, God won't frown on it!"

Peyton, unable to locate the captain and lieutenant, hastened back to the shed. Ten feet from the doorway, he could plainly hear Molly Klinner shouting and Gabrielle Johnson answering in a monotone. He shook his head, incredulous, certain that if he lived to be a hundred, he would never understand the female gender.

Peyton rushed past the women and headed for John Wright, who was at the opposite end of the shed in animated conversation with Robertson and Beecher.

When Peyton drew near, John Wright wheeled around and faced him belligerently. "These two fools believe we should take a stand here in the shed, but I think we should fan out an' take cover anyplace we can—try t' catch 'em in a cross fire. What do you think, Peyton?"

Peyton assessed the interior of the shed. It was a windowless, open-end, slab-sided room, some twenty feet long by twelve feet wide. There was nothing available with which to barricade the open ends, and without such a bulwark, it would be impossible to defend.

"They'll ride right through this place . . . or they'll burn it down around our ears." He looked toward the depot. "The way I see it, the only chance we have is to put our backs together and fight a four-pronged frontal. And the best place to do that is the station house. We can man all four of the partial walls and use them as a fortification of sorts."

John Wright squinted at what had once been a twenty-by-twenty-foot-square, single-room log house. The fire had consumed not only the roof of the structure, which had ultimately collapsed inside the room, but also the top section of the walls, which had burned down to the bottom three or four runs of logs, leaving a perimeter of solid, hand-hewn timbers some thirty to forty inches high and twelve inches thick. They would need to clear a path around the inside of the room so they could kneel and fire over the barrier, but luckily, they had already removed many of the scorched timbers and loose debris when they searched the rubble for bodies.

The disadvantage of manning the station was that with only two people per wall, counting Molly Klinner and Gabrielle Johnson, it would be impossible to defend in a full frontal charge should the Comanche opt to overrun any given section of the waist-high barricade.

Wright was in the process of voicing that opinion when the captain and the lieutenant, disheveled and mud-spattered, raced into the shed. The captain's breath came in a ragged gasp. "Somebody stole our horses last night . . . probably when Lewis left his post unattended. We're trapped like fish in a barrel."

Lieutenant Pendleton gaped in surprise at his superior officer. The horses had been in the corral when they had taken their posts. Pendleton stepped away from the captain. "I can't speak for Captain Cramer, gentlemen, but I take full responsibility for the missing stock. I fell asleep at my post. I am sorry."

John Wright spat a stream of amber that hit the ground and splattered onto the lieutenant's boot. "Sonny boy, if you live long enough, you'll probably make a good officer." He turned to Captain Cramer. "This un never will. You're jest plain lucky them Injuns didn't take more'n them horses, Captain. Better men than you have woke up with their hair gone."

Wright pointed at the hill beyond the far end of the shed. "Evidently, you two soldier boys don't know we got company. You'd best take a look out there."

The soldiers hastened to the doorway and gaped, open-mouthed, at the sight on the hillside. Neither of them had ever seen a hostile Indian, and the horde of savages that walked their horses toward them were obviously not what they were expecting.

John Wright cackled aloud. "You boys been braggin' that you come west t' fight Injuns. Well, looks like you're goin' t' get your wish."

Gabrielle Johnson laid her hand on Lieutenant Pendleton's arm. "I hope you have made your peace with God, Lieutenant, because in a short while we're all going to die horrible deaths."

Molly pushed herself away from the doorpost. Die, indeed! She longed to slap Gabrielle's face.

"We are not going to die! I didn't keep this baby alive these past miserable months just so some heathen Indian could kill it." She brandished the revolver that Peyton had given her. "I am going to fight for my life and my baby's life—no matter what you people do!"

Gabrielle burst into tears. "We will all die. I know we will."

William Beecher, the drummer, unnerved by Gabrielle Johnson's wailing, turned toward Peyton Lewis. "Where the hell is Rucker and that nigger? They were supposed to warn us if Indians were in the vicinity." He pointed his finger accusingly at John Wright. "That's why you let the two of them venture out with the horses and the only decent gun, wasn't it?"

When Wright nodded, Beecher's face twisted into a furious mask. "Damn you, Wright, answer me!"

John Wright spit a stream of amber that hit dead center on the toe of Beecher's shoe. "I jest did, Bill. You got a problem with it?"

Peyton glanced at the Indians; they were less than half a mile away. Their painted faces, multicolored war shields, and feathered lances were now plainly visible, and they were awesome. He walked to Molly Klinner, and without so much as a by-your-leave swept her into his arms and stalked out of the building.

As Peyton carried Molly across the muddy flats to the burned-out station, Gabrielle ran to John Wright and clutched his arm. "What about me? Does Peyton not intend to take me with him?"

Wright's eyebrows flew up. "Why, the last time I looked, missy, you had two perfectly good legs and weren't about to have a baby. If'n I was you, I'd jest trot along after 'em."

Captain Cramer watched Peyton carry Molly into the station and lay her down behind the barricade. "What in the hell does Lewis think he's doing? Surely he's not intending to take a stand in there?"

John Wright gathered up his shot pouch and powder bag and started for the door. "Yep! He's holin' up in the only place that's got an open field of fire an' can't be burnt down around his ears. An' I'm fixin' to join him." He turned to Gabrielle. "You comin', missy?"

Peyton placed Molly on the muddy earth that had once been the floor of the room with her back against the log wall. He apologized for not bringing her blankets, but made no offer to return to the shed for them. She did not insist. He set to work clearing odds and ends of debris from what would be a crawl space around the inside perimeter.

Molly shifted her shoulders more comfortably against the logs. She could feel their cool dampness through her coat; it seeped into her aching back as though it were a soothing liquid, relaxing her taut muscles. The baby moved again, easier, more gentle, and she wondered if it, too, could feel the coolness.

Molly had her answer a moment later when a pain jerked her knees to her abdomen. Obviously it did not. She panted for breath. The labor pains seemed less intense, and she wondered if perhaps her nerves had been damaged by the brutal torment she had endured throughout the night, or—and she shuddered even to consider the possibility—perhaps this was only the lull before the storm.

John Wright, Gabrielle Johnson, and the four men rushed into the station. Everyone but Gabrielle, who stood in the doorway staring at the Comanches, fell upon the task of helping Peyton clear an aisle and prepare for battle.

The men worked quickly, and in a matter of minutes had heaved enough of the collapsed roof over the wall to form a path of sorts, where, if they were careful to crouch or crawl, they could traverse inside the perimeter with minimal effort and maximum protection.

The Indians had drawn to a halt a quarter of a mile out on the prairie. They sat their ponies like statues, unmoving, fearsome. Only the feathers in their braided hair, and an occasional swish of a pony's clubbed tail, showed any signs of life.

Peyton heaved one last charred beam over the barricade, then walked to the north wall where Molly lay. He noticed that her knees were drawn up to her chest. "You doing all right?"

She nodded and watched as he fished three fully loaded revolver cylinders from his coat pocket and placed them on the top log for quick access.

Molly squinted at him in the brilliant morning light. "Are they still out there?" She knew it was a foolish question, but she felt the need to ask, simply to hear his voice.

"They're not going anywhere." His answer was a monotone, for his mind was on the coming battle, wondering if, when the Indians charged, he would have time after the first cylinder was empty to knock out the barrel wedge and insert the second cylinder, or the third.

Molly sighed. "I knew they were still there. It was just a wish."

She longed for him to look at her, but he did not. She gazed at the sky. It was a robin's-egg blue, dotted here and there with feathery clouds. She shuddered; were those wispy, overhead plumes an omen? She watched the clouds dissipate and blow away as though they had never been. She grinned to herself. *That* was an omen! Still, she was certain they would see enough real feathers to last them a lifetime before this day was over.

Peyton laid his revolver alongside the extra cylinders on top of the barricade, then withdrew a second pistol from his waistband and went through the process of checking the percussion caps and powder charges to be certain they were also in proper firing order.

"While you're wishing, Miss Klinner, wish for the U. S. Cavalry to come busting over that hill with their flags waving and their bugles blaring. . . ."

Molly laughed aloud and gazed up at Peyton. "I never thought I would hear you actually embrace the United States Cavalry, Peyton."

He looked at her, surprised by the sound of her amusement, noticing that, for the moment at least, her face was free of pain. "I'd embrace Ulysses S. Grant himself if he would get us out of this mess."

Gabrielle Johnson, having heard Molly's laughter, made her way quickly down the aisleway and knelt down behind the barricade on the far side of Peyton. She raised the five-shot pocket pistol and sighted down the barrel at the Indians. Her hand trembled so badly that she was forced to rest the butt of the weapon on top of the log for support.

She smiled fearfully at Peyton. "I've never shot a firearm in my life."

Molly, having felt the baby slip again, sucked in her breath and dug her heels into the hard-packed earth. Her face strained with the effort of tightening the muscles of her abdomen. With the veins standing out on her temples, she clenched her teeth and glared at the young woman. "Then it looks like we'll both do something new before this day is over, Miss Johnson."

Gabrielle arched her eyebrows at Molly. "I sincerely doubt there is much you haven't already done, Miss Klinner."

That's the truth, Molly agreed, as she doubled over with pain. She gripped her abdomen firmly, as though the sheer pressure of her hands clutching her unborn child would stop the agony. An ever-widening stain inched its way down the fabric of her skirt from beneath her hips, and Molly arched her back. "Oh, God! My water has broken. Oh, my God!"

Bracing her back against the logs, she bore down with all her strength until her muscles felt as though they would rip apart. A long, shuddering cry forced its way past her lips. "The baby's coming! Now! Right now!"

From the far corner of the west wall, John Wright shouted to Peyton. "We're in luck, Lewis. They're goin' t' circle us 'stead of tryin' a full frontal. Them ponies they're ridin' are surefooted little beasts, but that mud 'tween here an' there is as slick as owl shit. They know that. They'll jest show off for a while . . . try an' rattle us." *If they was half as smart as they think they are,* he added silently, *they'd bide their time an' let the ground dry out a day or two.*

The Indians began their slow pace toward the depot, and John Wright thumbed back the hammers on his shotgun, then steadied its barrels across the logs. "But they ain't smart."

Molly strained even harder, and her lips drew back into a grimace that exposed both rows of her tightly clenched teeth. "Help me, Gabrielle!" Her eyes, oversized and distended with pain, fastened on Gabrielle Johnson. "Please help me. I can't do this alone."

Gabrielle gripped her pistol handle more tightly and stared at the savages advancing toward the enclosure. Molly Klinner's plea for assistance echoed in her ears like an explosion. She grimaced, hating the sound of it more than she feared the sight of the Comanches coming to kill her.

"I'll not touch you, Miss Klinner. I told you that. And if you had any pride or social etiquette, you would not ask, much less implore!"

Peyton caught Gabrielle by the arm and jerked her roughly toward Molly. "Social etiquette be damned! I don't give a hoot in hell about your personal convictions, Miss Johnson. A woman is birthing a baby and needs your help—and by God, you're going to help her!"

Gabrielle sneered at him. Anger and humiliation—toward him for belittling her and Molly for causing it—brought her chin up in stubborn defiance.

"I won't."

Peyton tightened his grip on her arm. "What kind of woman are you?"

Gabrielle winced with pain and jerked her arm free. "Not her kind! And obviously not your kind either."

All the while that Gabrielle Johnson was refusing to attend Molly Klinner, she was making her way around Peyton Lewis to where the pregnant woman lay. Kneeling beside Molly, she used the hem of her cloak to blot Molly's perspiring forehead.

"I have absolutely no idea how one goes about delivering a child, Miss Klinner. . . ."

Molly grinned weakly at the girl. As much as she detested Gabrielle Johnson, she was glad she was there. "I don't either,

Gabrielle. So I guess we'll just have to birth this one the hard way."

Three hundred yards from the station house, the Indians turned their ponies parallel to the building. One at a time, they nudged their mounts into an easy canter that eventually encircled the makeshift fort.

Peyton, leaving Molly in Gabrielle's care, walked down the path to the opening that had been the front door of the station. He piled several beams across the entrance, neatly sealing it off.

William Beecher, kneeling behind the east wall, nervously pointed his pistol toward the line of Indians and jerked the trigger. The bullet kicked up mud two hundred yards short of the savages. The resounding blast was drowned out by the laughs and war whoops from the circling Comanche.

Wright jumped to his feet and peered across the interior at Beecher. "For Christ's sake, Bill. Wait till they get in range. An' when they do, don't shoot into the mass. Pick one target an' keep your sights on it."

The Comanche, jeering at the defenders, quirted their ponies into a hard run and completed the circle around the station. A bird's-eye view of the area would have resembled a wheel rim without spokes, turning on a stationary axle, the burned-out depot.

In a show that was intended to intimidate their opponents, the Comanche, at full gallop, executed all manner of dangerous acrobatics. A rider, his hand knotted in his pony's mane, slipped to the ground as though he were falling, only to have the horse's momentum snatch him again to the animal's back. He repeated the performance from the other side.

Other warriors were standing erect on their ponies' backs, and one nimble Indian somersaulted over his horse's rump, then caught its tail and ran with his horse until a companion snatched the boy up by his free hand and flipped him up behind him, to ride double until, at full canter, the young man sprang again to his own pony.

It was a fine show of horsemanship, intended to awe those watching, and, indeed, if the ground had been dry, it would cer-

tainly have achieved its purpose. As it was, however, the downpour of the past two days caused the footing of unshod Indian
ponies to be uncertain at best and treacherous at worst, and
more often than not, when attempting a particularly quick movement, the ponies slipped, slid, or fell outright, sending their riders sprawling in the mud.

After several such incidents, and amid ridicule and catcall-
ing from the men inside the barricade, the Comanche reined
their horses to a slow canter and tightened the circle around
the station as though it were the noose of a snare that had en-
trapped an animal and was slowly strangling it to death.

When no further shots came from the enclosure, the Comanche ceased their charade, and the noose tightened again,
until the riders were not more than a hundred and fifty yards
away.

The silence, as they orbited the station, was even eerier than
their war cries—another effective Comanche mind game, for
Molly Klinner's imagination, as she lay in the mud behind the
barricade listening to the absence of sound, and thus the unknown, was driving her to near panic. She tried to climb to her
feet to see what was happening, but Gabrielle held her down
and ordered her to concentrate on having her baby.

Gabrielle Johnson, proud of her behavior concerning Molly
Klinner, peered cautiously over the barricade with the intention
of relating what she saw. Nothing in her young and sheltered life
had prepared her for the spectacle that met her eyes. The Comanche, looming fierce in the clear sunlight, took her breath
away. In spite of the lingering morning chill that the sun had not
yet burned away, the savages' bodies, stripped naked for war and
almost completely covered with multicolored paint, glistened
with a grease coating that caused them to appear as though they
had been varnished, much like the colorful oil paintings on canvas she had once seen by the great artist, George Catlin.

A young Comanche, seeing Gabrielle's head above the barricade, flaunted his manhood at her with lewd gestures, then
climbing upright on his galloping pony's back, fondled himself
while pointing his finger at her.

Gabrielle stared in mesmerized horror at the spectacle. He

was the first naked man she had ever beheld, and she had no
trouble understanding his intentions should she be taken cap-
tive. All of a sudden, losing her virginity under the most horrible
of circumstances was very real to her; and all her brave talk of
preferring death to deflowering took on new substance. If she
were captured—and raped—and lived through it, would she
have the courage to live, to face the shame, the accusations, the
cruel persecution and judgment of those who had not been
there? No! Unlike Molly Klinner, she did not believe she would
want to live under those conditions. Gabrielle sank down next to
Molly and turned wide, frightened eyes to her. "They are still
out there, Miss Klinner."

Molly was horrified by the expression on the girl's face. She
had seen that look before, in 1863—on the faces of the "decent
women" right before they died. Molly forced calmness into her
voice. "Whatever you saw out there, or are thinking, Gabrielle, I
give you my solemn promise that nothing will happen to you."

Molly's quiet pledge, instead of reassuring Gabrielle, only
acted as a catalyst that mocked and cheapened her fear. Who did
Molly Klinner think she was to insinuate that *she* could protect
anyone? She certainly had not done a very good job safeguard-
ing herself.

"I am certain, Miss Klinner, that you have seen similar ex-
hibitions of naked men . . . probably on numerous occasions. But
I have not. I do not even know how to describe such actions—
and would prefer not to comment on them."

Molly wished she had said nothing. Gabrielle would not listen to her any more than she had listened to Stella Kirby that
first time. The thought was fleeting, however, because the baby
moved again, and she was forced to arch her back and dig in her
heels as the pressure on her uterus increased, forcing the infant
ever downward. Perspiration ran in rivulets down her brow and
dripped from her chin like raindrops. Molly could feel her pelvis
expanding, and she dropped her head back and screamed.

Gabrielle wrung her hands and whimpered like a lost kitten.
She had no earthly idea how to assist Molly Klinner with the
birth, and she felt worthless, as a woman. She wanted to hide, to
cry, to pretend that none of this was happening. In short, she

wanted it to be over—the birthing, the battle, all of it. "Why don't the savages just rush us and get it over with!"

Peyton dragged one last timber across the doorway, then walked down the aisle and knelt beside Gabrielle. He gazed out across the wall at the plumed and painted terrormongers who were encircling the station, trying their utmost to panic those inside the fortification into making some sort of lethal mistake.

"Frontal attack is not the Indian way, Miss Johnson. They're like a pack of wolves. They surround their quarry, then circle and circle, keepin' the beast at prey. And when the victim is totally confused and terrified, they rush in and try to hamstring it. That's what they are trying to do to us, scare us into doing something foolish—like wasting ammunition, or trying to make a run for it, or surrendering outright."

Gabrielle pressed herself tightly against the barricade. "They're nothing but naked, savage beasts. I'm terrified, Peyton. I can't help myself. . . ."

Molly, her breath an irregular pant, cut her eyes to Gabrielle. "If you put a bullet in one of them, Gabrielle, a Comanche gets real unsavage in a hurry, just like any other man."

Peyton wondered if Molly was speaking from experience. She was certainly a strange young woman, tough and fearless in a feminine fashion—and obviously deadly if pushed into a corner. How many corners had she been pushed into?

Gabrielle Johnson's knuckles went to her mouth, and her eyes filled with tears. Surely Molly Klinner did not expect her to shoot another human being? The very thought was revolting. Sobs racked the girl's shoulders. Her mind darted hither and yon like a sparrow that finds itself in the shadow of a hawk with no place to hide. She hated Molly Klinner; she hated Texas; and she hated herself for the terror that had turned her into a sniveling coward. She jumped to her feet. "I can't stand this! I've got to get out of here!"

Peyton caught Gabrielle by the shoulders and yanked her down behind the barricade. "Don't you listen to anything anyone says, Gabrielle? I just explained to you that that's exactly what they want you to do—break and run for it. Divide and conquer."

Gabrielle added Peyton's name to her fast-growing list of

people to hate. With a trembling hand, she brushed tears from her eyes. Crawling over beside Molly, she buried her face in her hands and wept, a horror-stricken young city woman who wished with all her heart that she had never left Monroe, Michigan.

A warrior broke from the circle and cantered his pony toward the northwest corner of the enclosure. Lying low over his horse's back, he loosed an arrow toward the station, then slipped nimbly to the far side of the animal, leaving nothing but a portion of his hand and the sole of his moccasin as a target. The arrow buried itself harmlessly in the log wall.

Peyton took careful aim at the fleeing rider, but at the last minute he raised his pistol barrel and dropped the hammer to half-cock. Why shoot at a man he could not see?

Joseph Robertson, on the opposite side of the enclosure, jumped to his feet. "You got him, Lewis. I saw him fall." He pumped his arm, indicating a job well done. "Good shot, my boy. Good shot!"

Peyton scowled at Robertson. He had seen overly excited new army recruits raise their rifles to their shoulders only to take them down and reload them, not having pulled the trigger. That had been in the heat of battle, when hundreds of shots were being fired, when one could not so much as hear oneself think. Those men usually ended up with their weapon exploding in their face, killing not only themselves but also those closest to them. Peyton prayed the banker would come to his senses before the actual battle began.

John Wright, who had witnessed the incident from the west wall, peered over the interior debris at Peyton and shook his head. It was all that needed to be said.

A second Comanche, inspired because his comrade had not drawn fire, raced his pony toward the station. The man rode tall and proud, taunting the defenders with his show of contempt for their marksmanship.

Peyton held the Comanche in his sights until the man was thirty yards from the station, then squeezed the trigger. The ball smashed into the Comanche's hair-bone breastplate and somersaulted him over his pony's rump to splash heavily in the mud. He skidded and tumbled, then came to rest in such a broken, grotesque posture that all who watched knew he had been killed instantly.

The group inside the compound cheered lustily. A moment later, the angry, bloodcurdling screeching of the Comanche drowned them out.

Joseph Robertson, excited beyond reason, emptied an entire cylinder of wild shots at the circling mass. Not one bullet found a target.

Peyton sprinted around the debris and backhanded the banker across the mouth. Fighting hard to control his fury, Peyton jabbed his finger against Robertson's chest. "If you pull a stunt like that again, so help me God, Robertson, I'll shoot you myself. We need ammunition worse than we need fools like you!"

Robertson wiped a trickle of blood from his lips and shifted his feet embarrassedly. "I'm sorry, Lewis." He made a deprecating gesture with his hand. "I guess I got carried away. It won't happen again."

Gabrielle heard the altercation, and she immediately felt an affinity with Robertson. Peyton's open chastisement of the man burned in her breast like a firebrand. How dare he be so callous as to reprove a person for nervous excitement! She jumped to her feet.

"Leave the poor man alone, Mr. Lewis. He can't help being terrified. I assure you, sir, we are all scared out of our wits. And we certainly do not deserve your unjustified abuse—which you seem very quick to administer."

Peyton ignored her remark, but Molly Klinner was not so generous. Yes, the girl was terrified. Anyone with an ounce of sense would be, but that did not excuse stupidity.

"You might think Peyton was hard on that banker, Gabrielle, but the man wasted six chances to save our lives. I know I promised you that nothing would happen to you, but if we were to run out of ammunition and the Comanche capture us, I assure you, Miss Johnson, before they are through . . . deflowering you, you will wish a thousand times you had shot Mr. Robertson yourself."

Peyton squatted down beside Molly. "Shut up, Molly. Is it any wonder Miss Johnson is scared witless?" He poured a fresh charge of powder into the spent chamber, thumbed in a ball, then set the load with the swivel lever. "Get back to birthing your baby, Molly, and leave the defense of this station to us men."

Molly bit back a scathing retort. It lay like bile against the back of her throat, clamoring for release. In all her considerable dealings with the opposite sex, never had she encountered a man so frustrating as Peyton Lewis. Did he not see or care that her response to Gabrielle Johnson had been her attempt to anger the girl, to make her mad, so that she would fight should the occasion demand it? She sighed, then admitted to herself that she had defended Peyton because she had endured those same vicious attacks against her integrity most of her adult life.

Molly looked again at the sky. The wisps of clouds were drifting slowly by. They had a future; they were going someplace; while she lay there in the mud, trapped in her past, going no place. She sighed again. Peyton was right. He did not want or need her intervention any more than she had ever wanted or needed anyone to intrude on her behalf. She grimaced, tired of lying to herself. Even though she had never acknowledged it before, all she had ever wanted since becoming a woman was someone to champion her through the good times and the bad, to stand by her, even when she was wrong.

Peyton had done that twice. He had not abandoned her when he learned of her terrible background, nor—and the second occurrence was by far more important to her—when he discovered that she was pregnant. Indeed, the fact that she was with child appeared to be his only concession that she, as a woman, was important. As little as that concession was, she cherished it.

Twenty-one

Because the people in the station had drawn first blood, the Comanche, especially those who were on their first war party, flung themselves into a murderous frenzy that would have been almost comical had it not been a life-and-death struggle for all concerned.

Throwing caution to the wind, they quirted their ponies into a full gallop. As they streaked around the burned-out building, havoc ensued, more catastrophic even than their first endeavor. Ponies plowed into one another; some lost their footing and fell beneath the hooves of the others. Warriors in full war bonnets, horned helmets, or various other assorted headdresses, carrying shields and feathered lances, were thrown from their mounts to be pounded, kicked, and occasionally speared by one of their own or their companions' lances. Several men were left broken on the field when their thousand-pound ponies fell and then rolled over them. It was abject pandemonium.

The older Comanche, those who were seasoned warriors, avoided the fiasco and busied themselves with tightening the human girth until they were circling no more than thirty yards from the compound.

At ninety feet, the Comanche appeared as large as giants in

the sights of the impassioned banker and drummer. As their nerves began tightening, so did their trigger fingers, and in spite of John Wright's instructions to fire at one chosen target, they shot into the mass as quickly as they could thumb back the hammers on their revolvers. Their barrage of wasted lead knocked down two horses.

Gabrielle Johnson, her fear of being captured increasing by the second, huddled closely against the wall. The rough surface of the hand-hewn logs cut into her cheek. She did not feel it.

Arrows zipped over the barricade and buried themselves in anything that happened to be in their line of flight. As though God were smiling on them, not one defender was hit.

Powder smoke hung like a thick blue will-o'-the-wisp throughout the compound, and breathing for those inside became intolerable.

Molly coughed, and the mere strain of tightening her muscles sent her into another convulsion. Perspiration flowed into her eyes, burning and searing, blinding her. She coughed again, clenching her teeth to keep from screaming.

Her labor was constant now, the pain so great that when an arrow buried nearly a third of its length in the mud near her foot, she found herself wishing it had pierced her and ended her agony.

A second arrow smacked into a timber to Molly's left, its fletching quivering like a hummingbird's wings, drawing Molly's eyes in that direction. A splotch of color in the shadowed tangle of fallen roof beams caught her attention. Leaning sideways until she had an unobstructed view beneath the wreckage, her heart pounded up into her throat. She felt as though she would gag on it, for the splash of color beneath the blackened beams was the corner of a quilt protruding from an overturned baby cradle.

The enormity of the discovery crashed in upon her as though God, in His displeasure, was bent upon punishing her for her utter selfishness the moment before, when she had wished an arrow would end her torment. Shame, guilt, and an overwhelming sadness for the unfortunate woman and her family who had inhabited this station sent tears to her eyes. She could identify with the mother whose child had lain in that cradle, could feel her suffering—not for herself, because *her* safety would have been the last thing on her mind, but for her baby, for her husband, when she knew the end was near. Molly wondered if, in the last moments, the family had held one another, kissed each other good-bye. Suddenly she wished with all her being that the chasm between her and Gabrielle Johnson could somehow be breached, for it was vividly clear to her that their conflict benefited no one and robbed them of the one genuine circumstance they had in common—femininity.

In that instant, Molly made up her mind that, despite the fact that Gabrielle was a spoiled and self-centered brat, she would try one last time to bridge the gap that separated them.

"Miss Johnson—Gabrielle—I know we got off on the wrong foot, but can't we lay our differences aside? I . . . I like having you near. You are more a comfort than I have let on. . . . I'm sorry for the things I've said. Can't we be friends?"

Indignation rose up in Gabrielle like a living organism. Friends? Not in this lifetime! She could not believe the woman had the nerve to suggest such a thing, not after the way Molly Klinner had betrayed her, and every other person in the compound, by choosing to withhold the truth about being a soiled dove—and pregnant. For had she spoken one word about her condition, none of them would be here now. Bitterness drew her lips into an ugly line.

"Just because I am attending you during your . . . womanly needs, Miss Klinner, do not form the wrong impression. We will never be friends. Nor will we be close acquaintances. The moment this unfortunate situation is over, I pray to God above that I shall never be forced to endure the humiliation of being in the presence of a person such as yourself ever again!"

Molly stared at the girl. "A simple no would have sufficed, Gabrielle."

As though on cue, a pain more acute than any that had preceded it raised Molly's hips out of the mud. Her eyes widened until she was certain they would pop out of her head. Her pelvic bones grated against her flesh, and the baby moved lower into the birth canal.

Molly spread her legs as wide as possible. "Can you see the baby, Gabrielle? Is it visible yet?"

Gabrielle assured herself she would not look at Molly's private parts. It was indecent; it was despicable! Yet, in spite of her pledge not to, she stared wide-eyed at Molly's pubic area, mesmerized by the enormous amount of blood the woman was losing—and the crown of the infant's head that was plainly visible.

Gabrielle blushed and looked away.

Molly arched her back. "I can feel it moving, Gabrielle. It's trying to be born. It needs help . . . just a little help!"

Now that the infant's head was visible, Molly Klinner's fight to bring her child into the world was suddenly very real to Gabrielle Johnson—the embryonic awakening of her maternal instinct. Positioning herself between Molly's knees, she slipped her hands beneath the baby's head. "Push, Molly, push! The baby is being born. Oh, my word! The baby is being born!"

Peyton, oblivious to the miracle of birth that was being played out virtually at his boot tips, stood erect and sighted down his pistol barrel. Again and again he fired at flashes of red bodies on multicolored ponies until finally the hammer of his revolver fell on a spent cap. An arrow plucked at the brim of his hat. Another clipped his sleeve. Calmly, he knocked the barrel wedge from his revolver and inserted a fully loaded cylinder.

Molly strained and shoved and shuddered. She dug her heels into the earth, and her fingers clawed up handfuls of mud. Her hips arched and her eyes rolled—and then she spied Peyton Lewis standing above her as though he were indestructible, exposing himself to needless danger, and all the pent-up emotions that had been building in her these past hours exploded like a volcano, venting themselves the only way possible for a woman lying flat on her back. Molly Klinner showered Peyton Lewis with a barrage of molten epitaphs that could only have been acquired in a house of ill repute.

Gabrielle reddened with embarrassment, and Peyton Lewis stared down at Molly in shocked silence.

That short-lived tirade, however brief and distracting for Peyton, was sufficient; a Comanche charged his warhorse straight at the enclosure. At the last moment, when it appeared the animal would crash into the barricade, the warrior spun the pony to the side and sprang over the wall, to slam into Peyton. The Indian's momentum carried both him and Peyton into the collapsed debris.

As he fell, Peyton's head careened off a charred post, and the world spun sickeningly. Spots, like stardust, danced behind his eyelids.

The Comanche straddled Peyton and grasped him savagely by the throat. With a cry of triumph that was more animal than human, the savage drew his war club over his head for the killing blow.

Peyton heard the Indian's war cry, and intermingled with it, yet sounding as though it were far away, he heard a woman scream. He assumed it was Molly Klinner in the throes of labor. The last sound Peyton heard as he drifted into total nothingness was a blast that caused a terrible ringing in his head, and his last coherent thought was that his skull had split open.

Through the cloud of smoke that hovered near the muzzle of her pistol, Molly saw the surprise on the Comanche's face as he gaped at the puckered blue hole that had appeared just above his left nipple, where smoldering particles of black powder burned into his flesh, creating a permanent tattoo he would forever be unaware of possessing.

The Indian collapsed in a heap across Peyton's body and lay there twitching spasmodically as his life's blood poured like rainwater onto the earthen floor.

Molly fully expected Peyton to shove the Comanche aside and climb to his feet. When he did not move, she was puzzled. The thought fleetingly crossed her mind that Peyton must be dead; but that could not be true. If he were dead, she would feel it, sense it, taste it. Certainly she would be displaying a far greater hysteria than Gabrielle Johnson, who had jumped to her feet and was reeling backward in a panic-driven effort to put distance between herself and the bodies sprawled haphazardly just a step away. A fallen roof beam brought her up short.

Molly Klinner lay there, unafraid, as though she were totally detached from reality, as though Peyton Lewis did not matter, as though the Indian did not matter, as though she herself did not matter. And, indeed, that was the truth: not one of those entities was important to her, because ironically, and unknown to those in the compound, even Gabrielle Johnson, during the few short seconds it took for the Comanche to die, Molly Klinner had given birth. She could feel the infant between her thighs, a warm, wet weight, independent of her body. She thought it po- etic justice that while men all around her were bent on killing one another, she had fought just as diligently to bring new life into the world—and she had prevailed.

Molly rolled her head toward Gabrielle. For a long moment, she merely gazed at the girl, seeing a stricken sixteen-year-old child-woman unable to cope with the alien world into which she had been thrust, and for the briefest instant, she pitied Gabrielle Johnson.

Molly dropped her pistol in the mud and strained every muscle in her body in an attempt to push herself to a sitting po- sition so that she could lean forward enough to lift the newborn to her breast. With a whimper, she closed her eyes and sank back against the damp earth, too exhausted to manage even that small task.

Gabrielle, leaning heavily against the fallen beam, was hang- ing on to her sanity by the merest of threads. The blast of Molly's revolver, only inches from her face, had nearly deafened her. As a result, she was totally unaware of the second Indian who had vaulted onto the top log of the barricade and towered over the two women like a gladiator, his greased, muscled body glistening and rippling in the sunlight, his face, beneath his buffalo-horn helmet, a smear of vermilion and black paint.

The man's reptilian eyes flickered to Molly, who lay un- moving in a pool of blood, then to Gabrielle, who, with her eyes squinched shut, was clutching the timber as though she were afraid to let go.

Ignoring Molly, whom he mistook for a casualty, the Indian withdrew his scalping knife and dropped catlike beside Gabrielle. Catching the girl's hair in his fist, he snapped her head back against his chest and sawed the razor-sharp edge of his knife blade across her hairline. Gabrielle shrieked and dropped to her knees. Twisting his fist more tightly in her curls, the warrior dragged her upright. The will to live, to protect herself, to *survive* at all costs, came unbidden to Gabrielle, not on the wings of a dove, not slithering like a snake, but rushing into her like a falcon striking its prey. It would have made her furious at herself, had she been afforded the time to consider it, for that selfsame determination to fight for her life was the exact same sentiment that had sent Molly Klinner to the floor of the washroom to be held down by bayonet points, and later in the middle of the street when she disengaged her mind from what was happening to her body.

But Gabrielle Johnson connected none of those truths as she twisted in his grip until she was facing him. With a snarl of rage, she attacked the man like an enraged lioness, scratching at his eyes, kneeing him in the groin, sinking her teeth into the exposed flesh of his shoulder.

With a howl of anger, the Comanche chopped Gabrielle a hard blow to the temple and spun her around so that once again the back of her head was wedged tightly against his chest. With a vicious thrust, he forced the edge of his scalping knife under her hairline until it grated against her skull.

Molly used that interlude, while he was wrestling with Gabrielle, to muster the strength to pick up the heavy pistol and steady it against her thigh. It took both her trembling hands to cock the weapon. She tried to align the barrel with the Indian's head, but Gabrielle continued to struggle, and Molly was afraid to pull the trigger. As the blade cut deeper into the girl's hairline, Molly gritted her teeth and fired at the bridge of the Indian's hooked nose, which was mere inches above and to the side of Gabriel's head. The powder blast caught the girl full in the face, but the ball, while nicking the top of her ear, carried away the right lower section of the man's jawbone.

The Comanche flung Gabrielle aside and, holding his face intact with his hands, vaulted over the barricade and stumbled toward the circling Indians. A moment later, he was rescued by a horseman at full gallop.

Peyton plainly heard Gabrielle Johnson's screams, followed by a gunshot. He fought hard to regain his senses, but try as he might, it seemed an eternity before he waded, one layer at a time, through the muddled languor of semiconsciousness to the evasive light of full wakefulness that seemed to hover just beyond his eyelids.

His hand went to his pounding head and came away bloody. He became aware of a leaden weight pressing the breath from his chest, suffocating him, and he instinctively shoved the dead body from him. Taking several deep breaths, he wobbled to his hands and knees, and gazed about him. Everything appeared to be enshrouded in a multicolored haze. He blinked, then blinked again. Gabrielle Johnson came into focus. The girl's hair, singed and matted with blood, hung in strands across her face, and her eyes, which were naturally large, were made even more so because her long lashes and shapely brows had been singed to the skin.

Gabrielle brought her hand away from her forehead and stared at the blood smeared across her palm. Without so much as a sigh, her knees buckled and she collapsed.

Peyton's bewildered gaze moved to Molly Klinner, who was propped up on one elbow with a smoking revolver gripped tightly in both fists.

Reality slowly forced its way into Peyton's throbbing head. He recalled the Comanche warrior towering over him with a raised war club, a loud noise, which he now guessed was a pistol shot, and the screams. He looked in awe at the dead Indian beside him, at the bullet hole in the man's chest. Molly Klinner had saved his life. Amazing. He would have been even more astonished had he known that Molly had shot not one, but two savages—and that Gabrielle would be dead now had it not been for Molly's quick action.

At that moment, however, Molly Klinner could not have cared less about the lives she had spared, or the one she had taken. Her entire concern was for the life she had just brought into the world—the one that meant more to her than any other life ever could—and it lay unmoving between her thighs.

Peyton, unaware that Gabrielle had attempted to defend herself, looked again at the unconscious girl. The concessions he had made toward her—because of her northern upbringing, his willingness to accept her timidity, her abhorrence of firearms, her ignorance of the frontier in which they were traveling—were gone, replaced by a sharp contempt for any so-called sophisticated rearing that somehow excused one's individual responsibility and courage to defend not only oneself, but her fellow man, especially when said people were fighting valiantly to save her life. Even more distasteful to Peyton, who had never before encountered a woman such as Gabrielle Johnson, one who had obviously been shielded from life's harsh realities, was the girl's reluctance to assist Molly Klinner during the throes of childbirth, which struck him as not only shameful and unrighteous in a woman, but downright criminal.

Molly tilted her head toward Gabrielle. "Is she dead?" She was surprised she had even voiced the question, for in truth, at that instant she did not care.

Peyton retrieved his revolver, then crawled to Gabrielle and raised her to a sitting position with her back resting against the blackened timber. Palming her hair off her forehead, he studied the two inches of hairline that had been laid open to the skull. The girl moaned, but her eyes remained closed.

"No. She's not dead. She swooned because she got her hairline adjusted a little. She'll be fine."

Molly heard the disapproval in Peyton's voice, and oddly, she felt the need to come to Gabrielle's defense. "She'll never be *fine* again, Peyton. You know it, and I know it. And should she live through this nightmare, I believe she will be a fine addition to Texas."

Peyton wondered if the pressure of everything that had happened in the last few minutes had dulled Molly's wits. Gabrielle Johnson, and men and women like her, would never be an asset to Texas. He cuffed Gabrielle's face until her eyes fluttered open. When he was certain she was fully awake, he explained about the slash on her forehead, assuring her it was not life-threatening.

Gabrielle's hand went immediately to the knife wound at her hairline and came away bloody. She was forced to bring her hand to within a mere inch of her face before she could make out so much as her individual fingers. When she saw the blood, her eyes grew wide and glassy, and for a moment, Peyton was certain she would pass out again. He caught the girl by her shoulders and shook her savagely, snapping her head back and forth like a rag doll.

"Damn it, Miss Johnson. You are a grown woman. It's time you started acting like one!"

Peyton wished the girl would grow angry, shout at him, curse, take a swing at him—anything that would make her come alive, that would indicate the slightest interest in self-defense. She stared at him.

Molly saw the flicker of disappointment that crossed Peyton's face. She shook her head; he would truly never understand women.

Peyton released Gabrielle, then fished his bandanna from his trouser pocket. Folding the cloth until he had a strip some three inches wide, he bound the girl's head and tied off the bandage. She flinched as he drew the knot tight, but she did not cry out as he had expected. Peyton inspected his handiwork. It would keep her lacerated scalp in place and the blood out of her eyes. Again, he wished she would show some type of emotion, but she sat there, staring at him as though she had taken leave of her senses. He sighed, growing even more frustrated with her. He could hear shots being fired from every corner of the compound, and he knew he must get back into the battle before another Comanche decided to breach the wall, instead of sitting there playing nursemaid to a woman who should have been perfectly capable of taking care of herself.

Peyton climbed to his feet and looked down at her. "Damn it, Gabrielle, snap out of it. Get over there and help Molly birth her baby!"

Gabrielle peered at him through bloodshot eyes. Above the ringing in her ears and the roaring pain that was splitting her head, she had heard only a portion of Peyton's command. She squinted at him in an attempt to focus on his face. She could see only a vague image, a specter with no form.

Molly Klinner's mouth drew into an angry line. "Leave her alone, Mr. Lewis. She did help me."

When Peyton looked questioningly at her, Molly closed her

eyes and opened her legs to him. "My baby is here, and I can't even bend over enough to pick him up. I want to hold my baby, Mr. Lewis."

Peyton stared dumbfounded at the newborn nestled in the fetal position between her thighs. Having never seen an infant only minutes old, the sight was not what he had expected. The child appeared tiny, weighing less than five pounds. Its skin was wrinkled, with a purplish tint, splotched and shiny with blood and matter. It seemed to be all head, with hardly any length to its arms and legs.

Peyton grimaced. *Well, it sure as hell is an ugly little thing.* He reached for the baby, careful not to crush it as he lifted it from between Molly's legs.

When he offered the child to Molly, she reached out and stayed his hand. Her eyes met his. "Is it . . . alive, Peyton?" All the world's agony was in those four whispered words.

In that instant, Peyton became acutely aware that if the infant were stillborn, Molly Klinner would lie right there and die with it. That truth was jarring, because suddenly, Molly Klinner was more real to him than at any moment since his having met her—almost as though he were just now seeing the person she actually was. Like a revolving canister of tintypes, pictures of her came unbidden to his mind: the brave and outstanding things she had done in the past six weeks, which he had previously refused to acknowledge; her dogged stubbornness when she had tracked him through the snow in below-zero temperature; her covering Rucker with her body to keep him from freezing to death; the times when there was barely enough food to sustain one life, much less two, yet she had refused to eat until he and Rucker had finished; the burning of her family Bible and the five-dollar bill; the intimacy when she insisted he warm his hands between her thighs, the same thighs he had just touched when he picked up her baby. Yet not once had she ever complained.

Indeed, the kaleidoscope of vivid pictures that flashed through his mind was startlingly clear in its significance, and suddenly meaningful in its extraordinariness, for all Molly Klinner had ever asked was that she be allowed to accompany him to Texas where she could "start a new life." He understood her insistence now. It had never been for herself; it had been the baby all along—always the baby.

Without intending to do so, because he did not believe he still retained enough faith in a Supreme Being to call upon Him, Peyton found himself asking God to breathe life into the unmoving bundle of flesh that lay so still in his hands.

An arrow screamed past Peyton's face, burying itself in a timber next to his head. He flinched, tightening his grip on the newborn. The child whimpered, then screamed angrily. Peyton grinned crookedly at Molly. "It's a she, Molly . . . and she's fine."

Molly took the baby from him and held it protectively against her bosom. Another arrow smacked into a timber, and she instinctively covered the child with her arms. She felt it snuggle against her breast, and a soft glow of welcome that she had never thought possible surged throughout her, engulfing her in its totalness. No, not complete totalness, but almost.

Molly raised misty eyes to Peyton and studied his face. "I love you, Peyton." It was a simple statement, but it hit Peyton like a rockslide. Nervously, he peered over the wall, almost relieved to see a Comanche, sporting a buffalo-horn helmet, bull-hide shield, and spear, galloping his horse close to the enclosure. With Molly's words echoing in his ears, he rested the butt of his revolver on the top log, lined up the front and rear sights, and shot the Comanche through the side. He self-consciously refused to look at Molly when she asked if he had killed the Indian, and cursed himself for only wounding the man. It had been a clean, easy shot, but Peyton's mind had been elsewhere—on Molly Klinner. Her untimely revelation had unnerved him more than he cared to admit. Incensed that she would voice such a sentiment at that particular moment—and that he would listen or even care what she said—caused him to lash out at her. "No, goddamn it, I didn't. He's still in the saddle."

Molly flinched from the unexpected onslaught, and for a split instant, another scathing whorehouse retort hung on her lips. Then the baby made a sucking sound and moved against her breast, and the rejoinder was forgotten. A look of pure awe filled Molly's face as she unbuttoned her bodice and offered the newborn her extended nipple. As the infant snuggled contentedly against her, she wondered if the mere touch of her body consoled the child, made her feel safe. Impulsively, she reached up and laid her hand on Peyton's arm. When he glanced down at her, she blushed.

"I . . . I was curious to see if the act of touching someone you love makes you feel safe."

He frowned at her. That was twice in as many minutes she had used that word, and again he found it troubling, confusing. They had been together for weeks, and as far as he could remember, she had never indicated that he had been anything more than a ticket to Texas for her. It must be the baby; it brought out the maternal instinct in her.

"Well, does it?"

"Yes."

Twenty-two

Rucker and Ben heard the unmistakable sounds of combat long before they finally topped a rise high enough for them to see the battlefield. They reined in their winded horses and appraised the struggle taking place a mile ahead.

Ben pushed his hat to the back of his head and scratched his hairline. He idly wondered if he had picked up a louse or two since having met these white people. Probably.

Resting his forearm on his saddle horn, he leaned forward and studied the scene playing itself out before them. "It don't 'pear, Mista' Fletcher, them folks in that depot is makin' much of a 'pression on them Injuns."

Rucker fished the makings from his shirt pocket and began rolling himself a smoke. "They're makin' enough impression that those red devils ain't overrun 'em yet." He offered the sack of tobacco to Ben.

Ben waved the tobacco aside. "Jest a matter of time, Mista' Fletcher. Them Injuns out yonder ain't like the ones we met in the woods. Them's Comanche, an' they go plumb wild oncet they got the stench of blood in their nostrils."

Rucker searched the circle of red men for a vulnerable spot

where he might breach their line. He did not see a single place that appeared weak or undefended. "Can we ride through 'em, Uncle?"

Ben scratched the three-day-old stubble that dotted his chin. Yes, he definitely had picked up a louse someplace.

"Back in '36, Cap'n James Bonham rode through two thousand o' Santa Anna's troops fo' times. I reckon we can ride through a hundred Comanche oncet."

Rucker looked skeptically at Ben. "Are you tellin' me you were at the Alamo?"

Ben continued to study the Indians. "All thirteen days, Mista' Fletcher."

A hundred questions concerning the controversial death of the defenders of the Alamo raced through Rucker's mind, but he pushed the thoughts aside. There would be time for questions later. If not, it would not matter one way or the other what really happened at the Alamo.

"All right, Uncle." Rucker struck a lucifer and fired his cigarette. "Since you've seen it done four times, how do we do it once?"

Ben drew his Walker Colt and thumbed back the hammer. "Well, there's one thing that comes t' mind." He rotated the cylinder slowly to ensure each nipple was capped. "Co'nel Crockett said it right b'fore Genr'l Santa Anna swarmed the walls: 'When yo' ain't got no other choice, be brave.' "

"For Christ's sake, Uncle! Davy Crockett was killed dead-er'n hell."

Ben nodded. "So was Cap'n Bonham."

Rucker blew a smoke ring and watched it dissipate in the breeze. "Tell me exactly how Bonham rode through the Mexicans, Uncle."

Ben twistèd in the saddle and grinned broadly at the boy. "Cap'n Bonham didn't ride through that Mexican army, Mista' Fletcher. He jest flat rode over 'em."

Rucker jacked the Henry open just enough to ensure there was a cartridge in the breech. With a fine rendition of the Rebel yell, he spurred his horse into a dead run that took him straight toward the circling Indians.

* * *

Arrows and lances fell like hailstones in and around the small fortification. Even an occasional bullet hummed overhead, sounding like an angry bee in search of an unsuspecting victim, but it was arrows, not bullets, that claimed the first casualty inside the compound.

Simultaneously, a score of the flint-tipped shafts tore over the walls, to bury themselves inches deep in timbers, logs, or any object of substance that had the misfortune of being in their path.

Captain Cramer, defending the west wall, chose that precise moment to stand erect in hopes of getting a better shot at a savage who was galloping past not twenty yards from the compound. As Cramer drew a tight bead on the rider, two arrows found their way across the pile of debris and buried themselves nearly to the fletching in his back, their small flint points protruding six inches beyond the brass buttons of his tunic front.

Bubbles of blood frothed at the corner of Cramer's lips, then burst and speckled his chin as though he had the pox. He staggered sideways like a drunkard and fell face-first over the log wall, to hang there like a beacon of triumph for the Comanche bowmen. Arrows from all directions punctured the body until it resembled a porcupine.

A young warrior, determined to count coup on the dead man, raised his bow over his head and raced his pony toward the wall.

As the boy angled across John Wright's field of fire, the driver leveled his shotgun and touched both triggers. The Indian and his pony collapsed, a pile of mangled flesh and bones.

Wright quickly ducked down behind the barricade and began to reload. Shouts and howls from the Comanche rose to such a deafening crescendo that for the first time since the last time he had fought Comanche, his hands trembled so violently he spilled his charge. Cursing himself for wasting precious powder, Wright peered hesitantly over the barricade, fully expecting the entire horde of savages to come swarming toward the enclosure. The sight that met his eyes nearly caused him to throw caution to the wind and jump erect. Fletcher Rucker and Ben, riding stirrup to stirrup, were racing their horses down the same hill the Comanche had used two hours earlier.

Rucker, with bridle reins between his teeth, was leaning low over his horse's neck, a pistol in one hand, the Henry rifle in the other. Ben, his hat brim turned up in the front from the wind created by his galloping horse, had his revolver thrust out before him like a swivel gun on a ship's bow. Although Wright could not hear the muzzle blasts, he could see smoke and flame erupt from the weapons and the devastation they wreaked as they neared the circle of red men.

When Rucker and Ben disappeared into the throng of Comanche horsemen, John Wright's excitement overcame his wariness. Standing up in full view of the enemy, he snatched his bugle to his lips and blew the "charge." The resonant call rose clear and distinct above the Comanche war cries.

Rucker and Ben fired their pistols point-blank into the painted faces of anyone who got in their path, and for the first time in his life, Rucker thanked God for the size and weight of a coach horse. The animal barreled into the lightweight Indian ponies and either knocked them aside or bowled them over, trampling both horse and rider beneath its massive, steel-shod hooves.

John Wright's unexpected bugle call, and the shots fired from a quarter other than the fort, sent both the defenders and the Indians into a state of confusion. The Comanche, except for those at the precise spot where Rucker and Ben made their breach, had not the slightest notion what was transpiring. Nor did anyone in the enclosure, save John Wright, and he was straining his eyes to see if the two reckless fools would actually emerge intact from the circle of warriors.

Peyton climbed up on a pile of debris and peered over the fallen timbers to the south wall where John Wright stood, his attention centered on a cluster of milling Comanche who appeared to be in a state of bedlam. Indeed, Indians from every point on the compass were gyrating toward the area directly in front of John Wright. Try as he might, Peyton could see nothing unusual that would attract such attention.

He cupped his hands around his mouth to be heard over the din of shouting savages. "What's happening out there, John?"

Wright spun toward Peyton, excitement animating his homely features. "The damnedest, foolhardiest thing I ever did see, Peyton."

Before Wright could further explain, Peyton watched in openmouthed wonder as Rucker and Ben burst out of the milling Indians and raced their horses hell-bent-for-leather toward the station house.

It was a spectacular show, the coach horses running all out, their hooves jarring the earth each time they struck the ground, Rucker and Ben lying low on their necks, twisted in the saddle so they could shoot any rider who drew near.

Every man in the compound jumped to his feet, cheering, and Joseph Robertson became so excited that he flung his hat into the air.

Hearing the excited shouts, Molly clutched her baby more tightly against her bosom and attempted to pull herself up the log wall. It was then that she realized the umbilical cord was still attached to the placenta. Molly quickly searched the ground for the hatchet dropped by the Comanche she had shot. The weapon was wedged between two timbers. Jerking it free, she tested the blade's edge with her thumb, then, separating a long, thin hank of hair the thickness of her little finger from the greasy mass that crowned her head, she sawed it free with the hatchet blade. In the space of seconds, she had intertwined the hairs into a single thread, and with deft fingers tied off the umbilical cord. With a quick stroke of the hatchet, she separated the baby from the placenta. Again she attempted to stand, but her strength ebbed, and she sank to the ground. She reached out and touched the sole of Peyton's boot.

"Help me up, Peyton. I certainly don't intend to miss seeing history being made right before our eyes."

Peyton jumped down from the pile of logs, caught Molly beneath her knees and shoulders, and carried her to the corner of the enclosure where she would have a clear view of the race.

Molly braced her hips against the wall and peered over the south barricade. It was a thrilling spectacle: the two men, low over their horses' necks, racing at breakneck speed toward the station. She laughed, and longed to dance and fling her hat into the air as the men were doing, but she was too weak to do the first, and her hat had long since fallen by the wayside. Turning the baby so that it faced the excitement, so that she could tell the child in later years—she hoped—that she, too, had witnessed what would surely go down as one of the greatest rides in the history of Texas, Molly took the babys tiny hand and waved it at the oncoming horsemen.

· The dozen Comanche who gave chase were incensed. In their rage to overtake Rucker and Ben, they quirted their ponies cruelly, forcing the animals to the limit of their endurance. The men inside the compound congregated at the south wall and formed a firing line. They held their breaths as Rucker, Ben, and the Comanche, a horse length behind them, loomed large in their sights. As the warriors fanned out to draw alongside the two men, they rode headlong into a staggering hail of lead. All five guns inside the compound erupted simultaneously. The havoc was awesome: two Comanche were killed outright, and several more, both men and horses, limped from the field mortally wounded. The Indians who escaped injury broke off pursuit and galloped their ponies out of pistol range, where they drew rein and screamed insults at the two riders who were now at the compound.

, Rucker and Ben kicked free of their stirrups and dropped out of their saddles to hit the ground running. They did not slow down at the wall, but instead bunched their muscles and cleared the three-foot-high barricade in a leap that took them into the waiting arms of their companions. The defenders pounded their backs, shook their hands, and shouted wildly, hailing Rucker and Ben as heroes.

Nearly a hundred Comanche drew their ponies to a halt and stared bitterly at the station house. They were stunned beyond speech by the sheer impudence of the two riders who had breached their ranks. In years to come, around council fires all across the West, they, too, would recount the tale of the ride made by a white boy and a black man—proud that they had witnessed the phenomenon, for they respected courage, horsemanship, and cold-blooded trickery above all other human qualities.

At the time, however—and it would never be admitted by any Comanche present—the episode was so insulting and humiliating that when the initial shock wore off, it sent the warriors into such a windmill of confusion that they raced their ponies first this way, then that, not knowing what to do next.

Finally they wheeled their horses and trotted them to the top of a rise a half-mile to the east, where they halted and sat their ponies in animated conversation, a long line of naked men, the oil on their bodies causing them to glisten like rubies in the midmorning sunlight.

Rucker, amid much backslapping and hand-shaking, tugged his hat brim down to shade his eyes from the sun's glare and studied the Comanche as they gathered at the top of the mound. He was disappointed they had not chased him all the way to the compound, where the defenders could have reloaded and counted coup on even more of them; but the very fact that they had turned tail and run suggested that the folks inside the station had most certainly made an impression on them—a feat which, according to Ben, was nearly impossible. He intended to rub the man's face in it.

Rucker grinned at those around him and told them that they had certainly done some fine shooting, which was true when one considered that the warriors who were chasing him had been at least sixty feet away and moving at breakneck speed.

The men laughed and hooted, enjoying the praise, their spirits high now that the enemy had retreated and the two scouts had returned to augment their ranks and firepower. They could hold off the entire Comanche nation—and they said so.

Ben watched the red men on the hill and wondered if he should throw cold water on his white companions' party. The truth was, the defenders were patting themselves on the back much too soon. The Comanche would come again, only this time they would have blood in their eyes. Ben said nothing.

Rucker laughed, his young face alive with exultation. "Let 'em come, gents. Me an' old Henry here will speak lively to 'em." He patted the Henry rifle affectionately.

With Peyton and Ben walking beside him, Rucker made his way around the cleared walkway to where Molly sat. "Well, Molly, what'd you-all think of that grand entrance?" Rucker puffed out his chest like a strutting turkey gobbler. "You told me a little heroin' never hurt."

Molly's grin was stronger than she felt. "I don't know who's crazier, Fletcher—you or Uncle Ben—but that was the finest ride I've ever seen."

"Heck, Miss Molly, Ben's the crazy one. Ridin' through them Comanche was his idea. An' . . . well, I couldn't very well let him outshine me, now, could I?"

Molly shook her head in agreement. Not in front of Gabrielle Johnson, you couldn't! She laughed delightedly. She had told the truth: it was the most exciting, heroic, foolhardy thing she had ever seen, the very stuff of which history and legend were made—providing one lived long enough to tell the tale.

Rucker, wondering at Molly's pale and drawn appearance, doffed his hat.

"Beggin' your pardon, Miss Molly, but you sure do look like death warmed over. You been shot or somethin'?"

Molly drew aside her overcoat to reveal the newborn sleeping snugly against her breast. "I believe the 'or something' fits very nicely, Fletcher. I had a baby girl while you were gone."

She watched his face intently. She had told him about her pregnancy at the Wichita station, but now it was more than talk; the truth was there for him to see. She prayed she would not see disgust in his eyes.

Rucker gaped at the infant, too stunned to speak, but Ben pushed past him and peered owlishly at the child. "Well, now, Miss Molly, she's a real beauty. I ain't seen nothin' that purty since my pappy tied my first pinto pony to the door o' my maw's wickiup—an' that was some sixty-odd years ago." He appraised the child from several different angles. "Yes, ma'am, she's purtier'n a warhorse, she is."

Molly's face beamed. Still, she had not heard from Rucker. She gazed apprehensively at him, hoping for the best, willing to accept the worst.

Rucker slowly palmed his hat to the back of his head, and his eyes traveled from the infant to Molly. "Why, Miss Molly, you told me you was . . . expectin', but I sure didn't think you meant right now!"

"Well, I didn't think I meant right now, either, Fletcher. But the Almighty has a way of doing things according to His calendar."

Peyton studied Rucker and Molly closely. He was bothered more than he would have imagined because she had confided in his cousin that she was going to have a baby. Why had she not told him? Then the truth hit him. She had not taken him into her confidence because he had never shown the least interest in who Molly Klinner actually was. Peyton frowned darkly as that thought struck home. Was he interested? Surely not! He didn't have time for a woman—any woman—and most especially not a woman with a newborn.

Gabrielle Johnson, who had groped her way down the wall to where they congregated, squinted at Fletcher Rucker. Although she had not seen the ride clearly, she had heard enough to know that it had been outstandingly courageous. Curiously, however, the ride was not what impressed the girl; it was the fact that Molly Klinner had told him of her delicate condition, and he had not betrayed that confidence. That caught her attention, because it was the act of a true gentleman.

Rucker studied the baby, taking in her small stature and rusty, blood-splotched skin. "I ain't never seen a baby that tiny or that color." He frowned at Molly. "You recollect what I said that night in Wichita about motherhood, an' John B. Hood, an' Robin Hood?"

Molly remembered it well, but she was surprised, considering the amount of whiskey he had drunk, that he recalled any portion of that conversation. She nodded suspiciously, not certain she wanted to hear what he would say next.

He pointed to the baby and guffawed. "Well, I reckon we'll have to call her . . . Little Red Ridin' Hood."

Molly laughed. "Just you wait until she's cleaned up, Fletcher. A more appropriate name will be Cinderella."

Rucker's statement, however, brought to the forefront a

question that had begun to worry Molly: when did one bathe a newborn? How critical to the infant's health was the timing of its first bath? She gazed at those standing around her, afraid to ask.

Rucker looked beyond Molly to Gabrielle, who stood facing him with her back pressed against the wall. From the concern that quickly washed over his face when he saw the bandage around the girl's blood-streaked forehead, it was evident that Molly and the baby were forgotten. Rucker took a step toward Gabrielle, then stopped, uncertain as to what he should do next. "What happened to you?"

Gabrielle's hands fluttered to her powder-burned face.

Rucker took another step toward her. "You look like hell, Miss Johnson. How bad are you hurt?"

An exasperated sigh slipped between Molly's teeth. Rucker would do very well with women if he would just keep his mouth shut. Sarcasm edged her voice: "Getting half scalped never was any fun, Fletcher."

Rucker ignored Molly and took the girl's blood-splattered face between his palms. She had been in his thoughts constantly while he and Ben were scouting for Indians. She had even played a substantial role in his decision to ride through the Comanche war party. *I love this woman.* The realization that for the first time in his life he actually cared about a woman—really cared—was awe-inspiring. Many times he had fancied himself in love, but it had never been like this. *I truly love her!*

Although Gabrielle could not see Rucker's face plainly enough to read his thoughts, she heard them in the intake of his breath, felt them in the caress of his touch. Suddenly Fletcher Rucker took on an identity of his own, for she could see him plainly in her mind. She blushed, but it was lost in the wreckage of her face. Why was she shy in his presence? She did not even like Fletcher Rucker, and had not since the first time she met him. So why was she remembering him with such clarity? Confused, she turned and made her way slowly back the way she had come.

Molly had watched the play between Rucker and Gabrielle with interest. The romantic side of her longed to shout at Rucker to run and catch the girl, to take her in his arms and kiss her soundly. She bit back the suggestion, for, in her opinion, Gabrielle Johnson was not now, or ever would be, good enough for Fletcher Rucker.

Rucker reddened with humiliation as he looked around at those who had witnessed Gabrielle's public rejection. The most magnanimous moment of his life dissolved into nothingness as Gabrielle stumbled down the aisle. The glorious ride would still go down in history, but in that instant his first awakening of genuine devotion toward a woman was shattered as though she had cast a stone into the calm waters of a millpond. In its stead was a heart full of splintered emotions spinning out of control. To hell with Gabrielle Johnson. He had been a fool to risk his life trying to impress a Yankee city woman who thought a cow pie was some sort of beef dish baked in an oven. He groaned, angry with himself, and disgusted with her, for allowing himself to finally care about someone—to care about her.

Rucker turned on his heel and walked to where Peyton relaxed against a timber. Together they made their way to the west side of the enclosure, where the lieutenant and the drummer had dragged the captain's body back into the compound.

Rucker gazed down at the arrows protruding from Cramer's back. He felt no pity; the man had been asking to get killed from the time he boarded the stagecoach in Kansas—picking fights with strangers, finding fault with everyone and everything below the Mason-Dixon Line. Yes, the man had definitely harbored a death wish. Rucker knew, without a doubt, that when the time was right, either he or Peyton would have accommodated the man's craving.

Lieutenant Pendleton began pulling arrow shafts from Cramer's body. "It isn't right, him getting killed in an out-of-the-way place like this. He was a good soldier."

Peyton glanced at the corpse. A good soldier, but not much of a man. Perhaps one couldn't be both in times of war . . . but the war was over. "Anybody else hit?"

Robertson and Beecher shook their heads.

Peyton made his way around the enclosure where John Wright and Ben were sitting on the top log of the barricade watching the Indians. "What do you suppose they'll do, John?"

"They'll ride right over us this time, Peyton."

Ben leaned his elbows on the log next to Wright and studied the Comanche thoughtfully. "You didn't ast my 'pinion, boss Lewis, but I'm a-goin' t' put my two cents in anyhow. I b'lieve Mista' John done hit the nail on the head. They gonna come at us fast, an' they goin' t' mean business. If'n it was me who had that Henry rifle, I'd shoot the first Injun who ventured off'n that hill . . . jest as far out as Miss Molly's rifle will reach." Ben shrugged, then grinned at Peyton. "That can be plumb unsettlin' to a Comanche, seein' the leader go under when you jest plain ain't s'pectin' it."

John Wright scoffed at Ben. "I reckon you're goin' to tell us that the great mountain man, John Colter, told you that?"

"Naw, Mista' John. It were Kit Carson."

Rucker did not hear a word they were saying. In spite of his denunciation of Gabrielle Johnson, he could not get the girl out of his mind. The more he thought about her, the less angry he became. Finally, he hurried down the aisleway toward the north side of the compound where he had last seen her.

Gabrielle was standing at the spot where Molly had shot the Indian. She looked desolate in her solitude, her cloak wrapped tightly about her, as though she were alone on a windswept island, waiting for a sail on the horizon. She was crying quiet tears, the kind that are not to be shared. They had mingled with the blood that streaked her face, causing her to appear nearly as hideous as a Comanche in full war paint.

She heard, more than saw, Rucker pour water from his canteen onto his red neckerchief. When he dabbed at the blood and grime that all but concealed her pale skin and beautiful features, she retreated a step and stared hollow-eyed into his face. Her fingers crept hesitantly toward her eyes.

Rucker caught her hand in his and held it steady. "Don't touch your face, Miss Johnson. We learned in the army that you're sometimes better off not to get your fingers near cuts an' burns. Accordin' to the company surgeon, a body's a lot better off to let 'em bleed freely for a spell."

"I . . . I'm almost blind, Fletcher. I was deaf for a few minutes, but it got better, but not the blindness. I can't see, except up close, like now. I'm scared, Fletcher. . . . I'm so scared I can hardly breathe."

Rucker examined her face, her eyes, her singed hair and skin, the small wedge of flesh missing from her ear. A lump rose in his throat. He swallowed it. "Tell me what happened. Don't leave out nothin'. It's important that I know exactly what did this."

"I . . . don't know. An Indian . . . was cutting me . . . with his knife, and I was fighting with him. Then I . . . I couldn't hear . . . or see."

Rucker appraised her face from all angles, noticing that intermingled with the blood and grime were small blue-black burns, powder burns, as though a gun had discharged near her face. Her pupils were dilated and appeared to be seared over with a smoky film.

Rucker felt as though he would vomit. During the war, he had seen several men permanently blinded by the burning residue of black powder from a muzzle blast too close to their heads. Those who were fortunate enough to save their sight were permanently tattooed with indigo spots speckling their face where the powder was blasted into their skin. They had been a horrible sight, even after they healed.

"Miss Gabrielle, I want you to sit down an' tilt your head back an' hold your eyes open with your fingers. I'm goin' to rinse off the pupils. It'll hurt, but you got to keep 'em open. Can you do that?"

Gabrielle nodded.

Rucker flushed the girl's eyes with water from his canteen. She whimpered, but managed for the most part to keep them open. He repeated the process again and again. Then, telling her to shut her eyes tight, he sponge-bathed her face. Gabrielle sat perfectly still throughout the ordeal, even when he untied the bandanna and raised her blood-soaked hair off her forehead.

Rucker was glad that her eyes were closed and she could not see his face, for even though he worked hard to keep it expressionless, his mouth drew into a slash, and a deep pain for her filled his eyes. The Comanche had laid her scalp back, exposing nearly three inches of her skull.

Gabrielle flinched as he unintentionally opened the slash, but to her credit, she did not cry out. With her eyes still squinched shut, she raised her face to his. "I look awful, don't I, Fletcher? Will . . . will it be everlasting? Tell me the truth. I can take . . . the truth. I'm not nearly so vain as most people believe me to be."

Her disfigurement was sickening. The knife slash would heal, and her hair would cover the scar. The tattooing, however, was different. It would be visible for a lifetime unless, very quickly, before the burns began to heal, someone with a steady hand and a sharp needle picked the burned powder out of her skin and then scrubbed her with hot soapy water. Even then it was an iffy proposition.

"Well, the slash ain't so bad. You're goin' to need sewin' up by somebody who knows what they're doin'." He laid her scalp back into place. "It ain't life-threatenin' by no means, but it's sure as shootin' goin' to be uncomfortable for a while."

Again, he was glad she could not see his face or the tears that had filled his eyes. He knuckled them away. "You're still the best-lookin' woman in the whole state of Texas, an' that's the truth."

She dropped her chin to her chest, and he wondered if she might swoon.

Rucker took her hand. "Are you all right, Miss Gabrielle? Are you wounded somewhere else? Talk to me!"

Tears forced themselves from between her compressed lids and trickled down her cheeks. She made no sound.

Rucker was at his wit's end, having no clue as to what he should do. He longed to take her in his arms, to reassure her that all would be well, that she would be fine. But he did not know if that were true, and she had asked him to be honest with her. Frustration and fear sent his arm around her, and he bent his head to hers with every intention of kissing her, but at the last moment he drew back, afraid that he would offend her. He would have been amazed had he known that being held at that precise moment was what she needed more than anything else he might provide.

Rucker sighed. What was it Molly Klinner had told him? "Just be yourself." For lack of anything better to say, Rucker grinned at her and shrugged his shoulders. "Look at the bright side of it, Gabrielle." She raised her face to him. "It's too early in the year for blowflies."

When he saw the pain his words had caused, he sobered, and if she could have seen him, she would have been startled; for at that moment, he looked like his cousin, Peyton Lewis. "I'm sorry, Gabrielle, but there is a bright side." He touched her cheek affectionately. "Just think of all the stories you can tell your grandchildren."

"Tell them what, Fletcher?" Pain and anger rang in her voice.

"You could tell them about the great ride I made through a hundred screamin' Comanche to get back to you . . . folks."

She opened her clouded eyes and blinked incredulously at him. "I'm sure it was a wonderful sight, but . . . you seem to forget, I barely got to see it, Fletcher."

Rucker laughed. "By the time this is over, you'll have heard the story so many times you'll think you were makin' that ride with me!"

Gabrielle Johnson turned her face away.

Rucker reached out and drew her toward him. "Miss Gabrielle, take my word for it—one day you will look back on all of this and be proud you were here."

Rucker's patronizing encouragement enraged her. She squinted up at him angrily, and her lips drew into a sneer.

"I'll never be proud of this day, Fletcher! All I will remember is that I went to pieces when the Indians attacked; that I would not defend myself; that a woman in the middle of childbirth had the courage to forget about herself and shoot the savage who was trying to scalp me. I . . . I am a coward, Fletcher!" She removed her hands from his. "No, I don't believe I will tell my grandchildren about this day."

Rucker was dumbfounded. Molly had shot a Comanche? Incredible! There were damned few men who could make that boast!

Gabrielle squinched her eyes closed, and her face took on such venom that it chilled Rucker. "I hate the West, Fletcher. If I survive this nightmare, I intend to book passage on the first stagecoach traveling east."

Rucker, young and immature as he was, heard and understood the anguish and the shame in her voice. He could relate to her self-loathing because he, too, had succumbed to less than heroic behavior while in armed conflict during the late war. In his case, however, with the chaotic confusion of heated combat and men dying every instant, no one had noticed. Indeed, he suspected that periodic cowardice was the rule in battle, not the exception.

"Nearly everyone freezes the first time they go into battle, Gabrielle. Hell, I've seen a thousand seasoned troops break and run, for no reason at all . . . an' I've seen those same men stand up in the face of sure death and fight to the bitter end. There's no tellin' what a person will do from one moment to the next . . . but there's one thing for certain: we can change—for better or worse—anytime we decide to. That decision is ours to make or break."

He picked up the five-shot pocket pistol Gabrielle had dropped and held it out to her. "The difference is, Miss Johnson, it ain't everyone who gets a second chance to prove somethin' to themselves."

Gabrielle squinted at the weapon, barely able to recognize that it was her pistol. The abhorrence of firearms that had been drummed into her since childhood returned with full fury, shouting to her that the gun represented everything bad that was known to mankind: lawlessness, savagery, crudeness, barbarity—and death. She started to shake her head with the intention of refusing the revolver, but something in the set of Fletcher Rucker's features, what little she could distinguish even though he was only inches from her, held her frozen in place. She leaned closer and strained to see him better, needing to see him clearly. The outline of his face swam before her in a swirling pool of murky fog. Then the truth hit her. It was not necessary that she see him at all; the answer lay in *her.* It had been there all along. All it had taken to bring it to the surface was his unwavering confidence that she possessed all those noble and valiant qualities that seemed to come so naturally to people like him, and Peyton Lewis, and . . . yes, even Molly Klinner.

Her heart beat erratically. The pistol Rucker offered was merely a symbol of the second chance he spoke of, her invitation to share the lives of a people she did not like or understand. The revolver represented them, their way of life, everything they deemed good and necessary, everything the frontier demanded: justice and equality, law and order, protection from savagery and barbarity, defense for loved ones and self, and the difference between death . . . and life.

Gabrielle Johnson had never seen as clearly as she did that moment, and she shuddered uncontrollably. Molly Klinner had put a greater value on her life than had she. How shameful. No human being should ask that of another person.

She reached out hesitantly and took the revolver from Rucker. It felt cold and lethal to her touch. "I . . . I don't know if I can do it, Fletcher."

"Sure you can." Rucker bent his head and kissed her startled lips.

He left her where she stood and made his way to the south wall, John Wright's position, where the men were laying down their strategy to counter the onslaught that was in the making: eight hundred yards to the east, the Comanches were again walking their ponies en masse toward the station.

Peyton positioned the Henry rifle on the top log of the barricade. He squinted down the barrel in an effort to pick out the leader of the thirty-man vanguard that preceded the group of warriors nearly half a mile away. He studied the front line and finally determined that the leader of the mob was an imposing warrior wearing a full war bonnet that nearly trailed the ground. The man was astride a magnificent black and white pinto that pranced like a show horse.

Peyton glanced at John Wright. "You're the one with the eye of an eagle, John. I say the head man is that fellow riding the piebald. What do you say?"

Wright studied the approaching horsemen. "Yep, that's him for a fact. He's sportin' an ol' flintlock trade gun with scalps danglin' from the barrel."

Rucker rested his elbows on the top log of the barricade and strained his eyes in an effort to see the rifle. He twisted his lips and mimicked Wright perfectly. "Yep. You're right on the money, John. One of them scalps is blond an' the other is a redhead."

Wright guffawed loudly. "Fletcher, you need t' get you some spectacles. Them scalps is as black as Ben's ass!"

Ben narrowed his eyes at the Indians. "Most of 'em are, Mista' John. But they's one in the middle . . . it's a mousy shade o' brown."

John Wright shook his head stubbornly. "I don't think so, Uncle. Ain't no way I could've overlooked no brown scalp."

Rucker frowned at the two men, then looked again at the Comanche. At that distance, he could not even make out enough detail to tell that the rifle the man carried was a flintlock, much less the color of some alleged scalps dangling from its barrel. He turned to Peyton, who was attempting to get a sight picture on the Indian.

"Let that gent ridin' the pinto get real close b'fore you shoot him, Peyton. I want to see them scalps."

Peyton spoke without taking his eye off the front sight. "Ben says we've got to shoot the lead rider as far out as possible. You got any idea how far this gun will shoot, Fletcher?"

"Naw. I only fired it close up when we busted through the Comanches. But heck fire, Peyton, even if we drop him way out yonder, the others will ride over us anyhow. Their dander is up, an' they got egg on their face . . . an' to an Indian, that's a pair that'll beat a straight flush every time."

The Comanche nudged their ponies into a trot, then into a canter, and to Peyton's satisfaction, the pinto moved unmistakably to the forefront. Peyton looked up at Rucker. "You're more familiar with this rifle than I am. Why don't you try the shot, Fletcher?"

Rucker squinted at the Indian; the man was at least two

thousand feet away. "Hell, no. You always was better with a long gun than me. You shoot him."

Peyton stood up and stretched his muscles. He took several deep breaths, then sank to one knee and braced the rifle barrel firmly across the top of the barricade. He judged the distance to the Indians to be seven hundred yards.

Ben, who had walked to a corner of the barricade where he could keep an eye on two sides of the enclosure at once, watched the savages swarm off the hill. He hoped that Peyton knew what he was doing. "Any idea what the range o' that there rifle is, Miss Molly?"

Molly, who had sat down to rest on a timber near the northeast corner of the depot, shouted to Peyton that Caleb King swore the Henry rifle would shoot dead center at three hundred and fifty yards if the sights were held two inches above the target.

Peyton frowned skeptically down the barrel. He had never heard of a repeating rifle that was accurate at two hundred yards, much less nearly twice that distance. He said so.

Molly shrugged. "I'm just telling you what Caleb King claimed." Under her breath she added, "The day he intended to shoot you out of the saddle when you thought you were safely out of range."

Peyton brought the rifle to bear on the warrior. In spite of Molly Klinner's assurance that the rifle would shoot three hundred and fifty yards, he was hesitant to attempt such a shot.

Sweat beaded his forehead and trickled into his eyes. "How far out are they, John?"

"Five hundred yards, an' comin' fast!"

When the Comanches reached the bottom of the slope, their ponies were running full tilt toward the enclosure.

All eyes inside the compound were riveted to the warrior on the pinto pony. Every breath was held in anticipation. The suspense mounted with each stride of the warhorse.

"Four-fifty." Wright lay his double-barreled shotgun across the log. "Four . . ."

Peyton's breath eased through his teeth, and his finger took the slack out of the trigger. The front bead steadied on the Co-manche's hair-bone breastplate, then rose two inches.

"Three-fifty!"

Peyton's finger pressed the trigger, and the rifle bucked against his shoulder. Surprise filled his face, for he had not intended to try the long shot. Why had he? Because Molly said the gun was accurate, and he wanted to prove her right.

Peyton dropped to both knees and peered beneath the haze of powder smoke that hung in the breeze like a billowing blue-white bedspread on a clothesline, obliterating the quarry. To his dismay the Indian charged on. Damn Molly Klinner! As the sound of the shot faded into the distance and the powder smoke danced away with the breeze, the Comanche threw his arms into the air and tumbled backward over the rump of his pony.

A second later, the warrior directly behind the man who had just fallen grasped his chest and slid sideways off his mount.

John Wright jumped to his feet and crowed like a rooster. "Fine shot, Lewis! Fine shot! Bullet went plumb through that first un an' knocked the second un a-windin'. That'll give them red devils somethin' t' ponder on!"

Peyton levered another round into the chamber and watched as more than fourscore horsemen raced undaunted toward him. The sight surprised him. According to Ben, who thus far had seldom been wrong, the Indians should have panicked upon seeing two of their leaders go under. Well, if the Comanche were as "plumb unsettled" as Ben predicted, they certainly had a strange way of showing it. Indeed, if his shot had slowed the attack one iota he was unaware of it. He said as much to Ben.

Ben grinned sheepishly. "It ain't foolproof, boss. They's times when it makes 'em even madder'n they was befo'."

At two hundred yards, Peyton fired again. Without waiting to see if he had scored a hit, he jacked another round into the chamber, then sent a second bullet screaming into the front line of the advancing horsemen.

An Indian in a buffalo-horn helmet grasped his midsection and toppled from his pony. The warhorse directly behind him attempted to jump over the man's body, but it went down in a spectacular somersault that triggered pandemonium as horses and riders nearby fought to maintain their balance and footing. The other riders surged around them and charged on.

When John Wright called out, "One hundred yards," Peyton fired again. A man's head exploded, splattering brains and matter over the Comanche nearest him. When Peyton repeated the feat a moment later with the same results, the front line of horsemen shuddered and then disintegrated into mass confusion as men all across the field yanked their mounts to a sliding halt, and the riders behind them, not expecting the move, barreled headlong into their ponies and carried them forward as though they were riding the crest of a wave.

When the Comanche finally regained control of their wild-eyed ponies and brought them to a standstill, they were a mere seventy yards from the barricade.

Peyton was not charitable. He sighted on an Indian who, by his excited gestures, appeared to be their main orator, and sent a bullet through his bull-hide shield, knocking him from his pony to hit the ground faceup, his dead eyes staring sightlessly at his gawking comrades. Another shot followed, then another, until, with bloodcurdling screeches, the Comanche yanked their ponies around and raced them parallel to the barricade.

A cheer went up from inside the depot. Even Gabrielle Johnson, who was still standing where Rucker had left her and did not fully understand the significance of what had just occurred, managed a self-conscious hurrah.

Although Ben maintained his composure, his voice, when he spoke, betrayed his attempt at nonchalance. "Evidently, boss, it takes right smart more t' get a Comanche's attention than it does other kinds of Injuns. Why, if'n that had been Creek, or Sioux, or—"

John Wright snatched off his hat and slammed it against his knee. "That's jest plain ol' bullshit, Ben. A Injun is a Injun, an' it don't make no nevermind what tribe . . ."

Peyton stopped listening and levered another round into the Henry's magazine. Molly Klinner had been right on target with her three hundred and fifty yards. He climbed to his feet and called to her. When she stood up, he tipped his head to her. "Thanks, Molly."

Molly smiled at him, surprised, at a loss for words, painfully aware that his acknowledgement, brief as it was, was the first time he had ever verbally expressed appreciation to her—for anything. The baby began to wail, and she was relieved, for the longer she gazed at Peyton the more awkward the moment became. She patted the infant's back and crooned softly to it.

An arrow zipped past Peyton, then another. He dropped down behind the barricade and snapped off a quick shot. He could not tell if he had hit the target, because the sight of Molly Klinner standing straight and tall, with a Colt revolving pistol in one hand and a newborn baby in the crook of her arm, kept flashing through his mind. He laughed to himself with the realization that she was the kind of woman balladeers sang about, history heralded as a heroine, and some lucky man felt honored to take as a wife.

Yet Peyton knew, even as he thought it, that such distinctions, no matter how richly deserved, would never belong to Molly Klinner. Her shaded past would prevent it, even in Texas.

Twenty-three

The Comanche completed their circle and tightened the noose more quickly this time. Arrows, lances, and occasional musket rounds fell into the compound like grapeshot fired from field artillery. Both sides knew that this time it would be a fight to the finish.

Rucker threaded his way around the compound to where Gabrielle had taken refuge behind the northwest corner of the barricade. An arrow with a hammered metal point ricocheted off a log and clipped Rucker's coat sleeve. Another, with a flint point, shattered like glass against a charred timber next to his head. Rucker ducked, then grinned sheepishly at Gabrielle, who was watching him from where she crouched behind the partial wall.

"Hell's bells, Miss Gabriel, it wasn't this dangerous when I rode through the whole passel of 'em!"

Rucker knelt down beside her, took careful aim, and shot a pony from beneath its rider in hopes that its owner—a young warrior wearing nothing but a turkey feather in his hair, who in all likelihood owned just the one horse and prized that particular animal above all other possessions—would be hesitant to ride a replacement mount close enough to the station to get it killed. He was wrong; the young Comanche caught a riderless black Appaloosa with a white blanket that completely covered its rump and swung upon its back. In less than a heartbeat, he had loosed another arrow at Rucker that pinned his hat to the charred beam.

Rucker snapped off the arrow shaft and flung it to the ground. Angrily, he planted his hat firmly on his head. Calling to Peyton, who, along with Molly Klinner, was manning the corner of the northeast wall, he warned him to beware of a kid headed toward him riding a big black Appaloosa with a white blanket.

"See if you can pick him off, Peyton. The wormy-lookin' little son of a bitch has got his distance with that damned toy bow an' arrow of his, an' he's goin' to kill somebody!"

On the west side of the station, Joseph Robertson cringed behind the barricade and cursed himself for a fool. Lewis had been right earlier when he told them to conserve their ammunition. Now, when he needed them the most, he was out of bullets.

An arrow, having been shot straight up, reached its pinnacle, then dropped like a stone into the compound. With an ear-piercing scream that nearly sent Gabrielle Johnson into hysterics, Robertson fell on his side and grasped the arrow that had suddenly plummeted through the fleshy portion of his upper thigh. William Beecher abandoned his post and ran to the banker.

Robertson, ignoring Beecher's attempts to render aid, cried out for John Wright's assistance until, finally, Wright left the south wall and scrambled around the aisleway to him. He took one look at the wound, put his foot against the man's buttocks, and pulled the arrow free.

Wright shook the arrow in Robertson's face. "Damn it, man, you ain't hurt! It jest took a little meat an' hide off'n your leg. Nothin' important."

Across the compound, Peyton studied the mass of Indian ponies galloping past. There were sorrels, bays, pintos, buckskins, grays, and duns of nearly every hue, but nowhere did he see a big black Appaloosa with a white blanket.

An Indian riding a scrawny, ewe-necked buckskin, its black mane and tail platted and bobbed for war, reined out of the circle and galloped close to the enclosure. When the Comanche notched an arrow and drew his bow, Peyton sighted the Henry on the man's chest and squeezed the trigger. Wood chips splintered from the warrior's bow as though it had sustained a small explosion. The Indian fell from his pony to hit the ground in a well-practiced roll that immediately brought him to his feet. A companion raced his mount past the man and, without breaking its stride, caught the warrior by his wrist and flipped him nimbly up behind him. Riding double, they angled away from the station toward the safety of the ridge to the north.

Peyton sprinted down the aisleway until he had a clear shot at the two riders. Taking careful aim at a spot between the rear Indian's shoulder blades, he pulled the trigger and watched both men tumble to the earth, shot through and through.

Molly, squatting a few feet from Peyton with her back pressed against the wall, drew her baby more snugly against her chest. She gazed up at Peyton as he levered another shell into the chamber. "Promise me something, Mr. Lewis."

The tone of her voice, or perhaps the absence of tone in her voice, prompted him to hunker down beside her and study her face. Her eyes were distant, as though she were there only in body, not in soul. He waited for her to speak, but words were not necessary; what she had in mind was plainly written on her aggrieved face. The finality of it chilled his spine.

Molly smiled sadly at him, so calm in her demeanor that it bordered on serenity. "When the Comanche overrun us, Peyton, promise me that you will not let them take me or my baby alive."

Although Peyton had anticipated her request, was even prepared for it, the reality of actually hearing her put it into words left him livid with anger—not at Molly Klinner, not even at the Comanche, but at mankind in general, the very same mankind that had devastated an entire nation and destroyed a unique way of life in a senseless political war between the North and the South and was now engaged in another battle that would end with the stronger nation decimating the weaker one. This time, however, the loser was not the South; it was the red men, the entire Indian nation.

Peyton wondered idly if the annihilation of the Southern white men, and now the western red men, was a conspiracy by the Federal government to eradicate all peoples who did not believe exactly as it did. Surely not—at least where the Comanche were concerned—for it could not be entirely wrong to eliminate a race of people who were so utterly savage that a young mother would prefer that she and her child be quickly assassinated rather than submit to their capture.

Peyton looked away from Molly. Could he shoot her and the child? Not if he was dead first—and he knew in that instant that the Comanche would have to kill him to get to her.

Peyton's lengthy silence, his refusal to meet her gaze, brought Molly's head up. Her voice took on a note of urgency. "You know what they do to women and children, Peyton. Please, promise me that you will do as I ask!"

"It won't come to that, Molly."

"And if it does?"

"It won't."

Molly picked up her pistol. There was one round in the cylinder—one bullet for her and the child. She looked sadly at Gabrielle Johnson. She had made a vow to the girl to protect her, a vow she could not keep. With a shuddering sigh, she drew the baby up over her heart and placed the muzzle of the weapon against the infant's small body. "Never mind, Mr. Lewis."

As the battle raged on, the Comanche war cries soared to a crescendo that bordered on fanaticism. Their horses brushed past the barricade so near that one could smell their heated bodies, could taste their lathered skin, could feel the earth tremble when their hooves struck. Those inside the compound knew with sinking hearts it was simply a matter of time before the Indians worked themselves into such a frenzy that they would ride straight down the bore of the guns pointed at them.

Gabrielle Johnson raised her head until her eyes cleared the top log of the enclosure. The Comanche swept past seemingly an arm's length away. They reminded her, what little she could see of them, of the jockeys she had once observed riding thoroughbred horses at a race track in Syracuse, New York. It had been an exciting time, and she had placed many wagers. This time, however, she and the people inside the compound were the purse.

Rucker, his face bleeding from splinters sheared off a timber by a lance, walked to the fallen beams where Gabrielle peered over the barricade, and hunkered down beside her. "They'll rush us shortly, Gabrielle. When they come over the wall, shoot fast, and shoot to kill."

Gabrielle pushed herself more closely against the barrier. The five-shot pistol hung limply in her hand; it had not been fired. "I can't do it, Fletcher! I can't shoot human beings. . . ."

Rucker's patience snapped. Catching the girl by her shoulders, he jerked her to her feet and flung his hand toward the Indians. "Those goddamned Comanche out there don't give a hoot in hell that you're from Monroe, Michigan, Gabrielle. An' they would laugh in your face at your squeamishness about killing people, because they thrive on it. It's what they live for. An' the longer it takes for a person to die, the better they like it!"

Rucker's unexpected attack left Gabrielle stunned. She felt betrayed. Rucker had been so kind and considerate toward her. So understanding. So gentle and protective. The gash at her hairline oozed new blood, which trickled down her forehead and dripped onto her singed eyelids. Her lips trembled.

Rucker released her and stepped back. "If they get their hands on you, Gabrielle, you'll wish a thousand times that you had personally killed every last one of the bastards yourself. I'm not sayin' that to scare you. It's just plain fact."

Gabrielle stared numbly at him. "I know, Fletcher. Molly Klinner told me the same thing. I . . . I . . ." She raised the pistol tentatively. "What would you have me do? I can't see . . . and even if I could, I've never fired one of these in my life. I . . . I don't know how to fight."

Rucker snapped off a shot at an Indian who was only a hairs-breadth from the barricade. He missed. He turned to her and held up three fingers. "How many fingers do you see?"

She squinted at his hand. "Three, I think."

He nodded. "All you got to do, Gabrielle, is let the Indian get as close as I am. Hold your fire until you can see up both his nose holes, then shoot where you're lookin'."

Gabrielle peered hard at Rucker, wishing she could see him more clearly. Surely he was jesting? No, he was not.

"All right, Fletcher, I'll try."

Acrid layers of burnt powder smoke waved like banners through-out the station, searing lungs, watering eyes, obliterating their view of the battlefield. The noise that accompanied it—guns popping, horses neighing, people talking, screaming, crying out—was so loud and intense that conversation was an impossi-bility.

Peyton squatted down beside Molly Klinner and jacked open the breech of the Henry rifle. He showed her the empty chamber and cocked his brows at her in a silent question.

Molly raised her face to him. All the emotions known to man were in her eyes: love, hate, compassion, fear, courage, life . . . and death. She touched her lips to the top of her baby's head. He had his answer.

Peyton laid the empty rifle aside. When he drew his revolver and again faced the horsemen, that very same apathy toward human life that empowered the Comanche with the ungodly ca-pacity to inflict cold-blooded atrocities on their enemies flowed through him like an icy wind. In the space of a heartbeat, Peyton Lewis became as savage as the most barbaric Indian who ever lived. Gripping his Spiller and Burr revolver in one hand and his bowie knife in the other, he waited for the Comanche to breach the wall.

It took only minutes for the warriors to realize that the deadly rifle fire had ceased. At first they were wary that it might be a trap, but when a young brave raced his pony to the north side of the compound and sprang from his horse onto the top log of the barricade, and the rifle remained silent, others became bolder, and they, too, charged the station.

The Comanche who had jumped onto the log wall peered down the aisleway at the northwest corner where Peyton was firing steadily. Then he swung his attention to the northeast corner, where Gabrielle Johnson stood alone. She could see his form in the bright sunlight, but she could not tell which way he was looking. She took a step backward, then another. The warrior raised his war club and trotted down the wall toward her.

Gabrielle's world stood still. She would never forget holding her breath until he was towering over her, nor the stench of his rancid body grease and other vile odors that gagged her until she was certain she would vomit, nor the sound of his voice when he dropped his head back and shrilled out his victory cry as he drew the club over his head for the kill. She would remember, even in her dreams, pointing her revolver at what she prayed was his hooked nose and squeezing the trigger. Lost to her forever was the sight of the ball smashing into the skin beneath his chin and exiting between the curved buffalo horns of his headdress, for all at once he was engulfed in a swirl of blue smoke, and when it had cleared, he was gone—poof!—as though he had never existed.

Gabrielle blinked her eyes wonderingly. Where was he? She gazed around her, but she was alone. Had he been a figment of her imagination? A specter created by her fear? Surely not.

Timidly, she made her way to the log wall and peered over the edge of the barricade. Her heart leaped into her throat. The Comanche was lying spread-eagle in the mud below, his filmed-over eyes staring directly up at her. Gabrielle's first reaction was a grand sense of pride in her accomplishment. She had protected her side of the fort, saved her own life and perhaps others' as well. Then the fact that she had killed a man hit her like a punch in the stomach, and she sank to her knees and retched up everything she had eaten the day before. Her hands trembled so badly that she dropped the pistol. Again, she retched—and again—until there was nothing left but dry heaves.

Rucker, having moved to the corner of the southeastern wall, had missed Gabrielle's entire ordeal, for, on all quarters,

Comanche were attempting to breach the barricade, and like
everyone in the compound, he had his own worries. A battle-
scarred Comanche lying low over his pony's neck and flailing the
animal unmercifully with a rawhide quirt was racing directly toward Rucker, his spear thrust out before him as though it were
a medieval jousting lance. It was obvious by the set of the man's
face that he intended to impale Rucker, even if it meant dashing
his pony headlong against the log wall.

When the rider was ten feet from the perimeter, Rucker
squeezed the trigger. The pony raised its head at that precise instant, and the bullet caught the horse a glancing blow just above
the eye. The impact of the .36-caliber ball drove the animal to its
knees in the path of an oncoming rider, and the two horses col-
lided, going down in such a frenzy of kicking and squealing that
both riders were crushed beneath them.

Rucker spun toward a third Indian who raced his pony to
the northeast corner of the compound and vaulted over the wall.
He screamed for Gabrielle to beware, but she was facing away
from the man, totally unaware of his presence. Rucker sprinted
down the corridor. Halfway to Gabrielle, he jerked to a halt,
steadied his pistol barrel with his other hand, and shot the Comanche through the back of the head.

Gabrielle whirled about, her eyes the size of saucers, and
Rucker fully expected her to swoon, but a moment later, when
another savage came over the wall, she snatched up her pistol
and shot the man through the chest. When he did not fall, her
lips compressed with grim determination, and she shot him a
second time, then a third.

The wounded Comanche made a desperate lunge for her
throat, but his hands, already without feeling, caught the neck-
line of her dress and ripped the fabric to her waist. For the first
time in her young and sheltered life, Gabrielle Johnson's proud,
flawless breasts were exposed to a man's inspection. The Comanche never saw them. Gabrielle pushed the muzzle of her revolver against his nose as Rucker had instructed, and the blast
propelled him backward as though he were a puppet on a string.
The man was dead before his head touched the ground.

Gabrielle drew her traveling cloak across her bosom, then

cut her cloudy eyes down the north wall to, of all people, Molly Klinner, appalled that the woman might have witnessed her indecency. She was relieved, then astounded at the sight she beheld, for in spite of her obscured vision, she was able to ascertain that Molly Klinner was paying no attention to the battle, but instead was sitting with her cheek pressed against the crown of her baby's head.

Gabrielle's eyes widened in horror as two dim forms vaulted the logs and dropped down beside Molly. She raised her pistol and pointed it in their direction and pulled the trigger. The hammer fell on a spent cap.

Ben, using the nine-inch barrel of his empty Walker Colt as a club, charged into the Indians and carried them sprawling into the pile of roof timbers.

Molly screamed and pushed herself more tightly against the wall. She watched the life-and-death struggle being played out by Ben and the two savages, acutely aware of the consequences should Ben not emerge victorious. Being careful that the muzzle of her pistol was against the infant's back and pointed directly at her own heart, she cocked the weapon and waited.

The three men rolled and tumbled, hacking, cutting, slashing. Blood streamed down Ben's body from multiple knife wounds, but he fought on, even though it was obvious to Molly that he could not last much longer.

His strength waning with each drop of blood that spurted from his wounds, Ben viciously smashed the heavy butt of his pistol against one Comanche's head. The skull shattered like an eggshell.

Even before the dead man began to fall, the second Comanche caught Ben by his hair and snapped his head back just far enough to wedge the razor-sharp blade of his scalping knife against the black man's throat.

Ben dropped his pistol and grasped the Comanche's wrist with both hands. The veins at his temples stood out like fishing worms, and his arms trembled as he labored to turn the Indian's knife aside. Slowly, amid quivering muscles and gritted teeth, Ben's strength ebbed, and the Comanche, with sheer brute strength, forced the blade into Ben's throat.

Molly watched in horror as blood welled up, then streamed down Ben's neck. She tried to look away, but she could not. Fully aware of what the future held for her and the baby should she fire that one last bullet, she raised her pistol and steadied it against her knee. The ball shattered the Comanche's spine.

Molly laid the pistol aside and drew her baby more closely against her bosom. Crooning a lullaby, she rocked it lovingly.

Ben, on hands and knees, clawed his way over the bodies of the Indians, and for a moment stared into her face, thinking how fine a woman she was, telling himself that it was an awful waste that she was not black, telling her aloud: "Yo' jest a damned fool white woman, Miss Molly. Yes, ma'am, yo' jest the damnedest fool woman I ever have seen. Yo' done gone an' wasted yo' only bullet on a no-'count nigger. Now what are yo' goin' t' do when them Comanche overrun us?"

In spite of the fear that was threatening to choke off her breath, Molly smiled at Ben.

"You know what they always say, Ben? Without damn fool women like me, smart men like you wouldn't know how intelligent you are." She laughed throatily. "Anyway, I'm depending on you to protect me."

Ben nodded. *When they take this place, you won't be here. They won't make you suffer, Miss Molly.* It was a promise.

Had Molly looked closely at Ben, she would have been privileged to witness a phenomenon few white people had ever seen in the man's eyes: respect. But she did not look.

At the southwest side of the station, three Indians wielding war clubs, hatchets, and skinning knives bounded over the barricade as though they had spewed forth from the bowels of hell. They fell upon William Beecher with a vengeance, hacking and cutting until his skull was crushed and his body dismembered. With howls and screeches, they bounded toward Joseph Robertson, who was dragging himself by his arms along the ground toward the corner of the building where John Wright was frantically reloading his shotgun.

Just as the savages closed in on the wounded banker, John

Wright palmed back the hammers of the gun and touched both triggers. The blast of the overcharged load of double-aught buckshot at such close quarters nearly disemboweled the three Comanches. When Wright swung the yawning bore of the empty weapon toward another half-dozen warriors who were breaching the wall, the men leaped back astride their ponies and raced out of range, where they regrouped and yammered and gestured about the carnage they had just witnessed.

Other Indians, aware that something important had transpired, dashed their horses out of gun range and rode hurriedly to the place where their brethren were congregating.

Gabrielle heard the cheers of the men inside the compound. She wondered what it was about. She heard someone shout that the Indians were retreating. Laughing and crying at the same time, she jumped to her feet, feeling that sense of pride and accomplishment that is an integral part of a personal victory, not because she had bested the Comanche but because she had confronted an even more terrible enemy—fear and cowardice—and had emerged triumphant. All at once, she had the grandest desire to kiss Fletcher Rucker's mouth. She looked down the wall toward the spot where Rucker had been just a minute ago.

A young warrior boasting a single turkey feather in his hair, riding a black Appaloosa, watched his comrades regroup out on the prairie. With the intention of joining them, he slipped to the off side of his warhorse and made one last dash past the barricade, aiming his bow in the general direction of the north wall. He loosed his arrow and without waiting to see where the missile struck flipped upright on his horse's back. Using his bow as a quirt, he flailed his mount into an earth-shaking gallop toward his companions.

Gabrielle's smile froze on her lips. She sucked in her breath, astonished, for suddenly what appeared to be a bundle of feathers was protruding from her traveling cloak at a spot just above her breast. Where had the feathers come from? She had felt no pain, had heard no sound. How did they get there? Her pistol slipped from her fingers and clattered to the ground; she could not understand that either. She gazed out over the prairie and

through the mist that swam before her eyes saw a horseman galloping away from the compound. She attempted to shout at him,
to demand that he come back and explain what he had done to
her. When she opened her mouth, no sound came forth. Then,
as though her body had no will of its own, her knees buckled,
and she slid down the wall until she was kneeling at its base. For
a long moment, she rested her forehead against the cool, damp
logs. They felt good to her parched skin.

It took all her effort to turn her body so that she could lean
against the wall. Why was she so tired? She closed her eyes and
took a shallow breath, then another. "Fletcher?" It was a whispered plea. Dimly aware that he had been by her side only moments before, her eyes searched the barricade for him. Her
vision misted as though the compound were filled with smoke.
It thickened.

"Fletcher, oh, Fletcher. I'm hurt. . . ." Not one person in
the enclosure heard her.

Gabrielle Johnson's eyes closed and remained that way.

Twenty-four

Fletcher Rucker had joined Peyton, John Wright, and Lieutenant Pendleton at the corner of the southwest wall, where he, too, evaluated the war party as it churned in confusion like bees in swarm. He frowned when he noticed the young Comanche riding a black Appaloosa in an all-out run to join his tribesmen.

"I thought I told you to shoot that little son of a bitch before he killed somebody, Peyton."

"You did, but that's the first glimpse I've had of him."

"That kid must have shot ten arrows at me . . . put holes all in my hat."

The boy raced into the mass of horsemen and disappeared.

Ben, with a bloody bandanna knotted around his throat, moved up on Peyton's other side. He gestured toward the Comanche. "They'll rant an' rave fo' a spell, but they'll finish what they started, boss."

Peyton had little doubt in the truth of Ben's statement, and that brought up a very real concern. "How many rounds of powder and ball have you got left, Ben?"

For the first time since having joined the travelers, Ben had been addressed without the derogatory "Uncle." He liked the sound of it; yes, he liked it fine.

"I jest reloaded all I had left, boss. I got three rouns'." It was a statement more than just an answer, for the truth was, he intended to use two of the loads on Molly Klinner and Gabrielle Johnson.

Peyton sighed. John Wright had one shotgun barrel charged and capped; Rucker only had two loaded chambers in his Shawk and McLanahan; the lieutenant had four rounds in his army Colt; and he, Peyton, had one. The banker, who lay propped against the wall nursing a grossly swollen leg, an indication that the arrow he had taken in his thigh had been poisoned, was completely out of ammunition, and had been throughout the last siege.

Peyton glanced over the debris to the north side of the enclosure. Neither Molly Klinner nor Gabrielle Johnson was visible.

Lieutenant Pendleton eyed the riderless ponies that dotted the landscape. Some were running wild, others stood loyally beside their dead or wounded masters, and a few grazed peacefully on the new grass that had sprouted in the last few days. "Perhaps I could capture one of those horses and ride for help?"

John Wright waved the suggestion aside. "Them's Injun ponies, son. They get one whiff of a white man, an' they're gone. Wouldn't make no difference nohow, 'cause they got scouts watchin' the trails. They'd get you afore you'd gone a mile." Wright peered at Ben. "How 'bout you, Uncle? You got anything to add to that? You always got somethin' to say."

"Name's Ben, Mista' John. An' no, sir, yo' done told it true. The lieutenant wouldn't get a mile."

John Wright draped his arm across Ben's shoulder. "Now listen here, Ben. I ain't never called a nigger by his given name afore."

Ben nodded. "I ain't never called a stove-up stagecoach driver my friend befo', neither." The two men laughed. It was a good sound.

Peyton made his way down the corridor and squatted beside Molly. "When they come again, Molly, there won't be much time for conversation. . . ." He touched her hand hesitantly, then closed his fingers tightly around hers. "I just want you to know that I'm sorry for the way this has turned out." He reached down and gently laid his powder-blackened hand on the baby's head. "I'm sorry for you both."

Molly took a deep breath, then exhaled long and slowly through her pursed lips. "I'm sorry, too, Peyton. I . . ." It was on the tip of her tongue to tell him that she wished they could have gotten to know one another better, to have had a chance at some semblance of a real friendship . . . anything.

"When this is over, Peyton, if you are still standing, take a long look around you." Tears welled up in her eyes and over-flowed down her cheeks. "What you are searching for is right *here* . . . in Texas. You told me you would find it here, and I . . . I truly believe you will." *Look at me!* she cried silently. *I am here! I am here.*

A clear and precise picture of the overturned cradle be-neath the wreckage was suddenly a vivid image in her mind. When the end was near, had the mother and father of that child knelt beside one another as she and Peyton were doing? Had they embraced? Had she kissed him good-bye?

Molly's arm went unbidden around Peyton's neck, and her lips found his, warm and tender at first, then passionate and hungry, for without his being aware, he was the first man *she* had kissed since she was twelve years old. When she released him and lay back against the wall, Peyton climbed slowly to his feet and stared down at her. Without a word, he rejoined the men at the west wall.

A half-mile from the compound, the Comanche sat their ponies and argued heatedly over their next move. Some, pointing out their numerous losses of both man and beast, were for quitting and going home. Others were in favor of waiting for nightfall and attacking on foot, and still others reasoned that the de-fenders were all but out of ammunition. They called attention to the fact that there were no longer any rifle shots, few pistol re-ports, and even fewer shotgun blasts. They spoke of the two white men they had killed, and the disgrace they would suffer were they to return to their tepees with no scalps or plunder. Fi-nally, a wind-dried, prune-faced old man squinted at the sun; it was directly overhead and cast no shadow. It was a good time to die. He began his death chant, and, one by one, the others joined in.

En masse, the horde of Comanche kneed their ponies into a full canter and rode straight toward the station. Had the circumstances been different, the vivid spectacle of the buffalo-horn helmets, greased and painted bodies, exquisitely decorated bull-hide shields, feathered headdresses, scalp-strung lances, and multicolored horses with their platted manes and clubbed tails would have been a beautiful, thrilling sight. This time, however, it was bone-chillingly terrifying. It was the end.

Peyton, Rucker, John Wright, and Lieutenant Pendleton squatted behind the west barricade where the brunt of the assault would occur and watched them come. Peyton and Rucker cocked their revolvers, and John Wright thumbed the left hammer of his double-barreled shotgun to full cock. The lieutenant gripped his pistol tightly in his sweaty, powder-burned palm. The Indians swept toward them. Through the soles of their boots they felt the earth tremble as nearly four hundred unshod hooves struck its surface.

If there was fear in the men who calmly awaited certain death, it was well disguised. Peyton Lewis loosened his knife in its sheath and turned his revolver cylinder to make certain that when he cocked the weapon, the single charged chamber would be in position. Fletcher Rucker fished the makings out of his shirt pocket and began rolling a cigarette. John Wright uncoiled his whip and stretched it out on the top log of the wall, its handle pointed toward him for quick access. The lieutenant picked up Captain Cramer's hat and brushed particles of dirt from its brim. With a shrug, he placed it rakishly on his head. "Hell, our red brethren will never know I'm not a captain." No one paid any attention.

Ben, who had not moved to the west wall with the rest of the men, shoved his revolver into his waistband and gathered up a scalping knife and a war club. He squatted beside Molly, stared at the sun, and recited the Apache death chant under his breath while Molly Klinner sang a lullaby to her baby.

Joseph Robertson, nearly out of his head with pain and fear, cringed against the damp east wall and with a shaking hand drew a Philadelphia derringer from his coat pocket. Opening his mouth, he placed its stubby muzzle between his teeth.

Fletcher Rucker glanced toward the corner of the northeast wall where Gabrielle Johnson lay. He started to call to her, to tell her not to worry, that everything would be fine. At the last second, he closed his mouth; for, while he did not consider himself overly religious, he did not want the last words he ever uttered to be a lie—especially to her.

Peyton stood up and gazed toward the north wall. The only person visible was Ben. Pursing his lips in thought, Peyton studied the revolver he held casually in his hand. One bullet. Had he saved that round on purpose? He looked again at the north wall. Ben was talking to someone Peyton could not see, someone who, not an hour before, had asked a very personal—and final—favor of him. With a sigh of resignation, Peyton started around the compound to where Molly Klinner was waiting.

Rucker caught Peyton by the arm. For a long moment neither man spoke, both remembering French's station, that day not long ago, but now seeming like ages, when Peyton had told Rucker to never again put his hands on him.

Rucker smiled, his fine even teeth glistening in his battle-weary face. He offered Peyton his revolver. "It has two rounds left." His meaning was plain: Molly Klinner and Gabrielle Johnson. He shrugged. "I . . . I just ain't got the guts . . ."

Peyton studied his cousin. The boy was growing up; he was even becoming a man Peyton could like, possibly even admire. Peyton traded pistols with him. When he stepped away, Rucker again caught his arm. "I want my Shawk and McLanahan back when this is over, Peyton. Don't forget that."

Peyton grinned and with a nod indicated the Spiller and Burr Rucker was holding. "My pistol's worth more than yours any day of the week, Fletcher."

Rucker watched Peyton pick his way through the debris toward Molly Klinner, then turned his attention to the Comanche. They were five hundred yards away and coming fast.

Molly's pulse beat erratically, and a great sadness enveloped her when Peyton walked down the aisle. His return could mean only one thing. She sighed involuntarily and gazed into his eyes. Words were unnecessary.

They stayed like that, peering into the windows of their being, bonded together by one of the most powerful forces on earth, that invisible chain that binds a man and a woman into one when their souls intertwine.

A soft smile dimpled Molly's cheeks. She had learned years ago that at the right moment, a man's eyes told a woman what his lips refused to say—and Peyton's eyes had said enough. A rush of passion for life that fills one who is facing certain death surged through her.

Ben discreetly turned his back on the two and studied the sweeping line of unbridled death that raced toward them some three hundred yards distant. They would be here shortly, and they would overrun the station. If, when that time came, something happened that prevented Peyton from fulfilling Molly Klinner's last request, then Ben would do that; he would be the last man standing. His face took on a peaceful expression. He might not have lived as *long* as some, but he had lived *more* than most. He was prepared to die.

The Comanche thundered on, looming larger and larger, intending to hit the barricade like a wave and wash right over it.

Above the rumble of hoofbeats, John Wright kept a running count of the Indians' progress. "Two hundred yards. One-fifty." When the count reached one hundred yards, Joseph Robertson pressed the muzzle of his derringer deeper into his mouth and pulled the trigger. Not one person in the compound turned to look.

Peyton stood over Molly, a fierce protector. He had made up his mind that when the Comanche hit the wall, he would shoot Molly through the back of the head, then rush to Gabrielle Johnson and do the same. It was as simple as that.

He glanced at the newborn. The infant would not suffer; the Comanche would simply bash in her skull. Peyton took a deep breath and thumbed back the hammer on Rucker's revolver. Molly closed her eyes; in a few seconds it would all be over.

As John Wright called out, "Fifty yards," and prepared to touch off the final barrel of his shotgun, hoping the buckshot would spread wide enough to wreak havoc on a few of the charging savages, an astounding phenomenon occurred: the Comanche, whom someone had once dubbed the "greatest light horse cavalry in the world," implemented an oblique movement that would have made a West Point graduate proud. In unison, the riders pivoted their mounts to the north and pushed them unmercifully toward a rise on the prairie that overlooked the crossing at the Red River. Beyond was their sanctuary, the Oklahoma Indian nation.

As the sound of the pounding hooves of the Comanche warhorses diminished, a hush swept the prairie like a soft breeze. One could not see it, one could not feel or taste it, but one could certainly hear it. The silence was deafening.

After several seconds ticked by without incident, Molly Klinner pushed herself to her knees and peered over the barricade. The prairie was empty.

"What is it, Peyton? Where have they gone?"

Stunned, Peyton shook his head. "I don't know, Molly. They just veered off to the north and . . . rode away." He eased the hammer down on his pistol.

Molly looked at Ben, who she believed had a natural instinct for what Indians would and would not do. "Will they come back?"

Ben watched the hill where the Comanche disappeared as though he, too, believed their hasty flight was somehow a ruse. "Comanches are kind'a like longhorn cattle when they stampede, Miss Molly. They's the only ones who know 'xactly why they do it—an' they ain't talkin'!"

Molly nodded as though she understood every word Ben had said, then swung her gaze to the rise, fully expecting the Comanche to sweep back into view.

The seconds dragged by, and nerves drew taut. All eyes were on the hill.

A moment later they heard the faint blast of a bugle, and, two miles to the south, an eastbound stagecoach, flanked by a squad of United States Cavalry, rumbled over a swell in the prairie.

Peyton looked at the gun in his hand. Suddenly it was too heavy to hold. He was remembering a day, weeks before in a snowstorm, when he had held a gun to another head and pulled the trigger—only to find, moments later, that it had been unnecessary.

Peyton's hand shook as he shoved the pistol into his waistband, for had the stagecoach come one minute later . . .

Molly saw the look on his face, the same self-incriminating expression as the day he had shot the horses. She reached up and took his hand. "Scary, isn't it? Somebody is watching over us. As I said before, in spite of you being a bank robber and me being a harlot, somebody likes us."

Peyton thought about Rucker being shot, Caleb King's death, the horses, the hardships during the snowstorm, the stagecoach trip, the station. He glanced down the aisleway at the bodies of Captain Cramer, William Beecher, and Joseph Robertson. "Well, we're in Texas, Molly. I hope the price we paid to get here was worth it."

Molly brought his hand to her cheek. "We're interlopers in Texas, Peyton. And yes, we paid a high price." She gazed up at him. "There's two kinds of interlopers in this world: the kind who crashes a rowdy party with the intention of dominating it—that's us taking Texas—and the kind who waits until the party's safe, and then they crash it—that's people like those who voted to wait until they had an army escort."

Peyton looked down at her. "So you think we're interlopers, do you? And we're going to tame Texas?"

Molly shook her head. "Nobody will ever tame Texas, Peyton. We are merely going to subdue it, so that one day the timid, like Gabrielle, like Beecher and Robertson, can live here without fear."

"Well, at least it sounds good. Who knows? You might even be right." He did not believe for a minute that they would subdue Texas in their lifetime.

Molly watched the Federal soldiers spur their horses forward and gallop toward the station. "You had better hope General Grant isn't leading those cavalrymen, Mr. Lewis."

Peyton looked questioningly at her, and Molly smiled at him. "You told me to wish for the cavalry, and I did, remember? You swore you would hug General Grant himself if they came to our rescue. Well, there they are."

"If Grant's with those soldiers, I'll kiss his mouth, Molly!"

Try mine, Molly pleaded silently. *It's softer, sweeter—and closer.* But she said nothing. If he ever kissed her again, it would be because he initiated it, not she.

John Wright snatched up his brass horn and blew a long answering blast. Then he and the lieutenant leaped over the wall and trotted out to meet the cavalrymen who were surveying the dead and wounded Indians and ponies that dotted the landscape. Even the untrained eye of the newest recruits had no trouble seeing that a fierce battle had been fought here. The "Battle of Burnt Station" would be the talk of Texas for the next fifty years.

Peyton walked slowly toward the south wall where the banker lay stiffening in death, his eyes staring sightlessly at the powder-blue sky. There was no need to hurry; he knew exactly what he would find.

Fletcher Rucker peered toward the north wall in search of Gabrielle Johnson. He was mildly surprised when she was nowhere to be seen. With an embryo of concern marring his brow, he walked down the aisle, and with each step he took, he fought the urge to bolt into an all-out run for the corner of the compound where he had last seen the girl. Finally he did run.

He found Gabrielle slumped against the wall with her chin on her chest. A great quantity of blood, nearly hidden from view by her heavy cloak, puddled in the hollow created by the slight swell of her breasts.

Rucker dropped to his knees beside her. An ache filled his heart, then spread slowly throughout his being, and the excitement he had intended to share with her now that they were safe died on his lips.

He carefully lifted her chin off her breast and tilted her head back so he could see her face. Her closed, lashless eyelids, translucent as onion skins, accented her sickly, chalky skin, which was cold to his touch.

Fighting to control a terrifying urgency that was pushing him toward panic, Rucker removed his neckerchief and dabbed at her forehead where the scalp wound had bled through the bandage. Each second that ticked by stretched his self-control more thinly until finally he drew her against his chest and cried out in grief-stricken rage.

Gabrielle's eyelids fluttered open, and she gazed up at him. She blinked, then blinked again, baffled that her eyes refused to focus properly. A searing pain in her chest caused her to grit her teeth to stifle the shriek that was building in the back of her throat.

"Don't hold me so tight, Fletcher. I think I've been shot . . . with a spear or something."

Relief flooded through Rucker as though a dam had burst in his chest. He eased Gabrielle down against the wall, his eyes roving over her in search of a shaft. He could see nothing.

"Where are you shot, Gabrielle?"

Her eyes were beginning to glaze, and her breathing was labored. "I don't know . . . There was something stuck in me . . . some feathers. I think it broke off when I fell. I . . . I must have swooned." Her voice was becoming faint.

Fletcher slipped his arm beneath her shoulders and gently drew her forward until her cheek was pressed against his chest. The sight of her back brought knots to his jaws; three inches of arrow shaft protruded from a spot just below her shoulder blade. Even as he watched, her life's blood trickled down the wooden rod and dripped off the tip of a small flint point to splash silently in a crimson pool at the base of the wall.

Rucker carefully maneuvered the girl forward until she was stretched facedown on the earthen floor. Without so much as a word of warning, he placed his knee in the small of her back and, gripping the arrow shaft with both hands, pulled it the rest of the way through her body.

In spite of Gabriel's brave determination not to cry out, the pain was so unbearable that when she did scream, it was heart-chilling.

The unmistakable sound of a woman in agony sent shivers up Molly Klinner's spine. She debated going to the girl's aid. What could she do? She had just given birth, and was more weak and exhausted than she would have believed or ever admitted.

Even while assuring herself that there was little she could do to help Gabrielle Johnson, Molly was shedding her overcoat and wrapping the child in it. Carrying the bundled infant to Rucker, she laid it in his arms. Then, sinking to her knees beside Gabrielle, she unceremoniously stripped the girl to the waist.

Molly was glad Gabrielle was unconscious, for the entry and exit punctures were ragged and ugly, and the shocked flesh of her chest and breast had already turned an angry purple, an indication of internal bleeding. Molly went to work to curb the flow of blood.

Twenty minutes later, the eastbound stagecoach drew to a rocking halt beside the remains of the depot. A businessman and his two young sons, en route to their home in St. Louis, along with two men in western attire, disembarked from the vehicle, to stare in openmouthed awe at the bodies of the seven Comanche whom Peyton and Ben had dragged out of the fort and laid in a line along the base of the west wall. Even in death, the warriors appeared fierce and threatening.

When the eastbound passengers found that a woman was wounded and another had just given birth, the businessman raced to the stagecoach and shouted to someone inside. Three women emerged from the coach and, in a matter of minutes, had taken charge of Molly Klinner and Gabrielle Johnson.

They forced laudanum down the wounded girl's throat and made her swallow it, then cleaned and bandaged the arrow punctures in fresh linen. Wrapping Gabrielle in a blanket, they ordered the men to carry her to John Wright's coach, where they stretched her full length on the seat. In spite of Molly Klinner's protests, the women insisted that she recline on the opposite seat. As they ushered Molly toward the coach, they were

forced to pass near the body of Captain Cramer. A hush fell
across them when Molly broke away and walked to the corpse.
They watched in disbelief as the young mother knelt and scraped
up a handful of damp earth. Drawing herself to her full height,
she squared her shoulders. "Captain Cramer, if you can hear me
from the gates of hell, I just want you to know what dirt—that
you can't wash off—feels like. It's how I've felt ever since you
kicked down the door to Miss Kirby's washroom." Slowly and
methodically she sprinkled the soil on his lifeless, upturned face.

Molly rejoined the group, and without explanation walked
to the coach. Although the women said nothing of the spectacle,
and were kind and considerate as they made her comfortable on
the seat, Molly could not help but wonder if the good ladies
would have been so generous had they known the truth about
her background. Glancing out the open door at the captain's
body, a peacefulness stole over her, and she realized that she
could not care less what the ladies thought. Not now. Not ever.

Peyton, Rucker, Wright, and Lieutenant Pendleton carried
the bodies of Captain Cramer, Joseph Robertson, and William
Beecher to the coach and lifted them to the roof, where they
were covered with blankets and lashed securely to the luggage
rails.

The cavalrymen, along with the St. Louis couple's two sons,
ages eight and ten, stripped the Indians of their earrings, neck-
bands, knives, bracelets—anything of value—as mementos, because without a doubt, the seven Comanche lined up alongside
the ruined building were the most numerous "hostile Indians"
any of them had ever witnessed killed in one battle. Then, under
orders from their commander, Major Anthony Zimmerick, the
soldiers bent their backs to the task of unloading William
Beecher's trunk and other baggage from the Butterfield's luggage boot. Dragging the Comanche corpses to the rear of the
coach, they grasped the bodies by the armpits and ankles and, as
though they were loading bags of meal, flung them onto the
floor of the boot.

When they threw the fifth Indian onto the pile, the body, already stiffening with rigor mortis, slide off the stack and fell to
the ground with a sickening thud. The soldiers caught up the

corpse, and on the count of three swung it again onto the heap. That time it stayed.

Peyton walked angrily to Major Zimmerick and jutted his chin toward the boot. "What do you think you're doing, Major?"

Zimmerick, caught off guard, studied Peyton carefully. "We're sending these hostiles into Gainesville with your stagecoach, Lewis. They'll be publicly displayed. Hell, folks will come from miles around to view these heathens." He shrugged. "I've been stationed in Texas for over year, and these are the first warlike Indians that I've seen. Why, General Custer himself ain't never been this close to a hostile Comanche. It'll be a holiday when these bodies arrive in Gainesville—yes, sir, a sure enough circus!"

Bile rose in Peyton's throat as his mind raced back to mid-October, 1864, outside of Albany, Missouri, where Bloody Bill Anderson, the leader of a band of Confederate guerrillas, was killed in battle by several shots to his body and head. The Federal soldiers had flung Anderson's body on a wagon bed and hauled it to Richmond, Missouri, where it was put on "display" at the Ray County Courthouse. A "circus atmosphere had prevailed." After photographs were taken and people from far and wide had "viewed" the remains, Anderson's body was beheaded and his genitals severed. Union soldiers then tied Anderson's naked torso behind a horse and dragged it through Richmond's dusty streets.

Peyton's gaze held unwaveringly on the Union officer. For the second time that day, he considered the actual motive behind the actions of the Army of the United States of America and the parallels between the Indian nations and the Confederate States. Was it not enough that the Northern aggressors beat their foes into submission? No! They must obviously feel a need to embarrass and humiliate them beyond human endurance. Perhaps that was how a true coward decimated a weaker nation.

Peyton tried to put his concerns into words. "These men are warriors, Major, not sideshow freaks. They should be buried here, where they fought and died. They should be treated as soldiers who fought for their homes, their people, their rights. They deserve to be buried with dignity."

The major shook his head. "Sorry, Lewis. These hostiles are going into Gainesville where they'll be displayed for public view."

Peyton sighed with the realization that his attempt to reason with the officer had only exacerbated the man's contempt for the vanquished, and he felt that cold, dead nothingness that preceded a battle, chill the fire of bitter resentment that had ignited inside him. With calm resignation for what was to come, he drew his revolver. "They'll be buried here on the battlefield, Major . . . where they fell."

Seeing Peyton's threat, the squad of Federal cavalrymen left the rear of the coach and quickly flanked their officer. Their movements were precise and controlled. In unison, their hands palmed back their holster flaps and gripped their pistol handles.

The major glanced around him at the show of force, then smiled condescendingly at Peyton. "Go on about your business, Lewis. You might have just whipped a handful of Comanche, but surely you're not fool enough to take on the United States Cavalry all by yourself."

Rucker stepped up beside his cousin. "Peyton ain't by himself, in case you ain't noticed."

The Union officer studied the cool young men facing him. He had seen their kind before, during the war. They asked no quarter, nor did they grant any. Rebels.

John Wright shook his head incredulously. Lewis and Rucker were loony. Two against a dozen. Yet, even as he thought it, he was walking toward them. He came to a halt at Peyton's right, and for a long second stared at Major Zimmerick. Then, cocking both hammers on his shotgun even though only the left barrel was charged, he raised the muzzles so that they took in the cavalrymen fanned out around the officer.

Ben drew his Walker Colt from his haversack and moved to the far side of Wright. His pistol was pointed toward the ground, but everyone watching knew it could be snapped into action in an instant.

Zimmerick assessed the black man, taking in his Federal army clothing and shoes and the Colt gripped loosely in his fist. In spite of his attempt at self-control, rage suddenly engulfed the major, and he pointed a trembling finger at Ben. "What do you think you're doing, you ungrateful bastard?"

When Ben merely stared at him, Zimmerick became even more angry. "We freed you, nigger—us, the United States Army! And how do you show your appreciation? You draw your weapon against your liberators!"

Ben's face took on the hue of damp wood ash as the major's accusation struck home. For an instant he wavered as his lifelong indoctrination in subserviency threatened to send his chin to his chest as it had so many times before in the presence of white authority. Then he squared his shoulders. "Mista' major, sir, I never was no slave—won't never be one—but I been half Indian all my born days." Ben looked at the bodies piled in the stage-coach boot. "An' I reckon when I die, I'll still be half Indian."

Zimmerick turned to Lieutenant Pendleton, who stood near the rear wheel of the coach. "What about you, Pendleton? You intend to play turncoat like this nigger?"

Pendelton crossed his arms over his chest. "I won't lift a weapon against the United States Army, Major, but in this situation I won't side with you, either. I will warn you, however, that you are putting yourself and your men in needless jeopardy. I can tell you from experience, sir, that unless you are prepared to kill or be killed, you had better rethink your position. These people don't bluff worth a damn . . . sir."

Inside the coach, where she had heard the exchange plainly, Gabrielle Johnson, lying on the coach seat, turned her head sleepily toward Molly, who occupied the bench across the aisle. Gabrielle's voice was nearly incoherent from the laudanum she had drunk. "I think we should go out there and stand with the men . . ." She attempted to draw back the quilt that covered her, but the effort left her spent, and she lay back exhausted.

Molly wondered which "men" Gabrielle was concerned about—the Northern cavalrymen or the Southern?

When Molly voiced the question, Gabrielle squinted at her, attempting to bring her face into focus. As befuddled by the opium as she was, she understood perfectly the reasoning behind Molly's inquiry. Yet, after what they had just been through together, the fact that Molly felt the need to ask annoyed her.

"I'm speaking of Fletcher and Peyton, Molly . . . of course."

Molly raised her eyebrows at the girl. *My, how a person does change.* Gabrielle's suggestion did possess a certain merit; Peyton and Rucker had stepped into it again. Then John Wright's statement, "They ain't no man worth his salt goin' to stand still for a woman meddlin' into his business," forced its way into her mind and hung there like a painted signpost warning passersby of a poisoned waterhole.

Molly sighed and leaned back against the coach seat. "No, Gabrielle. What's taking place out there is men's business. We are going to stay right here in this stagecoach and let them solve their own problems."

Then she laughed aloud at the absurdity of her statement, at the sheer impossibility that she, Molly Klinner, would not involve herself in Peyton Lewis's troubles no matter how poisonous it might be to their relationship—if there was such a thing. Placing the baby in the corner of the seat, she reached for the Henry rifle that lay on the floorboard beneath her feet.

Major Zimmerick's startled gaze moved from the muzzle of the rifle that suddenly appeared in the coach window to the powder-burned face of the woman behind the gun. She appeared perfectly capable of shooting him. He was amazed at these people, and he shook his head as he reassessed the motley group confronting him: two young, former Confederate toughs; an old, used-up stagecoach driver; a black man who refused to be intimidated; and a young woman who had just given birth. It was incredible!

Dropping his hands to his sides, he grinned at Peyton. "Where do you want these sons of bitches buried, Lewis?"

Peyton looked out across the landscape to the hill where the Comanche had materialized at sunup, splendid in their wildness, beautiful in their magnificence. "Have your men dig the grave on top of the rise, Major . . . and, although I'm much obliged for your help, we who killed them will do the burying."

Peyton swung his eyes toward the stagecoach, where Molly watched him from the window. Their eyes locked for a long moment, then he spun on his heel and walked toward the hill.

John Wright peered up at Molly. "You sure do work hard at

runnin' a feller off, Molly. Lewis was beginnin' to take a shine to you, but then you go an' spoil the whole shootin' match."

Molly drew the rifle back into the coach. She smiled to herself, thinking how wrong John Wright was, for he had not seen what lay deep in Peyton Lewis's eyes: acceptance, finally—and maybe something else.

"I wasn't meddling this time, John. I *sided* with Peyton because he was right, and . . . and because I was proud of him."

"Pride goes two ways, Molly. You might do well to remember that." Was that a flash of amusement she saw in his eyes, or a glint of contempt? Then he was going on: "I've got a notion, however, that whether he wants your help or not, you'll always be there for him. An' maybe that ain't half bad . . . no, ma'am, not half bad a'tall."

John Wright left Molly wondering at his words as he hurried off to help the eastbound driver cut two of the newly arrived horses out of harness and hitch them to the Butterfield so they could haul the bodies to the top of the knoll.

In less than an hour from the time the eastbound coach had arrived at the station, the men had opened a shallow trench on the Texas hilltop and buried the seven Comanche warriors. And less than thirty minutes later, Wright's stagecoach was heading west, toward Gainesville. And the legend of the Battle of Burnt Station was off and running.

As Lieutenant Pendleton, along with a private whom Major Zimmerick detailed to accompany the coach to Gainesville, climbed into the saddle, the major caught Pendleton's horse by its headstall. "Tell me, Lieutenant, would that woman have actually shot me?"

Pendleton laughed easily, then leaned on the pommel of his McClellan saddle. "Her rifle was empty, Major. In fact, I would wager a month's pay that there wasn't over one or two rounds in any of their guns."

The lieutenant turned his horse toward the stagecoach, then reined up and twisted in the saddle. "Was she capable of shooting you? She would never have batted an eye, sir."

The lieutenant saluted the major, then spurred his horse into a canter and galloped down the road after the stagecoach.

Twenty-five

April 8, 1866

A hush hung like a pall over the people who lined the main thoroughfare of Gainesville, Texas, when the battle-scarred stagecoach limped into view an hour after sunset. In some ways it was a funeral procession, for the stagecoach, pulled by two matching grays, was acting as a hearse for the three corpses laid out side-by-side on its roof.

The coach was pierced in numerous places by Comanche arrows, many of which were still protruding from the woodwork. The driver of the vehicle, along with the two young men who rode the seat beside him, were powder blackened so badly that they were very nearly as dark as the Negro who sat on top with the three bodies.

Two mounted cavalrymen, one of whom was a young lieutenant fresh from the East named Theodore Pendleton, who wore his battle-stained uniform as though it were a badge of honor, accompanied the coach as a guard. A third trooper, who had been dispatched ahead of the coach to alert the residents of Gainesville of the Indian attack and its casualties, watched their arrival from the porch of the saloon. He had come to Texas with General Custer, and not once in the months that he, and four thousand other troopers, had been there, had he either seen or come in contact with one hostile Indian. He envied Lieutenant Pendleton and wished that someday he would be fortunate enough to engage in such a battle. It must surely have been a soldier's dream come true.

Stepping off the wooden saloon porch, he joined the townspeople who clustered around the coach as it drew to a halt before the blacksmith shop, where the bodies of Robertson, Beecher, and Captain Cramer would lie until coffins could be made.

Before the stagecoach had come to a complete halt, the women of the town had already snatched open its doors and were assisting Molly and the baby down the metal fold-out step, while on the opposite side of the coach, gentle hands lifted Gabrielle onto a litter. Both women were whisked away to designated homes that anxiously awaited the heroines' arrival.

Amid the revelry of celebration, Peyton Lewis, Fletcher Rucker, John Wright, and Lieutenant Pendleton were ushered off to the saloon for drinks all around.

As Peyton stepped up on the saloon porch, he noticed Ben standing alone in the street. "You coming?"

Ben looked down at his worn brogans. When he raised eyes to Peyton's, they were evasive. "Naw, boss. I b'lieve I'll mosey down t' the livery stable an' wash some o' this stench off'n me. A man's pretty ripe when he can't stand t' be downwind of his own self!" He turned and sauntered down the street toward the stable.

When Peyton walked into the tap room, the first thing he noticed was a sign above the bar: NO NIGGERS OR INDIANS ALLOWED.

Peyton sighed. Ben was both Negro and Indian, and he, Peyton Lewis, had forgotten that truth—but Ben had not.

For the next two days, Peyton was constantly on the move, purchasing new clothing, personal items, foodstuff and supplies, saddle horses and pack animals—and plenty of ammunition.

The third day, at ten o'clock on the chilly morning of April 11, 1866, more than seven weeks and 550 miles, as the crow flies, from the Clay County Savings Association in Liberty, Missouri,

Peyton Lewis knocked on the door of the Samuel Horton residence, and when Mrs. Horton answered, he asked to speak with the widow, *Mrs.* Klinner.

Mrs. Horton guided Peyton to a spacious kitchen at the rear of the large frame house, where Molly sat basking in the heat of a cast-iron cookstove, rocking her baby. At the sight of Peyton looming tall in the kitchen doorway with hat in hand, Molly rose demurely to her feet.

During that instant before conversation, each beheld the other in mutual astonishment. Peyton Lewis's dark, unruly hair had been shorn off his neck and slicked down with pomade, and his lean face had been shaved smooth without leaving so much as a nick in his wind-tanned skin. He sported a new cotton shirt tucked into brown corduroy trousers, which were in turn stuffed into shiny, knee-high mule-ear boots. The only reminder of the hard-eyed young man who had stopped at Caleb King's soddie some fifty-six days earlier—Molly was amazed, for it seemed a lifetime ago—was the worn army holster whose flap had been cut away for quick access to the Spiller and Burr Confederate revolver it housed.

Molly blushed as though they were strangers, which indeed the two young people now facing each other were.

"Won't you come in, Mr. Lewis?" Then she laughed nervously, her eyes cutting to Mrs. Horton, then back to him. "I . . . I was afraid you had intended to leave without saying good-bye."

Mrs. Horton made a discreet apology, and with a swish of her full skirts made a hasty exit.

Peyton stared at Molly. Her hair, piled loosely on top of her head, had been brushed until it shone like burnished bronze in the morning sunlight. Her skin, which had been hidden beneath layers of soot and grime ever since he had met her, glowed with a soft, rose-petal vigor that spoke of youth and good health. Her dark eyes were bright and alive—and beautiful.

The white, high-necked blouse she wore was starched and ironed, and her gray woolen skirt swept the floor. He noticed the tip of a small, black, high-buttoned shoe poking out beneath the hemline. Molly Klinner was breathtakingly lovely, and Peyton Lewis found himself debating whether or not the transformation from sow's ear was the result of motherhood, hot water and soft soap, or rest and nourishment—or a combination of them all. He would have been astounded had he asked, for Molly would have answered with one simple word: love. For a child; for a man; for a new way of life. He did not ask.

Molly looked quietly at him. "Fletcher and Ben have come by every day. I had hoped that you would."

Peyton shifted his weight, suddenly uneasy in her presence. Why? They had shared every misery known to man or woman: cold, hunger, fear, death—and birth—events and emotions that usually bound people together. So why were they suddenly strangers?

Molly could have answered that question also, but again he did not ask. Had he inquired, she would have pointed out that, yes, they had shared misery aplenty, but they had never shared a true intimacy—not even the birthing of her baby. That was the barrier that stood between them like an insurmountable wall: they had never so much as held each other's hands or kissed each other's lips with a passion born of need, of desire . . . of love.

"Would you stay for coffee?" *Please stay,* her eyes beseeched.

He shook his head. "I'm packed for travel. My horses are out front. I just came by to say good luck to you . . . and to give you this." He held out a parcel wrapped in butcher's paper.

Molly's smile was brave on the surface. Inside, she had gone to pieces. Laying the baby gently in a cradle Mr. Horton had hurriedly fashioned, she forced her hands not to tremble as she accepted the heavy package.

Peyton bent down and touched the sleeping baby's face. "I'm curious, Molly. What have you named her?"

Molly laughed, a fine husky sound from deep in her throat. "I don't suppose my mother or father will ever know or care, but I named her Christi Jo, for her grandmother, Christine, and her grandfather, Joseph."

Peyton nodded. Christi Jo Klinner. It had a good ring to it. "Well, like Ben said, she's a beauty . . . just like her mother."

Hesitantly, he took Molly into his arms and held her tightly for a brief moment. Then he turned and walked out of the room. That was as close as Peyton Lewis had ever come to being intimate with Molly Klinner.

Peyton rode to the Taylor home, where Gabrielle Johnson lay fighting for her life. Mrs. Taylor met Peyton at the door and invited him into the parlor. Rucker sat in a cushioned chair talking to the Reverend Taylor.

The reverend climbed to his feet and offered Peyton his hand. Mrs. Taylor walked toward the kitchen. "May I get you a cup of coffee, Mr. Lewis?"

Peyton smiled fleetingly at the lady, uneasy at being in a preacher's house. "No, ma'am. I just stopped by to see Miss Johnson. But I'm much obliged for your offer."

Mrs. Taylor's smile was an apology. "Dr. Brown was just now here, Mr. Lewis. He gave Gabrielle a healthy dose of laudanum. She'll sleep most of the day, I'm afraid."

Rucker climbed to his feet, his eyes shining with excitement. "Miss Gabrielle is a lot better, though, Peyton. She may even be able to get out of bed by the end of the week."

That was good news, and Peyton grinned his pleasure. Then he sobered.

"Would you step outside with me, Fletcher?" He glanced toward the Taylors. "I beg your pardon, Reverend, ma'am. But I need to talk to Fletcher for a moment in private."

Outside, Peyton studied Rucker from beneath his hat brim. Rucker had changed over the past month and a half, had matured, had in many ways become his own man. Although he still retained a certain amount of the little boy in him that would very likely be a part of him his entire life, Fletcher Rucker, for the first time since he and Peyton had been children together, was taking charge of his future. Peyton was proud of him.

"Sure you won't change your mind, Fletcher, and ride on with me?"

There was a light in Rucker's young, handsome face when he looked toward the bedchamber where Gabrielle Johnson lay. "I reckon I'll stay with Miss Johnson until she's well enough to travel." He shrugged. "Which way I go from here will depend upon her, Peyton."

Rucker went on to explain that it had been quite a blow to

the bedridden girl when she learned that her trip to Texas had been in vain. General George Custer and his entire command, all four thousand men, had been mustered out of service at the turn of the year. General and Libby Custer—whom the cavalrymen referred to as the "Queen of Sheba"—along with most of the general's staff, including Gabrielle's brother, Major Paul Johnson, had quit Austin more than a month earlier for reassignment in the East. Indeed, even the cavalrymen who accompanied the eastbound stagecoach were civilians on their way home.

"Gabrielle came out here on a wild-goose chase, Peyton. She's alone in Texas, an' I reckon I'll see she gets home . . . or wherever she wants to go. I aim to ask her to marry me."

Peyton shook his cousin's hand. "Good luck, Fletcher. No matter what you decide, if you ever need me, I'll be somewhere down around Houston or Austin."

Peyton, his packhorses strung out behind him, rode to the livery stable and dismounted beside Ben, whose cane-bottomed chair was propped back against the open stable door. The Negro was dozing in the morning sun.

Ben righted his chair and climbed to his feet. "Well, boss, yo' jest missed Mista' John Wright. He hitched hisself up a fresh team 'bout a hour ago and rolled outa here for Dallas. Said he was s'posed to deliver that coach to the territory agent, or somebody. Said the Butterfield folks owed him a heap o' money, an' he intended t' collect it. Lieuten't Pendleton went with him to cor'borate his story."

Peyton had talked at length to the two men the night before; indeed, they had closed down the saloon bar at three o'clock this morning. Peyton squinted at Ben. "Have you ever worked cattle, Ben?"

Ben rolled his eyes as though only a greenhorn, or a complete imbecile, would ask a question such as that. He was a Texan, wasn't he? He grinned. "Ain't a Texican alive, boss, who ain't chased longhorns at one time or 'nother."

"You want to go to work for me, Ben? I aim to start a ranch down around Houston way, and I'm going to need a good hand. Job pays thirty a month."

Ben hitched up his trousers and stood a little taller. Thirty a month to outthink cows was more money than he had made in his life.

"Afore I answer, boss, can I ast you a somewhat personal question?"

Peyton shrugged his consent. Ben dropped his head, then gazed up at Peyton through his thin eyebrows, his black eyes as brittle as obsidian. "It ain't none o' my business, Mista' Peyton ... but I reckon I'm just plain nosy. If'n yo're leavin' Miss Molly a'hind, 'cause of her workin' in a ... 'cause of her past ... well, boss, it's kind'a like C'nel Jim Bowie used t' say when he was rakin' in his winnin's from a good poker hand."

When Ben hesitated, Peyton frowned at him. "Get to it, Ben. What did Bowie say?"

"Well, boss, C'nel Bowie claimed that 'secondhand gold is jest as good as brand-new.' An', well ... what I'm tryin' to say, Mista' Peyton, is that Miss Molly is sho' nuff pure gold, an' she's solid, clear through."

Peyton shook his head in wonder. "You come up with some of the damnedest sayings, Ben. You sure you don't make that stuff up?"

"Well, boss, you know what they say: 'An old-timer is a man who's had a passel o' interestin' experiences—some of 'em true!"

Both men laughed.

Ben walked inside the barn and returned with Molly Klinner's Henry rifle. "She said yo' was to have this, boss." He gazed apologetically at Peyton for a long moment, and Peyton could see what appeared to be an internal conflict in the black man's eyes. When Peyton took the rifle, Ben removed his hat and absently brushed a speck of dirt from its crown.

"T' answer yo' question 'bout hirin' me on? Boss, I'm rightly flattered that you'd ast, 'cause I sure can't think o' anyone I'd rather work fo' ... but I got somethin' I got t' do first."

Peyton nodded his understanding. John Wright had mentioned to him the night before that Ben had decided to stay with Molly Klinner until she was settled into a place of her own. He told Ben what Wright had said.

Ben held Peyton's gaze; there was no apology on his face. "She saved my life, boss."

Peyton felt an unexpected loss. He had grown to like the black man and would miss him more than he cared to admit. He shook Ben's hand, feeling his strong, callused palm, the grip of an honest man, a loyal friend. "The offer stands, Ben, anytime you're ready."

Peyton swung into his saddle. His horse danced sideways, anxious to be on the road. Suddenly he felt the need to explain himself—something he rarely did. Leaning on his saddle horn, he gazed down at the Negro.

"There are times in every man's life, Ben, when, for various reasons, gold is just too heavy to carry. At times like that, a smart man stashes his riches someplace where they are safe—with someone he trusts. You understand what I just told you, Ben?"

Ben grinned at Peyton and said nothing. There are times when silence can be a speech.

Peyton touched his hat brim. "Take care of her, my friend."

Pivoting his horse, with his pack animals strung out behind like a caravan, Peyton rode tall in the saddle down Gainesville's main street.

Molly Klinner sat in a rocking chair on the Hortons' front porch and watched him ride away. She lifted the new, leather-bound, family Bible Peyton had given her—to replace the one they had burned the night of the blizzard—from the butcher's paper that lay crumpled in her lap, and pressed it lovingly to her bosom. Curiously, she did not touch the leather pouch that also lay there, heavy with the weight of five hundred dollars in twenty-dollar gold pieces.

Molly's eyes took on a faraway look. "I'll see you again, Mr. Peyton Lewis."

It was a promise.

Inside the house, the baby whimpered and began to cry. Feeding time.

EPILOGUE

"Mr. Lewis?" Kate Edmons repeated the name for the third time, suddenly wishing she had not climbed Spindle Top at all, had not invaded Peyton Lewis's private world, had not attempted to intrude just to get a story.

"Mr. Lewis?" He focused his cool eyes on her. "About your trip to Texas, sir . . ."

A smile touched Peyton Lewis's lips, and Kate Edmons thought *Yes! He is listening to me at last.* Then, to her mortification, she realized he was not looking at her at all, but gazing beyond her, to the bottom of the hill where a new, six-horsepower Duryea phaeton motor car built in Reading, Pennsylvania, was chugging to a halt.

Kate Edmons watched with interest as a lovely, auburn-haired woman, who appeared to be in her early to midthirties, stepped out of the automobile and turned to take the hand of a taller version of herself, who at that distance might have been mistaken for her older sister.

The driver of the car, a well-dressed man in his late thirties, with an air of importance about him, jumped to the ground and caught the arm of an ancient black man who, with the use of a cane, was working his way down out of the back seat.

Behind the Duryea, a fringed surrey drawn by a stylish pair of matching grays reined to a halt. A tall, thin, blond man about Peyton Lewis's age stepped out of the carriage, then handed down a woman who, even at a distance, was obviously a rare beauty. Arm in arm, they joined the others.

Peyton Lewis swung his gaze to Kate Edmons, and again she had the disconcerting sensation that his cool gray eyes were piercing her most hidden thoughts. Her heart fluttered. *I'm a nineteen-year-old reporter,* she told herself, *yet every time he looks at me, I feel like a schoolgirl with a crush.* Then she remembered having heard that Peyton Lewis had that effect on most women, and she silently chastised herself for being just another one of many.

Peyton tipped his head, indicating the people waiting at the base of Spindle Top.

"My family, Miss Edmons."

Kate tore her eyes from his and stared at the group gathered at the bottom of the hill.

"My goodness!" The words came unbidden as she scrutinized the tall, elegant woman who was returning her gaze with interest. She must be Malinda Klinner Lewis! Kate blushed, recalling the spicy rumors she had heard throughout her growing-up years concerning the infamous Molly Klinner.

She studied Molly intently, seeing her through the eyes of a journalist. Try as she might, however, she could not envision such a beautiful woman, with obvious class and an unparalleled social standing throughout the entire state of Texas, ever having worked in a brothel during the War Between the States. Incredible!

Kate's gaze swept to the younger woman standing beside Malinda Lewis. That must be Christi Jo, who was supposedly born during an Indian attack at some place called Burnt Station. And next to her, Senator Samuel P. Johnson, her husband.

Kate's excitement grew as the professional writer inside her took possession of her wits. Her breath whistled through her teeth as she swung her attention to Fletcher Rucker, who, legend had it, had ridden roughshod through five hundred savage Comanche. The elegant, refined woman on his arm, wearing small, dark, gold-rimmed spectacles, could be none other than Gabrielle Johnson Rucker, who for many years was hailed from the Red River to the Panhandle as the most beautiful woman in Texas. Some of the old-timers up around Gainesville still argued that Mrs. Rucker had been half-scalped and pierced through her body by a Comanche arrow. They said she had lost most of her eyesight that same day. She had been only sixteen years old at the time.

God, what a story I've stumbled onto. Almost as an afterthought, Kate took in the old black man standing with the family. Who could he be?

"Miss Edmons." Peyton Lewis's soft Texas drawl caught her full attention. She turned quickly to him. He was watching her closely. "There is a story here, ma'am, if you are interested . . ."

Kate Edmons wet her pencil lead with the tip of her tongue and flipped her pad open to a clean page. "Okay, Mr. Lewis, shoot!"

Peyton Lewis grinned crookedly at her. "You indicated, Miss Edmons, you want a story about 'true' Texas heroes, like Sam Houston, Moses and Stephen Austin, Lovin and Goodnight?"

The young reporter nodded, her face animated.

Peyton took her by the shoulders and turned her around.

"See that old black gentleman?" Kate nodded, uncertainly. "That man is named Uncle Ben, Miss Edmons. The best we can tell, he's somewhere around a hundred years old. He was at the Alamo when it fell to Santa Anna in 1836. He knew Davy Crockett, Jim Bowie, William Travis. Why, Miss Edmons, Ben was acquainted with nearly all the 'Texas heroes,' including many you failed to mention—because *he* was one of them. Uncle Ben's your story, ma'am. He *is* Texas."

Peyton tipped his hat to the girl and took her arm. As they walked down the hill, he laughed. "My wife once said, years and years before you were born, Miss Edmons, that those of us who came to Texas after the War Between the States are nothing but interlopers."

AUTHOR'S NOTE

Although this story is a work of fiction, much of it is based on real people and actual facts and events. The names of some of the characters have been changed, as have a few of the locations. The inspiration for the story came to me while I was reading a transcript of a gentleman, a hero, who lived during the times and in the places mentioned in this novel. I thank his family, who wish to remain anonymous, for allowing me the privilege of interloping into portions of their ancestors' lives, both before and after the Civil War—indeed, even beyond 1901. It was a most arresting narrative.

It is interesting to know that:

- Jesse and Frank James, along with ten other men, did, on the snowy, wintry day of February 14, 1866, rob the Clay County Savings Association in Liberty, Missouri.
- Jesse James did lock Greenup and William Bird, father and son, in the vault.
- Jesse James did shout, "Birds are supposed to be caged."
- The robbery did net some sixty thousand dollars.
- Jesse James did, for no apparent reason, shoot and kill young George Wymore as he was crossing the street.

- The incidents related in this story concerning Brigadier General Thomas Ewing and the Burnt District of Missouri are historical fact.
- The murdering of the male population of the razed countryside and townships is factual.
- The incident concerning the old brick building on Grand Avenue and Fifteenth Street in Kansas City, Missouri, is factual. Among those civilians imprisoned there were Frank and Jesse James's mother and sister; William "Bloody Bill" Anderson's three sisters, Mary, Jenny, and Josephine, relatives of Cole Younger; and many others. On August 14, 1863, the building did collapse. Josephine Anderson was killed: Mary Anderson was maimed for life. Injured were the James women, Cole Younger's cousin, and others.
- William Anderson was killed in 1864, and his body did suffer the depredations described in this story.
- "Doc" Jennison and his Kansas Jayhawkers did burn, loot, and rape. The people in Missouri called the chimneys rising out of the charred remains of the Burnt District "Jennison's Monuments."
- The small mention of General George Armstrong Custer and the "Queen of Sheba," his lovely wife, Elizabeth, and their stint in Texas is factual.
- The Custers, along with four thousand troops, were stationed in Houston, and then Austin, until the end of 1865. Custer's army was dismantled and sent east at the beginning of 1866, a full decade before the Little Big Horn massacre.
- "Uncle" Ben was picked up on the side of the road and given an off-and-on, lifelong job by a young interloper in Texas (Peyton Lewis was not his real name).
- "Uncle" Ben did serve time in a Texas prison because of an incident concerning his wife.
- A Negro "boy" did survive the carnage at the Alamo in 1836. The word "boy" was applied to nearly all male Negroes until they reached late middle age, when they were referred to as "Uncle."
- Peyton Lewis (not his real name) did become a millionaire in

the oil business when Spindle Top changed the Texas landscape forever in 1901.

• Kate Edmons did write "Uncle" Ben's story, and it did appear in the *Waco Times Herald*.

—D. K. W.